The Forgetting Tree

Also by Tatjana Soli

The Lotus Eaters

The Forgetting Tree

Tatjana Soli

ST. MARTIN'S GRIFFIN NEW YORK

This is a work of fiction. All of the characters, organizations, and events portrayed in this novel are either products of the author's imagination or are used fictitiously.

 Printed in the United States of America. For information, address St. Martin's Press, 175 Fifth Avenue, New York, N.Y. 10010.

Illustrations by Gaylord Soli 2012

www.stmartins.com

The Library of Congress has cataloged the hardcover edition as follows:

Soli, Tatjana.
The forgetting tree / Tatjana Soli.—1st ed.
p. cm.
ISBN 978-1-250-00104-7 (hardcover)
ISBN 978-1-250-01934-9 (e-book)
1. Ranch life—California—Fiction. 2. Marriage—Fiction. 3. Self-realization in women—Fiction. I. Title.
PS3619.O43255 F67 2012
813'.6

2012028236

ISBN 978-1-250-02042-0 (trade paperback)

St. Martin's Griffin books may be purchased for educational, business, or promotional use. For information on bulk purchases, please contact Macmillan Corporate and Premium Sales Department at 1-800-221-7945, extension 5442, or write specialmarkets@macmillan.com.

First St. Martin's Griffin Edition: September 2013

10 9 8 7 6 5 4 3 2 1

For Gaylord with love

How much land does a man need?

—Tolstoy

That odd capacity for destitution, as if by nature we ought to have so much more than nature gives us. As if we are shockingly unclothed when we lack the complacencies of ordinary life. In destitution, even of feeling or purpose, a human being is more hauntingly human and vulnerable to kindnesses because there is the sense that things should be otherwise, and then the thought of what is wanting and what alleviation would be, and how the soul could be put at ease, restored. At home. But the soul finds its own home if it ever has a home at all.

—Marilynne Robinson, Home

The Forgetting Tree

Prologue

He was a respectable and loyal man, Octavio Mejia, the father of six children, and he had been late to leave that day, treating an infestation of whitefly on the newly planted Valencia trees. It was a Friday evening, his daughter's *quinceañera,* and he hurried the stick shift into reverse and stepped hard on the gas with his heavy, rubber-soled workboot even as the car bounced over a small mound under the lemon tree where he had parked for shade.

Forster and Claire had insisted he go on with the family celebration even though they would not attend. But he also was in mourning for the missing boy. Did they not see? Octavio had worked hard his whole life and mainly had a mountain of bills to show for it. The *quinceañera* had cost his whole paycheck for two months, Forster chipping in a hefty bonus, and even then, his wife, Sofia, and his teenaged girls were not quite satisfied that it would outshine the neighbors' recent parties.

It was late, the week so merciless it was one only the devil could be responsible for. He, Octavio, the only one cleared to do basic maintenance on the ranch to keep things alive. The police had finally allowed the irrigation stations to be turned on again, the rusting wheels screeching in protest, the hollow thunder of water tumbling down dusty tunnels after two weeks lying dry during record heat. Lizards, believing they had found homes in new cool caves, now dropped and rolled through the deluge of water like judgment, either saved out the end of a pipe or drowned against the wall of a sprinkler head, stunned by the sudden, unfathomable change to their world. As slowly as the police covered the land, it would take them a year to pore over all 580 acres. The immediate perimeter of fifty acres around the house and sheds yielded nothing. The ranch turned a parched, closed face to them. Water meant that the fruit would be saved, the harvest sold, and the bills paid, but it also meant that whatever marks might be left from that night would now be washed away forever.

No, he did not notice the mound, the freshly turned earth, thinking only of gophers, eternal bane of farmers, as he prepared to drive home. But he stopped the pickup truck a few yards away, the engine idling, and tried to recall something that buzzed, teased, at the edge of his memory. He snatched an orange on the dashboard, wedged against the windshield to keep it from rolling back and forth or dropping to the floor to be crushed beneath his boots. It was impossible to tell if the lack of water during the hot weather had done damage. Orange trees died from the inside out, the hurt not visible until long after the crime.

Absentmindedly, not hungry in the least, he peeled the orange, gnawing at the spongy pith beneath the rind before dropping the peel outside his window. The taste was bitter. He had worked the ranch his whole life, eaten its fruit, breathed its air, sheltered under its shade, worn its dirt like a second skin. He was as much a product of the land as the fruit, and yet it had turned strange against him. The roundness of an orange. He remembered what was nagging him. The night of Claire's birthday an odd thing had happened—a small silver globe went missing. But what did that have to do with anything later? The sorry sight of

Claire, found when she did not want to be found, weighed heavily on his tongue. That it had been his pickup driving up the driveway. Easier if it had been a stranger. Try as he might, he did not think that they could pretend, go backward in time to the friendship they had had these many years. The bond they had formed over the land. It was as if the boy had vanished into thin air. As if the land were cooperating in letting him hide.

The sun was in Octavio's eyes, and he had to shield his face to look up at the towering tree as he ate the wedges of succulent fruit. He was in the oldest section of the ranch, where the ancient lake grew smaller each year because of drought. He seldom came as far, the unmaintained roads making the passage slow and rough, but one of his newly enforced duties each night would be to padlock the back gate leading to the lake. He had forgotten the night before, rushing home for a final dance instruction.

When there were fires, the lake was used to fill fire trucks, or, more recently, water-bomber planes. Before that week, kids from the high school would sneak down there to talk or drink, and the Baumsargs had turned a blind eye to their goings-on. In his time, even Octavio had made the pilgrimage with Sofia when they were courting. The Baumsargs' lake had been a rite of passage for the young people who grew up in the area. Another thing that would now end.

The neglected lemon tree had grown to a monstrous height, almost even to the pitch of a barn roof, and the unpicked fruit had grown obscene—globular, swollen lemons the shape of footballs, hydrocephalic tennis balls, or further deformed into bizarre shapes resembling gourds, or small, ghoulish animals. Unlike the prim, tended rows of Valencias, Washington navels, and newly planted Eurekas, this was original rootstock left to its own devices. His grandfather had brought the original seeds to the ranch, named the tree Agua Tibia. Octavio thought of it as the patriarch of the orchard, its vigor too crude for the more delicate, cultivated, grafted generations. A section of fruit caught in his throat, and he coughed till it went down.

Much past its prime, the tree was woody, its fruit inedible. Its only purpose now shade. No one tended it. The fruit fell to the ground, rotting and enriching the soil till a fecund, gentle hill rolled away from the trunk. Around it formed a scrabbled, lush garden straight out of the Bible, composed of overgrown coyote bush, Russian thistle, goldenbush, sagebrush and curly dock, needlegrass and wild morning glory and Indian paintbrush. Stray seed of California poppy and nasturtiums. Horseweed grew so wild and untamed that the cottontail rabbits ran in and out unafraid of human contact, while quail worried their way back and forth across the seed-strewn path. One glimpsed near-sightings of roadrunners, coyotes, red-tailed hawks, all lusting after such abundance.

The tree reminded Octavio of the Mexico of his father's time, reminded him even of the California of his own youth, the way it would never be again. Cutting it down would be like cutting off an arm, sundering oneself from one's history. A way of life disappearing, and now this. A stray trail of juice trickled down his chin, and he roughly wiped all evidence away. He was late. The gate could wait one more night. He was heartbroken. He must pull himself together.

The boy's disappearance made him sick. Everyone had always commented that he was wild over Joshua, spoiled him, defended his misdeeds, and the boy loved him back like an uncle. He had taught the boy to drive in that very pickup, its floor usually littered with his chocolate-bar wrappers and comics. But did that necessarily make him above suspicion? The ground itself had turned poisonous, had swallowed him up, and wouldn't show Octavio where he had gone.

The low sun poured bands of dusty gold down the dirt alleyways of trees. The farm had been worked by his grandfather, his father, and now Octavio, and in the important ways that mattered, the ways that had nothing to do with money or paper titles, he felt it belonged to him, or he to it. Something devastating had been done to them all, but he could only probe the extent of the damage like a toothache.

Part One

Chapter 1

Claire did not believe in the evil of the world, and so when it touched her, at first she did not recognize it for what it was. No pointing red tails and pitchforks as in the movies, not even malice in the heart. Evil as simple as an accident, as boring as the aftermath it brings. Forster saying death would have been easier than enduring what followed. A small, domestic evil as random as lightning, as devastating to those touched by it.

She had longed for home—a place of connection and belonging and family—for so long it was hard to believe that her struggle to attain it was about to be consummated. Eighteen years since she first came to the ranch. Her only regret that Hanni, her mother-in-law, wasn't there to share the moment she finally got it back for the family, because what was the worth of something unless it lasted through one's desire for it, a whole lifetime if need be, or beyond it, into one's children's lives also? She couldn't imagine anything better than Josh or one of the girls taking over when the time came. She looked around at all that was hers: the blush of sunset on her blossoming citrus trees; Forster, coming down the steps from the porch two at a time, wrapping his arms around her. Hers—his love—also.

"Hurry, the girls have a surprise for you. Pretend you don't know."

Forster was throwing a party, a Claire-will-live-forever party, since she hated birthdays and their reminder of time passing. Yes, about to have everything, but time itself had escaped her, moved on, made her a little more leathery, a little more tired than she wanted to be. At last she had time to spend with the children, just as they were growing up and going away.

Everyone had been invited, everyone came, barbecue for over two hundred, pushing at the seams of the farmhouse, spilling over onto the lawn, eddying around the rose gardens, the shadowy edges of the stalwart orchards. Her mother and father had driven down from Santa Monica—witnesses to her hard-won good fortune. She took a long look around as if she were about to depart on a journey and would need this memory: the citrus fruit hanging heavy with juice; the leaves on the trees turned ever so slightly toward the last rays of sunshine, showing their faintly silvered backsides.

In the kitchen, the caterer was scolding a newly hired waiter who'd come in late and ungroomed. In her room, Gwen, sixteen, put on lipstick and mascara for the first time. The guests walked along admiring the healthy rows of trees, the food-laden tables, as Lucy led the younger children in a game of hide-and-seek. People ate as much as they could bear and drank more. Unnoticed, Joshua snuck out from the bar with a bottle of vodka hidden away in a newspaper. Everyone was giddy with the rare sense of work put aside in favor of pleasure.

* * *

As Claire stood admiring the paper lanterns strung across the lawn, her lawn, rocking in the faint breeze, the banker Relicer sidled up to her with a plate stacked high with ribs. Even under the magic golden pink of sunset, time had not been kind during the last ten years she had been in business with him. He looked as severe and expiring as in his mahogany-lined office—aged, pale skin and caved-in cheeks that spoke of a life of frugality.

"It's a beauty," he said. "What you've accomplished with our money."

"Money didn't accomplish this," Claire said, feeling smug with the last check to him in her pocket. She would put it in the mail after he left. "It just kept developers away long enough for it to provide." Impossible to explain that the land was alive and fertile. It just needed coaxing along.

Relicer gnawed at the rib beyond simply getting the meat off, intending to suck the very marrow out. A tardy waiter came by and in offering a napkin almost flipped the paper plate on the banker's shirt. Claire frowned, noticed the waiter's greasy blond hair, his unkempt nails. She would complain to the caterer. The young man apologized, but the expression on his face, small eyes and large nose crowded together, wasn't the least sorry.

"The money wasn't exactly a gift." Claire looked down at her feet. The moment of sweetest revenge. They would no longer be needing his services; the trees were bowing under the weight of their record harvest; prices were up and the loan would be paid off and the Baumsarg ranch would never be beholden again. A happy birthday indeed. Forster had been right that the place never felt as much theirs since the debt, but Claire knew that sometimes necessity made one temporarily do the wrong thing.

The most devastating revenge: the thin envelope with its single stamp, a check for the full amount, and a simple note requesting the closing of the credit line. Gwen made her way over to the rescue. "Come on, Mom. Cake time."

Claire looked back at Relicer, happy to be abandoning him. "It's a hard job living here, not a vacation."

As she walked with her daughter, she noticed the girl's first attempt at makeup. "I wish you'd wash that off. It makes you look too old." When Gwen frowned, Claire relented, putting her arms around her shoulders. "And too beautiful. What happened to my little girl?"

A mountainous tower of frosting masquerading as a cake was wheeled out on a cart, and by it stood Lucy and Gwen, unhappy that Josh was as usual nowhere in sight to sing his part. Raisi, Claire's mother, offered to go looking for him, but Octavio took charge. The girls sang "How Sweet It Is" in harmony, one part missing, and it sounded strangely romantic and dreamy coming from their mouths instead of the usual James Taylor version that Forster loved to play. Did the girls mistakenly think that Forster's favorite song was hers also? The girls didn't know differently because Claire had no time to listen to music, much less have favorites, so on Saturday nights, exhausted from a long day doing errands that had been put off during the week, she deferred to Forster's taste.

"Where's Josh for the picture?" Claire asked. He had hit a new stage of rebelliousness that was unfathomable after the docile joys of raising daughters.

After a half hour's search, Octavio found him drinking vodka with older boys in an irrigation ditch.

"There are going to be consequences to this," Claire said when she found out. "This is not acceptable. Those are teenagers. Not ten-year-olds."

Josh looked at Octavio, betrayed. "But they said—"

"You missed cutting my cake. Singing the song your sisters prepared. You weren't in the family picture. Things are going to change."

A charmer, Josh held out an orange as a peace offering. It used to be a joke between them when he got in trouble. The most precious thing for the family and the most common.

"Not going to get you off the hook this time, mister."

"We can always take another picture." Forster held the camera, not paying mind to his son's ruffled hair, his crooked smile, his fingers making rabbit ears behind Lucy's head, and at the time Claire was angry that the pictures were too silly to use for the Christmas card. "Behave!" she said. Forster was distracted after overhearing Claire's conversation with the banker, a double impotence—the farm's loan and this man's presence lording the fact over them. Forster remained sullen until she reminded him that this would be the last time they would have to entertain the man. "You can give him the check yourself."

Claire handed him the envelope, then gave him a thumbs-up. "We need you in the picture—"

"Let me take it," Raisi said, stepping out of the line.

"You have to stand by Dad," Claire said.

"Allow me." Relicer had appeared from nowhere and offered to take the family snapshot. A bad omen. Forster reluctantly handed over the camera. But the old man fumbled with the buttons until the dirty-haired waiter reappeared. He put his hand on the banker's shoulder. "I'll take over, Pops."

Claire again noticed the dirty fingernails, and Raisi noticed, too, her eyes clouding. Octavio started toward the waiter, sensing the women's discomfort, but Sofia called him. "Go," Claire said. She would handle this herself. The caterer would get an earful soon. Forster escorted Relicer to the car, handed him the envelope, and watched him drive away.

The night after her birthday party, Forster was late coming home from a machinery exposition out in Pomona. Her parents had left that morning to return home. A night of hot moonlight and citrus perfuming the air. Claire had worked late in the fields with Octavio. Listless from the heat, the kids begged to eat a dinner of party leftovers out on a blanket on the lawn.

After the meal, they played cards while she went to the barn to recover a wrap she had left from dancing the night before. Late into the night, Forster and she had danced in celebration of ending the Relicer part of their life. The caterer had bawled a waiter out, demanding to look in his bag before he left. When the silver globe was found in it, she came to the barn to inform them she was calling the police. Never seeing the man in question, Claire had stopped her, telling her to escort the man off their property with a warning not to show up again. A blemish on an otherwise perfect night. They kept dancing. Now ribbon and confetti lodged in the gravel like stars, flashed through the grass like comets, turning the world topsy-turvy.

From the dark surrounding groves, three men appeared, as if they had metamorphosed from the very trees—two Hispanics and one masked by a baseball cap and a bandana from the eyes down. They mumbled about looking for work while the bandanaed one squinted through the darkness at the house, farther up the drive.

Impossible that a house brimming with hundreds of people the day before could be empty and helpless tonight.

"My foreman, Octavio, is here. He will take care of you."

But the bandana man seemed hostile to what he sensed was a lie. One of the Hispanic men, wearing a dirty, reeking T-shirt, had a stagger that she thought was a deformity until she noticed the same heaviness in the stride of the other. Drunk. She pictured the loaded rifle safely on the top shelf of the closet in the entry hallway. How perfectly, uselessly far away it was. Even if she reached it, the child-lock would take extra precious seconds to unfasten.

Out of the corner of her eye, Claire saw Gwen walking down the drive looking for her. A cold sweat formed under her arms at the sparkle of a moonlit blade in the hand of the bandana man. She bluffed, "Octavio, where are you?" until he hushed her with a shave of metal. They must smell fear on her like dogs.

"He's gone home," Gwen yelled back.

The bandana one touched her arm with the cold flat of the blade as he stood partially behind her. His breath was hot and sour; she could smell his unwashed skin as Gwen came up to the group.

"Qué linda. Bonito pelo," said the staggering one as he reached to touch Gwen's hair. Quickly she stepped back, eyes widening as she registered that none of these were their usual workers. Far away, Lucy could be heard arguing with Joshua. Claire saw it, too, for the first time, her daughter's new curves, now a young woman rather than an awkward teenager, and it put a vise on her heart.

"Go back to the house, Gwen."

"No!" the bandana one said. "Keep her." He signaled to the other, who locked his arms around Gwen's narrow shoulders in a bear hug. When she struggled in a spasm of panic, he shook her like a rag until her body went quiet. He held her with one arm and punched her on the side of the head with his other hand. She yelped in pain.

"Let her go back." Claire put herself between the men and her daughter, her body forming a protective shield.

Raspy laughter from the other two, and the bandana one nodded. "Let's all go see what's in the house."

Her thoughts stopped, sputtered, jumped, grabbing. "Money," she said, the suggestion of what they might otherwise do intolerable.

"Let's go."

"Not here. It's at the bank. Tomorrow."

The bandana one laughed, and she knew this was what got him off, the humiliation. He clapped his hands, an understanding between them. "We'll need a hostage. Otherwise you'll tell the cops."

"Touch her and the deal's off."

"How do you figure you're calling the shots?" He stopped, contemplating. "Okay, let the girl go. Keep quiet, cutie, or Mama isn't coming back."

A car motor broke the silence, headlights sweeping the trees just short of them as a pickup went up the drive to the house. Octavio returned or Forster come back early? The men ran, pulling Claire with them to the deepest part of the black-bitter orchard. Afraid for herself, more afraid for her children, she let out a cry. A mistake. They shoved her on the ground, a boot kicked her side. "Shut up!" They would kill her. Kill them. Mouth gagged with thick fingers and dirty cloth.

"How does the rich *puta* feel now? Want to order me around now?" he said, as a fist crushed bone.

Rage, hatred, welled through muscles that should have had the strength of new steel. Unacceptable to her that she could be pinned down so easily, that she could not fight back. That she had ignored Forster's warnings of keeping a gun close by. Like a dog, she bit an ear and was punched. Kneed a groin and was cut. Would gladly have died fighting back, except the maternal kept her from sacrificing herself.

A small voice, not Forster's, not Octavio's, broke through. The worst pain yet—Josh had somehow found them. "Mom?"

She screamed and grabbed hair. A hard knock to her head. As she lost consciousness, she heard a scurrying and then one of the men winded, butted in the stomach. "Grab the little fuck!"

* * *

Recalling those next hours, so frightening, consciousness intermittent, all thought evaporated. She was on the same plane of existence as an animal being led to the stockyard, pure physical dread, and afterward, months later, she understood her mother's terror escaping across the border, how for so many years she was unable to talk of it. Terror was intimate, entwined in the moment, not translatable.

Afterward, her mouth filled with salt from blood and sweet from blood. Seeded in the dirt, her fingers plowed earth she loved but was now separated from. Divorced, dismissed, expelled from. Was this the feeling of being thrown out of that first, perfect garden? Her farm, her trees, and yet she had been rendered helpless. She woke from unconsciousness to the comfort of a warm rain that turned out to be piss. All bets off because she had fought, and they had gorged on their power over her. She would never forget the spiked hatred in their laughter. Their carelessness. Their lack of fear in repercussion. She lay on the ground, unable to move. Broken arm, torn life. Later (how long? time untethered), alone, she melted into the ground, a superficial burial. Until she remembered Josh.

Chapter 2

The calling voices of the girls were like fingers poking in the darkness. Purple groves that took the dark shapes of men. Leaves in slow swoon on the trees. Her trees, her orchard, but unable to protect her. Broken Claire lay in the dirt as the irrigation came on, the drops sharp and caressing. The earth underneath her fed to mud, but still she lay there. Waiting until the pain washed away. It would never wash away. Curious cleansing of water against evil.

Importune time to be shown eternity, but the stars swung like heavy gates overhead, a celestial unveiling. She saw stars with her eyes closed—a mystery. A mystery, too, why she couldn't force herself back to the groves, the earth, her brokenness, but kept spinning above. It made sense that heaven would offer itself to those most in need of its vision, not those secure in starched kneel in church pews.

Octavio called her name, but she refused to answer. Did not want the girls or anyone to see her. She in a swale of blackness, hidden. Later she woke to his scooping arms as she struggled blind against him, ineffectual against him, too. He carried her back to the house, but he could not return her.

The house was brightly lit, morbidly festive, as they entered.

Forster locked Claire in yet another set of arms. "You're safe." Safe hardly.

Behind his shoulder, through her swelled eyelid, she saw policemen and other people. "Are you okay?" "Just some scratches. More scared than anything else." The doctor took her away. Broken arm, bruises, slight concussion. The house was crowded with strangers, confusing her, as in a dream. Was this still a cruel continuation of her birthday party? A known face, Mrs. Girbaldi, her unlikely confidant, stood by the stairs, owl-like eyes blinking out of her unmade face. Had Claire ever seen her without makeup before?

"Terrible, terrible," Mrs. Girbaldi chirped.

"Where's Joshua?" Forster asked.

"Where are the girls?" Claire answered.

They sat on the couch, Lucy and Gwen holding hands. Faces tracked by tears. When they saw her, they jumped up and rushed to be comforted. Buried their heads so hard against her ribs that already hurt badly, but she didn't care. She hugged each of them, held them away. "Are you all right?"

They nodded, unsure, the damage invisible but felt.

"Where's Josh?" Claire said.

"He's not with you." Forster making a statement.

"She was alone," Octavio said.

"He ran to look for you," Gwen said. "Octavio called the police."

"Where's Josh?" The idea growing in Claire's head that all these strangers were to fill the vacuum of his absence. She searched for Forster's hand, stumbled across the room to the door. "We need to find him."

"They have search teams setting out. You need rest."

"Josh is still out in the orchard." Claire shook her head, fear tightening the muscles. "Where they took me."

Octavio stood as if made of wood, helpless, silent.

"Come," Forster said to him. "Show me where you found her."

* * *

During the first hours of Josh's being missing, Claire convinced herself it could all be a misunderstanding. Did she really remember his voice in the dark, the headbutt, or was it her imagination that later inserted it into the scene? A cosmic blip that would soon right itself. Her son, the baby of the family and the only boy, was spoiled, no getting around that. Maybe he was up to his favorite trick—pinching a chocolate bar meant to be shared with his sisters, stealing it and hiding out in the orchards to devour it in peace.

As teams of volunteers and police began to scour the acres of orchard, Forster called neighbors, the parents of Joshua's friends, all in the off hope that Josh had simply run off, cadged a dinner with friends, not called home. Forster prayed for the irresponsibility he usually punished the boy for. Darkness of real night settled in, a penetrating darkness the boy could not tolerate without his night-light before sleep. At ten, Claire still indulged him this.

When Claire's parents arrived, having turned around within an hour of arriving home in Santa Monica, she collapsed into her mother's arms. "He's afraid of the dark."

Raisi looked at her bruised face. "Oh, my girl, what has happened to us?"

Claire shook her head. "They wanted money—"

"Hush," Raisi said, nodding toward the girls.

Raisi watched her granddaughters wandering lost in the living room with smudged faces and reddened eyes, with shorts and T-shirts too insubstantial for the evening's cool. She signaled to Claire's father, Almos, to look after their daughter, and then she went to work. Herded the girls into their bedroom, drew warm bubble baths. Went into the kitchen and expertly made dough for cookies. Started a pot of coffee and served it to the volunteers congregated on the porch. Made a sort of order from the chaos.

She knew the value of trifles such as warm socks and hot cider in the face of devastation. Claire could count on her. At first Raisi had been a skeptic of this life her daughter chose, but now she was proud of what had been accomplished. Wrong that after such careful work, it could all so easily be undone. She would not tell Claire her experience of life—that this was the way of the world, to unravel everything one loved most. It was always only a matter of time. She prayed it not be so, but her heart ached with the probability.

Raisi found Claire in Josh's bedroom, curled underneath his narrow single bed. She made her get up and lie on the mattress, under the posters of airplanes and baseball heroes. Josh swore the family to secrecy about the stuffed animals that he still kept, because even though it was babyish, he wanted someday to be a veterinarian. Raisi sat on the bed to stroke her daughter's head, seeing the discolored skin and swollen eye and temple, her arm in a sling. Hours later when Claire woke, a question in her eyes.

Raisi shook her head. "He's not home yet."

"I'm scared."

"Be brave for the girls."

Claire closed her eyes, wishing that this strength *were* inherited, genetically passed down through the nerve endings, absorbed in the tissue, exhaled in the breath. Raisi, who had escaped Hungary during the uprising, who had lost all her extended family—mother, father, aunts, uncles, brothers—an entire country gone in one swoop of exile. Halfway around the world in Los Angeles, Raisi found and married a man, Almos Nagy, from the same small district village as herself. He ran an antiquarian bookshop in Santa Monica, a dusky backwater of a store that barely made enough to sustain them. Each afternoon, a half-dozen expats would gather and talk about what they had left behind. Things and places and people that over the years no longer existed except in memories.

Almos and Raisi had one daughter and, grateful, were afraid to push their luck for more. They had learned to conserve, to hoard, to save for a time of need. After she'd traveled thousands of miles, Raisi's life had ended not terribly differently from that if she had stayed in place, except for the longing. Which Claire had inherited, but her nostalgia extended to things not yet gone.

As a teenager, Claire had chafed at the dull, unrelenting routine of her parents—breakfast, lunch, dinner, always rotating between the same predictable choices, regardless of seasons, with only small concessions to the holidays. But now in the days of waiting for Josh's return, routine was a lifeline that kept the whole family from going under. It returned Claire to the past, trying to find the wrong turn that had caused this.

"Go take a bath," Raisi said.

Claire hesitated.

"I'll get you if there is any news."

In this way, Claire was prodded to go on with life.

The first restless night passed with no clues to Josh's whereabouts. Dawn broke with an ache. The next day, all the workers were ordered to go home, and the farm had an eerie, deserted feel as forensic experts took over, going back over every inch of earth in the daylight, sifting soil in places, looking for signs. They worked meticulously from the farmhouse out, so at their current rate the ranch would be done in years if not decades, while each moment mattered to Josh. Claire walked over the farm, scoured the earth where she had been found, not even able to find her own black drops of blood on the soil. The police demanded the water be turned off even though it was a record heat wave, not wanting evidence contaminated. Octavio cranked the big, shuddering wheels of the pumps closed.

Raisi took care of the girls, cooked and cleaned for the family, but the smell of food being prepared in the kitchen was a betrayal to Claire, and an even bigger betrayal when her stomach responded. She thought it unspeakable that life would dare go on with her son not there to eat his dinner. She sat at the table picking at a plate of macaroni and cheese.

Lucy, reading a book at the table, looked up at her. "We're just like the people in *The Cherry Orchard*."

Claire stared at her. "Why do people have children?" she said, then clamped her hand over her mouth in shame. "I didn't mean that."

"I know Josh will come back," Lucy said, patting Claire's hand with her own childish one.

Claire looked at her. "Why?"

The intensity of the stare made Lucy's face burn with guilt. "This is his favorite." Pointing her fork to the food.

The spoonful in Claire's mouth turned toxic. She ran to the sink and spat it out because, somewhere, her boy was hungry. Her stomach full when his was not.

The hours passed in a trance, the farm abandoned as the searchers, more desperate, skipped areas now, made looping excursions farther and farther out, past the lake, the fenced ditches, the neighbors' land. For once, Claire stayed inside, unwilling to go out into the groves. Raisi spent her time in the kitchen or in the living room, brushing out the girls' hair, stringing it with ribbon, teaching them parlor card games she had learned as a young girl. Dropping their usual teenage sangfroid, the girls now acted clinging and childish.

Claire and Forster fell into bed each night stunned, sleeping fully clothed, with shoes nearby. One night, there was the smallest tap on the bedroom door.

"Josh?" Claire said, bolting upright in bed.

Gwen came in, her cotton nightgown glowing in the dark. "We can't sleep," she said. Lucy sulked behind her.

"Bring your sleeping bags in," Claire said, hiding her disappointment. She watched over them as they arranged themselves around the bed, the bags like cocoons with the unformed girls inside. Since the disappearance, Lucy, thirteen years old, had started to suck her thumb in her sleep. It bothered Claire how meek the girls had turned, how serious-faced. But how could it be otherwise? Her mother was right. If she wasn't careful, she would lose them also.

A lifetime in each cycle of hours. Now Claire fought her increasing despair as one day passed into the next by forcing herself to go with Octavio to roam the grounds, both of them gloomy about the burnt edges of the thirsty leaves. If they didn't turn the water on soon, the fruit would be destroyed. Should they pick early and risk having the wholesaler reject much of it? Impossible without bringing in a full team of laborers. The false drought depriving the trees of their lifeblood, their air and nourishment. A whole season's worth of work, the entire crop, gone. If it went longer, the trees would die and need to be replanted. Enough to put them out of business.

Claire hid in the girls' room, reading them story after story, and when her voice cracked too much, they took turns reading. "What would you like? Something new?" But they did not want a story they did not already know the outcome to, did not want the complexities of the adult world. They reverted to their childhood, known classics: *Black Beauty, The Secret Garden, Anne of Green Gables, Jane Eyre.*

* * *

Housebound, cloistered days, the sound of classical music, the smells of her mother's cooking, returned Claire to her own childhood.

Their apartment was over her father's bookstore. One had to wind one's way through rows of shelves to find the staircase to get there. She would come home from school with friends and be embarrassed by the foreign smell of their apartment, the ever-present smells of cabbage and burning votive candles, her mother's rosary and thick nylons that made her look ancient and severe compared to the stylish mothers in tennis skirts and sneakers. Their home even sounded different. No big-band records or Sinatra. Instead, Liszt's Hungarian Rhapsodies played continually till the vinyl records crackled, and as a child Claire thought that was the sound of the past itself.

Another thing that marked them as foreign—the Nagys were a reading family and derived their knowledge of the world first through books. Subsequently, Claire found she only really understood a subject if she read about it in print. Close to Hollywood, all their neighbors worshipped movie stars, but they instead worshipped writers. A house of freely mingling nationalities—the Russians with the French, the South Americans with the Deep Southerners with the Irish. Dostoyevsky nestled against Borges, Zola communed with Faulkner and Joyce. As well, there was no discrimination between the living and the dead, and when school friends asked about the pictures of the grim men (Kafka and her father's favorite, Márai) in the living room, Claire lied and said they were distant great-uncles.

The gloomy apartment was crowded, the small rooms overwhelmed, filled with a past life bigger than their present one: towering antique armoires from Austria, featuring fixed forms of birds in flight and flowers native to the Black Forest. No longer being fashionable, these were picked up cheap at estate sales. An armoire in Claire's room was made of darkest wood and covered a whole wall, featuring a black bear with a gaping maw in which Claire used to hide a single grape. A tarnished Polish samovar with its potbellied blue flame boiled away on a sideboard each Sunday, while Raisi served Viennese pastries on china to the neighborhood ladies, scandalizing them by giving the grown-ups thimblefuls of eye-burning slivovitz, plum brandy, poured into crystal goblets stained the red, blue, and gold colors of church windows.

Almos tried to learn golf, planned days at the beach, bought a barbecue, but Raisi stubbornly clung to the old ways as if she were still in a place of scarcity, still in a place of cold, blowing winds.

Now Claire looked at the things inside her own house so painstakingly gathered, including the chest with the black bear, the samovar, the books. Had that really been her, trying to create a home so hard? A museum of family? She, after all, wasn't an exile like Raisi, or was she? Had she inherited the damage of loss the way the children of soldiers inherit that specific heartbreak?

Guilty about falling asleep for a few hours after the first week, Claire woke to the news that a piece of paper had been left in the mailbox, no observers, with a demand for ransom. The police immediately went into action, interviewing all the workers again. "I need to talk with you," Claire said to Forster.

"What?"

They went outside to the porch. "I offered them money."

He paused, considering, and his slow deliberateness maddened her. "I don't think—"

"What if I gave them the idea to take Josh?"

"Stop it."

"We need to get the money."

"The police said no."

"He's not their son."

"Let them handle it."

"My fault. Our son." Claire ran into the house. Punched the numbers of the bank and demanded to speak with Mr. Relicer. She was told he was in a meeting. "This is an emergency," she yelled. After too long, he came on.

"Mrs. Baumsarg, we heard—"

"I need money. An increase."

"Yes, well . . . the line was closed at your request."

"Open it again. Can I pick it up?"

"Under the circumstances, it wouldn't be responsible."

The answer was so in character, Claire hung up.

She ran back to Forster. "Let's sell the farm. We can get money fast." He walked out of the house, slamming the door. For the rest of the day, they did not speak. When Claire walked into the kitchen, Raisi stopped chopping vegetables and took her aside.

"You must stop this."

"What?"

"Pitying yourself. We don't know what happened to Joshua. But I see what is happening to the rest of the family. Do your job—hold things together."

Then it occurred to her at last, the obvious choice. She went to Mrs. Girbaldi, the wealthiest woman in the county. "It's a horrible thing to ask for. You have the right to tell me no," Claire said. "Nothing is more precious than a child," Mrs. Girbaldi said. The two of them went to the bank. A withdrawal wasn't even recorded since she had enough cash in deposit boxes to satisfy the amount. The bag was placed in the location specified, a lonely stretch of highway toward the desert, in the crook of a tree. The women went to a diner for coffee, and when they drove back, the bag was gone.

After an hour, they had still heard nothing. Back home, Claire stood vigil on the porch, unable to tell anyone what she had done.

That night, Claire turned her back to Forster, only waking when Lucy tugged at her. The child mortified that she had peed in her sleep, soaking her sleeping bag. Claire took her into the bathroom, running the bath and washing her as she had when she was a little girl.

Lucy rested her head on her mother's shoulder. "Is it our fault?"

"What?"

"We let Joshua go away."

"Never think that."

"Will the bad men come back for us?"

"You'll be safe. I promise," Claire said, bringing her to their bed and letting her sleep nested between them.

The next morning, Forster announced he would call the developers.

"I've taken care of it."

All through the next morning, all through the next week, nothing. Then Octavio was allowed to turn the water back on, and the sprinklers ran, breaking the hard, cracked dirt, and still they heard nothing. As if, collecting the money, the kidnappers forgot their part. Claire kept replaying that night. It had been Octavio's pickup going up the driveway. When did Josh decide to go after her?

At the Mejia *quinceañera* party, his daughter Paz wore a long blue gown. Her skin was milky, the crown of paste jewels on her black hair catching the light of candles, making her look as if flame were sparking off her body. It all came down to this, and whatever was out there in those dark fields, Octavio needed to protect his daughter, his whole family, from it. Despite the loud music, his father was dozing on a sofa pushed into the dining room. It was the old man's new trick—the ability to sleep constantly, under any conditions. Octavio squeezed his father's shoulder gently and only got a sleepy shrug in reply. He opened a beer and drank the full thing down in one gulp.

"Tavi, take it easy. The night has just started," Sofia said, walking past with a tray laden with food. "People are paying attention."

Sofia had never cared what people thought when she let Octavio take her to the lake all those years ago, but life changed. The house was crowded beyond standing room with relatives, and relatives of relatives, and friends, neighbors, only a small number of whom Octavio recognized, and the heat inside grew thick and pushing. He would go broke entertaining strangers, all people whose opinion his Sofia suddenly cared so much about. Not once did she suggest canceling for Joshua. Where had his gentle wife's heart gone? Nevertheless, Octavio stopped in awe at the sight of his firstborn child; his eyes grew watery. Twenty years from this night, would Octavio himself be tucked away on a sofa, worn out by life, while his Paz threw the *quinceañera* for her own daughter? It exhausted him, the endless cycles of life, like the harvest.

"Ah, *Papi,* not now. No tears."

Paz had replaced his young Sofia in her gentle concern for him. What worse hell could there be than to lose one's child, one's future? His love of Joshua was just as fierce as if he had been blood. Octavio shuddered as if a cold breeze had crossed his hot skin. Worse than the worst thing he could imagine, which was losing one's land.

The band tuned up for the first dance, the one reserved for father and daughter. Octavio had learned steps with a dance teacher, who gave Sofia and the girls lessons, but he was too tired to practice every night for it to do much good. Now he clumped across the floor, his footwork even more cloddish compared to the princess steps of his Paz. He was self-conscious, mortified by the bright light and the attention of all these strange eyes on them. Let Paz have the light, only outside was he himself, among his trees, one with the earth that he tilled like prayer. Eat the orange, taste the sweet juice that was like liquid light; he wasn't too shy to take credit for that. He stepped on Paz's satin slipper right before the music stopped, but she pretended she felt nothing. A good girl. They ended to applause, and Octavio was released to go outside, cool off, and hide.

Paz was circling a group of older teenagers who ignored her, trying to make eye contact with a boy she favored, when she heard them talking about two young men from Apatzingán, Mexico, involved in a crime with a local *delincuente* who was always in and out of jail. News traveled in the neighborhood more reliably than in the newspapers, but even second generation felt no inclination to go to the police. *Policía* were still thought of in terms of their homeland, a force that could just as easily bring more trouble than less. Instead, it was preferable to close ranks and take care of trouble from within if possible. The Mejias were not much part of the community; they were considered a bit conceited, barely a step below their beloved employers so that they took the disappearance as a family matter. Sofia was determined to remedy this to get her daughter married even if Octavio was determined to turn a blind eye. This grudge allowed the guests to gorge themselves on the food and drink without guilt.

Paz wished to move off and forget such talk on her special day, but the words *boy* and *money* stuck in her ear and nagged. Her father's heart had been heavy the last weeks; he scowled and kicked out of his way her younger brothers and sisters. Pretty, childish Joshua, who always flirted with her, was missing, and a bad outcome would not be good for any of them. Like a bird, Paz flew to her father, and he in turn herded the boys into a closed bedroom, despite Sofia's begging that it was time to cut the cake, that he was ruining the family's night. That he was always more interested in the Baumsargs than his own family.

Octavio's fists clenched and unclenched, his uncles and brothers behind him, rumbling like thunder in the mountains. These were young, innocent kids, thinking they were cool by being in the know of gang talk in the neighborhoods. They had only heard wisps of gossip. Two no-goods were passing through and had met a small-time criminal named Denny Larsen at the local bar. Just out of jail for burglary, using a fake ID, he had found a job with a local caterer and worked the birthday party at the Baumsarg ranch. He bragged it would be an easy robbery. Start-up money for getting in the drug business. Octavio understood what had nagged at him earlier about the stolen silver globe—it had been found in the bag of a waiter, who was promptly fired. The Baumsargs refused to press charges.

Octavio went down the porch steps of his house, the house he had grown up in, where he raised his own family, and yet the steps felt unfamiliar. He knew with certainty that nothing would ever be the same. Blood pounded in his head something fierce. If he didn't know better, he would say that he was having a heart attack, but this was an attack of a more intimate kind. His brother Avelino clutched a broken-edged baseball bat. A cousin held a pipe. Octavio had seen nothing that dark night, but the air had felt menacing as it now did. An electrical charge brushed over his skin like the feel of fur. The memory of a broken female body on the ground was replaced by the standing form of Paz, in her beautiful, shining blue gown that matched the night, sparks coming off her hair from the paste diamonds.

"Papi?"

"Call the police," Octavio said under his breath to Sofia, who came out to see why he insisted on disgracing them in front of everyone they knew. He charged off with a roar like a bull, to save what had already been lost.

As Claire sat at the kitchen table with Forster, her parents, and the girls, a truck roared to a stop in front of the house. Forster looked up but did not rise, as if he had a premonition that this was something he did not want to rush to meet. Octavio walked straight in, as was his habit. Paz trailed behind in her blue satin gown and tiara, ribbons in her hair and satin shoes. She cried as Octavio pulled her by the arm.

"We must talk," he said.

Gwen and Lucy, already in pajamas, stared at the girl, who now appeared a stranger. They had grown up together, played in the orchards and in each other's house. Beauty that Paz was, Josh developed a wild crush on her. Now she stared back in all her adult finery, badly out of place, and she wanted to hide.

"You look pretty," Lucy said.

Paz stared back without staying a word.

Raisi herded the girls up to bed, closing the kitchen door behind them. In their room, they worried out questions.

"Why did she come?" Gwen asked.

"She probably wanted you to see her beautiful dress," Raisi said, guessing from the foreman's seriousness that the real answer was far worse. "Since you missed her party."

"She looked like a princess," Lucy said. "Did you see she had lipstick on?"

"Why was she crying then?" Gwen persisted.

Raisi sat on the edge of the bed and covered her face in her hands for a moment. The world was a lure and a trap, a trap and tragedy. She had found this out as a young girl and never been disabused of the knowledge, although there was no acting on it, only enduring it. She got up to make coffee for the real mourning that she feared would now start. "Best to get dressed, girls. There won't be much sleep tonight."

The sheriffs came out and cordoned off the property, not allowing anyone on without permission. Police vans parked on the highway road. Floodlights were carried out to the remote area by the lake. Yellow tape unspooled and wrapped from trunk to trunk like a child's game. The two sheriffs' cars blocked the road to the orchard, careless and crooked, as if their drivers were in a great hurry.

The stark light of the searchlights gave the lemon trees and the fields around it an otherworldly feel, like a photo negative. Minus one child, the insulated Baumsarg world cracked open, the X-ray revealing a diseased inside. Octavio stood by the patrol car, his face contorted by pain. Claire sat in the back of one of the cars, her head bowed as if at a confessional. Each breath a labor. She was angry at the hurry that came too late. As if Joshua were lying under his blanket of dirt holding his breath. As if any of them could still be saved.

The officers stood knee-deep in dirt, one sheriff slope-shouldered and one potbellied with an aching back, shoveling, and then Forster let out a moan so strange it did not seem likely to come from such a large man, more like the noise of an animal trapped in the high mountains, leg caught, helpless.

He pushed them aside, parted the last inches of dirt with bare fingers. Then yelled for everyone to turn away in shame. Claire stumbled out of the car. The sheriffs, sweating, turned and with smudgy fingers stroked their felt hats. In the etched shadows, their expressions turned blank. Such outlandish grief made them dumb.

A glimpse of pant leg that turned out to be dirt-encrusted jeans. The bright red of a Keds sneaker that Josh had insisted on buying, so that he could spot his shoes easily for gym class. A pain charged through Claire's body, and she knew with certainty that she would never recover from the sight. It grafted itself, unwanted, onto her. A cicatrice of grief.

Octavio fell on his knees in front of her. "Forgive me."

A distaste, like bile. "What are you talking about?"

"I should have somehow protected him. I didn't know enough."

That was the final blow. Not even the death of Josh that destroyed, but her inability to save him from harm—a parent's first duty—was what undid her.

Chapter 3

The land was the first thing to understand. The Baumsarg family's citrus ranch was one of the most valuable pieces of land in Southern California—580 acres of groves, with a ranch house and numerous outbuildings of wood with corrugated-tin roofs that flashed in the sunlight like semaphores. The majority was planted between Valencias and Washington navels. The Valencias that spring were blooming white blossoms and in fruit at the same time, the novelty of which delighted Claire. Acres and acres of perfumed white, orange, and green.

Claire felt she had arrived in paradise when she married Forster and first came to live there as a young bride. Both sides of their family were from immigrant stock, raised for hardscrabble adversity and expecting no better, but always persevering. The promise of land made the hope fresh for Claire, made her feverish with dreams and plans, even as it had grown stale for the inherent family.

She did not know the ranch was already in peril by the time Forster and she first met at UCLA. An awkward, gangly blond of German descent, Forster carefully maneuvered a cup of punch through a boisterous crowd at a university social to bring it to her without losing a single drop. She was the shy girl at school, and his attention overwhelmed her.

"You have the most delicate hands," he said. How to explain that the moment he saw her, it was clear-cut that she was the one, but he had to pretend the knowledge away.

In the bathroom, the other girls had teased her over his attentions. "He's a rube. He's got dirt under his fingernails, in his ears. A farmer boy." Claire came out of the bathroom less flattered by his attentions, more wary.

Sensing he might already be losing her interest, he blurted out, "Would you like to go outside?"

She would. Away from the curious eyes, the ironic, curled smiles. In the dark, the spring air was fragrant. They stood on the stone patio and gazed into the gloom of eucalyptus trees to avoid each other's eyes.

"It smells so nice," she said, thinking how to make a quick exit.

"The oranges are blooming. I've grown up with this smell every spring of my life. I'd be lost without it." She looked at him more closely. His clothes—khakis and polo shirt—were old but quality. As he was oblivious to what he wore, they seemed picked out by someone else, maybe a mother?

"Tell me about your farm," she said.

"I'll tell you about the whole valley. My great-grandfather got the first seeds from a tree on the Agua Clara ranch. He started all the stock on our ranch, and the whole county borrowed from it. So there is a single patriarch tree that generated the whole county." His family had owned the large farm for three generations, including other land besides; he had never considered any other life. Development was encroaching, and with record droughts over the past years and subpar crop yields, the family had had to cannibalize and sell the other pieces of land to keep the main citrus operation going. Instead of being past its prime, he saw the valley where his family's farm lay as a place of promise still not consummated. He envisioned making the farm larger, more productive, being at the forefront of new trends in agriculture.

It seemed an old-fashioned, nostalgic way to live, one that appealed to her. She dreaded the idea of working in an office. He reminded her of a poet or maybe a preacher, not a farmer, so his endless talk of planting schedules and load counts seemed out of character, quixotic, until she realized he was simply stalling. Although the patio light was dim, she looked slyly at his ear and saw that it was pink and clean.

"What are you smiling about?" he asked.

"Nothing." Because he sensed her interest was real, he had grown bolder and more expansive. Even to the edge of passionate. No one else had seen this side, which she had brought out. Part of what she fell in love with was her own creation of him. "Are you going to ask me out on a date?"

Over the months of their courtship—the first boy she went on a date with, the first she kissed—Forster explained the life to her, but she was simply looking into his eyes, dreaming of their life together. She had never been in love before, didn't know if this was it, but she liked the feeling of being a small ship riding in the wake of a larger one. He took her to the lake on the edge of the ranch, and they lay together on the hood of the car, the warm, ticking engine beneath them substituting for contact.

They walked through the rows of groves, and the beauty and silence were like being in a cathedral. She stood still, feeling her legs anchored to the earth. The quiet was like a hum, like the earth's own metronome, a sound she had not even known she hungered for.

Forster picked an orange off a tree, then took his pocketknife out of his pants and cut a helix of peel from the blossom end. "This is the part you always eat for taste," he said. After they had eaten half of the fruit—sugary, dripping—he tossed the other half away.

The quiet was so intense they heard the splash of a fish in the lake. If she wanted this, she would have to be the one to make a move. She took his hand and placed it on her breast.

After graduation, he returned to the ranch, worked from dawn till dusk, tirelessly, and bragged at being the luckiest man ever to have such work. Not wanting to be separated, she stopped her studies, a temporary state that turned permanent, giving up her dreams of becoming a teacher like her mother, content to share Forster's vision. Or maybe the desires of the ranch itself seeped into her dreams, usurped others, and became her obsession as well. Regardless, she was unprepared for the demands her new life would make on her.

"I don't know anything about farming," she said.

"You don't need to know anything. You plant a tree and pick the fruit." A truth that contained a thousand steps in between.

His family paid for the large wedding, while her mother sewed her wedding gown, an old-world dress of ivoried lace and seed pearls that all the women marveled over. Overwhelmed, Claire was aware of having come from a more tenuous background, less anchored, and that of course was the precise attraction of the ranch. Her parents had lived in their new country like polite relatives overstaying their welcome, even though they had been there thirty years. They didn't want to take up too much room. They always spoke of the old country as the real life, of California as some kind of purgatory, although they had long ago given up on leaving.

"Are you okay, *mézes*?" her mother asked Claire as they dressed in her future bedroom, overlooking the backyard filled with impatient guests. Most of them were ranchers and still intended to get work done before sundown. Leisure didn't come easily. Her mother, a schoolteacher, was unfazed by the Baumsarg family's relative affluence, counted in acres of land rather than degrees. Her father, a scholar and book dealer, couldn't reconcile himself to his only daughter's choosing a life of farming over that of the intellect.

"I love him, Mama."

Her mother looked at her shrewdly, realizing too late that they had made a mistake sheltering her so much. "Sometimes love isn't enough."

A thing to say to a bride on her wedding day, yet Claire knew not to take it personally. Her mother believed in keeping expectations low to avoid future disappointment, an immigrant's philosophy.

After the ceremony, food was laid out on wooden picnic tables along the lawn as far as the edge of the orchard. At one point during the evening, Forster's great-uncle, white-haired, mustachioed, stood up and started to sing, joined by his friends who formed a barbershop quartet. They looked out of the forties in their old-fashioned striped shirts and straw hats; they were a nostalgia act, singing at Independence Day events, football games, and once even appearing on a TV show in Hollywood.

I love you truly, tru-ly dear
Life with its sorrow, life with its tear

They honeymooned in Hawaii, not on the beach, but in the interior of the Big Island, on a friend's ranch surrounded with cattle and fields where Forster felt comfortable—farms, always farms. One night, Claire woke to an empty bed and open door. She went out and found Forster curled on a deck chair. The dew was heavy as drizzle, and he was shivering in the moonlight.

"What's wrong?" she asked, an alarm going off inside her.

"Look at you," he said, accusing, jutting his chin at her. She looked down, saw the moonlight rendering her gauzy nightdress almost sheer. "So beautiful. And I'm supposed to make you happy."

She laughed—relieved and troubled in equal parts—and knelt down to hold him. Her mother's words echoed.

Claire moved directly from her parents' house to her marriage house. Forster's mother, Hanni, laughed at her cosseted ways—the silver samovar and the large collection of books as a kind of dowry.

"We have a teakettle," Hanni said. "Don't need that big thing."

Claire shrugged, shocked by the rudeness of her new mother-in-law.

"Why all these books?" she asked, as Claire carried in the heavy boxes, unaided.

"Because there are none here for me to read."

"I tell my son to bring me a tractor, instead he brings me a shiny bicycle."

Hanni had been an attorney's daughter before marrying Forster's father, but the years had honed her into a rancher, with browned, wrinkled skin, sharp, angular cheekbones that reminded Claire of a hawk, a look in her eyes devoid of any vanity.

"You are so lovely," she said, stroking her new daughter-in-law's plump cheek with her calloused hand, accusing. "No wonder my son went crazy over you."

"We went crazy for each other." She would never become like Hanni. She would apply moisturizer, wear hats, would read every day, and practice the piano. She would write. The idea of losing the nascent life of the mind for a life of physical labor frightened her. She had told Forster that she wasn't ready yet to have children, that she would make an appointment with her gynecologist for contraceptives.

Hanni winked. "When I was your age, I went to parties. Had so many beaux. I cried every night for a year when I first moved here. What are you going to do out in the middle of nowhere?"

Claire's heart sank. The other girls at college laughed at her, leaving Los Angeles for a rural life, said she was from another age, a pioneer, a pilgrim. Taunted her that she would be barefoot and pregnant in no time. They didn't understand that she wanted more than anything else to be rooted, and the ranch gave her that. Eventually she would have her own family, one that would not be lost. She could always go back to her books eventually.

"My mother's parents had a farm in Hungary. My mother says without land, you are nothing." An exaggeration, the farm had belonged to cousins, but that quieted the old woman.

"It is a hard, narrow life," Hanni conceded. "But it can nourish. For the right person." Neither of them at all sure that Claire was that person.

Under Hanni's niggling supervision, Claire took care of the sprawling house herself, deciding this would be her domain. She washed dishes, ironed clothes, and mopped floors, partly drudgery but also a kind of communion. Forster taught her to take over the ranch's bookkeeping.

Exhausted, she would play scales on the piano late each afternoon. She read a chapter of a book each night before Forster came to bed and began to stroke the hem of her nightgown. Mornings she sat on the patio and filled notebooks with descriptions of the orchards, of the clouds, of the physical labors of her days and the sensual pleasures of her nights. But the demands of the house and ranch defeated her efforts. She never made it to the doctor. Within months, she was pregnant with their first child.

* * *

The original farmhouse had been built in the twenties by Forster's paternal grandparents, who lost a fortune in the shipping yards of Hamburg and had to emigrate to avoid creditors. Each successive birth and handing over from generation to generation had resulted in more rooms, more painted adobe brick and wood. The house meandered, organic to the demands made on it, much like a nest cradled in branches of a tree, or the underground warrens of gophers. Forster's uncle from back East had visited one summer and had the inspiration to build the only wraparound, screened porch in the area, not believing the neighboring farmers who told him there were no pests to hide away from in the dry, subtropical climate.

Hanni made a point to show Claire the details of the kitchen, commercial in size, with a ten-burner stove, brick fireplace, cast-iron spits to roast large cuts of meat, double refrigerators, and thick, deep, hammered-copper sinks, imported from Germany in a brief flash of affluence thirty years before, that had to be scoured with a special mix of lemon juice and salt that stung the hands.

Ugly and practical, this was not a modern, status-seeking, unused kitchen, but rather the center of a working ranch. Forster's grandmother and Hanni had served up three meals a day to a working crew of fifty men during the height of picking season.

In the early days, before the advent of the commercial *loncherías*, the women, with the help of half a dozen of the Mexican laborers' wives, had become adept at making homemade tortillas, large pots of beans and rice, great vats of chili con carne, or *chili verde,* long aluminum trays of enchiladas and burritos, with bowls of whole jalapeños and *zanahoria en escabeche,* marinated carrots, on the side. The women in Forster's family ghettoized their German recipes to Sunday dinner, with their *Kartoffelkloesse,* spaetzle, and *Schweineschnitzel.* The heavy old-world food became synonymous in the minds of their children and grandchildren with the boredom of rote church attendance, the tightness of clothes not meant for everyday, with dry ritual and starched table linen not meant to be spilled on.

Claire fingered the faucets that had cross handles with porcelain inserts that read HEIβE on one side and KÄLTE on the other. She resisted the urge to run out of the room with her swelling belly, to return to her parents' apartment, to her books. Frightened she had made a mistake, was losing herself before there was even a self to lose.

"This was all here before I came," Hanni confessed.

"Didn't you want to make it your own?"

"The ranch changes you, not the other way around."

Already Claire was growing tired of these homilies, but she did not run out of the kitchen that day. Slowly, over time, she came to love the sensibleness of the house, how it stripped her of small vanities one by one, made her come to hate waste and ostentation.

For the first months of the marriage, Hanni sat back and watched her new daughter-in-law work. The only half compliment she gave her was "Well, at least you don't have time to read all those books."

It was true that Claire felt herself losing a battle. She spent an hour trying to write about the sunlight through the leaves of orange trees, and it read like a student's clumsy primer with no hint of the real experience. But Hanni was wrong that she didn't read. Every moment she could, she stole away and spent it in books—the reading kept her from chafing over the narrowing of her current life.

Saturday afternoons, frustrated by her writing, tired of having only her mother-in-law for company, Claire began a tradition of baking a cake or pastries, lighting the samovar, and brewing tea. She sent out invitations to all the neighbors. At first Hanni resisted the fuss, not willing to put on nice clothes and waste time sitting in the living room, but when the ladies of the surrounding ranches began to stop by, the reintroduction of community, she relented. Saturday teatime became a staple over the years. In this way Claire met Mrs. Girbaldi, the biggest land dowager in the area, both shrewder and kinder than Hanni, who became Claire's confidant. Her platinum-dyed hair and powdered-white skin created a monochromatic palette, a paleness broken only by the features she chose to paint on, maroon lips and heavily lined eyes, which aspired to a standard of fifties bygone beauty that hid her sharp, businesslike mind.

Hanni complained privately that Mrs. Girbaldi liked to "play poor." Her father had been a ruthless businessman and acquired land cheaply; her husband was even more ruthless and greedy. When he passed away, everyone was surprised that Mrs. Girbaldi was tougher than either of the men. Talk was that not only did she want to break up her family's holdings, she wanted to zone for high density to maximize profits. Claire circled, only half listening to the gossip.

"Did you hear about the Hahn ranch?"

"No, what?"

"I shouldn't talk."

"Tell!"

"An actor—"

"Bought it?"

"Cheap. Some teenage heartthrob named Don Richards. Got it as a tax shelter. Old Hahn couldn't grow a weed."

"A pity."

"Too much time nursing the bottle."

"But another actor. When one comes, they all start to follow."

"That's the end of the place."

After their first, Gwen, was born, the couple walked the orchards each evening. At a leisurely pace, Forster carrying the baby, it took almost an hour to reach the lake. They usually watched the ducks swimming back and forth in the last of the sun. Claire was too new to notice that the water level was low, reeds were overtaking a larger and larger part of the lake, a drought that meant even higher water prices and rationing. Forster spread a blanket beneath the large lemon tree, and Claire nursed Gwen while he paced back and forth. Sometimes, midsentence, he stopped and stared at her. "What?" "I never knew it would be like this," he said, cradling the baby's delicate skull in his big palm.

In quick succession, two daughters were born: Gwen, then Lucy. Claire and Hanni had their days full with the duties of two babies. With each birth, Claire felt more happily anchored, rooted, into her new life. She forgot her former reluctance, forgot also her books, but the joy she took in mothering reassured her that she had made the right decision. Still, some nights, walking a crying child, she did have a sense of being swallowed up. In time, she promised, she would return to her books, keep digging for that deeper vein of life that she had abandoned.

Claire and Forster discussed this being the end of their childbearing, but both of them were so exhausted most days that contraception didn't seem necessary. The moment she knew she was pregnant a third time, she also sensed it was a boy. Joshua. Unlike the first two, this birth was difficult, and the baby was kept in intensive care for a few weeks. When they brought him home at last, he was colicky, hardly ever sleeping through the night, something Claire hadn't experienced with the girls.

One adult had to sacrifice sleep each night, or the whole house would. As Joshua grew older, he didn't like to eat, and it took all Hanni's ingenuity to feed him. But from the first moment, he was clearly the last piece of the puzzle, making the family complete. Not knowing that life was less than perfect before, after Joshua's birth life could be described in no other way than balanced. Perfectly, miraculously balanced.

With three small children, Claire insisted that Forster take Sundays off to spend with the family. They would load up the used station wagon with toys and food, then drive down to a quiet stretch of beach. Setting up under the shade of trees and umbrellas, Forster would take turns carrying the girls down to the water, where they shrieked and giggled, by turns terrified and happy. Faces striped with zinc oxide that faded with the hours. Claire watched Joshua, read, and dozed. At the end of the day, dazed by sun and salt, they piled back into the car. Tired, sticky, content.

Chapter 4

But even as their domestic life grew richer, it became clear that the lifeblood of the place was out in the fields, and conditions were growing more difficult.

After the Girbaldi ranch, developers had turned their voracious attentions on the Baumsarg land, with proposals for communities of houses, condos, midrises, and high-rises. Forster and Hanni held out—a small, stubborn blemish with their strawberry fields skirting the new highways, windbreaks of eucalyptus and pine, rolling acres of avocado and orange and lemon. Now the local politicians were getting in on the act, claiming that the water table was being depleted, that agricultural water rates would need to be raised, all at the behest of the well-heeled developers.

Forster had the idea of building a crude lean-to at the foot of an off-ramp, stocking it with crates of fruit and vegetables, a blackboard with prices. More than the small amount of money it earned, he wanted to make their presence felt in the community so that people would want to buy locally grown rather than imported. Besides alternating the usual crops of Valencias in spring and summer, Washington navels in the fall and winter, he explored branching out into lemons, avocados, tangerines, and even blood oranges. An effort was made to innovate and modernize:

wooden crates were replaced by cardboard boxes, and then recycled plastic. They stamped the family name below that of the grocer who demanded an exclusive on their harvest. All of it to no financial gain. Their lack of profitability only made Forster more intractable.

Claire heard these problems in conversations over the dinner table, at the Saturday teas, watched the effect in Forster's growing insomnia, his pushing himself to work longer and longer hours while she stayed preoccupied by the children, until Forster came home one night from the local bar, saying he would load his gun and go blast the local county-board supervisor. The man had been bragging, claiming he would drive all the last farmers out of the area in a few years. Forster accused Claire of not caring, cloistering herself in the house, ignoring the farm and their future. It was only partly true. She bit her tongue, wanting to say she had done her part, bearing the children and caring for them. The next Saturday afternoon, she motioned Mrs. Girbaldi outside.

"I need your advice. The farm's in trouble."

Mrs. Girbaldi looked over the trees, shaking her head. "You married into trouble. But now . . . get out."

"They won't."

"Then get out there. Stave off the inevitable. But it will be gone one day."

"I don't know anything about farming. I'm a housewife."

Mrs. Girbaldi tapped her polished pink fingernail on Claire's arm. "Learn the land. I did when George passed. Everyone except you hates me for selling out. But I saw that's the future."

"I can't lose my home. I'm scared."

"Nonsense. Farming is as much a part of mothering as feeding them dinner or reading them a bedtime story. You might just like it."

* * *

So Claire reluctantly gave over child-care duties to Hanni, endured the howls of departure from Gwen, tears from Lucy. Only Josh seemed happy and content both when Claire was close and when she was not.

While Forster was in town, Claire went out for the first time on her own to talk with the foreman, Octavio.

He looked at the ground and spoke in soft, mumbling phrases, not willing to look her in the face out of a mix of respect and discomfort. A woman boss out in the fields was not done. He worried how the men would react. But a careful alliance started when he realized she was as worried about the ranch as he was.

One day, he asked her to drive with him to the edge of the ranch near the lake, an area of old trees that were past their prime fruiting days. They parked under the monstrous lemon tree that towered above them, and Octavio seemed so solemn and filled with importance about the place, she remained silent.

"That is the reason we are here."

Claire looked at the tree, but chose not to spoil the effect by telling him they came there daily. She wanted his trust and loyalty. "How did it get that way?"

"That is the original. That's where they all came from."

"Why doesn't it look like the other trees?"

"This is the original rootstock. My grandfather planted it. This is what lives. All the grafts, the fancy fruit we attach, it lives only because of the strength of the original."

Claire didn't think it mattered who took credit for the beginning. Who continued the ranch was what mattered.

Together Octavio and Claire walked the fields, he teaching her the growing cycles of citrus and avocado, soil conditions, irrigation patterns. Explaining bud unions, the joining of scion and rootstock, the merits of sweet-orange versus bitter-orange stock. He was surprised that her interest seemed genuine, and he warmed to the task of turning her into a farmer. She spent such long hours out in the orchards her skin tanned dark, her hair streaked pale gold. Calluses formed on her palms. Now she wore jeans more comfortably than dresses. Sometimes she fell asleep in her clothes from exhaustion. But she learned. Yields were low, and excess land had been sold, down to the last, undividable five-hundred-plus-acre parcel. Packers took too large a share of the profit. Forster at first resisted her help and then, relieved, came to rely on it.

Despite the difficulty, Mrs. Girbaldi was right—she discovered the life suited her. Fit her in many ways better than it did Forster. While he saw only tasks to be accomplished, she fed regularly on the sensory. No longer in notebooks but in her body. Farming as physical an experience as motherhood. Small, intangible things. The burn of the sun mixed with the cool coastal air, the inked flutter of leaves, the hard, briny skin of avocado, grapefruit, and lemons. Oranges, small and green and unripe. It all gave such pleasure and tempered the hardship. The air at noon filled with the sting of citrus oil; the delicate golden skin of Meyer lemons, which broke easily under a crescent of fingernail. In the late afternoon, she took naps outside with the girls when they were toddlers, baby Joshua curled against her breast, all of them spread out on blankets under the trees like fallen, ripe fruit. She could, unbeknownst to Forster, place a pinch of orchard soil on her tongue and gauge the sweetness of the coming crop.

During those early years with Forster, she drank deeply from the well of their marriage, a balance of belonging and being needed, and she didn't miss the life she had turned her back on. Except for her books. The sorrow of abandoning domesticity turned to relief. She felt her whole being expand with the freedom of spending her days outdoors.

Forster teased that she would try to read a novel during childbirth if she could. He was about right because it was her only free time. As if observing another person's life, she looked back to the time of school and books, working in her father's store and reading away the long, idle afternoons, as meaningless now in the hard struggle of daily survival they faced. Her parents stopped asking her when she would return to college to finish her degree. A heresy to them that a course in soil science would have been more useful than one in English literature. But farming was so rich in the present that it was a chore to consider the abstractions of a book.

In turn, she joked that Forster rested from working out in the orchards by dreaming of working out in the orchards. As the summer worn on, he grew thin and then thinner. When lightheadedness took him to the doctor, stress was blamed. The doctor prescribed rest, a vacation, which was about as impossible to ask for as telling a bird to not fly. Claire tried not to show how scared she was. Despite their differences in temperament, the rigors of the work, she still felt a fierce passion for her husband that was returned. Escaping during the night, Forster and she would sneak out to the barn to make love in the loft, their only place of privacy, the slatted moonlight striping their bodies in silver. Life without him was impossible to contemplate.

She would take more on herself, try to keep the worst from him. She took Octavio aside, told him to give the bad news only to her. The foreman wondered if she understood the burden she was taking on.

One afternoon, while Claire fed Joshua on the back porch, Hanni came and set down a cup of tea. Roles had reversed, Claire more and more assuming the role of matriarch.

"I worry," Hanni stated.

Claire noticed the stoop in her back as she sat down. When had she grown old? "About?" Now Hanni's abrupt style of speaking was her own.

"We're losing money. It can't go on."

"Yes," Claire said carefully, wondering why Hanni had come to her, not her son, for this conversation.

"I can hardly say it aloud . . . should you talk to him about selling?"

"Why not talk to him yourself?"

"He's too proud," Hanni said, the usual mix of arrogance and humbleness. "You're not."

Claire could have gone to Mrs. Girbaldi, who understood money, but Hanni was wrong—Claire *was* too proud to admit their financial difficulties outside the family. After a sleepless night, Claire came up with a plan. Hanni and she fed the girls, gave Josh his bottle, then told Forster they were going into town to shop. Sofia came to babysit.

"Don't spend all my money." Forster grinned, but strain was in his eyes. He went on his way to the fields with Octavio.

Instead of shopping, the women went to the bank. The family only had checking and savings accounts; everything else was paid in cash, no credit cards. Feeling out of place, they stood clutching their purses at the counter and asked the teller if they could speak to a loan officer. Once they gave their name, a secretary appeared and shuttled them upstairs to a mahogany-lined office. The president of the bank, Mr. Relicer, a neurasthenic man in an expensive black suit, came in drying his hands with a paper towel. He moved sideways, crablike, around his deep desk, stooping with a small, curtsying bob.

"I don't believe I've had the pleasure of meeting you yet. I wasn't invited to the wedding. What's it been? Six years?"

"Eight." Claire shook his hand, his nervous dampness causing her to pull away and wipe her palm along the side of her dress.

"Coffee?" he said, but when she looked up, his eyes were not on her but on the secretary. She realized it wasn't a choice but an order. "Hold my calls. Baumsarg. I consider myself a bit of a Germanophile. The name means 'coffin wood.' In the Bronze Age, they fashioned a coffin out of a tree trunk. Strange, is it not?"

Hanni coughed and stared out the window behind him. No help. She had gone away to that high ground of Baumsarg mulishness.

"We're considering taking out a loan for farm improvements," Claire said.

"Very wise idea, Mrs. Baumsarg." The address confused Claire, thinking at first he was addressing Hanni.

"Please call me Claire. It would be a temporary thing. We should earn out enough extra to pay it back within a couple of seasons."

Mr. Relicer shrugged as if the fact were inconsequential, as if he were a dear family friend that they had never known they had.

"What amount are we talking about?" he said softly.

Now it seemed as if he were their doctor, and they were navigating the gory details of some wasting disease. "I'm not sure just yet . . ." she said, looking at Hanni for help.

He scribbled something down on a notepad in front of him. "Consider the request, within reason, a blank check. We are very interested in having the Baumsarg family as a client."

"Surely you aren't going to advertise the fact?"

They both laughed, he a little too loudly. She noted that he didn't answer.

Hanni stood up as the secretary came in to lay down a coffee service. "Where's the bathroom?" she demanded.

"This way," the secretary said. Hanni bolted without a word to either of them.

"Banks make her nervous."

"Why would that be?" They remained silent for the duration of his pouring the coffee. He scooped a heaping spoonful of sugar into his cup, stirred vigorously, the spoon making an annoying clink against the side. If he had been her child, Claire would have reached over and stilled his hand.

"I'm glad to have this moment in private," he said, and Claire flushed, feeling as if she were committing some vague infidelity. "The Baumsarg place is such a gem. I drive by it on my way to work each morning. I live in the development down the highway, Pepper Tree Estates?"

Claire nodded, noncommittal. Thank God Hanni was in the bathroom. Old man Fuller had sold off his ranch years ago, and the developer turned it into the hated tract housing of Pepper Tree Estates. The locals all tried to drive another route so as not to pass by it. A faux-rustic sign of defeat. Fuller had made a fortune, retired to Montana, and now raised buffalo as a hobby. They bad-mouthed Fuller, but they also knew he had caved to the inevitable.

"It's just wrong, to me, to not leverage such a valuable asset."

"I think we need to get more automated, farm on a bigger scale." Claire drank her coffee, her hand shaky. It had been a mistake to come alone. Relicer probably thought Forster was too proud and had sent her, that they were already that desperate.

"Maybe it took someone new, fresh blood, to take initiative. To unlock the value of the place."

"Write down your terms," Claire said. Her head had started to pound. Hanni was making her way through the door. "We better be going."

"What about your coffee? I have some chocolates from Switzerland I'd like to share."

She felt that every extra minute in that office was costing them some exorbitant percentage of interest. "So kind, but we're wanted back. Young children, you know how it is."

"I understand." He stood at his desk and studied her a moment. "I'll have papers drawn up for a simple line of credit. The farm appraised as collateral. I'd be glad to drop by with the papers on my way home. For Mr. Baumsarg's signature. Since we're neighbors."

Claire shook her head. "I'll bring the papers back."

He said nothing for a moment, simply scribbled on his notepad as he stood. "I'll put down a flat amount, and when you want more, just call me."

"Thank you."

"It shouldn't be a problem for a pretty wife like you to convince your husband."

So he had seen through her ruse. She dug in her heels. "Forster was just too busy to come himself."

Mr. Relicer made a slight moue. He held out his hand but did not come around the desk this time, forcing Claire to retrace her steps, lean over the wide desk to shake his hand, which now was dry and hot. She felt as if she had been misled, the previous damp palm a ploy.

"Good-bye, Mrs. Baumsarg," he said to Hanni, speaking loudly as if she were a great distance away, or deaf. "An honor meeting you."

She wagged her fingers at him over her shoulder as she fled back out the door.

That night, sitting up in bed, Claire broached the idea.

Forster jumped up as if scalded, paced the room. "The farm has never had debt."

"I understand." She was already weary, knowing the contours their argument would follow.

"That's how we've stayed independent. My mother would die if she knew."

Claire waited a long, pregnant moment. "We're on the verge of bankruptcy. We need it for payroll, equipment. Fertilizers. New tree grafts. Just to stay competitive."

"I'll be the first generation to mortgage the place, to put it in debt." Forster knelt in front of her. "I'm confused."

"We have to try this."

"If it doesn't work?"

She ran her roughened palm down the side of his face. "No choice but sell."

That first winter there was record rainfall, and the spring yield was double. They paid the loan down halfway. The next fall, a second crop of lemons in, Claire felt a sense of accomplishment as she and Forster watched triple the usual number of packed crates, stamped with the Baumsarg name, being loaded on trucks.

Forster just took her hand, nodded.

But the following year was dry again. Only a few inches of rainfall. Drought conditions and some of the trees dropped fruit. Red scale infestation. Claire called Mr. Relicer, and the loan amount was promptly increased. As an afterthought, she invited him to their annual Memorial Day picnic, sensing the need for his goodwill. This seesawing would continue year by year for the next decade.

Summers she worked outside from dawn till dusk under the goad of debt, but even in California winters there was work to be done, especially as they implemented rotating crop harvests so something would always be coming to market. As the years passed, she was not there to take the children to the school bus, nor was she the one waiting for them in the afternoon. She did not bake cookies for them, Hanni did that, nor was she around to supervise homework. As soon as they were old enough, their after-school chores consisted of helping work the ranch, and their first memories of their mother always involved the groves. Frequently her first interaction would be to kiss their already sleeping faces good night. Josh liked to form a cave under his bed and sleep there, so she would climb down on her hands and knees, claustrophobic with the mattress only inches from her face, to kiss him good night. Usually he was cheating, staying up late, reading a comic with a flashlight. Sometimes they read together.

"Time for bed, Josh."

"My name is Steve Rogers."

"Okay, bedtime, Steve."

"I'm really Captain America," he whispered.

"Now."

"I have to defeat Red Skull for the safety of mankind."

"Mankind can wait till morning."

She missed the children but felt she could recover her time with them later when things were easier.

One Christmas Eve temperatures threatened to drop below freezing, so instead of opening presents, Forster and she took the children out with them to tend the few remaining smudge pots illegally tucked away in difficult corners of the farm, stopping to listen to the humming of the big wind machines that would protect the nascent crop, tempting the children with the idea that Santa might make his way through the rows. Instead of lumps of coal, Joshua threw oranges at his sisters and hid in the dark. When he came out, his face and arms were black from the oily soot of the smudge pots. "Captain America to the rescue." Claire scolded and laughed. Still days after, the handkerchief he blew his nose with turned black.

During this time, the surrounding farms continued to be sold, most at sky-high profit, more and more farmers surrendering, retreating farther and farther inland in search of cheap land, but more importantly in search of the freedom of a disappearing way of life. Split-level wood-and-brick ranch houses went up, then these, in their turn, gave way to large, gleaming mini-mansions with glass walls that deflected rather than invited. Indigenous eucalyptus and California pepper trees were chopped down; Italian cypress planted. Golf courses were carved out of the landscape. Fences went up, gates with intercoms and cameras, patrolled by snarling, box-headed dogs. A seismic change had occurred by the time Hanni no longer knew the names of their closest neighbors.

Once a year, Claire oversaw the repainting of the farmhouse's white clapboard walls, the glossy coating of the trim and window sashes, as neighboring, now dated, ranch houses were torn down to make room for the new rage of Tuscan villas. As out of place as seeing an elephant grazing in the desert. Like a herd of elephants, their sheer numbers destroyed the delicate balance around them. Like weeds overtaking a garden. At first, land parcels were divided in five-acre plots, then divided down to two, to one, cut in half, then halved again, until the land could barely contain the outer walls of these monstrosities. Home prices and land prices rising, the Baumsarg place became an eccentricity, a gentleman's pastime, an anomaly. A fortune in dirt.

Except that they had to earn a living off it. A devil's choice: to be wealthy but lose your place, or be poor and be rooted.

* * *

At the yearly parties put on by the family, Mr. Relicer was an obligatory if unwanted guest. He came the earliest and stayed the longest, never declining the grudged invitation. At the beginning of each month, the statement from the bank arrived, and Claire wrote out the check for interest, which was steadily taking a bigger and bigger bite of their earnings. Debt had become unavoidable, predictable as drought or pests. Claire's mood would be dark those days of bill-paying, and she would go out alone to walk the farm. Their small valley was still not part of the great suburbanization that was consuming the rest of the area in tract housing and minimalls. They were still a throwback to the rural roots of the area, a backwater of the past. A last holdout. But for how much longer?

On those walks she often dreamed of the land's returning to its sparsely filled former self, with adobe-bricked haciendas, or colonial Spanish stucco. Better than that, though, the landscape should be unshackled of human design entirely, remain empty, except for rows upon rows of avocado, orange, and lemon, or further back in time to grapes and black walnut, apricot and almond. But even human cultivation was not the beginning; in the beginning, the land was vacant of everything, the hills barren except for scrub and chaparral, the land unfilled, suffused only with air and sunlight, a state that some might call paradise.

With Josh now eight, Hanni realized that her role had become ornamental, that Claire had filled it and then some. Hanni decided to finally take the world tour she always dreamed of. The Saturday teas had convinced her that there was indeed a world beyond the ranch, beyond Southern California, and no matter how unlikely it was to surpass home, Hanni was determined to pass judgment before her wits left her for good.

In Thailand, bewildered and made homesick by the unfamiliar, the chance comment of a fellow traveler sent her to visit a citrus orchard.

The heat that day was overwhelming, the dead weight of humidity something Hanni was unused to, and after climbing a slight hill, she felt faint. The local farmer helped her sit down in the dirt, her back against a tree, shaded from the intense sun. He took out a small, sharp dagger and plucked off a deep green orange. He cut it in half. Hanni was surprised that inside it was ripe and juicy.

The farmer had a mild, worn face. He walked barefoot through his orchard; clearly he'd spent his whole life there. Hanni felt at home for the first time since she'd left. Through a guide, he explained that the temperature never dropped enough to make the outside peel orange, although the fruit was ripe. Hanni acknowledged California's riches—the cool evening temperatures that produced the glorious color.

The experience determined her on a new course: visiting other citrus farms. She would go to the Middle East to see their orange groves, then to Italy, specifically Sicily, where blood oranges thrived in the volcanic soil. Maybe after that Spain.

The idea that the same activity was going on in unknown places of the earth, places in which she had no language or custom or anything else in common, made Hanni unimaginably happy. It gave her a feeling like that of people who experience religion, an unexpected communion. But preparing to leave Thailand, she was bitten by a sand flea, and days later she was so ill she had to cancel further travel plans. The hotel manager was frightened that the old, white lady tourist might die in the room, requiring all kinds of remedy and rituals to erase the bad luck.

By the time Hanni arrived back home, she was delirious. Forster and Claire checked her into the hospital with a 105-degree temperature. An expert of tropical diseases from the university said there was no cure, only hope.

Hanni did not resent the foreign-borne disease. She considered it yet another land, another room, she had not yet entered in life. The ideas of illness and idleness as alien to her as the idea of death—destinations to keep open-minded about after such a long and work-filled life. It was her folly in leaving where she belonged, however temporarily. Shock like that of a transported plant. She comforted herself with the thought that maybe heaven consisted of orange groves.

In her last hours, fluids refused to stay in her body. Her face appeared wooden, mummified; her lips shriveled as if seeking counsel within. She took Claire's hand.

"I didn't believe in you at first," Hanni said. "But you turned out to be the right person. The perfect choice." Claire cried, but Hanni shook her head. "What I'm saying now is between women who have given their blood and sweat for the ranch. Let it go."

Claire thought fever had taken over the old woman's mind.

"Its time is past. Take Forster away."

"This is our life." Claire mourned Hanni's passing as if she were her own mother, but never told Forster her last words, reasoning they must have been said in confusion.

With the bequest from Hanni, Forster, Claire, and Octavio decided to make the biggest gamble for the ranch's independence yet: branch out into organics with its higher profit margins. Rather than its being a blessing, Claire felt a sense of foreboding in using the money in a way Hanni clearly had not sanctioned. And yet, what kind of an inheritance could not be used in the best interests of the heir?

They financed a new ten-acre parcel of lemon trees adjoining theirs from yet another farmer who had sold out and moved inland. At the auction, the farmer took their lower bid because he wanted the place to remain farmland as long as possible. If it was successful, the change to organic would be Hanni's legacy. The turnover meant the soil would have to be amended with natural fertilizers and pesticides, no chemicals, until it tested clean under the guidelines, taking at least three or four years. If Claire had learned nothing else, it was that miracles took grueling work and utter, saintly patience.

Chapter 5

Kidnapping the boy had been an afterthought that went bad, they said at the trial. After Claire promised money, panicked, the men grabbed him as a kind of insurance policy. When she heard that, her guilt was complete and permanent. Josh had been unafraid, Denny Larsen said. "He yelled and called me Red Skull." A detail that broke her heart. He died that same night, when he tried to run away. The staggering one tackled him, and the boy fell, accidentally hitting his head on a rock. Not knowing what else to do, they buried the body at the farthest corner of the ranch by the lake. Small consolation, at least he had not been long at their hands. They waited for the body to be found, and when it wasn't, they decided to try for the ransom. It seemed beyond cruelty to Claire that her little boy was already gone while she had frantically gathered the money.

After Forster lifted the boy from the earth, Claire could not bear to hand him over to strangers again. She asked Octavio if they could drive him home one last time in his pickup, the boy's favorite place in the world. All farm children learned to drive tractors and pickups early, and within the confines of the ranch Octavio allowed Josh to sit in his lap and steer the wheel, and then drive himself. Now he handed the keys to Forster to drive while Claire sat in the truck's bed, next to the swaddled body. "Come," she said, but Octavio shook his head and walked.

"My heart breaks," he said at the house, head bowed between Claire and Forster, after the body had been driven away. Octavio felt guilt, not that he had done anything wrong, but that he had been under the tree earlier and had not known. How was it possible that he had not sensed anything?

Claire could not explain her deepening despair after the arrest of the men and learning the truth. The facts were flat and dry, disappointing in a way she could not describe. Denny Larsen got the idea of burglarizing the house while working the party. They had never intended to hurt anyone. The outcome random as an act of nature. They did not have the driven power of evil that the act deserved.

It was the headline story in the local news, and the church overflowed with both known and unknown faces. A feeling of expectation was in the air that the Baumsargs appear broken, in some way show the shame of victimhood. Claire stood alone, stranded at the door of the church, until Octavio rose, gave her his arm, and escorted her to her seat. She walked with a kind of unadorned, bone strength, sat regal and remote in the front pew, until Forster arrived with the girls. When asked to say a few words, she stood in the front of the church in silence for such a time that Forster got up to rescue her.

"'I am going to him and he will not come back to me,'" she quoted, and allowed Forster to lead her away.

She refused to have the reception at the ranch after the funeral; instead it was held at the recreation room of the church. The crowd showed an undeniable fascination at the horror of the crime. Looky-loos who wanted to gawk at them in their grief.

When Claire came back to the house, she threw off her shoes, dragging herself from room to room in her mourning dress. Sounds came from Josh's room. Dizzy, she tiptoed to the door, opened it, and found Paz and the girls playing with his trains and cars, passing a liquor bottle. Even in laughter, they looked so forlorn and abandoned, her motherly instinct to scold evaporated. Why *not* mourn in this childish way?

The girls, red-faced, froze when they saw her in the doorway. They had been giggling and, she suspected, were a little drunk.

Claire sat down on the floor next to them. She pointed to the bottle of Baileys Cream.

"Do you like that?"

Lucy shook her head in a noncommittal way, as if the bottle had forced its way into her hand. "Not really."

"When I was your age, we drank vodka and orange juice."

"Really?"

Claire nodded.

"We shouldn't have been drinking," Gwen said.

Claire shrugged. "Our parents couldn't smell it on our breath."

"We pray for him," Paz said.

"That's good." She liked that the verb was in the present tense, that Josh was still alive in those terms.

"Mr. Relicer gave me a twenty-dollar bill," Lucy said. "Do I have to give it back?"

"No, definitely keep it."

After the attention from the outside world ebbed away, a stasis enveloped the family. Like the series of fault lines that riddled the land, the stillness was deceptive, hiding thousands of faint tremors that originated deep inside, that silently displaced the ground without shaking it. On the surface, nothing of note. Everything that went on happened within, subterranean reckonings.

Claire emptied Josh's room, packing all his belongings in boxes, storing them in the barn, intending to move Lucy into the room so the endless bickering over a shared room would end. Then she changed her mind and moved all his things back in, frantic when she didn't remember the precise place of each object, consulting the girls, who fought over their conflicting memories of the placement of a pencil cup, a baseball mitt.

The overdue harvest was quickly picked and sent out. A curious by-product of the Baumsargs' tragedy, the fruit stand was overrun with people, and for the first time they sold out by noon each day. In a macabre act of souvenir-collecting, people coveted the cardboard boxes stamped with their name. Because they had lost so much time, they recovered substantially less fruit than they hoped. The defeat went unnoticed by Claire.

Not once did she go out and supervise the harvest. It was as if the trees and ground that she had loved had betrayed her. There was also a further isolation: Octavio no longer came into the house. Paz invited the girls over, but Claire told Gwen to turn down the offer. She didn't want them out of her sight.

"We can't turn into prisoners here," Forster said.

Since the funeral he had let her do things as she saw fit, but her behavior was finally wearing on him. He allowed that her sorrow was making her act out. The unspoken accusation was that he had not been there to protect them. But still, she was turning paranoid in her grief.

Claire looked up from the apple she was peeling. "Maybe it's time for us to move on."

* * *

She canceled the Saturday teas, no longer wanting to bring the community onto the ranch. From then on, contact with the outside world would be held to a minimum. She took over the tasks of caring for the girls from Raisi. Together as one unit, she and the girls moved from breakfast room to living room to bedroom and back. Hardly during the day did one of them separate from the others, and when they did for any length, Claire grew panicky. They were not allowed to work at the fruit stand; they were not allowed to go outside, period, unless in a group, moving together like a small, wary army.

After a few weeks of living under siege, Raisi packed her bags to leave. "It's time you were on your own again."

"But I need you here."

"What you *need* is to heal those girls."

"They're never out of my sight."

"Do you see? They're becoming afraid of life."

Claire shifted in her seat. "The world is a bad place."

"Good and bad. You can't protect them forever."

Without Raisi, Claire stayed up nights in her rocking chair in the girls' room, waiting for the phantom men to come back, or others in their place. The girls slept crushed together in Gwen's single bed, no more squabbling over space. Awake at night, Claire heard noises, thought she saw dark, purpling shapes crossing the lawn outside. Even the trees made her grow numb with dread. Her mood was unalleviated by the fact that the three men had pled guilty, were sitting in jail pending sentences. The ransom money had been found in a house, untouched, and returned to Mrs. Girbaldi.

Sleep-deprived, Claire dragged through her days. When she finally fell into bed, she lay wide awake. She missed her mother, wanted to tell her she understood things about the past for the first time.

She had resented the nights as a child when her role was to comfort Raisi from her nightmares. They never spoke of these things in daytime, but it had frightened Claire to see her mother so fragile and weak. How could such a mother possibly care for her? It caused Claire to build a false strength, forget about being a child herself. Now that they lived apart, did her father play that role?

Raisi would clutch her blankets, waking from the recurrent dream of walking the frozen fields to cross the border. Despite the worsening conditions in Hungary before the revolution, Raisi's family had refused to leave. A young woman, she decided to cross into Austria alone. The iced ground crackling under her weight, the roulette fear of running either into a border guard, meaning imprisonment or worse, or into a fellow refugee, with the attendant danger of groups. After a night in the freezing cold, lost and almost freezing to death, she saw bonfires on the Austrian border, farmers burning their harvest bales of hay, then burning old wood, sometimes resorting to burning their last wagon, to provide signal to those who were lost. To guide the way to freedom, a new life. After the revolt was crushed, she lost all contact with her family behind a wall of silence. Fear of staying, fear of leaving. That constant sense of displacement had haunted Claire's childhood.

In a Red Cross tent after Raisi made it successfully across, she took it as an omen when a pretty, blond girl from California served her hot cider. This first human kindness determined where she applied for citizenship. Nothing else to do but let the past go. Every year on the Fourth of July their storefront prickled with flags, and Raisi stood rigid, hand pressed to heart, when she heard "The Star-Spangled Banner."

Place is important, she told Claire. In a time of need, place is everything.

But there was no signal fire to guide Claire. Place was destroying her.

Plans for new trees were suspended. They backed out of an escrow for additional acreage. At night in bed Claire held Forster's hand and spoke of selling the farm and moving to the more open Central Valley to start over.

"A fresh start."

"Running away," he countered.

"What's wrong with that?"

Rightly he rejected the chimera of moving on. Knowing that trouble and unhappiness moved with one, only belonging was left behind. He turned away from her in bed, crooked his head in his arm. For the first time, they no longer touched. Over the next weeks and months, even the idea of intimacy became awkward, except for a chaste kiss in front of the girls. In the closet, Claire shyly turned away in her faded bra when he walked in.

One warm fall day when the air was like crystal and the landscape saturated with light, Forster came inside and found the girls huddled in bed, reading. "Enough of this!" he said in high spirits. "We're going on a picnic." He insisted that they go to a favorite spot on a hill overlooking the lake. The girls and Claire reluctantly walked with their wicker baskets through the lines of the trees, carefully, as if on patrol, squinting in the bright light that hurt their eyes. Underneath the trees' shade, a group of workers were lounging after lunch, throwing a ball and playing music on a radio. Claire's mouth crimped tight. When the men saw the family approach, they jumped up, shamefaced, and took off their hats—understood that the period of mourning would never end.

Forster went and spoke a few words to them, while Claire imagined a current of glances and nudges passing among the men. Suspicion always lurked in her mind now—which of these men might be related to the ones in jail, however distantly? Might there be recriminations against the long sentences, revenge, however undeserved? The day changed for her—the trees cast a pall, the sky cloudless yet without sun. When they came to the path that led up the hill, they had to pass the lemon tree. Forster grimaced at his oversight—he should have taken them another way. He didn't blame a particular spot of land for their tragedy; rather, he felt the land, too, had been violated. Claire turned the girls around and marched them back home.

Essential to take care of Gwen and Lucy during this time, and Claire threw herself into a confusion of activity. She started by repainting their bedrooms, letting them pick their favorite colors. Gwen chose yellow, and Claire sewed matching curtains and counterpanes. Transforming Josh's room was the hardest. At Forster's insistence, Josh's things were boxed up again and moved out into the barn, to be donated to charity. Lucy was given his room, and she insisted on purple walls. After much negotiation, they compromised on lavender and planned to add a canopy bed for Christmas. If Forster had let Claire, she would have ripped up the floorboards, taken the walls down to the studs. Even so, with each brushful of paint, she felt guilty of erasing the past.

With the same fervor, she cooked breakfasts of French toast and pancakes, omelets, and scrambles, freshly squeezed orange and grapefruit juice. The breakfasts were so big and involved that the girls were frequently late for school. When it got too late, Claire allowed them to play truant. It was safer to stay at home anyway. Then she would let them watch movies while she brought them hot chocolate and caramel popcorn, treating them like invalids.

Isolated by what they had suffered—neither teachers nor counselors were willing to reprimand—the girls, so pale and tentative, got away with more than the wildest rebels. Gwen was caught smoking in the girls' bathroom. Lucy got caught necking with a basketball player during homeroom. While Gwen would eventually straighten out to the point of primness, Lucy plunged deeper into bad behavior. Caught with cigarettes, then alcohol, then marijuana. With the years, the power of her intoxicants grew.

"Aren't you spoiling them?" Forster asked. "They're going wild."

"They deserve spoiling."

One night they sat down to a roast, creamed corn, biscuits, salad, roast chicken, and a pizza. The table was so full, the counter held the extra dishes.

As the girls sat down at their places, Lucy looked around and saw the extra place setting. "Who's coming to dinner?"

Claire looked at Forster uneasily, and when he smiled, they both started to laugh. The strain wearing them thin.

"Just us." Claire took up the place setting, dumped it into a drawer, and went to the stove, hoping no one would see tears. Still not adjusted from the habit of thinking in fives.

"Can we go on vacation?" Lucy said.

No, thought Claire. She could not stop the irrational panic that they would be gone when Joshua returned. Fact helpless against maternal instinct.

Forster smiled. "That's the best idea I've heard in a long time."

They couldn't afford the money for the trip or the time spent away from the ranch, but even she saw escape was demanded. It was decided—a week down the Baja peninsula. It was perfectly acceptable that they needed "time away." If Claire said "vacation" to the neighbors, it would have sounded crass and unfeeling. So escape was labeled retreat. It irked her that she worried what others thought when no one knew her suffering, the depth of which justified any action with the ability to ease the pain. No one could know the middle-of-the-night agonies, waking up before remembering, and then having the knowledge invade the body with the force of a hammer blow. She didn't care for herself, but she resented a judgment of the girls. They should be affected by the tragedy, but not too much. Anything inappropriate, self-pitying, melodramatic, would be blamed on Claire, but a lack of emotion was blamed on her also.

The night before they were to leave, the Santa Ana winds, commonly known as devil winds, howled through the canyons, made the shingles slap down on the roof, the windows and doors moan. Claire dreamed Joshua was a baby again, and she had misplaced him somewhere. Laid him down on a bed or a couch or a pillow. Placed him in a reed basket or a wooden orange crate. She searched and searched, frantic. It was way past his feeding time, her breasts ached with milk, and he was nowhere in sight. Finally she heard him and rushed out into the orchards, following his cries until she found him beneath the lemon tree. As if he had been tending there from birth. Claire woke, her body in a sweat.

She left Forster in bed, worried in her rocking chair till daybreak pulled her out into the fields, the winds tugging against her nightgown, the humidity dropped so that she could hardly spit.

It was really too easy. The gasoline can in the barn. Matches from the kitchen. The long, dizzying walk down the dirt road, rising sun blinding her. Whispers in her ear that could have been wind. She forgot the mechanics of lofting the can—watching the loop of gasoline sparkle in the air and wet the lower leaves, dousing the brush underneath, staining the trunk dark, but still leaving the container only half-emptied. Thinking the lower limbs the most promising place for the flames to gain purchase, she threw on another loop just as the wind gusted, carrying the loop backward, raining on her. Face and arms stung as if attacked by a swarm of bees. Forgotten, as well, that the first three matches were blown out, how not until the driven fourth did a brilliant flower of light ignite, kindling of tumbleweed blossoming like a shard of sun. No, in her memory, the tree simply self-immolated.

She staggered back, too slow, heat singeing hair and eyebrows. Burning her cheeks raw as if from sunburn, as if from blood stroke. That was the moment she heard the high scream and came to herself. She could no longer separate sleep from waking or this zombie state in between. Heart stopped, her small boy ripped away from her like in birth. What had she done? She swatted at the fire, wanting to put it out, reverse time. Anything so that she could solve the conundrum of destroying what you love for the pain it has caused you. Heartsick, nightmared, she saw a rabbit wobble out from under the burning brush. His fur scorched away on one side, the other side untouched. He staggered, stopped, ran. "Survive," Claire whispered, begged. "Please survive."

Black smoke fanned itself into the unforgiving blue sky. A single, wide lick of flame reached from ground to topmost branch, a reversed lightning. Leaves dried out, then curled to gold, then black ash. The rinds of lemons grew rigid and tight, then burst, releasing a thick blood of juice.

The siren at the barn finally clanged. Pickups rattled to life. Footsteps and the calling of Forster and the girls. *Claire, Mother, Mom. Where are you? Where have you gone?*

Octavio roared up in his pickup with a crew, not looking at her but unrolling the faded fireman's hose, cranking the water. Another rescue. Forster ran to Claire.

"Thank God you're okay." He held her, then pushed her away, smelling the gasoline on her. Incredulous, he stepped back, the muscles in his jaw clenching.

"We have to leave here—" she started, but he moved quickly, slapping her across her cheek.

She agreed to voluntarily check into a clinic. For two weeks she either sat in her monk's cell of a room, or outside in the courtyard, watching a collection of turtles wade in and out of the fountain. The counselors gave her grief lectures, pamphlets about overcoming loss in twelve steps. In the clinic's living area, she uneasily passed by a painting of a rainbow over hills, a smiling person in a sunbeam at its end. She took her medication and played the part of patient, allowing them to feel pleased charting her progress. When Forster visited with the girls, she acted contrite. But inside, she was unmoved. A granite and implacable stubbornness formed—she balked at the premise that something so monstrous and unfair should be accepted, lived through, recovered from.

When the clinic released her, she felt smaller, dried out. Her elbows and knees bent stiffly. The terrible thoughts still infected her, but they were weakened by medication, did not have the power to rise to action. Nothing could move her, neither Forster nor the girls. This is what it feels like to be dead, she thought.

"It would do us all good to get away," Forster said.

Claire nodded, powerless.

"Octavio said he will handle things for a week."

In Mexico, they were disappointed at how desolate everything was, empty, like a moonscape. Forster explained to the girls that the origin of the word *desert* was from wasteland, which it turned out to be for them.

They could not afford two rooms so shared a single one with two queen-size beds. The girls piled in one, Forster and Claire in the other. Husband and wife, they lay side by side like patients in a hospital. Sometimes Claire wondered if the girls hadn't been there, would Forster have reached over, would they finally have been able to heal? Would she have apologized, and would he have forgiven?

The next day they drove a winding, potholed road from the gulf side to the Pacific side of the peninsula. East to west, the eternal search for renewal. But they were already at the end of west. Tired by the heat and the bumpy ride, they stopped at a turnout for lunch. Gwen and Lucy wandered away, and Claire settled down into medicated solitude, falling asleep in the shade of the cliffs. Now she slept endlessly—ten, eleven hours each day—and woke exhausted, longing for more.

Forster shook her awake. At first she mistook it for affection and felt a small gratitude inside her. Until he told her that Gwen came back without Lucy.

The next two hours were spent under the pounding sun, calling. Claire's eyes burned, she tripped over cactus, her head spinning. Chest pounding so hard she thought she would keel over. Half-crazed, drugged, she cursed at the grotesque possibility that another child could be taken. Not knowing which direction to go, they returned to the car. Forster shuffled between it and the cliffs where Gwen sat crying as he tried to soothe her.

"What happened again?" he asked.

"I went ahead to check out a water hole. When I turned back, she was gone."

"Was anyone else there? Any strangers?"

"No. I don't think so. I didn't see them."

"Why didn't you keep watch over her?" Claire yelled.

"Don't," Forster said.

"Then why didn't *you* watch her?" Claire accused him.

"What were you doing?" he said. "Sleeping." Only blame and venom left between them.

At last Lucy appeared in the distance, shimmering, unsteady, a mirage—sunburned, dusty, tearstained. Claire blinked, then blinked again, not wanting to trust anything until she was sure the girl was flesh.

"It's her," she whispered.

Together, they ran. Claire grabbed her, looked her up and down. "Are you okay? Are you hurt?"

"I'm fine," Lucy said.

"Where were you?" Forster asked.

"We were scared."

"I disappeared," she said, smiling a sly grin. "Like Josh used to do. It was just a game. I was coming back—"

"Don't ever do that," Forster said.

"You're ruining everything," Gwen shouted. "Making Mom and Dad fight." Gwen punched Lucy's arm. "I wish you didn't come back."

"No," Claire said. "You can't say that."

"We miss him, too," Gwen said. "Not just you."

Each of them like a jagged piece of glass to the other, unable to do anything but inflict damage. Three grief-worn female faces on the car trip home. Four wearied souls. Forster staring through the windshield, trying to forestall more harm. The trip no escape. Claire refused to pretend healing. Instead, the land reflected them back on themselves, and they could not bear up to the revelation. When they returned home, Forster moved into the guest room, the first step of his eventual leaving.

Other families survived tragedy. Perhaps it was a greater curse that they only appeared to remain intact, that they imploded, their collective outward gesture to become more polite, more considerate, distant as lone trees in a cleared forest, each grabbing a private circle of sun, together only in their solitude.

In the weeks after they returned from Mexico, an unheard-of thing happened in the orchard. Octavio was at a loss to explain: the leaves on the citrus turned a burnt yellow as if it were the changing of color during a New England fall. People drove by to take pictures of the outlandish sight. He assured the Baumsargs that he had taken the utmost care of the ranch while they were gone, personally supervising what he normally delegated to others. The leaves clung on for over a month, fresh and pliable but yellowed, then overnight every single one fell to the ground. A gold carpet upon which stood a barren stick forest. Not a sign of life on the trees, and Forster had the agriculture guys come over to take soil tests. There were guesses about mineral contaminants in the water table, a wind-borne fungus, unknown and unseen pests; the trees had gone dormant except for a strange thickening of the trunks. The bark turned hard as iron.

The orchard's shock deeply moved Claire, as if the land itself had turned sentient, mirroring her belief that the only true love was the one tested, put under duress, stripped, stranded, and beaten. The land reached out to her, and she accepted. No one else understood the problem—she'd survived, her son had not.

The following spring, the trees resumed their growth.

Part Two

Chapter 1

Fifteen years later, the Baumsarg family, too, had grown impregnable outer shells.

With the passage of time, Josh had been her son for less time than he had not been. Untrue—he would always remain her son—yet one time had the weight of feathers and one had the weight of lead. Often, coming across her image unexpectedly in a mirror, she didn't quite recognize herself. Who was this woman formed from sadness? Browned, wrinkled skin, weathered by the sun, and sharp, angular cheekbones. But she spent little time looking in mirrors, caught up in the management of the remaining 160 acres. Selling the larger share had been unbearable, but it was an amputee's choice—severing one part to preserve the core. The only other choice was to lose the whole.

The truism that time healed all was just as false as it was true, but Claire had found her way back to life through the land. When she had shunned public life all those years ago, the ranch had provided extraordinary haven. The ranching life—the deep silences of the groves, its strict schedules, its routine, the narrowness of its concerns, the necessary attention to variables of weather, cycles of fruition and decay—provided a relief that nothing else could.

It had been a mixed lot of successes and failure. She had survived, the girls were grown up, but Forster and she had parted ways years before. Unlike her experience of healing, the land had turned against him—strange, foreign, resistant. It had driven him away.

So when in the doctor's changing room, gossiping with other patients, drinking chamomile tea from paper cups, she heard her name called out for a further consultation instead of being okayed to go home (by proxy meaning she cleared), Claire was sure they couldn't possibly mean her, and then she grew angry. She didn't have time for this, what with replanting a section of avocado groves that had burned in the fires last fall, digging another well for the one that had gone dry. Relentless, the city was all over them, trying to raise water rates and drive them out of business. No, no time for sickness. It had been four years since she had been in for a checkup, and only Gwen's prodding had made her go in for the mammogram.

The quick sorority in the room disappeared, and again she was made separate from the group, this time ejected from the world of the healthy. The heat behind her eyes made her think of the wildlife shows Forster had loved to watch years ago, how a herd moved as a single entity until one of the members fell behind and succumbed to whatever chased. That act of surrender—she couldn't bear it. The one sacrificed by the group, danger averted, the weft of the fabric rendered whole again as if the disappeared had never existed. Animals didn't have the advantages—or was it a disadvantage?—of humans with their compassion. What lesson had the girls learned from the shows? They ran from the room. Ostrichlike, they pretended what they didn't see didn't exist.

The walk down the long hallway was like the stringing of beads, adding surgeon, radiologist, ultrasound doctor, nurse, counselor. She remained dry-eyed and skeptical. The tough iron shell that kept both the bad and the good at arm's length. In the back of her humming mind was the trump card of the unfairness of it. Surely she was immune to further insult. "There's been a mistake," she said. Not until the surgeon, workmanlike, guided her fingers under his, along her suddenly foreign skin, rotating the soft tissue at the top of the breast, a private place she had not paid attention to since nursing her last child, did her breath escape—as she felt a hard seed of mortality, no mistaking it, lodged within her.

"We can take the lump and test for margins," the doctor said.

She both heard and didn't hear. There was no fear. Her mind calculated what this would mean to the work schedule, if Octavio could handle the harvest alone. How much time did something like this take? "And then?"

"If the margins are clear, we won't have to take the whole breast."

"But it could change in the future. It would mean a constant waiting. Take it all now. I want it done with."

For the first time, he paused to examine her face. "That's unnecessary."

"That's what I want. If you won't do it, I'll get someone else. I don't have time for this."

"You don't have time for cancer?"

What she hated most about the disease was her inability to hide it. Undergoing chemo and radiation, she would have front-and-center invalid status. The help she needed to ask for would come with a price. Her greatest fear: the family's impatience with her refusal to sell off the remaining land. Forster had allowed her to keep the operation going, yet even he didn't seem pleased with her stubbornness. She flirted with the idea of just ignoring the whole thing for six months till she got her projects done around the ranch. Once the news got out, she would lose her leverage. In this case, not acknowledging a thing, not talking about it, rendered it less powerful. If only Raisi were around now. Claire dismissed the statistic that her own mother had died of breast cancer ten years before. No, she would get the operation over with right away.

Within days of the diagnosis, Gwen and Lucy flew in from various compass points on the map. Their presence in the hospital room literally lifeblood. Missing them, denying that missing, had dulled Claire. Despite the circumstances, she feasted on their company while at the same time wondering if maybe she could work the guilt angle on one of them. They hovered over her after the surgery, exchanging gossip with each other. Distraught and distracted in equal parts. Cell phones buzzed, laptops flickered. Their eyes searched for reading glasses, lipstick, magazines, death.

"Thank God I got you in when I did," Gwen said. Her glorious blond hair now butchered short, chin-length. Junior partner at her law firm, mother of two, she had taken on the mantle of the matriarch in charge of all the major and minor dramas of the family, organizing social gatherings, and being overbearing to her younger sister. "This is nothing. Early detection. Totally survivable."

Lucy, recently moved to Santa Fe, was wearing a heavy patchouli perfume that overpowered the small room. Thin in her faded jeans and boots, her bare, tanned arms revealed tattoos. Six months before, she had finished another in a long line of rehabs, and everyone was hopeful that this latest fresh start would take permanent hold.

"Is it possible," Gwen said, sneezing, "that you not wear that around me? It's giving me a headache."

Lucy looked at Claire and burst into tears. Still the baby of the family. Her emotions always on the surface. "I'm going for a cigarette. Call me when the doctor comes."

"I thought you quit," Claire said. The tumor had not been found early, but she wouldn't mention that.

Gwen hid at the end of the floor in the lounge, teleconferencing with her office until the doctor appeared. She returned to watch the nurses empty drains and tubing, and she helped them coil the hoses back up, pinning them on the inside of Claire's nightshirt, careful and steady. She had a look of resolve in her eyes, ready to take on this new challenge. She helped Claire into the bathroom, rolled her IV in after her.

"We should have caught it earlier," Gwen whispered. Long ago, she had become the little mother of the family while her parents struggled to keep the farm solvent. Often Claire caught her washing Lucy's face, mending her clothes, braiding her hair. Gwen would fix a snack for Josh or help him with his homework. When a girl he had a crush on turned him cruelly away, Gwen went to the girl's house and bawled her out. Claire could gauge her failures in mothering by Gwen's remedying the oversights.

Once Josh had come crying to Claire, a bump on his head and a half-moon-shaped gash along his cheek. The girls had been sunning in the orchard, and they had talked him into climbing an apricot tree to pick ripe fruit that was out of reach. He fell off the topmost branch. "They told me not to tell," he cried. In a fury, Claire yelled at Gwen even as she felt the burden placed on her unfair. She was still a child herself. "You know better. It's your job to look after them."

In the hospital room, the light hurt Claire's eyes. "I want out of here," she said. The painkillers were wearing off; the nurses slow and stingy on their rounds. She begged that the blinds be lowered to a gloom, but even the blue of the television made the room appear hazy, smoke-filled, disturbing her. She longed for her own house, her own bed. What was happening with the fields in her absence?

"You just got out of surgery."

"Recovery is the same anywhere."

Lucy sneaked in a fifth of Knob Creek, and just as when they were teenagers, Gwen resisted, lectured, then finally gave in. "Just this once, for nerves. I've got it under control." They took turns drinking shots out of the water glass on the nightstand. Lucy stroked her mother's head. "When you're out of here, I'll take you for a real blowout."

Claire chose not to lecture. "How is the new job?"

"What does it matter?" Lucy said, waving her hand at the machines surrounding them. "With all this?" She wanted to be a painter now, after wanting to be a singer, and before that a chef. Some strange role reversal had occurred between the girls. In school, Lucy had been the straight-A brilliant one, and Gwen had struggled and worked for B's. Now Lucy was adrift, caught up in one thing after another.

"This is nothing. An inconvenience." Claire didn't want this to be another excuse for her daughter to fail again.

Because of the size and spread of the tumor to the lymph nodes, a radical mastectomy had been necessary even without Claire's draconian instructions, but the surgical team was offended when she refused the simultaneous reconstructive surgery.

"Mom, that's medieval, walking around with a gash across your chest," Gwen said. Her wealthy divorce clients took their plastic surgery seriously, and she offered a whole Rolodex of what she called "boob men" to call.

Claire found it alien and strangely hopeful at the same time, as if packaging might be a cure-all for any calamity. "It's okay the way it is," she reassured Gwen. "If I decide to pose for *Playboy,* we'll rethink it."

The girls laughed and passed another round of drinks, relieved that their mother would not fall apart on them.

"I want to go home. I can't sit around a hospital room for a week."

"You have cancer," Gwen said. "Forget the farm."

"You can take care of me. What could that involve? There are things that need to be looked after." That strange maternal twinning of love and thwarted expectation.

Forster came to the hospital, bowlegged under the weight of a gigantic arrangement of roses and lilies that sucked the air out of the room, made it smell like the dregs of an emptied perfume bottle, like the hall of a mortuary. The nurses ticked their heads in disapproval as if he'd tracked in crescents of dog shit on the bottom of his boot. Given his squeamishness in all matters of the body and heart, his visit was the more unexpected. He had come alone, without Katie, his second wife.

"Who died?" Claire asked, pointing at the flowers.

"I see I came for trouble."

"Get me out of here," Claire said. "There's so much going on. Octavio needs my help."

"I already talked to him. Everything's fine. This time of year, things are slow."

Claire frowned.

Forster rarely visited the farmhouse, not wanting to drive through the long rows of citrus trees leading to it, rejecting the smell of his beloved blossoms in the spring, going to the length of driving the long way around the county road to avoid the loading trucks whose picking schedules he knew by heart, as they filled with fruit crates stamped with his own name. Katie confessed he went to the absurd extreme of forbidding orange juice in the house.

After forcing Claire to stay on the ranch, he had been the one to leave, a point she never let him forget.

Now he chose to live in an apartment, looking over the ocean, a desert of water, devoid of one square inch of soil. Perhaps an attempt to return to his seafaring ancestors' roots? He ignored Raisi's mantra of the importance of place. Such a decision smacked to Claire of a denaturing beyond even discussing. She felt pity for him. All his other poor decisions—investing in a car dealership, a fast-food restaurant, both of which went under—appeared in its long light. He was a man of the soil, trained in the rhythms of growth and harvest. Turning his back on the place he was from, he rejected a way of life. Because of the one loss, creating another.

In the hospital, the girls each bowed a submissive head for a brush of his lips across their forehead, then escaped downstairs to the hospital cafeteria. "Do I smell bourbon in here?" he asked to their giggling, retreating backs.

What they were squeamish of witnessing was not the hostility between their parents (there was none), but rather the open display of affection. No matter how long the absence, Forster and Claire reunited as tenderly as if still married. The distance between them had kindled within Claire an affection as strong as in the first days of their courtship that she was at pains to hide. The acrimony, the blame—suffocating when they were still married—had faded away.

How to explain that after twenty or more years, a marriage, if it had ever been real, could no longer be sundered by a piece of paper. In two decades—the same time it took to raise a human being—a marriage became its own entity. Life intervened, yes, a decision was made that life together was too painful, but the marriage itself lived on, a kind of radiological half-life. After the death of Josh, when Claire refused to consider trying to have another child, Forster escaped to his beach apartment and a new wife. Not so unusual to drown oneself in otherness—the ocean, when you are a man of the soil; youth, the state of having everything that will happen in front of you, when already so much has passed.

It surprised everyone when they did not immediately have children. After two years, young Katie paid Claire a visit. A sweet girl, ten years older than Gwen, she cried in Claire's lap as she explained that Forster offered to divorce her after he made the abrupt decision to have a vasectomy. Claire believed that Forster came around to her way of thinking. Every child deserved to be wanted for itself upon coming into the world, not merely to replace what had been lost. But still, there was the problem of this girl-wife.

"I don't know what to tell you," Claire said, "except that he is a good man. In spite of all that."

Claire and Forster's marital bond was welded strong by the girls, whom they had successfully raised, but was equally forged by failing the one child—the intolerable offense of not rendering the world harmless to him. They had failed, and if they were lucky, neither of them would create such scarring ties again.

"You can't leave just yet," Forster said, settling back into a hospital chair by the window, his eyes avoiding Claire's face.

"I need one of the girls to come home for a while."

She felt she had aged unbearably in his eyes, that he recoiled at the lines and fissures etching her face. Had he already resigned himself to yet another death? He looked as strong as a decade earlier, his face browned, his eyes calm. Even the sprinkling of gray in his blond hair simply made him seem more solid, more able to endure. Maybe in running away from the ranch he had made a bargain with the devil? She could ask Forster for anything and he would do it—unspoken but suspected that he would even leave Katie if it came to that—but he refused to live their old life on the farm again. They were locked together like two pieces of a puzzle that created a gaping hole when put together. Alone, they could choose to ignore the emptiness, but together they created an absence.

"You look good," Forster said.

"Liar," she said.

"Not bad to me."

"Help me get out of here. Be my alibi."

"What do you need?" he said. "Give me something to do."

"I ask for one thing, and you refuse."

"Christ, you have cancer. Forget about work for a time."

" 'Highly survivable,' according to Gweny."

He flinched at the remark. "Don't be so hard on her. She loves you." His face crumpled. "I'll see what I can do, okay?"

"I need to go home."

He got up to make his escape, before more things he could not give would be requested. "You're the invincible one. Don't let us down."

"That's right. Tough as nails."

"What about the farm? Gwen mentioned you're worried about it."

"I just need a friendly face around."

"I can do that." He hesitated, and she suspected the real purpose of his visit. "Maybe it's time to let go of the place?"

"No."

"Claire—"

"I'm lying in a hospital bed. Are you really going to talk about selling the farm now?"

The truth was that she had dug her way back like a feral animal. Scratched and clawed those around her, metaphorically ate her young by demanding what they could not give. Make no mistake—survival was not a pretty business. It was bloody and ruthless and necessary, and afterward the best most could do was to try to forget. There had been the first survival, and this was nothing in comparison.

Through the next days at the hospital, the girls circled, fluttering around Claire in their attempts to take hold of the situation, once again waiting for what would come next. As a young mother, Claire had the guilty thought that perhaps it would have been preferable to have had only one child, so that parent and child would be best friends. Siblings were always more distracted by each other, more concerned with their own constant jostling for status and position, the attending barbs and slights and hurts, to have Claire be anything more than a distant, dispensing figure.

On the day of her release from the hospital, the afternoon was like a bell, clear and hollow, with the usual white-blue haze caught in the creases of the foothills, along the long floors of the valley. A deceptively simple landscape because the haze usually hid the complication of the nearby mountain range, the capped peaks of the San Gabriels. Their existence due to the catastrophic pressure deep beneath the ground. Only on rare, Santa Ana–wind days, the humidity dropped to zero, the barometric pressure so high it caused headaches and nosebleeds and crazy longings, did the mountains appear, a presence that on most days remained invisible.

The pain drugs made her nauseated on the drive home, the traffic stop and start, gridlocked, winding out of the city. Forster drove, and Lucy sat in the backseat, distractedly biting her nails while staring out the window. A paper bag lay between them for Claire. Gwen went through paperwork in the passenger seat, reading out options of clinics around the country, rates of success, side effects of treatment.

"Please stop," Claire said.

"Choices have to be made," Gwen said.

"Leave it for now," Forster said.

"But you said we should decide—"

"Not now."

"What?" Claire asked. "What are you talking about?"

"The chemo, Mom."

She felt a weight on her chest, the first hint of panic. "Stop at the bookstore on the way home."

"We'll do that later," Gwen said.

"I want some new books for tonight."

"You don't have enough unread books?"

"She wants to stop, we'll stop," Forster said.

Gwen and Lucy gave each other the Crazy Mom look over the front seat. Turning into the bookstore parking lot, a young man in a pickup tailgated them, and Forster cursed under his breath. Claire turned around to watch the man through the back window. A manic thumping of bass from his car vibrated through theirs, *boom, boom, booomm,* a seismic pound, like blood slamming through one's body, as he threw them the bird, irritated at their slowness. Her face burned—how could he be so rude, so stupid, didn't he see cars stopped right in front of them, that there was nowhere to go—didn't he understand that she was dying?

Claire had not acknowledged the idea of dying even to herself, so intent was she on getting home, on *appearing* to Forster and the girls, pretending a strength made up in equal parts of politeness, denial, and strange, wild longing.

In a hurry, the young man, so far removed from the idea of death that it mattered to him only that their car was blocking him from where he wanted to go, slammed on the horn. Would he act any differently if she told him she had cancer? As they pulled into a space, she rolled down her window.

"I'm sick!" she yelled.

"No shit, lady. How about getting out of the way?"

The girls, mortified, shushed and gestured quiet with their hands. *Be quiet, be still, Mother.* They collectively panicked at any sign of confrontation, violence.

Claire let out a few choice expletives, and the man made gestures, gunning his car, leaving them in a dust of exhaust fumes and burning rubber. *Mother,* the girls said. *How could you?*

Years before, playing her part of rancher's wife, she had hosted picnics and hayrides on the farm for seniors, disadvantaged children, people with disabilities, sent crates of oranges, avocados, and strawberries, did her part as long as she herself could keep a distance, preferring to play the part of dutiful mother and wife, the friend who made casseroles, sent candy and flowers, found gifts that were neither too much nor too little. Able to take other people's grief and misfortune and her own charity in bite-size pieces. But she had lost the taste for social niceties, now preferring gut-swelling confrontation, with all its dangers. *Mom, you should never do that. No. Dangerous.*

The girls could view Claire's heart at will, as children always see through the deception of their parents. She appeared to them as wide-open and mundane as their living-room sofa, comfortable and a bit disdained for its utility. Since Josh's death, they carried on the conceit that Claire was as self-sufficient and contented as they wanted her to be. A necessary blindness that each new generation took on, in order to concentrate its energies on the future, its own fate, rather than the past and its mistakes, the provenance of the parents. Claire accepted the fiction, but also knew that the past required just as much attention. Would not let them out of its grip until it received its due. Her daughters were still too young to know this.

"We're just saying we want what's best for you," Gwen said,

returning to her point as if the interlude had not happened. Patient and relentless as she was with her clients. Was that what they taught in law school?

"I'm going to the local hospital. I'm staying on the farm for treatments."

The girls, united for once, frowned.

Chapter 2

When they pulled down the long driveway and drove through the rows of grapefruit trees, Claire felt a flutter of life for the first time since before the winnowing of the illness started. Forster waved and walked down the path to Octavio's outpost in the groves. Gwen yelled at Forster's retreating back that he stay for dinner. Claire bent down and ruffled the fur of the neighbor's dogs, endured their frantic jumping, noses and tails thumping against the dressing taped tightly around her chest, swaddling emptiness. That's the way it felt to her, not a presence, death, squeezing against her chest, but rather a vacuum to be filled. Contact, touch, connection, the dogs were oblivious to the mortality that made her daughters' touches shy. The sharp pain that was dull at the same time, promising a long, dreary convalescence, but Claire didn't care as long as she was back home.

"This is where I need to be. This is where I'll recover."

"We understand," Lucy said. But they didn't. Lucy had never felt homesick for the ranch once she left, and only Claire's insistence drove her back for visits. For the daughters, the ranch had always been a place of hard work and then later sadness. Neither of them had inherited Claire's love of the land.

* * *

The possibilities had been mulled over privately between Lucy and Gwen for days. Lucy had a new job, albeit minimum wage, working in a gallery in Santa Fe. She'd lose it if she didn't start right away. Also, there was no clinic close to her. Gwen had her job, a husband, and two children to think about, but Sacramento might be workable. Between her Kevin and her, they could handle taking Claire to her appointments.

At the kitchen sink, Claire turned the KÄLTE handle and let the water run a minute down the side of the sink before filling her glass. The water tasted icy, different from anywhere else, especially the lukewarm chemical flavor at the hospital. It came from their own well, a deep, artesian source that was drying up: traces of eucalyptus and orange and limestone, perhaps the mineral taste of bone.

As Claire drank glass after glass, dreamy, content, the girls circled round her, wary, waiting. She smiled, gulped air. At last she could breathe. Gwen took the role of leader. Claire nodded at the rightness of this, while water dribbled down her chin, sobered by this glimpse of the future once she was gone, the rude shock of the world's reordering afterward.

"What are we going to do about the farm?" Gwen asked. "It's getting harder for you to manage alone. Especially now."

"Octavio is here." Claire filled another glass to stall them, surprised that it had been brought up so bluntly, but to Gwen's credit that was her way. When she was a little girl, she always found one and only one solution to whatever problem came up and stolidly clung to it no matter what. Living alone, Claire savored getting lost pondering the great infinitude of fixes available to any problem, basking in the possibilities rather than employing any single one of them and getting on with solving the thing.

With her strawberry-blond hair and creamy skin, Gwen had

always been striking, and her deliberate adult dowdiness of flat heels and baggy dresses irritated Claire. A throwback to Hanni? Or was it due to the night of the attack? Did Gwen blame herself for Josh's being taken? Or was Claire responsible, putting too much responsibility on her? Whatever it was, Gwen's adult self seemed determined to drain the pleasure out of everything around her.

"The farm is fine," Claire repeated. "But it's time for one of you to come back."

"What about the cancer?" Lucy said. Gwen frowned at her sister's clumsiness.

"Am I going somewhere?"

"We have to think about the treatments." Gwen patted Claire's arm. "This is an optimal time to sell. Before the county starts making demands for access roads."

Claire shook her head, dizzy at this outlandish misunderstanding. "I didn't ask for anyone's help."

"We're your daughters," Gwen said. "Of course, we'll help. I talked to a real estate agent who said that the Owens's land went for a record price."

Their relentlessness made Claire feel as if she were being buried alive, hurried to the end. "It wasn't your right," she said, desperate to get away. "I'm going to check the garden."

Undeterred, Gwen dogged her outside. "You said you need family near."

The ring of Meyer lemon trees hadn't been picked, and now the skin hung dark yellow, shrinking back on the fruit. "What I *need* is someone out here with a basket. I'm going to make lemon pie."

"Mom."

"I never told you to move away, but I didn't stop you either."

"No one except you wants to be here anymore." Gwen squinted into the evening sun, as if it had placed itself just to irritate her. Away from Lucy's scrutiny, she became petulant, childish. "I don't see how. Even if the farm's managed by Octavio and Dad, what about the house? Who's going to clean? Cook? Who's going to take you to doctors? Who is going to be responsible?"

"My head's spinning."

"Exactly. Your head's spinning. I can't leave everything behind. That leaves Lucy. Enough said."

"It'll get taken care of. How do you get through a day with all your worrying?"

Gwen flushed, and Claire remembered fights they'd had as she grew up. "It gets taken care of, Mom, because someone else worries about it and does it. Not you."

"Unfair."

Claire longed for Forster to guard her against this bullying. She was tempted to go find him but resisted. Odds were that things were going to get far worse in the future, and then she'd have no choice but to ask his help. Now she should try to hold siege alone.

"I want to spend time together. Have the children see you more," Gwen said.

"Is that what this is about? Me being gone?"

"Don't be melodramatic."

"This is just a bit of unpleasantness to be got through. People survive cancer every day. If it gets worse, then we'll rethink things."

"If that's the way you want it. I'll just take the kids out of school. Take a leave of absence. Tell Kevin that I have to come—" Gwen's voice cracked.

Nothing could not be remedied, no matter how late, by love. In this case, by giving in, and yet Claire couldn't render it, the habit of independence too deeply established. The thought of an invasion unnerved her. She did not have it in her to deal both with cancer and Gwen's wheedling her to sell the farm. Didn't illness absolve one, allow one to be selfish? So she relented, backed down, cajoled, sacrificed the battle for the larger war.

"You can't uproot yourself. What if I hired someone to take care of me? How would that be? Would that make you feel better?"

"*Hire* someone?"

"Temporarily. Just to get me through. A stopgap."

"Pay money?" Gwen said, offended by the suggestion.

Claire could not say it aloud, that money sometimes was by far the easiest price to be paid.

"You've always done everything yourself."

"I know, Gweny. It's just temporary."

"It's not right." Gwen shrugged. "We'll think about it, okay? I'll go start dinner."

"How come you don't feel differently about the farm? It's your home, too."

Gwen shrugged. "You never understood. All we could talk about when we were kids was getting away. It was so boring and isolated. And then our family broke." She walked inside.

Claire picked lemons. It was good to be home, even under the circumstances. When Lucy came out with a basket and helped her pluck them off the thorny branches, she was content.

"Remember when you gave us a penny a fruit?"

Claire smiled. "I even remember when it went up to a nickel."

"We were happy."

She looked at Lucy. "Why doesn't Gwen remember that?"

"It hasn't been for a long time now. Happy, I mean."

"Things change."

"Maybe it would be better to sell, after all?"

Lucy had always been the child most like her. Impractical, a dreamer, emotional, so this felt like a betrayal. "Did Gwen send you out?"

"Like I ever cared what Gweny thought." Lucy snorted a laugh. "But don't you think the place is, well, kind of haunted, or something?"

"This is where you all were born. This is where we belong, like Grandma said."

"Maybe she was wrong."

"Hanni was not wrong." How had Lucy intuited Hanni's last-minute change of heart? Not that Claire would ever admit it.

"I don't see that either you or Dad was all that happy here."

"We'll set up interviews for a cleaning lady Monday. Get someone installed right away." Claire would take up the mantle, insisting on her immortality, insisting, mostly, to remain where and how she was.

The truth was that standing in the orchard looking at a grown-up Lucy, the present did not feel real. She did not feel real to herself. The deforming fact of her missing breast, the new possibility that she would be no more, were mere fictions. Instead, it was more like taking on the role of a character in a play, forced to make the character's circumstances one's own. But this distance allowed her a clarity of purpose.

Lucy sighed and turned back to the house. "I should help with dinner."

"Be on my side, baby." Claire hugged her.

"I always was. You just didn't see it."

Alone, the last of the sun on her skin, the moment took Claire back to her early days, peeling an orange as she walked through the rows of trees, dropping a confetti of rind behind her, eating the sun-warmed fruit, the girls small and playful as puppies, running in their coveralls through the trees—seeing eternity down the rows the long way, seeing only the next bushy trees across—yelling, laughing, *You're it! You're it! You're it!*

She sat on the lawn with Raisi, legs crossed Indian-style, with Josh in a bassinet under the jacaranda tree, purple blossoms floating slowly down like a benediction, landing in their hair, on the baby's blanket. Jacaranda blossoms fell, or was it the coral tree in the front yard? Roots like a banyan tree's, orange-red blossoms like sickles, like small crescent moons of blood.

Nothing had changed except time. Lucy was wrong because once it had been a happy place, unhaunted, and they had been happy there. She was sure of it. Time had corrupted things.

It started with Josh's death, tainting the rhythm of their days in ways not anticipated. In the mornings, she lay in bed, unable to rise, the weight of sorrow pressing her down further and further into her bed. She stopped packing the girls' lunches, letting them make their own. Forster, too, withdrew, spending less and less time on the farm, less time being a father, no time as her husband. Was their mutual pulling back the reason the girls clung so close to each other, the reason they left home so early and stayed so far away? Could it be that those three men first setting foot on the ranch were catalyst enough to set in motion a chain of events inexorable, not capable of being recovered from? Or was there something brittle and unsound within the family, something diseased, something they could not have known or fixed, something that might never have come to light of day except the fates unkindly exposed it?

That first night back from the hospital, Forster, Octavio, and Mrs. Girbaldi stayed for dinner, and the table was filled with food as it had been in the old days. Claire loved the feeling of the kitchen filled again with life. She pulled out her lemon cheese pie from the oven, set it on the counter to cool, the scent sharp and healing as sunlight. But she couldn't eat—a piece of chicken brought to her mouth nauseated her, lying rubbery and repulsive on her tongue, her mind convulsed with the idea of its being dead flesh. Her entire will focused on simply not gagging. The pain drugs ruined taste—like walking around with a mouth full of pennies.

"Pass the salad," Forster said. "We need to discuss some things. We are all going to have to pull together."

"Mom's getting a maid," Lucy announced.

"Do you want me to talk with Sofia?" Octavio said. "She could come back from Rosarito. Or should I ask Paz?"

"Isn't she in school?" Claire said.

"It could be arranged," Octavio said.

"I don't want anything to interfere with her studies."

"Finally," Mrs. Girbaldi said. "This place was always too much to take care of by yourself."

"I wouldn't call her a maid," Claire corrected.

"What else do you call someone who washes your floors?" Lucy said.

"Not your boyfriend," Gwen said.

The girls' catting was like the background noise of a television, muffled yet reassuring.

"She'll do some cleaning," Claire said. "But also driving me, cooking meals, running errands. A nanny for adults."

"Still, it's a stranger." Lucy had remained quiet while she might have been called on to stay, but now she pouted at not having been asked.

"Unless you have Paz," Octavio said.

"Usually maids are strangers," Claire said. "Until you get to know them."

"Like a man," Gwen said to Lucy, "before you've slept with him. Lucy doesn't know some of them *after* she's slept with them."

"You just said she wasn't a maid."

Claire sighed. "Let's call her an assistant." But to assist in what? Illness? A handmaiden for illness.

"You're not going to like a stranger in your house," Gwen said.

At that moment Claire wanted so badly to please the girls, to show her gratefulness at their coming. "Here's the deal. After I've finished all the treatments and am healthy again, I've decided to put the farm up for sale."

Gwen's face lit up. "You're serious?"

"Yes." It was as easy as that. Peace would descend for the limit of her treatment, and she would deal with the rest later. She was surprised that deception was so easy and could give such pleasure when truth almost always led to disappointment.

"That's good," Forster said. "Really good. I'm surprised."

Even Lucy gave her a wary yet pleased nod, convinced her mother was finally shaking off the ghosts of the past.

For days women from an agency came in a long, supplicant line of battered cars, oversize models from a decade or more earlier that Claire recognized from when shy boys had picked up the girls for dates. The women came shuffling in, wearing scuffed shoes, most speaking halting English. A young, sweet-faced girl, Angelita, had good references, but not till half an hour passed did she reveal she was pregnant and would leave early for Mexico. Dolores, a middle-aged, heavyset woman, wanted access to a gym for three hours a day to lose weight. A Scottish nurse, Moira, with purple lipstick, was born-again and insisted on installing religious pictures in the house. A Vietnamese lady wanted to move in with her aunt and three children.

Octavio again suggested that Paz do the job, defer her admission to law school, but Claire refused.

Claire spoke a fair amount of Spanish, enough to get the basics across, but this was more complicated. Many of the women didn't like driving. Most had to care for their own families at night even though the job description had stated live-in. The younger ones weren't educated enough to read English, follow medication instructions. Lucy was right. Everyone *did* feel like a stranger. How to admit that Claire was looking for a kindred spirit in these women while they were sensibly looking at this as a dull, servile, low-wage job?

Claire did not resent the new immigrants the way some of the old-timers did. She didn't yearn for the old days of Midwestern farmers, polyester-suited developers, bedraggled surfers, Velveeta cocktail-party canapés, and dinner theaters that featured *Hello, Dolly!* But she needed a real companion for this undertaking back to health.

After a week, despairing of finding anyone, Gwen wanted to hire a full-time nurse in addition to a cleaning lady. Mrs. Girbaldi, who treated them as a surrogate family, listened to the hiring woes while the girls cooked dinner.

Claire complained that she couldn't afford to hire two full-time new employees. "Besides, all the attention will make me feel like I'm sick."

"Why don't you take Paz once a week just to clean?" Mrs. Girbaldi said. "It would please Octavio."

"Maybe. Then I could look for an assistant only. Maybe a college student?"

Gwen frowned. "Not such a great idea. They'll be distracted—boyfriends, going out, future jobs. No way they'll do grocery shopping."

Lucy sighed, filing her nails. "I could come home."

"No," Claire said. "You're excited about this Santa Fe job."

"Thing is, I met a girl today. At the coffee place." Lucy continued filing her nails, while the rest of them stood around the kitchen.

"Yes? And?" Gwen finally blurted out.

"I didn't think you were listening." Used to being the baby of the house, Lucy was always off guard at being taken seriously.

Her brows furrowed as she pulled together the thought that she'd thrown out so casually. "I said I needed an extra shot because they always make the cappuccinos so weak, and this girl said, yes, not like in Europe. I asked her where she was from, and she said from Florida, by way of London and France. She learned to be a barista there. Born in the Caribbean. You should have seen the pattern she made in the foam—a perfect leaf. I think she said she'd studied political science at Berkeley. She wore the most beautiful canvas shoes from India, embroidered with all these sequins and—"

"Does this sound as bad to anyone else as it does to me?" Gwen asked, already turning away.

Mrs. Girbaldi sighed, tearing lettuce leaves, so much they had enough to feed twenty. "Let the girl talk."

"And she'd want the job why?"

"Oh, I forgot the whole point of the story—she got fired while I was there. She was crying, and I offered to take her for a sandwich to calm down. She hadn't eaten the whole day and was starving. She was hysterical—said she couldn't pay the rent that was due. She owed money to some boyfriend, something like that."

"I don't think so." Gwen continued peeling potatoes.

"Why did she get fired?" Claire asked.

"That was what was so strange. There was some old guy who came in every morning whose eyesight was failing, and she always brought him his coffee. That morning she took off with his briefcase—just left the store. The manager accused her of stealing until the old man came back and explained that she had returned it to him. She told the manager to f— off anyway."

Claire felt determined about something for the first time that day. "I don't want you giving up your job."

"I should to be here with you," Lucy said without conviction.

"This coffee girl isn't the kind of person we are looking for," Gwen said finally, wiping her hands on a dish towel.

"Why not?" Lucy said.

"Remember when Mom was out of bay leaves? And you went outside and picked leaves off the tree, insisting they were bay leaves?"

Lucy's face turned blotchy. "What are you talking about?"

"And Mom thanked you and pretended to put them in the soup?"

"Oh, my God. I was six years old!"

"For all you knew, they could have been oleander. You could have killed us all," Gwen said.

"Can you get hold of her?" Claire asked.

"Who?"

"The coffee girl!"

"I know the apartment I dropped her off at. But she was moving out," Lucy said. "Maybe I should drive over now? Get her name and cell number."

"You don't even know her name?" Gwen said.

"Minna. I think her name's Minna, okay? It's not like she wants the job. Bay leaves!"

The whole plan unraveling, the girls arguing, Claire's chance to stay at the farm taken and replaced by an unwanted, cobbled second childhood in a condo in Sacramento. "Go talk to her. I have a feeling about this one."

Lucy got her keys.

"What about dinner?" Gwen said.

"I lost my appetite." Lucy slammed the back door.

Mrs. Girbaldi hummed as she cut cucumbers. One of the traits Claire loved in her was her cool unflappability. Nothing, including their family squabble, affected her.

"Take it easy on Lucy," Claire said to Gwen. "She's still fragile."

"How long does she get away with that excuse?" Gwen banged the oven door shut on the potatoes and left the room. Despite her maternal solicitude, her taking charge, her furious cleaning and cooking in the house, she chafed against her self-appointed role.

"She's mad about me hiring a girl. Thinks it will interfere with me selling the ranch."

"Will it?" Mrs. Girbaldi was never sly about getting to the point.

"As if that's the only way she can be happy."

Claire turned away to set the table. Knife, fork, spoon. Knife, fork, spoon. Raisi's love of routine now her own. The farm would go on for a while longer, and she would go on for a while longer with it. She banged the glassware down on the table so hard it was in danger of shattering. Gwen and Lucy weren't the only ones with a temper. Sometimes people simply didn't understand what it was that created and sustained them. Regardless, this girl Minna would have to do.

Chapter 3

After an uneasy dinner spent listening for Lucy's return, the dishes had been cleared away, and Gwen, still angry, watched a movie while Claire played gin with Mrs. Girbaldi, pretending not to notice when she cheated by fudging on their long-running scorecard. Mrs. Girbaldi was on her third cocktail by the time Lucy returned with the girl from the coffeehouse. Driven by different motivations each, they rushed from different rooms of the house to gather in the entry hall to satisfy their curiosity.

The afternoon had blued to evening, and the only thing that illuminated was the small, overhead light from the open passenger door, as a tall, lanky form stretched out her legs. The girl stood in the driveway, turning once, and then again in a full circle, appearing satisfied as she surveyed the grounds around her as if she owned the place and had merely come to check on things, perhaps take a retreat, rather than to be in service there. They stood in line for inspection and greeting.

Claire admired this sense of confidence. What struck her first as the girl walked toward them was that, despite the dusk, she wore dark, oversize sunglasses, and this gave her both a glamorous and a pitiful air, making it unclear whether they were being visited by someone famous, determined to hide her identity, or, conversely, a blind person hopelessly dependent on the whims of strangers. Transformed, ebullient, Lucy bent her head near the girl's, whispering something low enough for only her to hear, and both of them giggled with the air of conspirators, reinforcing the feeling of her being just another in a long line of the girls' many friends who had come visiting over the years. Claire had to remind herself that the two had only just met, their intimacy seemed so natural, and this was yet another thing in the girl's favor.

When she entered the hallway and stood under the light, at last taking off the sunglasses, a moment's hush enveloped them. A perverse sense of pride went through Claire at Lucy's having felt no need to inform them that the girl was black, or at least biracial. She held out her hand. "Hello, I'm Minna."

The first to break the spell, Claire moved closer to shake her hand, first lightly, then more forcefully, cupping her frozen, thin fingers in her own. "You're ice-cold! Poor thing. Where have you been?" Claire felt an immediate desire to protect and moved closer still, wrapping an arm around Minna's shoulders as if offering refuge to one distressed—the girl had a vulnerability that evoked maternal instincts. Taller than Lucy, her body, although slender, gave an impression of muscularity. She had powerful, wide shoulders, and long, tapered fingers that looked as if they held musical promise. Her skin glowed the shade of coffee with milk stirred in, and her brown hair had the sleekness of being straightened and held to a shape not of its own volition.

"Come in, come in," Claire said, trying to erase the impression of their inspecting her by further and further kindnesses, ushering the girl into the family room, corralling her into the most comfortable chair, fluffing a pillow behind her back, offering a footstool, a bowl of long-preserved, dusty mints. In the girl's presence, the mints appeared hopelessly provincial. Behind her, she could hear Mrs. Girbaldi's throat clearing as if to say, *Who is interviewing whom?*

When Claire first looked at Minna, the green of her eyes startled her, unexpected and lovely, the soft hue of moss. As the girl took in the room—the floor-to-ceiling bookcases around three walls, stacks of books on every surface, including one tented open along the sofa's arm—she picked the splayed book up, twisting a delicate wrist, to read the spine. "*Tales of the Arabian Nights*? Are you a classicist, or are you drawn to the fairy-tale elements?"

Claire smiled. "I'm making up for a stunted education," she said, diffident as if she were being courted. "I love stories."

"Do you love stories or love *love stories*?"

Minna chuckled and stretched her long legs out in front of her, crossing them at the ankle. She wore a loose summer dress, but what drew Claire's attention were her expensive-looking gold sandals, the heels high, calling for a more glamorous occasion than the one she was there for. Her toenails were painted an iridescent red, her toes hanging over the front as if the shoes were a size too small. Her feet were long, narrow, aristocratic.

"You found me out. I love both."

"I already feel at home here," Minna said, granting them for the first time her wide, brilliant smile. "My great-grandmother was a novelist. We always had books around. At one point I wanted to be a librarian just to be able to read all day."

"Really?" Gwen said, as if this were an outlandish statement.

"What was her name?" Claire asked. Triumphant, she would not look at Gwen or Mrs. Girbaldi. Now, besides Claire's being transported by her exotic looks, Claire's heart quickened because Minna had entered her territory. At no time did she not prefer the imaginary to the real.

"Jean Rhys."

"Oh," Claire said. "Oh."

She swooned. It was as if the last thirty years were swept away and she was back in her college English lit class, reading Rhys for the first time. Her masterpiece, *Wide Sargasso Sea,* had turned all the Jane Austen and Brontë sisters books on their head. A prequel to *Jane Eyre,* it was the madwoman-in-the-attic's side of the story, the one that Jane so easily dismissed. After reading it, Claire felt that if one knew any person thoroughly enough, almost all could be explained and forgiven. What had happened to the girl who read that book?

"She was one of my heroes in college. I loved her books," Claire said.

"I never heard of her," Gwen said.

Minna looked at Claire for confirmation, and said, "She was well-known in the thirties and forties. Interest revived in her in the seventies with all the postcolonial Caribbean and feminist studies. Although she hated that label; hated the island and being lumped together with other women writers.

"She told my mother she was absolutely disappointed to have a daughter and no sons. More disappointed to have only granddaughters and great-granddaughters. Ironic, that we are a whole clan of women."

"Is she still . . . ?"

Minna closed her eyes for a moment. "She passed in '79. I hardly knew her. I have one memory as a baby, being dandled on her lap. I was fascinated by her false teeth, how she moved them around in her mouth." Minna laughed.

"Jean Rhys," Claire said. "Beautiful Antoinette, on that lush, sensual island. And Rochester, who comes to marry her."

They all sat in silence, mesmerized for different reasons.

Minna leaned forward, suddenly serious. "She had a large impact on me as a girl. She was a great heroine in Dominica, where we're from."

"Do you go home often?"

"When interest in her work revived, the royalties grew. The

family bought land around the original farm until we were one of the largest landowners. Then came the anglicizing. My mother decided to send me to England."

"How about some wine?" Lucy blurted out, and Gwen glared at her as if confirmed that her sister had lost her mind.

"I'd love some," Minna said, so quickly it was obvious that she was nervous. "Red if you have it." She sighed, glancing at Gwen. "Maybe not appropriate for a job interview?"

"No, no. It's fine. We're liberal here. Go ahead, open a bottle," Gwen said to Lucy's disappearing back.

"We grew up on our grandfather's coffee plantation. Took shopping trips to Martinique. A charmed life."

"So how did you end up working at a coffee shop?" Gwen asked.

"How rude!" Claire said. "Excuse my daughter."

"Are you aware," Mrs. Girbaldi jumped in, "that this is a job of great responsibility?"

Minna looked off into the corner of the ceiling for a long moment, as if making a particularly difficult calculation, and, once decided, looked at Claire.

"Lucy filled me in a bit. My mother had breast cancer."

Claire hated everyone in the room for their roughness, how they had forced this out of Minna. "Did she survive it?" Claire asked softly, as if she didn't want to wake something sleeping in the room.

"She died of something else."

The blood stopped and started inside Claire. She understood now the pull toward the girl, could see in her eyes that they were fellow sufferers.

"So I've been through cancer treatment before. I've learned to be careful in approaching the subject. Some people want to be direct and head-on about the whole thing. Others prefer a more indirect approach."

"My daughters think I'm being stubborn, wanting to stay on here alone."

"You talk about us like we weren't even here," Gwen said.

"You are stubborn, Claire. That's your strength."

Her using Claire's name should have alarmed, a premature intimacy, and yet it thrilled Claire and made her feel they shared an understanding already.

Gwen coughed. "Lucy told us you were taking classes. . . ."

Minna turned toward her, her profile sharp, suddenly businesslike. "I did my undergraduate work at Cambridge. I started my PhD in political science at Berkeley, but decided to take some time off. Too much stress."

"What are your future plans?" Mrs. Girbaldi asked.

Minna sat back and smiled, showing that she was answering these intrusive questions only for politeness. "I think I'd do well in diplomacy. My father served as a diplomat. There's always the librarian dream to fall back on."

"Wow, Cambridge," Lucy said, coming in from the kitchen, balancing wineglasses, not missing a beat as she shot a look to Gwen.

"England's a tradition in our family. Three generations. I want the advanced degree, but now I need some time off. The coffeeshop gig was just for some cash."

Later, Claire remembered being so dazzled that first meeting with Minna that the information offered up came to her piecemeal. So distracted was she by the timbre, the wave and lilt, of Minna's voice, like especially ravishing music that reached unexpected places. Definitely English, but something of hot sun and tropical waters, too. A slowness born out of heat and languor.

"I don't know why this would appeal to you," Claire said. "Taking care of a sick lady. But you won't have to clean."

Minna laughed, a deep belly laugh, head thrown back, perfect white teeth exposed. "I'm well acquainted with a mop. My *maman* made sure all of her girls kept a spotless house."

"You have sisters!" Lucy said as if that provided a final confirmation of her worthiness.

"Two sisters. Another house of women only, like yours."

A silence hung in the room. The family had long ago decided on omission rather than *Once we had a son, a brother. . . .*

Minna continued without seeming to note the pause. "I was the ugly runt of the litter. My oldest sister was a model in Paris. Now she's married. She lives in the south of France. In Cannes." Minna smiled and nodded, sipped her wine.

The conversation made Claire feel countrified, rough, and without style. She imagined the girls, if they had any sense, felt the same. A new silence stretched until it reached discomfort.

Minna sighed and continued as if the situation required it. "My middle sister lives in Florida. She invests in the real estate market. She has the most beautiful, modern house."

"You must miss them," Lucy said.

"I do. But when the three of us were children in Dominica, all we could talk of was getting away. It was so isolated and backward on the plantation. Can I tell you the funniest story?"

"Please do," Mrs. Girbaldi said.

"My oldest sister was an art student in London when she was discovered by a photographer for *Vogue*. All fine and well. But they wanted her to be more of a story. A sensation. So they invented this story that he had found her in Haiti, living in the slums and starving, breaking coconuts with her bare hands or something equally absurd. Very much like the stories of Iman being a goat herder."

"Why would they lie?" Gwen asked.

"I guess to make themselves feel progressive and liberal, feel proud of plucking one of a million from a fate of misery. The wild savage redeemed."

"But you aren't even from Haiti," Lucy said, outraged.

"People always mix up Dominica with the Dominican Republic. It's all the same to them. Close enough."

"I am so proud of my girls," Claire said, resolute, ready to close the deal. "They wanted to take care of me, but I don't want them upsetting their lives."

"Lucy told me that you are a very special family," Minna said.

"You're hired if you want the job," Claire said.

Minna opened her eyes wide, grinning, while Lucy jumped up and clapped, rushing to kiss Claire. "Good for you, Mom."

Gwen and Mrs. Girbaldi remained seated and silent.

"That's very kind of you. But perhaps you should speak with your family in private. It's a big decision, bringing someone new into your home."

"Wise girl," Mrs. Girbaldi said, before Claire could get in a word of protest.

"The job will probably last only six months. After Mom is well, she's selling the ranch," Gwen said.

"Sad to leave such a wonderful place," Minna said.

"Yes." Claire looked at this girl, her dark Cordelia.

Another too long pause in the room.

"Can you direct me to the loo?"

"Down the hall," Gwen answered.

Minna left the room, and they sat in a divided silence.

"I guess I'll start on the dishes," Lucy said.

"Not just yet," Gwen snapped.

No one moved, and they listened in silence to the sound of high heels going back and forth on the wood floor in the hallway, doors opening and shutting. Minna popped her head back in the room.

"Sorry, but I can't find it."

"I'll show you," Lucy said. "How about I make you a snack in the kitchen."

"Lovely, I'm starving."

"I can't believe how you are acting," Lucy hissed as she left the room.

Mrs. Girbaldi hiccuped. "A beautiful girl."

A few minutes later, Minna returned, gathered her purse and sweater. "I'm leaving now. Why don't you give me a call in town once you've decided."

"Could you wait in the entry for a minute?" Claire said. Then she faced down Gwen. "I want her."

"You shouldn't rush—"

"Why not? How much better do you think we'll know anyone else?"

"What about references?"

"She worked in a coffee shop."

"I wonder," Mrs. Girbaldi said, as she poured herself a glass of wine, "how well she'll adapt to life here. It certainly isn't Cannes, or Cambridge, or even Berkeley."

"Well?" Claire pushed.

"It feels funny," Gwen said.

"She's very smart."

Gwen frowned, threw her hands up in defeat. "It's your decision."

"Tell her to come in," Claire said.

And just like that, opposition to Minna crumbled like a house on a false foundation. Or perhaps, the resistance had been half-hearted; already Gwen and Lucy were making plans of escape. Even Gwen seemed satisfied that she had put up an honorable fight. A release of tension, a giddiness, enveloped them now that a solution had so propitiously fallen into their lap.

The next morning, Claire woke to the smell of coffee. In the kitchen, Minna was dressed in white polo shirt, white jeans, and white tennis shoes. True, the girls' intuition had been correct in that it felt odd to have a stranger living with her. The habit of solitude was entrenched. This was a shotgun decision—her only way to get what she wanted. Still, she felt a sense of astonishment and relief that Minna was made flesh, not a dream, despite the evidence the previous night when the girl went to Lucy's car and pulled out of the backseat all her worldly possessions packed in two cardboard liquor boxes. Her sudden appearance as companion so improbable that it distracted from Claire's preoccupation with her illness, a welcome relief. She poured coffee.

Minna was frowning. "Sorry, but where do you put your trash?"

"Trash? There's a can under the sink. For big stuff, there's a bin in the garage."

"I couldn't find it anywhere. You Americans, always hiding everything ugly away."

Claire gave a polite shrug.

"I walked in the orchard this morning. So beautiful. On Martinique we grew sugarcane and bananas mostly, but we had some avocados and citrus for the local markets. It reminds me of my island here. I squeezed a pitcher of juice for us."

"I thought you said your plantation was on Dominica."

"We had plantations on different islands."

"That's what I recognized in you," Claire said.

Minna looked up then, embarrassed.

"You appreciate the land."

"Your daughters are unhappy with my staying here?"

"Unhappy with me," Claire said.

Claire backed out the ancient Mercedes from the old carriage house that served as garage. Forster's family had insisted on buying American cars, starting during the war—a succession of Fords, Chevrolets, and then with Forster's generation Thunderbirds and

Mustangs. But despite their vehement patriotism during that period of the forties and fifties, fruit with the Germanic Baumsarg name did not sell; the produce had to be sent to a middleman, who relabeled the source, at a significant discount. They were krauts, enemies no different from the Japanese. Hanni had told stories to Claire about the deprivation suffered while she was a young woman, when the only butter available was lard colored with food dye.

Since the eighties, the choice had centered on the most economical. The diesel Mercedes belched a black cloud when Claire gunned it and shuddered at stoplights from its worn shock absorbers. The odometer had clocked over 250,000 miles, and the car still had its original, albeit peeling and fading, silver paint job.

Minna sat behind the wheel and ran her finger over the lacquered-wood dash. "Nice." She had put on a headscarf and large hoop earrings for the outing to the airport.

"Hardly nice," Claire said. "I hope you're good on freeways."

"I love to drive. I've driven cross-country five times. Up to Alaska once. Down to South America."

"Where to?"

Minna looked at her feet, suddenly shy. "Colombia. And Costa Rica. Peru, of course."

"You drove to South America?" Claire asked, incredulous, and Minna blinked, but before she could answer, the girls came out with their luggage. By the time the car was loaded, there was no room left for a fourth person. Lucy's suitcases took up most of the backseat, piled high with tote bags, so that Gwen had to squeeze in.

"Aren't you coming?" Gwen asked when she saw Claire hesitating in the driveway.

Minna sat behind the wheel, humming to herself as she checked her earrings in the overhead vanity mirror.

"Hurry, I'm tight on my flight time," Lucy said.

"Where will I fit?" Claire asked, waving her hand at the car.

"Maybe let your mother rest?" Minna said.

It was miraculous, the speed with which the barely accepted fact of Minna's caretaking was taken for granted and even relied upon.

The girls piled back out of the car to say their final good-byes, and for the first time Claire felt their imminent absence. The fear surprised her. She thought she had conquered it during the years of their college, the shorter and shorter visits, the growing distance of their adult lives. Had she made a terrible mistake in not selling the farm, not following Gwen's advice? Was Lucy right, had she stripped out all the happiness to be had from this place? But if she admitted to a mistake now, then she would also have to admit her earlier mistake in staying all those years before.

Panicked, Claire stood rooted to the spot, unhappy. She came within a breath of calling the whole thing off, revealing her cowardice.

Minna watched, two sharp lines like incisions forming between her brows. "The sun is making you dizzy," she said, and pulled Claire away from the car and into the shade, the girls following.

Perhaps Minna was right, perhaps the white noon sun was making her light-headed. Under the shade of a fig tree next to the front door, she tried to relax into the feeling of protection. Beyond, the sun still scalded, firing the fine dust in the air. It lit up Minna's headscarf, with its garish yellows, greens, and reds, cheap and harsh in the burning light. Who was this girl and why had Claire been so impulsive, so starved and willful, as to insist on her company? Standing in the shade, doubt shook her.

Minna had left the driver's-side door open, and the buzzing sensor made an anxious, insect whining in the background. Ignoring it, Minna folded her arms under her breasts and watched the leave-taking for a moment.

"I want you two to know that I will treat Claire as I would my own mother."

The girls teared up. Mollified, they pulled out Kleenexes and dabbed their eyes. They embraced Claire. Minna excused herself and went into the house. The girls drifted back toward the car as they traded final good-byes, admonitions, promises, encouragements, schedules. They would take turns visiting home.

When Minna came out, she was carrying a book. "This is for you."

Claire looked down at a first edition of *Wide Sargasso Sea*. She opened it to the title page and read the faded, spidery blue autograph. "This is too much."

Minna shrugged. "It was meant for you. Maybe I am superstitious, but sometimes I think certain people come into our life for a reason."

The taillights were at the end of the drive before Claire could thank her. Minna was right. She was where she had fought to be, having achieved her dubious goal, buried away in the middle of her groves. Claire turned her back on the car, her fleeing daughters, opened the book to the first page and hungrily began to read.

Chapter 4

They settled into a pattern of days.

Mornings were hardest. Knowledge of the cancer like a weight. Each morning Claire woke, the fact of the disease pressed down on her like a stone lid, like a tombstone, a covering of earth. She was accustomed to a cloistered solitude, had been reinforcing its walls for all the years since Joshua's death, freely perambulating the garden in housecoat and slippers, sipping her oversize cup of coffee as her fingers trailed elegiac lavender heads and spiky, stick-leaved rosemary, cradled flesh-soft roseheads and dimpled citrus. Her garden and the ranch beyond it had always given her such consolation, but now she gazed on it as one about to go away on a long journey. Paradoxical since she had fought so hard to stay on the ranch; it had ended being her sole victory.

But the atmosphere of the farm had changed. She felt eyes watched her. In addition to Minna, there was Paz, who came once a week for cleaning. They hadn't seen each other in a year when she came through the door. She went to Claire and buried her face on her shoulder. "How are you, *mi tía*?" Claire marveled at how self-assured she had become since she'd been away at college. "I wish you would have let me care for you."

"Give me my wish—your name on the door of a law office."

Paz blushed. "Among other things. It's official—Steven and I are marrying at the end of the year. You'll come?"

Of course, Claire thought, if I'm here. "Are you sure you have time for this?"

"Spending money." Paz laughed. "School's expensive."

Even during the times that no one was at the ranch, the possibility of it threw a veil of self-consciousness over all Claire did and saw. My lavender, she repeated to herself. My rosemary, my roses, my farm. But despite the insistence, it now seemed a changing and remote landscape.

The doctor sent thick booklets describing the procedures of chemotherapy and radiation, and Claire signed endless papers stating than she understood the risks, would hold harmless those who would poison her with the intention of a more ultimate health. She tried to distract herself with the activities of the farm, but it seemed as if her old life had been transcribed into a language she could not understand.

"What do you think about spraying the back field?" Octavio asked.

"Yes. I think so. I don't know. What do you think?"

"Should I ask Mr. Forster?"

"No. No need to. I'm fine."

"I think you do too much. You need rest to get back your health."

"I'm fine. This is what I need."

Instead of the farm, Claire plunged into the most private of worlds, the pages of a novel, for comfort. That old luxuriousness like a warm bath that she had not realized how much she missed.

The book Minna gave her was a weathered, smallish hardback. The pages yellowed and brittle and smelling, she imagined, of faded spices. Claire stared at the signature for long moments, feeling a thrill that the author had actually held this volume; it made the reading more urgent.

Rereading a book was a different experience from coming upon it for the first time. Especially if it was well-loved, like a favorite piece of music, it was capable of taking you back to a former self. In college, it was a revelation that the madwoman, Bertha, in the attic of *Jane Eyre,* might actually have an argument, might actually be a human being; moreover, a wronged one. That there were explanations for the crazy behavior. That the tall, dark, stoic Rochester might just be a misogynistic schemer. A newlywed when Claire next reread it, unpacking her boxes of books in her new home under Hanni's scrutiny, this time she was much taken by the sensuality of the island, and the newlywed status of Antoinette and Rochester. That, too, had been omitted from *Jane Eyre,* as if Jane were jealous of Rochester's erotic past. Now, all these years later, she identified with Antoinette's mother, Annette, her fear, a common fear of women through time, that her better days might be behind her. *How could she not try for all the things that had gone so suddenly, so without warning.* Then, so close to the relief of marrying Mr. Mason, the death of a son now doubly destroyed Claire. Claire had to lay down the book and take breaks while reading the passage in which Annette's son dies.

From the vantage of her older self, Claire knew that when disaster struck, no matter how long prepared against, it was always sudden, always took your breath away. That much she understood. Some might consider Claire herself a madwoman, one in a citrus orchard instead of locked up in an attic. But she understood why the mother insisted on riding out on her horse each morning in her shabby clothes, despite the jeers, why she kept walking up and down the glacis, keeping vigil over her abandoned Coulibri and all the things that were *now a thing of the past*. If one gave up the past, what was there?

In the year following Josh's death, the newspapers filled with the court case and then the sentencing of the three men, Claire had gone into town, alone or with the girls, and experienced repeatedly the hushed silence when entering a store or restaurant, the whispers, "That's her!" She had achieved a macabre, unwanted celebrity. The fruit stand sold out daily for a year before attention finally shifted away.

She would not allow her illness to turn her into an object of pity; she refused to be sequestered. Instead of staying in the house, she put on jeans and sneakers, a sweatshirt over her bandaged chest, snuck into the orchards, and took long walks along the snaking rows of citrus. She wore a large-brimmed straw hat, hiding her face, the skin that would be sensitized by the chemo. The workers who saw her, probably thinking that she was indeed a madwoman, dodged out of her way quickly, making her privacy so complete and absolute it was almost as if she were invisible.

Claire spent long hours reading on the couch, and Minna served her thick, frothy health drinks.

"I can't. I'm not hungry."

"This is important. Builds the blood."

Claire sipped and grimaced. "What is it?"

"Secret recipe from *Maman*."

The following Monday would be Claire's first chemo treatment, so she tried to luxuriate in the last days when she was still free to pretend away her illness. Mrs. Girbaldi was hosting her annual fundraiser for animals, and although Claire shrank away from the effort of having to socialize, she decided she should go because to attempt to live a normal life seemed essential for what lay ahead.

Saturday morning Minna and Claire sat over coffee and newspapers on the patio. Paz was mopping in the living room, and Claire did her best not to hover over the girl. The house hardly felt hers anymore. Not only did Paz's presence make her uneasy, she itched to correct details, such as the amount of oil used on the floor. Paz used too much and left behind a faint tackiness on bare feet. Not having control irritated Claire. When the mop handle clattered on the floor inside, she jumped, still groggy from having read late into the night.

Minna stood and looked out over the orchards. "This is a *God* place."

"Excuse me?"

"You are lucky to have this. There are powers here."

"It's true. I draw strength here."

"It can heal you if you allow it. *Maman* said trees healed you."

"I want to explain some things—just because I hired you doesn't mean I can't take care of myself."

"Of course."

"I don't intend to lie around being sick. I expect you to be productive as well. Live your own life, too."

"Something bothers you?"

"No. Yes," Claire said. "I'm not a pushover."

"Are you feeling uncomfortable with me?"

"I've had to be strong to keep this place. You should know this."

"That's hard to do always."

"Yes. But it's who I am."

Minna sipped her coffee and said nothing. Finally, she sighed. "Sometimes you have to give up power. For a time."

Claire worried that she had offended the girl. If she left, Claire would be back to square one with her daughters. She had become crafty in her grief, sly in her fanatical attachment to staying on the farm. Minna had slippery edges, which meant she might do better than most. A hunger was there that Claire could work with.

"It must have been amazing to grow up on the islands," Claire said, lightening the mood.

Minna blew on her coffee, which must have gone cold quite a while ago, an unnecessary, theatrical gesture. "It was a magic place. We owned things there like you do here."

"Did you appreciate it at the time, how special it was?"

"It was simply our life." Minna shrugged. "My *maman* preferred oil lamps at night. I would sit on her bed as she rubbed a cream made from coconut and flowers on my arms and legs and neck. She told me it would give me soft skin for my future husband someday."

Claire smiled. "An idyllic childhood."

"A way of life. People came for dinner and stayed a week. My parents had so many friends the house was never empty. I was never lonely there. Always a picnic or a party or an outing to go on. Like here, no?"

"We were happy here. Once." Claire knew there was no such nostalgia for the girls. To them the ranch was simply earth and fencing and buildings. They were oblivious that it had spawned them as much as Forster and herself. "I'll be out tonight."

Minna nodded.

Claire thought of her own first lonely nights on the farm. "Would you like to go with me?"

"Should you bring your help?"

"You're my assistant."

Minna looked up and grinned. "It will be a raucous party, I hope? I'll be your chaperone. Keep the men off you."

"More like I'll be the mother hen guarding her chick from the wolves."

"But I'm a wolf. Just like you, I can take care of myself." Minna stood and gathered the breakfast dishes. "Can I use the phone for a long-distance call to home? Just to let them know where I am. You can deduct from my wages."

Claire waved off Minna's suggestion, embarrassed by the mention of money and pay, dismayed how it ruined her effort at camaraderie, still so tenuous. She felt ridiculous, like having a schoolgirl crush, trying to make a good impression on this girl.

"I insist," Minna said. "We must keep business and friendship separate."

Claire was pleased by Minna's mention of friendship, implying that she looked at this job as something more than a way station. Despite Claire's protests to the contrary, she wanted a companion to go through her ordeal with.

Claire spent the morning in the barn with Octavio, going over the coming week's work. The basket price for avocados was down, but strawberry prices had skyrocketed because heavy rains in Oxnard had spoiled its crop. Both sobering and an act of grace to realize that the world went on despite one's private turmoil. Late afternoon, Claire came back from shopping to the eccentric sight of Minna sleeping out on the lawn. She lay flat on her back, her arms flung out sideways. Claire touched her on the shoulder.

Minna yawned awake. "What did you buy?" She jumped up like a teenager, eager to look through the bags.

"Go ahead," Claire said, laughing.

Minna pulled out three velour sweat suits. Tube socks. Orthopedic clogs.

"What's wrong?" Claire asked at Minna's obvious disappointment.

"What about something fun?"

"I'm preparing."

"Prepare for *after*. Buy a pair of stilettos."

"I was never a stiletto kind of woman, if you haven't guessed."

Minna laughed. "It's long past lunch. You need to keep up your strength. Let's eat the leftover salmon." In the kitchen, Claire sat on a barstool while Minna prepared food, and then they ate.

"I never eat this often."

"Now you will. Protein is important."

"So you'll come tonight? At least get to know the neighbors," Claire said.

"Sure."

"Do you go to the movies?"

"Now and then."

"Donald Richards will be there. He owns a place a mile down the road. He has a menagerie—cows, horses, llamas, goats, dogs, and cats."

"A Noah's ark."

"He's not a Noah. He tends to get falling-down drunk and flirt with all the women."

"Occupational hazard, I guess." The harshness in Minna's voice surprised Claire. "My sister was a model. I know a bit about that kind of life."

"What do you mean?"

Minna rose then, pushing the barstool back with her knees. "I should finish unpacking. I've been running around like a chicken, exhausted."

"I don't mean to be nosy."

"We're sisters. You can ask me anything." Minna sighed. "It hurts me to speak of her. My oldest sister and I haven't talked in years." She stood still, lost in thought. "She's married to a terrible man. An evil little Frenchman. Can't leave because she has two children with him. He drinks, and when he's had too much, he beats her."

The story burst out of her. The ugly, flayed thing lay on the table between them. Claire didn't know how to respond.

"Why does she stay with him?"

"Why?" Minna asked in a mocking tone. "I suppose because she isn't thin and young as she once was."

"A terrible reason."

"Not everyone was born owning a prosperous farm." Minna slapped the back of one hand in the palm of the other, a gesture of dismissal. "She puts up with it. Considers it her 'lot.' Allows him to call her his nigger."

Claire looked down, hiding her shock, not wanting to seem prudish, although despite all she had gone through, she did feel cloistered, naïve about the realities of the world Minna spoke of, unable to think of a reply.

"Wouldn't make a very good book, nuh?" Minna set her cup in the sink, staring out the window, oblivious to Claire's discomfort. "You're lucky to live in the middle of this grove. A little blind paradise."

"Not always a paradise," Claire defended, but Minna did not hear her.

Minna stretched her arms overhead. "That's why I'll never marry, not in this life. Voluntary slavery if it goes bad."

Claire took a long bath, and as the claw-foot tub filled, she confronted her naked self in the mirror. Not a vain woman, she had no explanation for the unaccountable vertigo she felt, as bad as if she were viewing her broken, bleeding self in a car accident. She had been avoiding this confrontation, but Minna's story had haunted her into meeting it head-on. She didn't want to be either trapped in an untenable situation or self-deluded. Would she ever get used to this? Or perhaps the bigger question, would she survive long enough to get used to it?

Perhaps a person who preferred fictions wasn't such a bad thing. She conceded the possibility that her daughters were more sensible and more loving than she allowed them to be, that their charity in taking care of her would possibly not have been entirely a burden, might even have rekindled their relationship. But Claire needed to stay on the farm, and they wanted to be done with it, and so she sowed the attitude that she was self-sufficient.

Their family had a long habit of silence. *Hush. Not now. The pain is too much.* Now she had a new secret. She had been loath to tell what the oncologist had diagnosed: her lymph nodes had been affected; the chance of the cancer's having *metastasized* (ugly, foreboding word she had been unfamiliar with) was high. The survival rate equal to flipping a coin. Make this time count, he counseled, and she would, by making sure her daughters were away and protected from new pain. Her gift to them.

Exactly what this girl, Minna, was about, Claire didn't guess, but she liked the girl's mixture of bravado and timidity. Claire's mind, fleeing the reality of upcoming chemo treatments, found refuge in the mystery of Minna. Claire created her glamorous and mysterious, and perhaps just the slightest bit spiritually wise, while not being overbearing, and that was exactly how she found her to be.

They met in the kitchen at six for the short drive over to Mrs. Girbaldi's. Minna walked in wearing a silk, spaghetti-strapped dress that draped to her ankles. The dress's background was black, the foreground filled with the most spectacular flowers. From a distance, the singular effect was that Minna stood naked, huge flowers in red and gold twined around her body. On her feet were the strappy, golden sandals. Claire stood breathless, in awe, before an ancient Mesopotamian queen.

Minna, confused by Claire's stare, shrugged down at her dress. "Too much?"

"No."

"It's a handoff from my sister. The model. After the babies it was too tight around the arse, you know."

"The hips."

"Yes." Minna smiled. "The hips. I appreciate the correction. I always try to improve myself. Be a lady like your daughters."

"The dogs will howl at your beauty."

They both laughed.

"In Dominica, the rich white people, the *blans*, have guard dogs that go crazy howling when they see a black person. But it's not because they hate us, it's because they smell their owners' fear of us. They try to show off and earn their keep."

Claire stood, not able to say a word. The girl took the words out of her mouth.

"Should we have a drink before we leave?" Minna asked. "I make a smooth martini. Your last chance to have alcohol for a while."

"Was your mother as beautiful as you?" Claire asked.

Minna looked at her. It was as if she comprehended Claire's desire for escape. "*Maman* had the most beautiful face you will ever see."

"Make that martini. I'll go get my wrap."

The phone rang—Gwen calling. Claire told her how attentive Minna was, how she was feeding her a special diet. "She even wants me to take up yoga and meditation. Can you imagine?"

"You sound good," Gwen said.

"Call me Monday night after my treatment, okay?" When she returned to the living room, Minna was standing stranded in the middle of the floor.

"Where are the drinks?"

"I couldn't find where you keep the alcohol. It's not in the bar."

"Locked kitchen cabinet. Old habit from when the girls were young."

"Everything is hidden away here," Minna said. "Why do you people hide everything away? Who was that on the phone?"

"Gwen."

"Checking on us, nuh?"

Claire paused. "I told her what good care you were giving me. Like another daughter."

"Oh, I don't want to compete with your daughters. I'll be like a son. Responsible, protective."

Claire was quiet, watching as Minna expertly chilled the glasses, then coated them in vermouth. She hammered the ice into small pieces before putting it in a shaker. Cut a long curl of lemon peel. "You're good."

"You guessed another secret. I worked as a bartender also."

They clinked glasses.

"To . . ." Claire floundered.

"To new life," Minna said. The martini was flawless, so smooth it went down like water.

Chapter 5

By the time they arrived, late and slightly buzzed, Mrs. Girbaldi's house was full, people queuing at the tufted-leather bar (built by her now-deceased husband decades ago when that was the style). Others strolled the long tables filled with pet-related items for the silent auction: oil paintings of stiff-legged Labradors and setters; ceramic statues and coffee mugs of poodles; pawprint-embossed picture frames; pet-photography gift certificates; plush-covered down beds; plated bowls; GPS-signal dog collars. Claire would donate money but was determined to collect no more clutter in her life. It was time to discard, lighten her load. Her new perspective made every object, mug or diamond earrings, look like junk.

Mrs. Girbaldi regularly hosted blue-chip charity functions and country-club gatherings; tonight there was a holdover from a benefit for Pendleton veterans—in attendance was a disabled marine in a wheelchair, whom she was determined to help find a job. The young soldier had been wheeled next to a serving table in the corner, ostensibly to avoid his being knocked into, but the effect was to isolate him in his cagelike chair. He sat, his horsey, handsome face alert, uniform pressed into knifed ridges, his chest covered in ribbons, while his big hands fumbled with a dainty-handled cup of punch. People passed and nodded in his direction—they were a conservative, patriotic, flag-waving crowd—but the wheelchair, or rather the woundedness that it connoted, made them shy. There was no denying a discomfort with his presence—it felt awkward to congratulate him on his service or to thank him for it. Afraid that it would beg the question of the price he had paid. Was he bitter? Would that bitterness explode against a luckless well-wisher? They were there collectively for simple pleasures. Claire was there to forget, even if only temporarily, and none of them wished to be faced with the moral vagaries of the harsh, larger world outside. So, cruelly, they kept at a remove from the young man.

The crowd was more casual than usual at Mrs. Girbaldi's affairs—older women with gray poking through their undyed hair; soft-voiced men; surfer types; youngish couples with toddlers in plush, reinforced strollers. Not the typical well-maintained, affluent, older crowd that financed local philanthropic undertakings. Amid this gathering, Minna stood out all the more.

A ripple of attention went through the room as they entered, and Claire enjoyed the vicarious glamour. Did Minna mind being the only black person to enter a crowded room? Did the double takes bother her? Claire watched and thought that if anything Minna thrived on the attention. Because, of course, her beauty trumped all. A couple passing leaned together and one said, "Probably down slumming from Hollywood."

Minna looked away as Claire tapped the man on his shoulder and whispered, "She's the great-granddaughter of Jean Rhys."

He nodded, satisfied.

After they moved off, Minna laughed. "Shame on you. Name-dropping. As if they even knew who she was. Do you want another drink?"

"Why not?"

Claire moved off to the edge of the living room, surveying the scene for anyone she knew. Conversely, she wished for no attention, no one to notice her compromised self.

As Minna passed the young marine, she bent down to him. "You can't possibly be interested in that punch. Would you like me to get you a Scotch?"

"That would be outstanding." He laughed, his face lit up, suddenly a young man again, not simply the object of pity. Minna knelt, and he looked at her with delight. All the others who talked to him had remained standing. Of course her attentions would be every bit as recuperative as any job. Minna talked, laying her hand on his knee for emphasis. Someone took a picture of them for the local paper, mistaking her for an actress.

At the best of times, Claire was an ambivalent partygoer, but now she stood paralyzed by the thought of her lopsided chest, shielded by the frail camouflage of a gauzy, knotted scarf. Perhaps Gwen was right and a "boob man" was in order. The absurdity of such self-consciousness did nothing to mitigate it. At her age, in her condition, what did it matter anymore?

Minna moved through the room toward the bar like a lioness prowling her territory. One noticed her skin, its burnished golden brown, her long neck, her powerful stride, her softly dropping feet like sleek paws. The sensation of her nakedness still lingered, but it held no hint of shame, rather a crude-cut beauty, lacking the slightest artifice. It was the rest of them, with their pale skin and bluish veins, their thin legs and bound breasts, who required covering, modesty, and shame. Minna disappeared to the end of the line out the door.

On the couch, holding court, sat Donald Richards. He and Claire had been distant friends over the almost thirty years of his owning the ranch, although he was only there part-time.

They pretended an intimacy at parties that was never followed up on. Claire imagined his debauched lifestyle had little in common with her cloistered one, but they enjoyed being bored together at parties.

The valley regularly attracted celebrities searching for the anonymity they had so eagerly shunned before fame found them. The longtime locals prided themselves on taking no notice of these Hollywood types, carrying it so far as to ignore them, and sometimes past that to outright rudeness. Often after enough ego drubbings, FOR SALE signs would spring up like dandelions, and the celebrities, full of the new hurtful knowledge that, after all, they wanted attention and fawning, would return north to where they would be courted.

One got inured to seeing movie stars in the grocery, or TV hosts pumping their own gas. One got used to the everyday fact that in person they were always shorter and had worse skin, that they were kinder and more fragile than one imagined.

Claire was fond of Don, even imagined they had a mild flirtation going over the years made of equal parts his compliments and her mockery of his stardom. She had grown protective of him. Like a particularly noxious weed, he persisted and flourished on neglect, and the whole community came to accept him.

His eyelids fluttered as Minna passed by while he listened with rapt attention to Mrs. Carsey (talking with hearing-aid loudness) about her late poodle. It must have been a handy gift to have, being an actor, portraying one thing in public while one's private self attended to its own interests. Minna took a drink to the soldier, stopping only briefly to talk, much to his obvious disappointment.

Don motioned Claire over with an impatient wave. "Who's your friend?"

"My new . . . assistant."

"Introduce. She looks like Halle Berry. But more rustic."

"She's way out of your league," Claire said, hurt pride and motherly solicitude neatly merging.

A line of autograph seekers had formed behind her. Donald's latest movie had been released the month before. Although he was in his late forties, he played a soldier in the First Gulf War. Claire hadn't bothered to read the reviews, although she noted in the posters that they had outlined his eyes in kohl, giving him an aging, dissolute Rudolph Valentino look that seemed at odds with the image of the wholesome, young American soldier he was supposed to be playing. In the movie, he goes AWOL, and while escaping into the desert, he meets and falls in love with a Kuwaiti princess, played by a busty Italian starlet. A jaded Romeo and a loose Juliet, and an indictment of war to boot. Claire wouldn't say it to his face, but she thought there would be more dignity in his growing oranges.

Unbelievably there was Oscar buzz, and Donald even testified before Congress about something to do with the war, although during the actual war he had been boozing and womanizing, in and out of rehab. Now he was talking about opening an elephant-rescue sanctuary on a couple of hundred acres in the Santa Ynez valley area of central California because the terrain was supposed to resemble elephants' habitat in Africa. All night long people came to talk to him about the Gulf wars and Afghanistan, preferring him to the real soldier.

When Minna came with her martini, Claire whisked her away outside.

"Where are you taking me?"

"To see our wards."

The lawn was filled with collapsible pens. Two dozen dogs from the shelter had been bathed, fluffed, perfumed, and beribboned, then put in one per pen to be adopted. People walked through the maze of fences, stopping to offer a pat on the head or a biscuit. The attention combined with the confinement wound the dogs up to a fevered barking that rolled in waves through the evening air.

"Whose dogs are these?" Minna asked.

"They're strays. Hopefully some will get adopted tonight."

"Why don't you take one? Save a life."

"I used to have five at one time. But now, no new responsibilities."

Minna studied the pens. "All prettied up and then maybe to have their hopes dashed." She stood close to a pen with a chow mix in it. His fur had been shorn, and his body was small and whitish, his red-tufted head looking oversize in comparison. She reached her hand in to give him a pat, but the dog grew impatient and leaped up against the fence. Minna grabbed his snout, clamping down the jaws, then pushed him back and let go.

"Are you all right?" Claire asked.

"Couldn't be sure what he'd do."

The people around them, realizing nothing had happened, chuckled, and Claire couldn't help a smile.

"Where'd you learn to do that?"

"In Dominica you need to be able to handle yourself around dogs. Some can be mean. Anyway, he leered at me." Minna smiled, making a face.

"These have all been checked out for temperament. Fostered."

"But you never can trust them totally," Donald said. He had followed them outside. "Claire has been trying to keep us apart."

Minna looked into her drink, stiff and prim as a schoolgirl, and Claire was embarrassed for the poor impression she was making. Now she was as eager for them to like each other as she had formerly been reluctant for them to meet.

"Minna's studying at Berkeley," she said.

"Really? My daughter's a freshman there. Where do you live?"

"I just started PhD work there. I did undergrad at Cambridge."

"Too smart for me," he said.

"Actually, Minna is the great-granddaughter of the novelist Jean Rhys."

Don looked blank.

Minna leaned on one leg while droning off the whole recitation in a bored, singsong voice. "Her best-known book, *Wide Sargasso Sea,* was a postcolonial answer to *Jane Eyre.*"

Don still looked blank.

"You know . . . Rochester?" she said.

"Oh, Rochester, sure. I'm not a totally illiterate actor. So you're an intellectual?"

"That was great-granny. I'm just a simple girl."

"I've been rereading the book," Claire said. "Rochester's obsessed by money and lust. A perfect role for you."

Don laughed. "What are you doing with boring old Claire?"

Stung by the insult, Claire debated what to tell him. She wasn't ready for full public disclosure.

"I'm a friend of Lucy's. I'm staying on the ranch for the summer."

"Dear," Don said, taking Minna's arm as he led her away, "come give me your sage advice on a dog I'm considering adopting. I want to name him Heathcliff."

She looked over at Claire, and they both realized they had been played.

"Sometimes first impressions are deceiving," Don said.

Claire waved them off. "Go. Tell him to take the dog. Save a life."

Minna gave Claire a strange smile. After she disappeared with Don, Claire went back inside and sagged down into a sofa, exhausted. The interaction had served as distraction, but now, alone, reality came down on her even more heavily than before. She didn't like lying about her cancer, but maybe it was better than suffering those pitying looks that the soldier had endured. She wanted to escape her own life. It had been a mistake coming, she thought, and just as she was contemplating sneaking out, Mrs. Girbaldi made her way over.

"They're all eating and drinking up a storm, but no donations or bids," she said. "Wrong type of crowd."

"Don's taking another dog."

"Good," Mrs. Girbaldi said, eyeing a potential donor at the cheese table. "He seems to have made a new lady friend, too. Be right back."

Claire ate and talked, drank and listened, constantly checking for Minna's return, ready to leave. Over an hour passed before she came back.

"Where've you been?"

"We took the dog to his house."

"I want to go home." Claire grabbed her purse and said curt good-byes.

Mrs. Girbaldi looked unhappy as Claire pecked her cheek. "Leaving so soon?"

"Nerves about Monday." In the car, alone, Claire turned to Minna. "You drove to Don's house?"

Minna looked straight ahead, out the windshield, petulant as a teenager. "Yeah. We put the dog in the yard and then we fucked on his couch."

Claire shook her head as if the girl's words had blurred meaning. "What are you saying?"

"I thought that's what you wanted. You threw me at him."

"What I wanted? I don't even know what that means. That you'd do something like that if I *wanted*?"

"Which part?"

In that moment, Claire knew she was in over her head. As much as she liked Minna's iconoclasm, she realized she was habituated to the opposite—people, including herself, who offered no surprises. Was Minna's wildness the right thing for her now?

"I enjoyed it if that's what you're asking," Minna said.

"How will I face him? This is a small community, everyone will know. He'll want to see you now." Then a new thought occurred to Claire. "Are you quitting me?"

Minna leaned over and rubbed Claire's arm up and down, rough and comforting as if reassuring a child. "I explained to him I don't want a romance now, okay? It was just recreational."

"Jesus." Claire looked at her. "You slept with him?"

Minna giggled, and then they both broke into roaring screams of laughter, a shredding, incredulous kind of hilarity that tore up the animosity between them.

"For your information," Minna said, when they could at last breathe again, "he doesn't know who Rochester is. Had him confused with Heathcliff. He said he could read our reactions, and he played us. He's very small."

Claire screeched, choking, and covered her ears. Her chest and stomach ached with the heaves of laughter; it was the first time she had laughed since her operation. "No more. No more, no more, no more, you bad girl."

That night Minna walked into the kitchen wearing pale blue cotton pajamas, face washed smooth, hair pulled back in a bun. It felt like going back in time to when the girls were in their teenage years. Claire heated milk in a pan, and they talked about the logistics of the coming week. Already, the events of the evening were fading, and they had eased into a routine of familiarity that was out of keeping with the short time they had known each other.

"Not to hurt your feelings, but I like you much better now that your daughters are gone. You seem . . . more yourself."

Claire laughed. "They're good girls."

"I love Lucy. She saved me."

"You're too young, but when you settle down and have

children . . . you love them more than your own life. But they grow up to be your jury. All the judgment of how you raised them, the mistakes you made. It's a lifelong sentence."

"You're a good mother."

"I don't think they see that."

They drank from their mugs.

"Can I tell you a secret?" Claire said.

"Of course, my sister."

"All I want, all I've wanted since . . . a long time, was to stay on this farm."

"It's not much of a secret."

Claire shook her head, impatient. "My daughters don't understand."

"No."

"They have no feeling for the land. Refuse to live here. They want me to leave, and sometimes I have doubts . . . maybe they are right."

Minna put her hand on Claire's. "Maybe you should offer the ranch to one daughter to take over. She runs it and gets to keep it."

"That would create hard feelings."

"It's their choice. Maybe there will be only one taker. Hopefully there will be one taker."

An hour later in her bedroom, book slumped against her chest, Claire awoke to the sound of a strangled voice. It took several minutes to shake off the impression that its source was not in her dream, which had been troubled, nor even from an overloud television, but real, and its source was Minna crying. She pictured Don come back, charged with lust, beating against the French doors. She ran into the kitchen with the only weapon in reach—her book—only to find Minna, her back to Claire, screaming into the phone.

"Mwen renmen-w, I love you . . . I told you—I take care of you as soon as I can. You push and push, Jean-Alexi, and I just disappear again, you hear me?"

How to account for the momentary conviction that Minna was an intruder in her house, even though she was wearing the robe Claire loaned her? Her feet were spaced apart, her shoulders hunched, as if enduring a strong wind, or preparing for a lash. That posture created a whole new idea of Minna from the one Claire thought she knew. She was speaking English quickly, mixed with a guttural, foreign-sounding language (maybe French?) whose words Claire couldn't pick out.

"Minna?" Claire whispered, more to hear herself aloud, wake up from an apparent dream, than to be heard. Minna turned, and the face that looked back at Claire was a stranger's—flamed eyes, tendons and bones swelled in rage against the surface of her skin. But it was the expression of fury—or perhaps the adrenaline of terror?—that took her breath away.

No dream. Claire turned away, as if she had been shown something shameful, something not meant for her eyes, as provocative as a vision of Minna and Don writhing on his couch. She groped her way back to her bedroom and lay rigid under her cover, scared, staring at the ceiling. More excited talking on the phone, something at last concluded, and the receiver was hung up. Perhaps Claire fell asleep, but after a prolonged period Minna, *her Minna,* kind and smoothed over, came through the door as if the other had never been. She carried a cup of herbal tea.

"Have a nightmare, *doudou*?"

"No," Claire said, looking out the window, at the dresser, anywhere but at her.

"Drink," she coaxed, and Claire reluctantly did. Minna leaned over her in bed, stroked her damp hair, plastered down by panic. "Don't ever be frightened of me."

Chapter 6

The late spring brought a fierce bout of tule fog through the orchard every morning. Minna and Claire walked like ghosts, barely visible one to the other. Trees slid by like apparitions, the only tangible thing the scent of the leathery white blossoms that foretold future harvest. The quiet brought a sense of invisibility.

The natural world colluded with this illusion: rabbits stood in their path, not flinching till they were almost close enough to reach out and touch them. Hummingbirds hovered close by their faces as if in search of nectar. One morning, Minna lifted her arm and pointed through the fog to an orange tree, under the branches of which a coyote lay curled sleeping as if enchanted.

They discovered a mutual admiration for silence, so on their walks there would be only the sounds of their feet against the earth, only the slight husking of their exhalations. For old times' sake, Claire would stoop down and take a pinch of dirt, place it on her tongue, taste whether it was too sweet or too sour, worrying about the harvest, although modern chemical tests made the practice obsolete. Minna did her divining in other ways—leaving a large glass of water in the kitchen with a piece of floating bread swelled, a portent of plenty, she insisted. She had heard Claire and

Octavio discussing the small yields of apricot and avocado that season, attributed to low bee pollination. Places, too, can be haunted; the spirits want to be propitiated.

"I'm not watching things closely enough," Claire said.

"You need to be watching only your health."

"The farm barely gets by. A bad harvest, and I'll have Forster complaining."

"This is Octavio's job. If he doesn't do it well, you should replace him."

Claire was surprised by her presumption, not sure how to react. "Octavio's good. And loyal. He's been through a lot with us."

"I don't like to see you worried."

"What about your worry? That phone call a few nights ago?"

"Can I tell you a secret?"

Claire nodded, not sure how much she really wanted to know.

"He's a distant cousin I had a crush on for a while."

"Why do you call him?"

"Why? Because I owe him money. Why? Because he's a voice from home."

"Maybe you should put him behind you."

Farmers, like as not, assess an operation not by its current crop, nor its location and climate, nor even its prospect, but direct their attention straight to the real wealth of a farm: its soil. The soil, far from being ignored as dead filler, is recognized as a live, changing, vital organism on which the life of the farm depends. The amount of rainfall, of sun and shade, of decomposing plants, of soil amendments, the rate of harvesting, all contribute to its vitality. Neglect it, throw away its careful balance, and life comes to a standstill.

Claire knew these things and wondered if the knowledge transferred to the human body—what was the effect of depression, poisons, surgeries, fear, and anxiety within her own body? Minna was on a campaign of strange means to realign Claire with the natural world, and as much as she claimed not to believe in its efficacy, she appreciated the effort and grew more and more fond of her. Her naïveté made Claire overlook the quirks that were coming out. Small things, such as when one morning finding an expensive crystal glass broken in the sink. She asked Minna about it, and the girl denied knowing anything.

"But that's absurd. It's only you and me here."

"Ask Paz."

"She hasn't been here in days."

But these were minor flaws. Mornings Minna ground spices with a pestle. She insisted that Claire anoint herself with a combination of lime and nutmeg, which made Claire feel she was a dish about to be consumed. Afternoons Minna planted dried leaves in the ground from a velvet bag she carried, explaining that four leaves of one, boiled in tea, fixed the kidneys, five could kill you. At night, candles burned everywhere, while she chanted prayers. Claire prayed only that Minna wouldn't end up burning the house down. Minna insisted on cooking one meal a week consisting only of white: chicken meat, white rice, white rum. For an inexplicable reason, no salt, which made it impossible to eat. When Paz scraped it out into the garbage, she made a face.

"I can cook for you. Mama and I can bring you good food."

"It had to be white," Claire said, realizing how ridiculous she sounded.

Later, alone, Claire teased Minna. "Do you really believe in all this? You, an educated woman?"

"They live side by side. The normal and the magic."

Claire wagged her head, unsure.

"Picture they live inside each other. You see what you have the ability to see, no more."

She told Claire that her grandmother on her mother's side was a high priestess. Her mother, a schoolteacher, scorned all that, thought it was what made the island backward, but after giving birth to Minna she suffered from a darkness. Depression, melancholia, or postpartum, whatever it was, she stopped caring for her baby, or anything else. The grandmother said an evil spirit inhabited her. They exorcised it in a ceremony, fed her herbs, and she was fixed. Afterward *maman* was willing to learn the old ways. She was a full priestess by the time grandmother passed.

Claire was thrilled with this revelation, the most Minna had told her about her past so far. Even though Claire remained skeptical of the folk remedies, none of it bothered her enough to put a stop to it, although her former healthy self might have been offended by such nonsense. In her sickness, her new vulnerability, she had grown superstitious, willing, within limits, to latch onto any promise of relief and succor, any magic trick capable of helping her find her way back to health. Wasn't it like hoping a cosmetic might erase the signs of age? She had as little faith in Minna's potions and chants as she would a palm reader, but with no expectation, she was pleased simply with the novelty of the undertaking.

After the first few weeks had passed, the honeymoon phase of the relationship, they had grown accustomed to each other's rhythms—Claire woke early, while Minna slept in. They both were incurable night owls.

Despite Minna's explanation, the phone call from weeks before still bothered Claire. Was it partly resentment about Minna's ongoing affair with Don? Claire had gone as far as to discuss it with Forster and Mrs. Girbaldi. Later she regretted this lack of faith on her part, wished she had kept her mouth closed. Predictably, the two had arrived at the same conclusion: Mrs. Girbaldi thought Minna should be fired right away; Forster thought that her explanation had been a logical one, which made it even more necessary to get rid of the girl. But the more everyone jumped to find fault with her, the more Claire was inspired to be loyal. Minna was like a stray that fears the world will turn on it again at any moment. Perhaps they would never understand certain things about her. How well did any human being know another, after all?

Claire slipped Minna's pay into an envelope and put it on the bombé chest in the entry hall where she left mail, although no mail ever came for Minna, and none seemed ever to go out. As Claire sat reading in the living room, Minna came in holding the check. Claire looked up from the book, embarrassed to be confronted with the bare workings of their relationship.

"I wonder if you could advance me a few weeks?"

Claire waited, but no explanation was forthcoming. "If you need it," she finally said.

Without making a decision to be deceptive, Claire neglected to pass on this news to Forster or Mrs. Girbaldi, already sensing that their misgivings would turn to full rebellion against keeping Minna. Did it really matter that she was paid in advance?

Minna's need for money seemed insatiable to Claire, who never observed her shopping or buying anything personal. It was a mystery what the money was for. How large could the debt to the cousin possibly be?

The girls' calls marked the week, taking turns every other day: Monday, Tuesday, Wednesday, Thursday. *How're you? Fine. How're you? Great. Couldn't be better.* Once in a while on Friday through Sunday, Claire called them, and they would answer, startled, apprehensive. "Everything is fine," Claire would say. "I simply miss your voice." And she did. Having someone in the house again, especially a young woman the same age as they were, made her long for the companionship of the old days.

She was too shy to talk to them of the torture of the chemo treatments, how her stomach was in knots the morning of the first treatment before they got in the car, how as she walked down the hallway to oncology, her body broke out in a sweat, and Minna, sensing her panic, held her hand and began to talk of their plans to plant a vegetable garden in the backyard.

The first few treatments she had not felt sick; the nurses had been hopeful she would be one of the lucky ones with few side effects, but after the third treatment they came with a crushing ferocity. She refused to burden the girls with how she would be so nauseated and disoriented on the way home, she vomited into a plastic shopping bag. Most of all, Claire felt she needed to protect them, as if they were still too young to be exposed to this kind of suffering. But Minna, younger than Lucy, insisted on sharing this burden. So on Monday: *How're you? Here, let me put Minna on.* On Tuesday: *How're you? Tired.* Wednesday: *Talk to Minna.*

Blossoms dropped off, replaced with small, green, marble-size lemons, just as Claire's hair began to fall out. Paz did the spring cleaning, finding strands of hair everywhere. Crying, she stayed outside, ostensibly to air the pillows for the outdoor furniture, even though Claire wasn't allowed to be in the sun. Feeling helpless, Paz was almost glad that Minna had the job of caring for Claire.

As the first speckle-skinned Blenheim apricots ripened, ulcers broke out inside Claire's mouth, and unable to eat, she sat on the linoleum kitchen floor, defeated, while Minna spooned honey in her mouth to sooth the burning.

"I can't do it," Claire said.

Minna held her forehead, her hand, held her body up when Claire was too dizzy to walk. She put her in a chair and rubbed her back while Paz hurriedly changed the bedding, then they both helped her lie down. "You will get through this. I'm going to make you a special drink, an elixir my *maman* taught me. It heals everything."

True to her word, Minna spent hours in the kitchen boiling all sorts of herbs, flowers, and plants. Strange smells issued from the kitchen, but when Claire tried to go in, she was shooed away. The elixir was addictive; it always tasted different, but always made Claire feel the same. Calmer, healthier. Unaware, Claire began her first steps into magical thinking, the idea that Minna's cures could indeed heal.

On the one day a week Paz was there, she and Minna found everything to fight about. Minna disliked how her things were moved around when her room was cleaned. She complained that too much detergent was used in the laundry, claiming it gave her a rash. Said dust was accumulating everywhere, bad for Claire's breathing, and what was the girl doing all day long anyway?

Paz told Claire that Minna left dirty clothes and dishes everywhere, that the bathroom was a nightmare to clean, that when she cooked in the kitchen, it was a disaster afterward—the sink clogged and a sticky tar burned on the bottom of the pots.

One day Paz snuck into Claire's room and woke her as she napped. "I don't think Minna is right in the head. She gets so angry, she's messy, she always is lying around, not working. This is not the right person to care for you."

"She'll get better."

"Let me come and care for you."

Claire took Paz's hands. "Law school is your father's dream. I want to live long enough to be at your graduation. Give me that."

Paz hugged her as they both heard the creak of the floorboard. Minna shifted her weight; obviously she had been standing there listening.

In May the fog lifted by noon, and then the sun, magnified by being denied all morning, scorched the edges of the rose petals, turned the skin on the figs a dark purple even though the flesh inside remained unripe.

In the evening, the fog returned, a salve on the bruised vegetation. The women waited for the cooler temperatures to work in the garden. Since Claire hadn't had the energy to plant seeds earlier, she cheated. Although she knew Forster didn't want to come to the farm or watch the ravages of her illness, she traded on his guilt and asked him to fill the back of his pickup with seedlings from the local nursery. When he unloaded and realized the women were facing the task of planting alone, he relented and picked up a shovel. All day the three of them transplanted tomatoes and squash and basil into Octavio's neat, ready-made rows.

Claire sat on her knees, winded, stabbing at the ground with her dull spade while Forster and Minna did the real work. In all the years she had grown vegetables, she had been too lazy to do the necessary labor of digging up the rocky, clayey soil, replacing it with rich topsoil. This omission cost her much each year in extra tilling and fertilizer and salt-burned plants. She waged a constant battle trying to supplement with compost—grass clippings, coffee grounds, banana peels, apple cores.

Now, a couple of inches down, the tip of her spade hit a rock, sending shock waves up her arm into her shoulder. The lymph nodes had been removed under that arm, and the doctor had warned her that bruises or cuts on the arm increased the risk of lymphedema, permanent swelling. Scared, she held it away from her trunk now, as if it were a dead thing.

"Are you okay?" Forster asked.

He tried not to look at her too closely. She felt even more sick, more ugly, around him. Why was a woman's love different in kind than a man's love? She loved Forster beyond husband, loved him in spite of his graying hair and the wrinkled corners of his eyes. She loved him in his weakness, in the clear knowledge that he would not be there through the worst. Her mortality, her illness, caused him to flee her now, in spite of loving her.

"Need some help?" asked Forster.

"I'm fine."

Claire tried to concentrate on the job at hand. Minna, natural and easy in the garden, effortlessly planted six seedlings for Claire's every one. What puzzled her was that one could not simply dig a hole the size of the root ball. She was used to pushing seeds into the muddy, late-winter soil with her thumb, not even bothering to use tools. Now, the recalcitrant earth broke up in stiff, clumped spadefuls, had to be dug twice as wide as it was deep, to reach far enough down without the sides collapsing, or a rock inhibiting the spreading roots. By the time Claire had a hole of sufficient depth, it resembled a small gravesite, large enough for a bird or a mouse. She thought of all the countless small pets that had been interred by the children over the years: mice, rats, hamsters, goldfish, snakes, birds, crickets. Hadn't there been a ferret once? Never a serious pet such as a dog or a cat that deserved a proper memorial.

"In fact, Claire does need help. The farm is too much in her condition," Minna said.

Forster flushed red but kept digging. "I suppose that's a conversation between the two of us."

Minna shrugged and turned her back on them. Exhausted,

Claire stared into the steep sides of her hole, mesmerized by an earthworm trying to tunnel his way back into darkness, when Minna gave a yelp of surprise. In her hand was an Indian arrowhead made of shining black obsidian, the small crescents visible where the edges had been pounded sharp.

"We find a batch every spring," Forster said, dismissive.

Minna dug another hole and found a tan shard of pottery. "Can I keep it?"

"You'll be sick of them in no time."

"This farm belonged to someone else before it was yours?"

"Well, I don't know who Forster's great-grandparents bought it from." The accusatory tone of Minna's voice irritated Claire. She considered the farm created out of whole cloth from the hard, barren alkali soil, created out of nothing, worthless really but for the hard work of Forster's family and her own. "I don't know how long ago Indians were actually here."

"Maybe the Chumash?" Forster said.

"My great-uncle on my father's side, the English side, had bought land on the far side of the island because it was cheaper. He was clearing the jungle for his coffee fields," Minna said. "They began digging up bones. All sorts of bones. He pretended they were animal ones because otherwise it would be considered bad luck, make the land worthless. Until they dug up skulls, and the lie was up. It turned out to be a slave burial site. But this uncle kept plowing, hiding them by throwing the bones in a big pile in the jungle. After he was done, the pile was high as a man, wide as four men across with outstretched arms."

"What'd he do with them?"

"Forgot about them." Minna rubbed her calf with her hand. "A year later his crops failed. A year after that, the plantation house burned down. They moved to town, and his wife and daughter died in an outbreak of typhoid fever. He went back to England, broken. Became an alcoholic."

"That's terrible," Claire said, gripped by the matter-of-factness in Minna's recitation of events. People used to making a living off the land had a natural sympathy for each other, knowing the hardship involved, even at the best of times. Especially in her illness, Claire was full of the idea of unfairness in all its permutations.

"What're you implying, Minna?" Forster chuckled. "Some kind of curse?"

"He was careless. He shouldn't have ignored the bones," Minna added, as if to ease the blow of her words.

Forster studied her for a moment, debating. "Who were you talking to on the phone that night, right after you first came here? When you were so upset?"

Minna's eyes widened, then narrowed. Claire cursed herself that she had confided in him; he could never keep a secret. "My cousin. I borrowed money from him. He wants it back."

Forster looked at Claire significantly. "How much are we talking about? Is he threatening you?"

Minna shook her head. "It's not like that. I call him because he's from home. A familiar voice."

"If there's a problem, you can tell us. We'll help if we can."

"None."

Claire hadn't told him about Minna's recent requests for advances on her pay.

"He talks to my family. They are angry I'm not in school. I say there are other things in life."

"Do you believe that?"

Minna smiled slyly. "It's okay to enjoy yourself when you're young."

After Forster left, Minna clucked her tongue. "You betrayed me. Told him about the call."

"It frightened me." The truth was that during the last month, the intimacy that illness necessitated had created a bond between them so that Claire no longer questioned Minna. Such distrust was in the past.

Although it had not been discussed, Minna assumed a right to be gone every couple of nights. At bedtime, she slipped out the kitchen door, and Claire ran up to the second-story hallway and peered out the window just in time to see a faraway pair of glowing headlights like predatory eyes, waiting at the far-off foot of the driveway.

In the moonlight, the tree trunks shone smooth and heavy as bones, and even the paths between the rows resembled the ribs of an animal long succumbed. The faintly rotting smell of oranges on the air made it difficult to breathe.

Claire longed to forbid Minna these visits. All those years of living by herself, and now she could not admit the clinging panic she felt on those nights, alone, the waves of fear. Wasn't she paying for Minna's time? At two in the morning regularly, she woke with a pounding heart, watery bowels, a feeling that if she continued to lie there in the darkness another minute, she would simply cease. If Minna was home on those nights, she would appear magically with hot milk and sing her back to sleep, or would massage her back and legs till she drifted asleep. Claire stopped short of picking up the phone, calling either the girls or Forster to complain. Clearly she was protecting Minna even if it was against what she herself wanted. In the calm of daylight, she admitted to the irrational panic, admitted, too, that she didn't own the girl's soul. A companion, an assistant, but not a friend, not a lover, not a slave.

On those mornings when Minna had been at Don's house the night before, Claire found her in the kitchen early, preparing breakfast, bruise-lipped, quiet and satisfied as a cat that has feasted enough to last for days.

"Aren't you tired of taking care of an old, sick woman?" Claire pouted. "What can there be for you here?" Miserable at herself for being so whining. In her worst moments, not only did she resent Minna's health, but also her youth, her beauty, even her previous night out. What she really resented was the unfairness of all those things ending in her own life.

"That's why I need to be with Don," Minna said, measuring coffee into a filter. "Do you never watch the mother bird fly away from the nest? The babies worry, but then she comes back with a big, fat worm for them to eat. If they all stayed in the nest, they would starve."

Minna owned only a few dresses, rotating so regularly Claire knew which day it was by the choice. What to make of a girl not having more than three dresses and a pair of white jeans to her name? Perhaps it was some bohemianism in her, or an asceticism that rejected material things. Which begged the question of what she did with all the cash she was getting. As a favor, Claire asked her to pick among the girls' old clothes and her own, explaining how the waste bothered her. Claire especially wanted her to try on a dress made of pale-green and pink silk. In her own opinion, she had reached the nadir of her attractiveness—hairless, unexercised, bloated, and pale—and was convinced she would never again do it justice.

Minna slipped it on. Underneath, she wore no bra, and her nipples were clearly outlined in the fabric as if the dress were designed expressly to accentuate her nakedness instead of clothe it, making her all the more alluring for both what it revealed and what it hid. She twirled on her bare feet, rising on tiptoe, and

Claire clapped as the gauzy fabric fluttered out from Minna's legs. Claire had not felt such childlike pleasure in a long time.

Minna went to her room and returned with a magenta printed scarf, which she wrapped around Claire's head despite her protests. In the full-length mirror, Claire had to admit that it was a better solution than her alternative of patchy, sad molting-bird baldness.

"Now we are real sisters." Minna laughed. "Exchanging skins. Why do you insist on making yourself ugly?"

The comment shocked, doubly so since it was her own complaint about Gwen. Was it true that children divided up and took the parents' traits? Yet it was true she had lost the knack for the physical. "I can't help it."

"I see no men here for you. You never talk of anyone."

"All that is in the past for me."

"That's ridiculous. No one is past the need for love."

That night Claire watched as Minna in the pale-green and pink ex-dress disappeared down the driveway.

Paz was sorting laundry a few days later when she came across the dress. She brought it to Claire, chiding her that she should know better, that it required dry cleaning. What if the *loca* (as Paz referred to Minna) had got hold of it for washing, she continued, the ongoing feud between the two turning her bitter. *Loca* would ruin it. Claire took the dress and said nothing. After Paz left the room, Claire held the dress close and caught a whiff of Minna's perfume, the patchouli Lucy had given her. She brought it closer to her nose, and there was also the unmistakable tang of sex.

Chapter 7

On those nights when she could neither control Minna's nocturnal wanderings nor control her own mortal panic, Claire rose, turned on the lamp, and read the novel Minna had given her. Finishing the last page only to start at the beginning again so that the conclusion became beside the point; she craved only the journey. The novel did not abate her fears, but instead made her feel that she was not alone in that fear. Ever since the chemo started and her attending physical deterioration, the past had moved closer, taken up physical residence beside her. She would not admit that she was perhaps looking for meaning in her suffering—why had she been so afflicted, both before and now?

When the wind blew through the trees, Claire heard voices, as in the old days when workers slept overnight in the bunkhouses. A lone avocado falling down on the roof rang out like the crack of a gunshot, and she felt at her chest for a bullet that did not exist. Creakings of the worn boards in the house convinced her intruders had broken in; in the novel she read about creakings of bamboo outside Antoinette's bedroom window. After a time she forgot which had actually happened and which had been imagined.

Having read it many times before, Claire now read the book as a proxy for Minna's background, of which she was so stingy. Rhys's earlier novels failed to interest Claire, but the last novel, set in Rhys's native islands, spoke about the solace to be found on one's own land. One always searched for one's own story in a book no matter how exotic it might seem.

The imagined Minna flourished to the proportions of a romantic heroine, rushing down the crushed-shell driveway of her Coulibri into the arms of some moody island boy, or perhaps an Englishman's son? Claire backed up, not wanting to turn it into some tawdry romance novel. From her privileged background, it was clear why Minna felt at home in the elite world of Cambridge, even girlfriend to a movie star, but at what price? Did her English suitor lust after her dusky beauty, but not love her for that same non-English blood, just as Antoinette's Rochester failed to love her?

None of this seemed any more far-fetched than the reality of contemplating her own disease, reading the drug side effects, the survival rates, on pamphlets and disclosure forms. Reading her blood count before each treatment, to see if she was strong enough to endure more. Without the fiction of the Sargasso Sea to lose herself in, Claire would have gone mad. She prayed for metastasis, not of death, but of life, the spreading of an imagined world that would cover over the deficiencies in the real one.

One afternoon on her way to the garden, Claire found Minna sitting on a stone retaining wall, swinging her legs and humming in a voice so low, so mournful, it sounded more dirge than pleasure. Her face was swollen lumpy from crying.

"What's wrong?"

"It's so beautiful here. But I'm still in a bad place."

"Poor girl, you're safe here!"

"I'm dead and drowned."

Claire felt a catch in her throat at the possibility something treasured might be snatched away. She knew about the pernicious effects of nostalgia. Raisi had been plagued with just such longing, until Claire's father saved up enough money to send her back for a visit, nearly twenty years after she had left. When she returned to California, she said little about the visit and never mentioned going back. Was it a great disappointment, the comparison between memory and always failing reality?

"What do you believe in?" Minna asked.

Claire, astonished at such a question, spread her arms to embrace the groves stretching out all around them. "Isn't it obvious? This is all there is!"

Minna gave her a look she couldn't read. "If I could just see the colors, you know? The smells. Just for a moment the sight of the ocean."

It became clear that Minna made her brave way through life on her charm, but it was a cultivated thing, a thing put on like a piece of clothing. Here the mask dropped, and Claire realized Minna was without protection, helpless against the world.

"We can fix that," Claire said, more desperation than plan.

Minna wiped her nose with the back of her hand like a child. "How?"

She looked around for some answer that would stop the tears. Years ago she bribed the girls when they were young with coins, trinkets, ice cream, anything to stop the crying. "I could take you to the beach? Or you could do up your room? Make it more like home? It can't feel normal being stuck in a teenager's room." Was Minna's power over her that she had turned Claire back into a mother?

At first Minna seemed unimpressed, but she sat in thought for a few minutes. "You wouldn't mind?"

"I'm asking you to do it. Make it yours."

"But when I leave . . ."

"That's a long way off."

Claire neglected to mention that Lucy's lavender room had formerly been Josh's. She hated going in there, despite the changes, always looking for what she knew she would not find. A good excuse to put yet another imprint on the room, dull its previous incarnations. The next day Minna, with new energy, dropped Claire off at the nurses' station a full fifteen minutes early for her chemo appointment. Minna couldn't hurry her through the door fast enough, and then she took off shopping. When she picked Claire up after the treatment, the backseat was filled with bags.

All afternoon, while Claire lay on the couch sucking on ice chips for nausea, Minna carried pails, brushes, and extension poles up the stairs to her room. Claire almost felt sorry for herself at the neglect, but at least Minna seemed to have forgotten her dirges and tears, her homesickness. The paint fumes grew so strong Claire moved to her bedroom and closed the door, but soon it wasn't even breathable there, and by necessity she escaped to the orchard.

Octavio watched her walk listlessly up and down the rows like a child orphaned in the forest. Finally he came and suggested she rest in his stand.

For years he had remained unfazed by Claire's mood swings, loyal to her wish to remain aloof to the outside world. Ten years before he had bought a house on Rosarito beach in Mexico with plans of an early retirement, but then Forster and Claire divorced, and the girls moved away. He felt responsible for Claire, never able to forget the sight of her in that dark grave of orchard. Years passed, Sofia had already quit her job and moved there, but he stayed on at the ranch.

"How is Sofia?"

"She has the grandchildren this week. Driving her crazy."

"How many now?"

"Five."

"Five! And me with two. We are getting old, my friend."

Octavio laughed. "Not until our grandchildren's weddings are we old."

Although they never talked of it, Claire knew he was waiting till he could safely shepherd her into the future, but she stubbornly kept falling to pieces on him. He would have to be brutal and finally just abandon her to her fate if he was ever to be free.

He led her to the shelter he had constructed from castoffs so that there was nothing that could be ruined or stolen. The place, an unlikely refuge, served its purpose and could be abandoned in a moment, like a child's makeshift playhouse. Claire found its transience a kind of perfection: patched outdoor umbrellas pushed together under the green gloom of a towering avocado tree; underneath, a roughly nailed table and collection of broken-down lawn chairs; a hammock stretched between two pepper trees; a dented cooler filled with ice water and sodas; a scratched-up boom box. It was the place workers could find Octavio for problems, where messages could be scrawled on scraps of paper and weighted under a rock on the table.

In her preoccupation with her illness, it surprised Claire that the farm functioned just fine without her. The workers had their own version of the farm, one as separate, yet real, as Claire's own.

"You would like some iced tea?" Octavio asked as he fished for a bottle in the cooler.

"Gracias." Claire sat and sipped while he did paperwork.

"De nada."

"Es dificil . . ."

Octavio nodded—his face a cross-hatching of deep creases from the constant sun—polite but wary, wanting to be of service but not to be too deeply involved. A carefully calibrated distance they had maintained over the years since the attack. Octavio made sure his sense of obligation stayed limited to the running of the farm.

"Problema del cáncer."

Relieved, Octavio stood up. "You want for me to get the girl?"

Claire shook her head.

"You like this girl?" he asked, clearly indicating he did not.

"She's very smart." Claire knew firsthand the animosity between Minna and Paz. "She's a city girl. Just not used to us country people."

Octavio shook his head and wiped at his mouth. "The workers see her in the orchard late at night. With Señor Richards."

Claire paused, but not so long as to appear that the news was entirely unexpected. "She's young, spirited."

"When you do not watch, she walks the farm like she is the owner. Orders workers to stop what they do to get her water. Orders one to hold an umbrella over her against the sun for hours. She calls them names."

Claire was shocked but did not want to appear so. In all her years with him, she knew Octavio always to be honest, and so she could not doubt the truth of what he said now. Her dilemma lay in what to do about it.

A diplomat, Octavio changed the topic to spraying schedules for the orange crop.

"Why was the last crop so small?" she asked. They staggered plantings and harvesting so that they had crops of oranges, lemons, grapefruit, avocados, or strawberries going out all year long.

"Minna, she said you ordered not to spray. She told me to wait another two weeks to pick. Many of the *naranja,* they go bad."

"It was an experiment," Claire said, furious and trying to hide it.

"I talk to Mr. Forster," he said, shrewdly guessing the truth of the situation.

"You will not."

"If you make me listen to this girl, I farm badly."

"Let me take care of things," Claire said.

Hours passed. She liked being out in the open air and had no desire to confront Minna just yet. Despite her anger, the drugs made Claire woozy, and she fell asleep. The workers stopped by on their way home, Octavio acting as adviser and informal bank, giving small cash loans as needed out of his pocket, writing everything down in a small spiral notebook he kept in his shirt pocket.

"You used to not write anything down," Claire said, when they were alone.

"Many years have passed." He winked and tapped his head. *"Viejo."*

"I'm sorry about my words earlier. I'm not myself lately. Things are going wrong, but I will fix them, I promise you."

"Maybe it is time for us all to retire? Both of us go live with our *familias*."

"I've been selfish. Do you want to leave?"

Before he could answer, they both saw Minna slam the front door of the house and walk toward them, calling out Claire's name. She wanted to intercept her, but felt too weak to move from the chair.

"She is here, Señorita Minna," Octavio called out. His face was stony.

A group of workers whispered as they watched Minna approach. Claire heard, *"La negrita."*

Minna looked at Claire with irritation. "You should tell me where you've gone."

"She visited with me," Octavio said, but Minna didn't look at him, or even register that she'd heard his words.

"Help me take her back to the house." Minna directed her words to the group in general, to the air, instead of to Octavio.

"I'm not a child," Claire said, struggling up.

"Help her!" Minna repeated, louder and more emphatic.

No doubt that she would slap him if Claire didn't do something. "Did you pass on my request to delay picking the Valencias?"

Minna stopped short. "Yes."

"And to not spray?"

Minna nodded, not daring to look at her.

"Well, it didn't work out so well. So we're going back to the old schedule."

Claire was standing, perspiring from the effort despite the coolness of the afternoon air. Octavio and Minna stood, rooted, at a standoff while Claire swayed back and forth like a pendulum between them. "Please, Minna, take my hand," she ordered, and almost collapsed into her arms. "I need to lie down."

Minna almost lifted her off her feet, her arm around Claire's waist. *"Luego!"* she hissed behind her.

They staggered back to the house, Minna seething.

"Put me down now," Claire said at the door. It took her a minute to catch her breath. "You will never give an order again having to do with the running of this farm. Do you understand?"

"But—"

Claire raised her hand. "I don't want to hear about it. I covered for you this one time only, but you aren't making any friends. You better start."

"They hate me."

"Stop giving them something to hate. Change your behavior. I don't want to ever hear about you abusing the workers again, do you hear? Don't think I won't fire you if I have to."

* * *

One of the mysteries in life was how one took for granted its joys—health, love, and happiness—until they disappeared, and then one was consumed in mourning their passing. There had been happiness in Claire's life, but it passed too quickly, overwhelmed by the drudgery of work, bills, and tending to family. There had even been rare moments of grace after Josh's passing.

Claire remembered one particularly bad day afterward when she had walked out alone to the lemon tree where he had been found. What had she been looking for? Grief and sorrow weighed her down, and she lay on the ground beneath the tree. Without a sound, Gwen came up behind her. Had she been following her? For how long? And why? Side by side they lay on the ground till they both fell asleep, so many hours that nature forgot about them in its midst. Claire woke and felt she was in an enchanted garden—dragonflies flew above her face, one bumped into her motionless knee, while Gwen slept the slumber of an enchanted princess, small twigs scattered in her beautiful long hair.

Claire lost herself in the blue of the sky, the white clouds emptying her mind. A hummingbird balanced in the air above her, in the silence his whirring the engine of the world. Would it be too crushing a burden to carry on one's life filled with the knowledge of one's luck, the richness of the gifts bestowed on one?

After the first month of treatment, Claire's hair had begun falling out, but one morning, she rose to find a majority of her hair had stayed behind on the pillow—a last, blond nest. She sat stranded in the bed. Claire did not consider herself as formerly possessing a beauty that was now lost. Her hair had always been too fine and thin, never growing past her shoulders. Rather it was simply that she had the eerie premonition she was losing parts of herself—as if an arm had come off here, a leg there—what would ultimately be left? Sans hair, sans breasts, sans pillowcases, checking accounts, orange trees, daughters, dishes, husband, son. How many parts equaled the sum total that formed the essence of each person? Certainly not hair—hair must be the least of the markers of one's being—yet there she was, stranded, hysterical, in mourning for her hair.

Minna came in with breakfast. "What's wrong? Are you sick?"

Claire shook her head and pointed, accusing, to the pillow, speechless. Mrs. Girbaldi was expected for lunch, but Claire wanted to hide forever in her bed.

"Oh," Minna said, and set the tray on the floor, sat on the bed, and took her in her arms. She rocked Claire like a child, till she was soothed. Claire felt too destroyed to be reserved or shy. She cried abjectly, all self-consciousness and inhibition gone. In just such a way, she had comforted her girls when, inconsolable, they grieved over the death of a pet, or some other long-forgotten misfortune. To them such grief was deadly serious, and she treated it as such. Likewise, no matter how foolish she might appear now, the sick had privileges. She would be forgiven by Minna. Rage and confusion poured out. When she finally settled down, Minna kissed her forehead and said, "Now that's over, we must get to work."

After Claire had dressed, Minna placed her on a kitchen stool (the same stool that Claire had used to cut Gwen's, Lucy's, and Josh's hair) and took out a small pair of silver sewing scissors and began to snip the last straggly remnants. Each cut strand carefully placed on an outspread cloth, added to that from the pillow, not allowed to fall on the ground, sparing her evidence of her weakening, disappearing self. When Claire had only a soft buzz cut, Minna took out a razor and a can of shaving gel. As the razor skimmed Claire's head, Minna hummed a tune Claire thought sounded like a lullaby she used to know. Claire looked out the window, pretending it was an ordinary haircut, pretending that all this was happening to someone else.

Ersulie nain nain oh! Ersulie nain nain oh!
Ersulie ya gaga gaaza, La roseé fait bro-
dè tou temps soleil par lévé La ro seé fait bro-
dè tou temps soleil par lévé Ersulie nain nain oh!

The phone rang—Gwen's day—and Claire motioned to Minna the excuse that she was asleep. Minna talked on the phone several minutes, then hung up.

"You must let them know you are okay," she said. "They will blame me." Minna brought out a small jar of red paste and rubbed it on Claire's head. "This is to soothe the skin."

Claire nodded, eased by the gravelly, warm feel of the tincture, like sand mixed in warm honey, compared to her chilled nakedness without it. Her skull felt small and fragile as an egg.

Next Minna took out a small pot of brilliant blue liquid and a small paintbrush. "This is for good healing. The hair will grow more beautiful than before. I will make you as beautiful as the goddess Erzulie."

Claire sat still and refused to think what she looked like, simply basked in Minna's attention.

A knocking at the door, and Mrs. Girbaldi, as usual, let herself in. When she walked into the kitchen, her lipsticked mouth dropped open. "My lord, you look like a Purple People Eater."

All three of them howled with laughter, and so Claire was able to survive into the next hour.

After lunch, Claire's newly bald head wrapped in the magenta scarf, Minna led them single file out over the lawn. She sang the same song she sang earlier, but this time it was clear to Claire that it was familiar only in her attraction to it. At each turn, Minna threw a small curl of hair, then she gave them each a handful to accompany her. Bits of Claire were scattered over the lawn. Out of the corner of her eye, she saw Mrs. Girbaldi turn away and wipe at her face. Was it indeed a rehearsal of a funeral? But Claire did not feel ghoulish. She imagined her hair lining birds' nests, squirrels' dens, rabbit warrens. She herself, formerly insubstantial and windblown, would become rock solid, sinking down into the earth, forming roots that fingered their way down into the soil. Her hair, herself, resurrected.

Mrs. Girbaldi, caught in Claire's need, stayed through the afternoon, read while she slept, made her famous corn-and-tomato soup for dinner. The phone rang, and Claire asked her to answer it. It was Lucy, alarmed by the news from Gwen that Claire wasn't well.

"What do they expect? I'm going through chemo," Claire said when the call was over.

"Why aren't you talking to them?"

"Whenever they hear I'm ill, we start with the selling of the farm again."

Mrs. Girbaldi shook her head. "But it's just land. Not kin."

"No! Those acres are as born from me as the children are. Maybe more so. The girls turned away from it all."

Mrs. Girbaldi shook her head as if something valuable had been dropped and broken. "They escaped, child."

"They betrayed."

For dinner Claire lit candles at the kitchen table, pulled out the cloth napkins, creating a minicelebration. When Minna came downstairs, she wore tight jeans, high heels, a glittery, low-cut camisole that used to belong to Lucy when she was in college.

"Night," she said, letting herself out the door, not bothering to look at the table with its three settings.

Mrs. Girbaldi spied on her out the kitchen window. "Where's she going?"

"A date," Claire said. "Just spoons? Or forks, too?"

"She goes out regularly?"

Claire shrugged. "Quite a few nights."

"That's not her job. Her job is to keep you company."

"This is a job, not a prison sentence. I can't expect her to take vows of celibacy, can I?"

"She spends the night? With who?"

A sly smile. "Don."

"That was quick work."

"I like having her here. It gets me through. And I have you, don't I?"

"Of course. And you have your daughters. Have you forgotten about them?"

"No."

"I think you have. This girl has bewitched you."

"That's ridiculous," Claire said, but wondered if it was true.

"Something I wanted to talk to you about. I was at the club, having lunch with Margaret Parker. You know Margaret?"

Happy to change the subject, Claire nodded, wagging in a noncommittal motion as one did with Mrs. Girbaldi's sprawling narratives, like genuflecting toward the points of the cross, indicating a familiarity, rather than intimacy, with said person.

Mrs. Girbaldi continued, undeterred, lowering her voice to a stage whisper. "Well, her cousin came down with the cancer."

Claire smiled at the idea that one could *come down with the cancer,* as if it were the flu.

"They took her to a clinic down in Baja," Mrs. Girbaldi continued. "They fed her all this strange stuff—I'm not saying what, but let's just say it was a struggle getting it down, and it would be illegal in this country. A month later, she went back to her doctors, and they examined her: the tumor was gone! They accused her of having it operated on. 'How could I do that,' Margaret asked, 'when you all said yourselves it was inoperable?'"

The story hung, unremarked upon, Claire's attention directed away as if Mrs. Girbaldi had burped.

Chapter 8

A week later, Minna invited Claire to her now transformed room.

The climate in California is ephemeral; the air brittle and self-effacing. Upon entering the room, Claire felt she had left her old world as she knew it. She understood for the first time the indolent pleasure of the wet and liquid air in those exotic novels that took place in the tropical corners of the world. Impossible to explain how a coat of paint could affect barometric pressure, but there it was. She was in a strange but longed-for land.

Two walls were painted dark greenish turquoise, a color that breathed the nearness of the ocean, its salty stick, the choking, crowding vegetation, and the torrential, silvered downpours of rain. Claire was positive if she touched these walls, her hand would come away slick, not with paint, but the breathing condensation of the equatorial climate. The walls modulated from light to shadow, as if one were looking down into the depths of a lagoon while sitting in a small, unseaworthy boat. A vertiginous experience that suggested to her the overwhelming feel of crossing a sea whose entrapping strands of kelp wrapped around rudders, propellers, anchors, hulls.

"You're an artist, Minna."

Claire had taken in only half of the room, and by far the half of lesser importance. The remaining two walls were painted a bold yellow, the color of blazing sun, bleached coral beaches, the stuccoed walls of mean villages. All manner of figures and symbols and words filled these two walls with a sense of menace proportionate to their unintelligibility. Claire reassured herself that it was only a matter of familiarity and comfort would surely follow. In a spirit of exploration, she excavated the nearest, largest of these words: OGOU BALANJO. Underneath it, smaller letters read SPIRIT OF HEALING. Then, like a bend in the road, a view that was formerly invisible presented itself: the drawing of a white woman, round-faced, with empty blue eyes and long strands of stylized, yellow hair. But one noticed this only much later because what riveted the attention was what she was holding—a salver at waist level, on which rested her two breasts. The chest area above the tray was blank as an unmarked map, scored only with two small *X*'s where the breasts should be, like the cartooned X-ed eyes of a dead fish. Above her head, written out in strips of Christmas tinsel, were the words SAINT AGATHA. Below her large, round, clawed lion's paws were the painted words PATRON OF BREASTS.

"Is it magic?" Claire asked.

"It's the beginning."

"She's me?" The figure was so monstrous—a mockery or a kindness, she couldn't decide—that she felt unmoored as if punched. She stood there, stranded, as Minna waited to catch her swoon, helping her onto the floor. Claire kept looking up, hypnotized by the figure, who only grew in power when observed from that vantage.

"I've upset you?" Minna sat on the floor next to her and held her hand. "These are powerful *majik, sanp.* To heal you."

Claire nodded, sickened and awed, mesmerized by the eyes of the woman, flat and placid. She felt that if she sat there long enough, looked hard enough, she would find the answer to many things that had eluded her. Meanings so covered by time and evasions and half-truths that they were all but forgotten. The more time she spent looking at Saint Agatha, the less fantastic, the more normal, she appeared, until it was Claire's own bare walls, her timid Germanic landscapes and faded English botanical prints in the rest of the house that lacked reality.

"She's beautiful?" Claire whispered, feeling unqualified to judge even that because the figure was so far beyond the dull concepts of beauty or ugliness.

"You like her!" Minna jumped up, excited as a schoolgirl, and waved her hands back and forth across the walls as she described her future plans for more drawings, as if the surface of the walls weren't already buckling under their duty. Her happiness took away all Claire's opposition, the menaced feelings of alarm. Of course, they were just drawings, primitive renderings no more powerful than pictures in a magazine, book, or cave. Harmless.

But after that first visit, Minna's door again remained resolutely shut. Somehow Claire understood that the powerful contents needed to be bottled tightly, sealed like a drug or alcohol. The room was so foreign now that for all practical purposes it had ceased to exist as part of the rest of the house and became like the exotic grafting of the lion paws on Saint Agatha, or the grafting of more delicate fruit on rugged rootstock. As time went on, such permutations on the everyday began to seem more and more possible. Another of Minna's pictures that Claire had barely had time to glance at on her way out of the room: a fish tail attached to a woman's lower body. The house, too, had become mermaidized.

Gwen arrived, a combination of long rest weekend and inspection. She was pleased by the pristine quiet of the ranch house, disturbed by her mother's waning appearance. She carried in a large box with a bow from the car.

"A present?" Claire opened it to find a Styrofoam head with a blond wig perched on top of it. "Oh, no."

"You're going to need it, so might as well get a nice one."

All day long Gwen's voice could be heard in the living room, on the phone to clients. Minna hid away, mostly in her room, presumably painting. "So she's an artist now?" At night, Gwen drank down a whole bottle of wine while Claire sat on the sofa listening to her complaints about her underemployed husband, her long hours at the office. The bitterness in her voice left Claire exhausted.

They quieted when Minna left for a date with Don.

"Great. She's here a couple months and has a movie-star boyfriend."

"She's had a more difficult life than she's let on."

"Those," Gwen said, pointing her finger out the window at Minna's disappearing back, "are the kind of women who get what they want."

Saturday night Claire became feverish. After consulting with a nurse on the phone, Gwen helped Minna bathe her with cool washcloths, then watched as Minna brewed up an elixir that Claire eagerly drank down.

"What's in that?" Gwen asked.

"My *maman* taught me folk medicine. Natural ways to bring healing."

"Got anything for stress?"

"I can make something for you."

Within an hour, Claire's temperature was down, and she slept comfortably.

"I'm so glad we decided to hire you," Gwen said.

"Do me a favor?" Minna asked.

"What?"

"Don't trouble your mother with your problems. She talks about you and Lucy all the time. She worries. If she felt you were happy, it would ease her mind."

Gwen weighed her options and decided not to be insulted. She had not let on her shock in the change she saw in her mother—the new frailness. It hit her full force, her mother's mortality, so hard to reconcile with the steel-minded mother who had raised them. The idea of her failing to heal scared Gwen.

"Minna's worth her weight in gold," she said to Claire the next day.

"She fights with Paz. Octavio doesn't trust her." She tried to minimize her feelings for the girl.

Gwen wasn't fooled. "She's taking good care of you. I'm happy you're in good hands."

Living with the vicissitudes of her rebellious body, Claire lost her taste for ordinary diversions. Minna was her midwife, introducing a whole other way of existence. While Claire could no longer tolerate watching the news on television, or listening to Mrs. Girbaldi's neighborhood gossip, she could sit outside for hours watching the trees, her thoughts swirling like a leaf riding a swift current of air. The old urgencies of the farm, which had before so preoccupied her, Paz's complaints, Gwen's and Lucy's constant dramas, all began to mercifully recede.

Time, too, lost its normal sequence. Minutes became dense, rich as whole lifetimes. Claire would leave an afternoon of daydreaming filled with ephemeral wisdom as if she had been away on a long year's journey and come back with a box filled with treasure. But she had gone nowhere, traveled no farther than a few footsteps. She hated the word *detachment*, but there was that—a shifting as if from a northern to a southern exposure—the whole world appearing newly draped.

* * *

Still, when Claire went out into the judging world, to the hospital or more rarely to the grocery, she clapped on the wig that Gwen had bought for her, or she wrapped her head in the colorful scarves that regularly arrived like bouquets from Lucy, or she wore Forster's old baseball cap, brim pressed low to her bare head, but this was for the world's sake, not her own. Patients dressed as much for others as themselves. They knew the battle being fought, grew proud of their scars, but the nonsick were visibly relieved not to be confronted with rude reminders of mortality. So the diseased attended to their illnesses discreetly in their shrunken, compromised world.

Only at home did the world open out for Claire, spread its toes to dig down into the cool infinite. She loved to sit with her head uncovered, to feel the air move against her scalp, to be attuned to the exact moment a sunbeam touched her forehead, something that in her un-stripped-down state she had been oblivious to. It occurred to her, as dispassionately as watching a cloud cross the sky, that this deep joy she felt in the ordinary might be a prelude to her death.

In her more optimistic moments, she did not believe that the cancer would kill her, but she did feel privy to a great secret that changed everything else: namely, that someday, sooner or later, something would. This was the kind of impossible knowledge that one pays lip service to, but it was like explaining the feeling of being in love, or the pangs of childbirth, or the ache of fear or loneliness. One can only know such things from the inside out.

After a difficult night during which Claire hardly slept, Minna and she walked through the orchards earlier than usual, the tule fog dense as ever. Claire, bald-headed, dressed in a clownish, marigold-colored robe given to her by Mrs. Girbaldi, thought she must appear like a supplicant Buddhist nun.

"I hate the nights," Claire said.

"I am always happiest in mornings and afternoons, never at night," Minna said. "Ghosts haunt one then." Suddenly Minna veered off and headed to an area that Claire had been careful to avoid. She dragged behind, trying to think of excuses not to continue.

"We've never walked here," Minna said.

"Nothing of interest." Claire stopped at the place the asphalt road gave out, but Minna insisted on walking down the gravel path.

The asphalt road faltered, crumbled into large bits of rock and gravel, further broke down to sand, then scraped into raw dirt and rough clay. Ants colonized part of the gully, and electric-blue thistle flowers crowded an uprooted eucalyptus, out of whose roots wild willow smothered the path leading to the wash.

Claire was torn between following and returning alone to the house when she heard Minna's cry. Reluctantly she approached. Minna stood stricken in the clearing as if she had seen a gravestone. Claire coughed, ready to come up with some fatuous story, but Minna waved her off. She waded through the bracken and undergrowth, lush from neglect.

Claire had not visited the tree in years, and Octavio avoided cultivating a large area around it until it had become enchanted in its abandonment.

"We should be getting back," Claire said quietly and futilely. With no sign Minna had heard her, exhausted, she sat on the ground, her back to Minna and the tree. "I'm feeling bad, if you care," she shouted.

No response. Claire turned just in time to see Minna place her hand against the trunk, as if taking its heartbeat, as if searching for clues inside for the sad state of abuse on the outside.

"Minna!" Claire yelled, but the words pushed back down her throat. She closed her eyes and must have dozed off because she woke blinded and overheated by the sun. Minna glared down at her, eyes bleared, swollen. She knelt and with an outspread hand touched Claire as she had touched the tree, and Claire shrank away as if she were being branded with a bloody imprint.

"This is the God wood," Minna said. "The tree of good and evil. Your tree of forgetting."

"I don't want this."

"Pauvre amie. This is where it happened. A son who died here."

"We don't talk of it," Claire whispered, as if their words might bring down the sky.

Minna's eyes were bright with excitement. "This is why you stay."

Claire turned away, aware now of footsteps and the sound of low voices. Five of the workers stood at the head of the road with their pruning tools, ready to begin the day. Like thieves, Claire and Minna stood and stumbled past them, Claire whispering, *"Buenos dias"* and *"Discúlpeme,"* covering her poor, exposed head with one hand.

When they reached the house, Minna pulled two lemons from her pocket. One lemon was rounded, with a deep cleft running through it so that it was like a crenellated heart, or perhaps two lemons that grew into each other's space and conjoined. The other was blackened and hollow, a victim of hanging unpicked from the previous years.

"What are you doing?" Claire asked, horrified by the sight.

Minna shrugged.

"You can't bring those in the house."

"It's only fruit."

"Get rid of them." Claire was enraged that Minna would defile the tree, disinterring the fruit, and at the same time shamed at her own irrational reaction. "How did you know?"

"Places are marked by what happened there. Sometimes they are cursed by bad luck, sometimes they become sacred, but either way they are marked."

They did not speak for the rest of the afternoon. On schedule, the tule fogs rolled back in at sunset and blanketed the hot fields, cooled over Claire's temper. They pretended, unsuccessfully, the blaze of the day and its events had never been.

Chapter 9

Syringes of Adriamycin the deep color of cherries or blood. Claire dreamed in red and woke with dry heaves. Methotrexate the deep yellow of egg yolks. Whole cocktails of medicines—mix the Taxol with the cisplatin, shake the Cytoxan with the fluorouracil. Face reddened and bloated, chest and arms rashed.

She woke with the conviction, like a toothache, that if she went in for her treatment that day, she would be weakened beyond the point of recovery. She picked up the phone and called Mrs. Girbaldi.

"Nan, tell me about that clinic. . . ."

Minna came into her bedroom, busy, hardly looking at her as she laid out Claire's clothes and went back out. She was talking about saints and symbols she had looked up in a book to paint on her walls, walls that had long ago been filled. "Coming for breakfast, your ladyship?" Claire heard the slap of her bare feet down the hall and was still under the covers when she returned.

"Come on, sleepyhead."

"I'm not going today."

Minna stopped. "It's not an either/or proposition."

"I'm serious. I can't do it today."

"I'll have to call the doctor. I'll have to call Gwen. . . ."

"Please."

"It's my *responsibility*. My *job*. It's your life we're talking about, *doudou*. I would be negligent."

"If I go today, it'll kill me."

"What if they don't believe me . . ."

"You believe me," Claire wheedled, grabbed Minna's hand. The girls had pulled similar stunts when they were little, and she never once gave in. But she knew Minna was inexperienced. Claire schemed she could trade on Minna's changeable heart.

Minna hesitated, stroked Claire's hair. "I'll say we had car trouble. I'll reschedule."

"Not this week."

"Don't be greedy." Minna stood thinking. "Get dressed for breakfast before I change my mind."

They sat in the kitchen. Claire obediently stirred syrup into her oatmeal, drank her coffee, and poured more.

"I want to try a clinic in Mexico Mrs. Girbaldi told me about."

"What's going on with you?"

Claire sagged down into her chair. "I'm starting to forget what I'm living for. I want to go away somewhere exotic and forget . . . this."

"Oh, *che,* exotic is on the inside. Back home, we sat around bored to death with all the green of the jungle, all the blue of the ocean. Each last one of us would have cut off our right arm to be in California."

"But you could have left at any time."

Minna drank her coffee. "Someday I will take you. A place very far, with steep mountains and waterfalls. Where the flowers open only at night. Their perfume is so strong you forget all the pain in your life."

"If I make it that long."

"You will make it. I'll take in enough life for both of us. We are like those plants—I can only survive if you survive." Minna got up to clear the dishes. "Now I have to go tell lies."

Claire, giddy at her temporary freedom, did not question what Minna told the doctors. When the phone rang, Minna shook her head and let it ring. Then she made her own calls. An hour later, Claire saw Don's car pull into the driveway, and her throat caught, thinking Minna would leave with him, but this time he drove all the way up to the house and wrestled three straw beach hats out of the trunk. Mrs. Girbaldi was in the backseat ready to go.

"What's going on?"

When Don saw Claire, his face broke into that smooth, movie smile that revealed nothing. "Let's go have some fun, little sweetheart."

Mrs. Girbaldi patted her hand. "We're going to go get a miracle."

After they crossed the border, traffic moved quickly through Tijuana, and soon they were on a desolate, winding road, burnt tan fields on either side, the land dropping away to the empty blue ocean. It was hard to remember a time when the land around the farm had been equally bare, the possibility of not having to look through a barricade of houses crowding out any glimpse of distance—mountains or water. But it was not as barren as on her previous visit all those years ago. Was it a coincidence that she always found herself in the desert at low points in her life? She wondered if that trip had turned out differently, if they had somehow come together again as a family, would the future have turned out better? Now Baja had aspirations—half-finished stucco developments everywhere, like a blight, trying to replicate the urban sprawl north of the border.

"Did you know I came to Cabo in the fifties?" Mrs. Girbaldi said. "It was just a little fishing village then. We all drank in a bar on the sand. Sinatra, Crosby, later on Bobby Mitchum."

"You met Robert Mitchum?" Don asked, turning around so that the car swerved.

"Hey!" Minna said.

"I danced with Mitch on the beach many times. He said I was as pretty as Lana Turner, if you can believe that." One could tell by the way she said it that this memory had nourished her through long decades.

Minna turned around and squinted at her. "He's right. Most definitely."

"Silly." Mrs. Girbaldi laughed, delighted. "You don't even know who she was. Anyway. He *was* a charmer. He died of lung cancer." Realizing what she said, she looked guiltily at Claire.

"It's okay," Claire said. "I haven't forgotten. People die."

"Yes, they do. Problem is, sometimes they forget to live," Minna said.

They passed two beer breweries and then a donkey pulling a wagon of mud bricks. When they stopped for gas, Claire got out and stood looking up and down the broken sidewalks. A three-legged dog nimbly picked his way down the road. A place one could lose oneself in. She fantasized that if she ran away, if she bargained not to return to her old life, the cancer would vanish in trade. This hardscrabble town was not a place that accommodated sickness. Death, yes. Decay was visible everywhere—the bleached signs, the unsold dusty cans and bottles in the cashier's window, the trash-clogged gutters.

"Do you need to take a pee?" Minna asked.

Inside the filling station, the men stared hard through the glass at Minna until she glared back and their gazes crumbled away. Claire passed by invisible. One could not blame them. Playing with paper towels and squeegee, Minna helped Don wash the windshield. Her dark skin blazed in the harsh sun, the bright coral tank top she wore in astonishing contrast. Her teeth, as she laughed, like rare pieces of polished ivory. It occurred to Claire for the first time that Don was in love with her. How could he not be? How could any of them not be dazzled by her?

In the dank bathroom, there was only cold water and soap like gritty sand to wash her hands. Claire avoided the cracked mirror.

The road veered inland, and the ocean dropped from sight. The air grew hotter, sparse grass giving way to glittering-hard desert floor. Don sang cowboy songs from old Roy Rogers films, while Minna sat next to him, dissolved in laughter, trying to sing along.

For stretches of time, Claire forgot her illness altogether, lost in the thrill of movement, in the lust of Don and Minna for each other, in the cheerful prattling of Mrs. Girbaldi.

"Where are we going?" Claire asked.

"First we need to eat."

Although the air appeared still, far off in a field Claire saw a whirling of wind as it funneled sand up into a cone. It danced shakily back and forth like a drunken top, a miniature tornado, then landed on a bush, which became possessed, electrified, branches stretching and shuddering. She did not wonder at the credulity of the ancients in explaining such a sight as an act of providence. Although she was amazed, she did not point out the sight to Don or Minna or Mrs. Girbaldi, hoarding the vision until she could decipher its significance. Even riding along in their modern, air-conditioned car, Claire would not have been surprised to see the bush burst into flame, to hear the voice of God. In her illness, she had fallen outside the constraints of time and logic.

She recalled Lucy's disappearance all those years ago, and

their panicked reaction. Claire should have walked out into the desert without turning back until she found her. So clear in hindsight that Lucy had just wanted to be found.

Don drove them through the gates of a resort along the ocean, and they entered another world, the fake movie version of Mexico Claire had long ago expected—palm trees, fountains, and red-tiled buildings. But the simplicity she also expected was nowhere in evidence: the parking lot was filled with expensive imported cars; the lobby stood marbled and sleek. Here Minna's glamour was the norm rather than the exception. They were seated on a terrace overlooking the bay; oily, listless waves dragged forward and back, back and forward.

A lovely, plump waitress, with heavy, oiled hair that coiled like a snake down her back, greeted them. Her uniform was straight out of a B movie—white peasant blouse with an elastic neckline pulled down over her shoulders, ruffled skirt in red and green that accentuated her full hips. When she recognized Don, she giggled, asking for an autograph.

"Only if you bring us menus."

She bowed, hurried away.

They ate large, moon-shaped pieces of Mexican papaya, the rose-colored flesh served at room temperature. The fruit tasted overripe, even the smell made Claire queasy, but she kept spooning pieces in her mouth, forcing herself to swallow because she didn't want to appear sick, didn't want to break the spell of reprieve and be forced to return home. Didn't want the day to ever end. The waitress brought a tray full of margaritas from the manager. Claire picked up a glass and drank, although she wasn't allowed alcohol. The girl stood by Don, telling him how she enjoyed his latest desert picture.

"Dear," Mrs. Girbaldi said, "can you let the man dine in peace?"

Irritated, at first Minna ignored the girl. Then she began to ask her for things: salt, a napkin, another order of chips.

"Is there anything else?" the waitress said, sullen.

A fork, bottled water, another with bubbles. Till the girl caught on and stayed out of reach at the bar, mooning over Don from afar.

"Annoying," Minna said.

"Source of paycheck," Don said.

They ate ceviche and fresh grilled mahimahi and local lobster until Claire felt sick but would not dare refuse a bite.

Minna smiled. "Somebody must be feeling better."

"This is lovely. Like it was forty years ago," Mrs. Girbaldi said. "Let's toast."

Everyone raised a glass. "To the past."

Minna lifted her glass. "To the future!"

Don took a snapshot of them at the table, Claire with her arm around Minna, smiling as if they were ordinary tourists on a pleasure jaunt. When he left to use the telephone, Claire held Minna's hand.

"Tell me we never have to go back."

"I'm honored you included me in this escape." Mrs. Girbaldi drank down her margarita.

"Let's walk on the beach," Minna said.

"No," Claire said, but it was too late. Minna had already pulled her to her feet.

"Count me out," Mrs. Girbaldi said. "I'll order us another round."

They walked along the sand, around a bend that hid the restaurant from view. A breeze came up and rattled the dried-out palm fronds overhead. Claire's arm that held her hat in place prickled as the blood left it.

"Let's wade in the water," Minna said.

"It's too hard." Claire motioned to the hat.

"Take it off."

"No!"

"No one cares."

"I won't." Impossible to explain the damage of seeing one's disintegration reflected on the faces of strangers. Far from wanting to attract attention, Claire wished to be invisible.

"Okay, look." Minna pulled off the coral top she wore. Underneath, her white cotton bra did not pass for a bathing suit. She hiked her cotton skirt up and knotted it on the side of her hip. Her thigh was rounded and heavily muscled, like a runner's.

"Easy for you," Claire said.

Minna held out her hand, and reluctantly Claire took off her hat.

Once it was gone, Claire had to ignore everything, concentrate only on nature, to save herself.

The water was cool; it tugged and sucked against her legs, luring her out to the darker, purple-blue depths. Claire was not brave enough to look back at the shore so she waded, knee-deep, and stared out. She had never felt so exposed in her surroundings, naked and peeled, a turtle unshelled. Absurd that a hank of hair insulated one so much from the world. She had experienced this exposure before, in a much more devastating form. How had she ever recovered from the stares after Josh's death? Hadn't she been singled out and forced into the part of victim then, too? Wasn't it the same—the internal, private agony and then the public one added to it?

"This reminds me of home," Minna said.

"Tell me what it is like."

"A pink house on top of the hill."

"Pink?"

"A beautiful pink house, with a red-tile roof. Windows arched and trimmed in white. And bougainvillea—red, purple, and gold. Bird-of-paradise bushes that brushed against each other like chimes in the wind. Hibiscus flowers as big as trumpets."

Claire closed her eyes. "I want so much to see it."

"The inside cool as a cave, even on the hottest day. The oiled wood floors smelled of lemons. The greenhouse, hot, humid, smelled of flowers and earth."

"Take me."

"Leta, our cook, loved me. Famous people came to eat her dinners and said that her dishes were better than the finest restaurants, not only in Roseau, but in Port-au-Prince or Kingston."

"Maybe she would have cooked something I could bear eating."

"She said her secret was knowing to put both sweetness and saltiness in each dish. She was more than a cook; she had magic. She told me the sun was a sweet orange in the sky."

Unlike Claire with her parochial life, Minna dreamed of a specific place because she was already at home in the larger world. Claire imagined that the bookish sophistication of Cambridge and the hedonistic pleasures of her sister's Paris had taken Minna further and further from the simplicities of that pink house. The exotic, the fantastic, possibly even the transcendent, held no surprises for her. Claire, on the other hand, had buried herself on the ranch until anything outside its borders frightened her. Now she felt alienated inside her own body.

When finally they waded back to shore, a Mexican family quickly turned around to walk in the other direction, the parents shoving their children along in front of them. The children turned back, jeered. A scene from the novel came to Claire: children taunting Antoinette, singing, *Go away, white cockroach, go away, go away.* Minna, oblivious to the snub, tied a scarf around her head, then put on her shirt. She handed Claire the straw hat. But Claire dropped it onto the sand. No more hiding.

* * *

When they returned to the restaurant, Claire made her way to the bathroom to patch together some semblance of a presentable face. After being in the company of Don and Minna, after being filled with new places, scents, food, after her revelation on the beach, she was under the illusion of returned health, and the death mask that stared back from the mirror shocked her. As if she could outrun her fate. Not a glimmer of health to be found no matter how she searched: shrunken head, skin bluish white like a ghoul's. She wanted her hat back. What was this conceit of theirs that she belonged among them, the living, the loved?

Claire dried her hands, determined to go find the hat, or if it was gone, buy another. She took a left that should have been a right, found herself down a dimly lit hallway stacked with cases of cerveza, bags of frijoles and *arroz*. At the end of the hallway, she saw the back of their pretty, plump waitress on her knees, the heavy, oiled hair like a snake down her back. Don leaned against the wall, his pants down.

For a moment what she saw did not register. She stood stranded, confused as if in a dream, but Don's eyes made her back away, made her trip over a box in her panic. The waitress turned. Claire fled, ran, as their laughter chased her. It wasn't they who were mortified but Claire.

When she returned to the table, Minna's eyes widened. "Are you okay?"

Claire nodded, speechless. Sat down and drank her water, then Mrs. Girbaldi's.

The waitress came to deliver the bill and lavished a Cheshire-cat smile while presenting a wedge of flan on the house as Don came and sat down. Did Claire detect sadness in his eyes, or resignation?

"How kind," he said, reaching up to straighten the waitress's crooked blouse.

"Where have you been, Donald?" Mrs. Girbaldi said. "We'll be late for our appointment."

"Can I have your autograph, Señor Richards?" He signed a menu when she returned with change, leaving a piece of paper among the bills on which her name and number were written. When she turned away, Minna snatched it up and wadded it into her palm.

"What if I wanted that? Jealous?" Don asked.

Claire had rarely seen him so pleased. No sadness, certainly no mortification.

"Not at all. It's a respect thing. Between women," Minna said.

On the way out, the waitress stood at the entrance and again smiled. "*Buenas tardes,* Señor Richards. Please come visit again. I'm here every Tuesday through Friday."

Even Claire fumed that the waitress treated them as beneath acknowledgment. *White cockroach.* Minna went up to her, stood close as she shoved the paper down the girl's blouse, holding her in place by stepping down on her foot. Before releasing her, Minna ground down her heel, and the girl screamed.

The owner came running.

"I'll sue you," the girl said. "It'll be in the papers."

Confused over what had happened, the owner, a bent-over old man, took the girl to a chair, then hobbled into the bar for ice.

"I don't think so," Claire said. She felt a thrill of adrenaline go through her.

"Why not?" the girl said.

"Is the owner your father? Or an uncle? Does he know what you do in the back hallway?"

"Come close, *ti* sister. You and me need to seriously talk." Minna leaned closer to the girl and spoke rapidly in whispered tones until the girl jerked her arm loose and escaped, limping away.

"I didn't know you had it in you," Minna said, putting her arm around Claire.

"You protect your own." Claire couldn't have imagined getting involved in something so tawdry, yet she felt thrilled by her own actions.

In the lobby, Mrs. Girbaldi looked shook up.

Don was smoking a cigarette. "So you speak Spanish?"

"Just socially," Minna said. "The islands are full of pidgin French and Spanish."

"Yeah, I saw. My lady is full of mysteries, isn't she?"

"That little preview in the hallway that Claire interrupted could have made you famous. Her boyfriend over there behind the bar playing cameraman."

Don stared hard at the young man cleaning glasses. "You're not even jealous."

"I'm only jealous of something I want and can't have."

They drove farther down the coast, stopping at whim at what captured their fancy—clay statues of dogs and tin mirrors and paper flowers—anything certifiably useless and unneeded, despite Mrs. Girbaldi's protests about being late.

"This is Mexico. Time is elastic," Don said.

Finally they arrived at the clinic: a tiny, pristine building that sat on a white, prim beach.

The director of the clinic came out in a starched lab coat. He was overly tanned, his thinning hair bound in a small ponytail. He would have looked more in place in a down-at-the-heels nightclub. *"Bienvenidos!"* he said, as if they had arrived at a resort for a holiday. A young girl in a short sundress served them small glasses of pink juice from a tray. They sat on white sofas, the sliding doors open to the beach, and an overweight, older nurse came out and took Claire away to have blood work done.

In the doctor's office, Claire felt dizzy as she took off her clothes to put on a cotton smock. The nurse, too, was sweating in the heat. When she noticed Claire's nerves, she smiled and patted her hand. With the most delicate touch, she pulled a syringeful of blood. Minutes later, the doctor came in reading her records, shaking his head. His teeth were bleached an unnatural bluish white. He held her hands out, studying her nails, pulled her eyelids down and looked at the tissue.

"You are not healthy."

"An understatement," Claire said, then leaned over and retched.

After an orderly cleaned up the mess, Mrs. Girbaldi and Minna were brought in. The doctor frowned at them. "You shouldn't have traveled with her. Brought her here like this. We can't help her in this condition."

"Please," Mrs. Girbaldi said. "We can pay handsomely."

"Your cell count is dangerously low," he said to Claire. "You need a hospital. There are drugs that will build the blood back up, but first you require a transfusion."

A black wave was coming over Claire, darkness like water rising quickly around her.

"Help her," Mrs. Girbaldi pleaded.

Don came through the door. "What's happening?"

The doctor took her pulse. "What's your blood type? Is anyone a relative?"

"What's wrong?" Don said.

"I'm a universal donor," Minna said. The doctor flicked his eyes over her. She dropped her voice. "I was screened recently."

The doctor shook his head. "You must sign a release. If she dies here."

"Oh, no." Mrs. Girbaldi started crying.

"Why didn't you tell me—" Don yelled at Minna.

"Shut up."

"I'll never forgive myself . . ." Mrs. Girbaldi moaned.

"Let's do it," the doctor said.

Hours later, Claire was lying in a queen-size rattan bed, watching the sunset over the ocean, a regular faux-vacation. Minna sat next to her.

"How is my *doudou*?"

"I was wrong to make you do this."

"Now we have the same blood in our veins."

"You saved my life."

"We saved each other's. Don will sit with you while I make arrangements for a hotel. Mrs. Girbaldi is exhausted."

Don came in, sheepish, and Minna passed him without a word. His hands shook when he touched Claire. "You scared us."

"It was all my fault. Not hers."

"Thank God nothing happened." His face showed strain, the usual veneer worn off.

"Minna's my angel. You don't deserve her."

"I don't." Don sighed. "I've never met anyone who didn't care about the bullshit, you know what I mean? Even with the lies."

"Lies?"

"You know. Her stories change all the time. I tell her she can trust me."

"The details change. Her actions speak for her, don't you think?"

Claire fell asleep, and when she woke, the windows were dark. She was alone. The lights were dimmed, and an unfamiliar nurse stood in the corner, head bowed as she ironed Claire's dress, mumbling, *"Padre nuestro . . . ahora y hasta la hora de nuestra muerte."*

The next morning, Claire asked a new nurse for her dress and shoes, as well as watch and earrings, but they were nowhere to be found. More lost things. The doctor, eager to get rid of them, wheeled Claire out in her cotton hospital gown and plastic flip-flops to the front entrance.

"When you are stronger, come back. We have a new therapy with fetus cells."

Claire nodded.

When Don's car pulled up, Mrs. Girbaldi and Minna sat in the front seat with him as if they were sightseers.

"Such a shame," Mrs. Girbaldi said. "I liked the view here."

"It's a bad place," Minna said. "They are a sham: ripping you off with their miracle cure."

The drive home was a blur, as if Claire were being pushed by a tailwind of mistakes. She pictured old black-and-white movies where the hands of the clock fly around the dial.

Minna reached back and put her hand on Claire's knee. The nurse's words kept echoing in her ears, *la hora de nuestra muerte . . . nuestra muerte . . . muerte,* as if she were telling a truth no one else was willing to admit. Claire clung to Minna's arm, would not let go, *as you would cling to life if you loved it,* as if Minna were her air and light and blood.

Don called the oncologist, who arranged to meet them in the emergency room.

"I will not treat you if you do anything like this again," the doctor said.

"It was my choice to make this mistake," Claire said. "I earned it."

She spent the night hooked up to IVs. Don drove Mrs. Girbaldi home while Minna, bare feet curled up under her, slept in a chair in Claire's room. In the morning, Claire felt a tingling on her chest and arms and looked down to discover sunburn.

Their trip into the exotic changed many things. Changed

Claire's fear and Minna's roving. She no longer left evenings. Claire didn't know if Don's car no longer waiting at the end of the driveway was cause or effect. For her, the trip somehow had a liberating effect. She no longer felt unequal to her medicine. She went to the hospital by choice rather than sentence. Outwardly her world contracted, but experienced from the inside, life on the farm grew richer and more precious in ways she'd never imagined.

Her truancy was duly reported to Gwen, who phoned with the studied coolness Claire was sure her children received when caught red-handed at something forbidden. The delicious secret was that no punishment was possible, or rather the most severe punishment possible had already been meted out. As if that weren't enough, she had almost caused her own demise. What could Gwen do to make her suffer more than that?

Exorcised, Claire returned to treatment. Well-behaved, she listened to music through her earphones and nodded to the oncology nurses in their funny cartoon T-shirts. She would follow the treatments to their natural conclusion. Minna, chastised, stood in the doorway, checking on her, in the unlikely event Claire would try to bolt for another escape. But Claire had lost the desire to flee: like a bird too long domesticated, she would stay in her cage despite the wide-open door.

Chapter 10

As with all things forbidden yet tried, the trip was not without repercussions. At the next chemo session, Claire's white cell count still hung stubbornly low. The doctor, still smarting over what he considered the betrayal of her trip to the clinic, decided to stop treatment for the time being. An undercurrent of blame was palpable as he filled out her file, as if her rebellion would be the cause of her demise rather than a reaction to it. Claire was to stay at home and receive daily injections of a drug to build back up her blood.

Chastened, Claire played the part of obedient patient and tried to self-inject, but she could not stand to watch the needle plunge under her skin. The nurse sighed at this squeamishness and instructed Minna on how to give the injections. Already in the hot seat for her part in the "runaway" trip, as it was referred to by the girls, as in, "Mom ran away from home," Minna was grim about the job, her usual playfulness gone. She practiced shooting water into oranges for hours and hours, until she felt comfortable with the procedure, until she reached the point at which Claire could not feel the bite of the needle when Minna fed it under her skin, performing the procedure as a kind of sleight of hand.

The other effect of the rogue trip was that Gwen decided they should have a family gathering over the Fourth of July. They hadn't all been together for a holiday since their teenaged years, and it was long past time.

Claire couldn't deny a certain excitement in watching Paz scour the house clean, the feeling that things could be returned to normal at least for the long weekend. The house had fallen under a kind of a luxuriant torpor during the last months, Claire so distracted by her illness and Minna's dramatics that she had failed to notice that Paz had indeed become lax as Minna complained, that dust was in the corners and cobwebs in the windows. Bald-headed and frail, Claire readied the bedrooms, set up cots and sleeping bags in the sunroom for the grandchildren, while Paz washed floors and windows, scrubbed toilets and showers. When Claire commented about the state of the house, Paz said, "There is only so much I can do one day a week. Minna tells me, 'Leave this, leave that.'"

Claire brushed it off, not willing to let anything get to her. She felt a new determination to overcome her illness, felt maybe it was time to make amends.

During all of this, Minna was more morose than usual. "Everything okay?" Claire asked, but didn't wait for an answer. She had grown familiar with what she called Minna's blue periods, times when she was so silent and sullen that Claire learned to stay away. Minna had requested a full month's pay that morning.

"What do you need all this money for?"

Minna looked displeased with the question. "A cousin needs an operation."

"You're going to have to start saying no. You can't give what you don't have."

"Why aren't you resting?"

"You and Paz are doing all the heavy work," Claire said, although in reality Minna had done little.

"Not true. I saw you cleaning. I saw you baking. You're going to get sick, and I'll be blamed again."

"Minna!" Claire was annoyed. "It's good for me to have distractions."

"So that's no to the advance?"

"I'm not comfortable with it."

Some milestones let one know where one is, are able to promptly sink one to the bottom of life like an anchor. One occurred the moment Gwen walked through the front door, her children straggling behind her. The first thing she did on seeing Claire, standing there proudly bald, was instinctively reach an arm back to shield the children, wanting to warn and admonish at the same time. It was then that Claire felt truly sick, scared, deluded by her earlier confidence. She stayed on her feet through sheer will, betrayed by Minna's assurances, *Looking better. Better and better. The best each day.* Claire excused herself and hurried to the closet, wrapping Minna's magenta scarf over her head, hoping that would bring some relief to her appearance.

"How're my babies?" she said on returning. Smiled and smiled, because smiling through the death mask was all she could manage.

But the children had caught a glimpse of her naked disease. Her granddaughter, Alice, four, looked at her, and her lip started to tremble. "Where did your hair go?"

Sensing panic, Minna took over: carried bags, gave candies to the children. Shock neatly covered over, disguised. With a marked coolness on both sides, Gwen took Minna's hand. Unable to take her anger out on her mother, she blamed Minna for Mexico, allowing if not instigating it. Don was negligent, but he was also a stranger and a movie star; Mrs. Girbaldi, eccentric, was equally out of reach. Only Minna was within arm's reach of retribution.

"This must be little Alice," Minna said. "Pretty as her mama."

Tim, stolid as his father, hid behind Gwen's leg. He had obviously inherited an opinion of Minna from his parents.

When Gwen and Claire were alone on the porch, balancing ice teas in their laps, Gwen burst into sobs, such a disturbing sight from her self-contained daughter that Claire took her in her arms, reassuring her that after all she looked worse than she felt.

"I had no idea you lost so much weight," Gwen said.

"It's the ultimate diet."

"I can't believe that in your state . . ." Gwen wagged her finger as if it was obvious to both of them just how bad that state was. "I can't believe under the circumstances you pulled this Mexico stunt."

"I don't know I'd call it a *stunt.*"

"What else?"

"Most people on chemo continue working, or raising a family. They have to. I went on a day trip. I had to."

"Minna was irresponsible."

"My idea. I forced her. I had to—for here." Claire put her hand over her heart.

"Your health comes first. What's the point otherwise?"

What's the point if the heart isn't involved? Claire wanted to say.

At the noise of a car, Gwen hurried to the door. Lucy's rental car came down the driveway, and Gwen ran out to intercept her. It didn't matter. The minute Lucy walked through the door and saw her mother, her face dropped. She was the one unable to hide her emotions. It was stupid for Claire to pretend any longer that she wasn't really so sick, but now she was preoccupied with hiding the signs of the illness: keeping her head covered with scarves or caps; applying eyebrow pencil and rouge to try to add life to her face. She felt ghoulish but didn't know what else to do. All her excitement over the visit had dissolved and was replaced by a wish to return to solitude.

Although the house was full to bursting, Claire received less attention now, a fact she gratefully accepted, returning to the normal state of family, and no longer the invalid centerpiece. It could have been fifteen years before except for the addition of Minna. She and Lucy reunited like long-lost friends and spent hours on the back lawn, smoking cigarettes and gossiping. Lucy looked better, stronger, than in years, and Claire felt some vindication in leaving her in Santa Fe. All the bedrooms were occupied, a constant coming and going from room to room, slamming of doors, except Minna's, which remained resolutely shut. At odd, stolen moments, Claire looked at her, helpless, feeling unfaithful to the house's former silence and dreaminess.

After a few days passed, Minna asked if she could take the weekend off to visit friends. Claire did not believe she knew anyone in the vicinity and felt hurt that she referred to being with them as a job, something to be shirked.

"You should spend time with your family," Minna said. "You don't need me." As part of her leave-taking, she prepared one of her herbal drinks, which Claire had become addicted to, full of hibiscus flowers and mysterious herbs that dissipated her nausea. When Gwen asked for her own, Minna went back into the kitchen to make a new batch.

"I didn't mean for you to go to so much trouble," Gwen said, but did not stop her either.

Minna showed Gwen how to give the injections, frowning at her work on the orange, correcting her till she was satisfied. "More gently, otherwise you'll bruise her skin."

"You know the oncologist won't treat Mom because of Mexico," Gwen said.

"She was sick before Mexico."

"Not for you to decide."

"Nor for you."

Gwen sighed. "I appreciate your friendship with Mom. It's made a big difference."

Minna nodded.

"Maybe we were wrong to insist on her selling. If this place is that important to her. She's halfway through her treatments."

"I'm aware of that."

Before Minna left, she gave Claire a massage with special oils to ease her aches and pains. They sat on the bed afterward, enjoying the evening breeze through the window.

"Where are you going?"

"Santa Barbara. Don's idea. To see the land he's buying for the elephants."

"Of course, you're going away with him."

"He thinks he loves me." Minna giggled. "Drink up." As Claire finished the last thick, green sludge from the bottom of the cup, Minna got up and straightened things on the dresser. "I don't want to mention it, but I must. Gwen talked to me. She wants me to convince you the farm should be sold."

Claire put the cup down hard. "She never quits."

"Should you think about it?" Minna studied herself in the mirror. "Don has mentioned me moving in with him."

"Is that what this is about? You want to leave me?"

"I want you to make the right decision for yourself. I worry that you might stay here just for me."

"I'm staying until I'm well. With you or without you."

"As long as it is what you want, *che*."

That evening, Don's car pulled up the long driveway, and he kissed the girls on the cheek before he drove Minna away. They watched wistfully as the car departed.

"Some girls have all the luck," Lucy said.

"Just happens that all lucky girls look like that," Gwen said.

Claire had forgotten the routines, how much noise and activity she used to accept as normal: the television always on, phones ringing, music thrumming at all hours in the house, and since the girls' tastes rarely matched, competing strains of Bach and the Stones. The children scattered toys all over the floor, and Claire had to pick her way around in order to not slip. They cooked or ate out, went shopping, to the playground, beach, and movies; every day was a long, exhausting series of activities. Sometimes it seemed to her they were afraid to ever be still. Had that been her life before?

The newspapers, the celebrity-gossip magazines, the fashion magazines multiplied on the coffee table. When Claire flipped through them, the glossy images depressed her, made her feel beside the point with her balding head and lopsided chest. Alone with Minna, an alternate universe had shown itself, shutting away the outside world. But that world was the medium, the barrage of sensory information, that her daughters lived in, like fish in water, and they thought it eccentric of Claire not to be able to name a single clothing designer, a single makeup line.

"Why can't we just sit and talk?" Claire said. "When do I have you here?"

"Talk about what?"

"I don't know. Like in the old days."

"I don't remember talking in the old days," Lucy said.

Gwen looked over and saw the disappointment on her mother's

face. "I remember lying outside at night on the road. Cars never came by. The stars were bright because the city lights were still far away. We had so much freedom back then; my kids have none of that. But all we could talk about was how bored we were, how we couldn't wait till we were old enough to go explore the world.

"Okay, turn the radio off," Gwen said to Lucy. The silence hummed. "We were kids. We talked about what we were doing. We never asked about you. We didn't think about what your life was like."

"You were my life," Claire said. "You and the farm."

"You were a good mother."

Claire was silent for a minute, savoring the words. "It makes me sad. Living apart. We hardly know each other anymore. Why can't you make arrangements to come back here and live for a while?"

A different silence now around the table.

"Here?"

"Why not? Plenty of room. I'm still going to sell, eventually."

"This isn't where our lives are."

"Come on, Gwen. You're always complaining how hard you work. You and Kevin could spend more time together. Time with the kids. Like your dad and I did. It was a good place to raise a family. You just said so yourself."

"I don't want that kind of life," Gwen said.

She looked at Lucy.

"The place feels haunted. I told Minna as much," Lucy said.

"You did? When?"

"I don't know. Before we left that first time. I thought she should know about Josh."

Claire felt a dropping in her stomach. So it had all been an act at the tree. For a moment, just the time it took to inhale a few dizzy breaths, she felt an anger strong enough to sever the relationship. But did she ever, even for that barest moment, believe that Minna actually had powers? Of course not. So she was just as guilty of willful blindness. Wasn't the truth that they were going through a ritual, enacting it for each other, and themselves?

"I don't understand why you two want to live like you are from nowhere, unrooted. How many people in this world have that? Minna understands the preciousness of place."

Claire retreated into her books, plunged back into the Rhys novel to fuel her imaginings of Minna.

The mineral-hard ocean and the palms and the untainted green of Dominica, the jagged hills that so fascinated and appalled Rochester. Were there brilliant parties at her family's plantation, an approximation of burned-down Coulibri? Was the isolation of Granbois like that of the Baumsarg farm? Where did Minna meet the handsome boy who broke her heart? She had hinted about him, how he kissed her in a greenhouse on the estate of her pink house. Claire had decided on unrequited love for Minna because after thinking at length about it, she could come up with no other reason for Minna's friendlessness, her moods, the mournful look in her moss-green eyes, glimpses caught when she was unaware of Claire's watching. The more she read, the more she thought she understood Minna, and even though her absence had only been days long, Claire could not wait for her return, to compare the imagined Minna against the person made flesh.

Of course Claire knew that this was futile, knew these were sentimental wonderings on her part, that even the smallest, no-nonsense glance from Minna would confirm the vainness of her fantasies. She could hardly see the reality of her own daughters because of the network of memories, loyalties, loves, and jealousies that they resurrected and laid to bed, over and over, during that holiday weekend.

She had wanted family since she was a little girl in the small, dark apartment over her father's bookstore, and this family had been created through, because of, the farm. She was angry that they didn't see that. Angry that they didn't accommodate the high price paid. Valued that life so little they were unwilling to keep it going. What was out there that was more important than what was on the ranch? It was impossible to be in their presence—the undertow of the past was too strong, a constant replaying of some infatuation, some slight. Only with strangers, new acquaintances, could one gauge who one was in the present, try on whom one might become.

The girls' behavior was to pretend nothing had happened, that Claire was not sick, that everything was the same. But something *had* happened—Claire had changed. The experience of the disease had opened her up, made her want to reach out, but they still insisted on the mother who required nothing of them. They were more fascinated by Minna.

Exhausted by the heat, they idled away long afternoons on the porch by conjecturing about her.

"What do you think he sees in her?" Lucy asked. No question *who* they were speaking of.

"What doesn't Don see in her?" Gwen said. "She's a mystery. I'll give her that."

On the afternoon of the Fourth, Tim played morosely with a stick in the driveway. A careful child, not wanting to give away too much of himself, miserly for all his six years due to Gwen's cautious hovering. It infuriated Claire that Gwen forbade him to go into the orchards. "It's the safest place a child could be!" But Gwen wouldn't budge. Claire despaired at her tentative, unsure grandson.

"Are you going to see the fireworks?" Claire asked him when Gwen finally relented long enough to go inside for his sunblock.

He shrugged. Claire had only seen him a few times a year since he was born, and he was still wary of her. Obvious that grandchildren needed to be charmed, unlike one's immediate children, who were more or less hostages to one's love.

"Mom says I have to stay here. She says you might go away like Mr. Grumbles."

"Who's that?" Claire said, a sinking feeling in her stomach.

"The goldfish." He wiped his nose with the back of his arm. A moment later he sneezed five times in a row.

"Gesundheit!"

"Mom says I'm allergic to plants."

"But the world is full of plants."

"That's why Mom says I should stay inside."

"Aunt Lucy is going to take you to the fireworks. Do you know why?"

He shook his head, noncommittal, not willing to risk showing excitement.

"They are going to have cannons there, and I need you to tell me how loud they are, okay?"

He looked cheered but still untrusting. Gwen's child.

"Tell your mom I am not going down the toilet like Mr. Grumbles."

As the week progressed, Claire grew more and more exhausted, a hostage to the activity in the house. Forster came by and surveyed the citrus crop, spoke to Octavio. When he offered to take them all out to lunch, Claire begged off.

"How come you never visit when I'm alone?" she said.

"Your Minna doesn't appreciate visitors."

Claire nodded, not believing him. Alone in the glory of her empty living room, she sprawled on the couch.

On the coffee table, Gwen had left a stack of books she'd brought about cancer survivorship that Claire refused to read. Now she skimmed through them, intending to dump the whole pile in the trash as soon as everyone was gone. She calculated her best bet was to stay as ignorant as possible of what could happen. She thumbed through a pamphlet on alternative medicine Lucy had included. Formulas for vitamin combinations, herbal elixirs, teas and pastes and poultices. Offers for copper bracelets and crystal charm necklaces. Discounts on pyramid structures built out of lightweight PVC that could be suspended over one's favorite chair or bed, so that the healing energy of the cosmos would be diverted to cure one. Remedies included bleeding with leeches, diets of macrobiotic food, injections of shark cartilage or third-world embryos, or even a payment plan for prayer directed to one's recovery, as if lobbying would improve your odds for holy intervention.

Instead she flipped through the growing piles of women's magazines.

GET 10 YEARS BACK

WE KEEP OUR PROMISES

LIFE IS BETTER WITH BEAUTIFUL SKIN

She blinked her lashless eyes, sucked in her hollowed cheeks, too busy keeping alive to worry about being beautiful.

FOR SKIN SO FIRM

YOU'LL WANT TO SHOW

IT OFF AGAIN

There was nothing she wanted to show off. The airbrushed models made her feel more decrepit by the moment.

LIVE LIKE IT'S ONE BIG PREMIERE

She tossed the magazine down, disgusted and demoralized in equal parts, and a sheaf of white papers fell out. It was an appraisal of the property done a month before. Paid for on Gwen's credit card. Why, no matter what Claire tried, did Gwen stay so determined to sell the farm? Minna hadn't been lying.

Claire needed to go through the rest of her treatments, become a model patient, survive, for the simple reason that she had not yet taught the girls what was important in life. Could it be possible her mothering was still not done?

Head spinning, she went to the kitchen to make tea from the last of the mixture Minna had left her. As she leaned over the stove, watching the kettle, a whish of air blew the flame high, high enough to lick the cuff of her housecoat. A singe of flame spun her around and straight into her ten-year-old son. Her eyes swam, and she savagely brushed the blur away, but still he stood in front of her. Fresh and sweet as her dreams, mischievous, and just the smallest bit weary, as if he'd had a poor night's sleep. Yes, she recognized that, and it broke her heart. Did the dead tire from the grieving constantly calling on them, not leaving them alone to enjoy eternity? Her heart lifted although she knew this was an unthinkable mistake, an error so treacherous that if she allowed herself to believe, it would wreck her.

Many times she had dreamed her boy would return, had returned, that it all had been a horrible mistake. Always unchanged, although his sisters and Claire had aged, and everything else around him had been transformed by time. Even as she reached out for the longed-for hug, she lost consciousness.

The sun was in Claire's eyes when she woke, still on the floor. Gwen was running for the phone, yelling directions. The afternoon passed quietly in the emergency room. Gwen stood by her gurney, holding her hand. "I'll never forgive myself."

"For what?"

"Not preventing this, for going to lunch."

"Don't be silly. You can't always be there just in case." Even when one was there, one could not always prevent bad things from happening. How long would it take till she herself believed that?

That night, back in her own bed, Claire poured the vitamin drops Minna had left for her on her tongue. Hours later her throat had swelled so big that she could hardly breathe, her chest a vise twisting the breath out. Her skin turned raw with rash. Back in the emergency room before sunrise, the girls and the grandchildren sleeping on chairs in the waiting room, Claire's blood count again plunged. The on-call doctor asked what she had eaten, then took an analysis of the vitamin drops. Some unidentified compound in the drops had caused an allergic reaction. He threw the drops away, shaking his head.

"Your cell count is low. Your immune system is weak. Stay away from crowds." He glanced at Tim, who was sniffling. "She needs to be isolated from anyone sick."

"We're her family," Gwen said.

The doctor looked up from his clipboard. "Germs are germs. Do you want your mother healthy?"

"Of course."

"Then have the kids stay at a friend's. And why did you take her to Mexico?"

"It wasn't our doing."

"You need to take care of your mom," he said. "She needs you all on board."

"That's complicated," Gwen said.

"Of course we will," Lucy said.

Chapter 11

A quick family meeting was held around the breakfast table, and it was decided that Gwen would leave early with the children. Mrs. Girbaldi would drive them to the airport. As the girls washed the breakfast dishes, Claire heard Gwen whispering to Lucy, "I'll have her checked out, too."

"Have who checked out?" Claire said.

"No one," Gwen said.

"Turn around," Claire said. "Sweetheart, quit going behind my back."

"What do you mean?"

"I know about the appraisal of the ranch."

"I'm protecting you. Has Minna convinced you to stay?"

"Don asked her to marry him." Another untruth blurted out. "She hardly needs me."

Gwen shrugged.

"You're my daughter. I love you. But this jealousy . . ."

Gwen blinked her eyes rapidly. "Why do you like her more than us?"

"That's ridiculous," Claire said, even though she suspected it might appear that way. "Before I passed out . . . I saw your brother." She had intended to keep this a secret, suspecting their reaction, but in her desperation to win them over, she found herself ruthless.

"I just can't do this. This morbid stuff," Gwen said.

"It's a sign. I knew you wouldn't understand," Claire said. "I want you to come back here to live. Children need to live here again. It will be like the old days."

"No one wants the old days back, except you."

Gwen passed instructions to Lucy on how to give the injections, but Lucy's hands shook so badly that she jabbed the needle in like a dart, with such force that it left small, grape-size bruises on Claire's skin. The grandchildren were herded out the door. Both glanced backward, wondering, she was sure, if they had done something wrong and Nana was sending them away.

"Have them call me on my cell phone," Claire said.

They stood on opposite sides of the glass window in the living room.

"Alice, will you send me pictures? So I get better?"

The little girl nodded, but she was so young that out of sight was out of mind.

"Gwen, get them some markers." On Claire's side of the glass she drew a happy face. Once they realized they wouldn't get in trouble, the children went wild with the forbidden pleasure of drawing on the glass.

"Can you draw some hair on? Pretty hair for me?" Claire said into the phone.

"Oh, boy." Gwen laughed. "We're going to have trouble at home now."

Tim stared at Claire, not hiding his fascination at how bad she looked, what might be happening inside her, what his mother told him. He started to draw round bugs with scowling faces. "These are the bugs that are eating you," he said into the phone. "The cancers."

Gwen grabbed him. "That's enough."

"No, no," Claire said. "Let's *X* them out. She put a green *X* over one; Tim drew a yellow one over another. "That's a good boy."

He remained silent, then drew a fish in a bowl that Claire suspected was Mr. Grumbles.

"See," Claire said into the phone. "Come back from the dead."

When everything was packed, Gwen made a last attempt. "It's not too late, you know. To leave. Not too late at all."

"I need to stay here."

Gwen pulled away. "I'll call your doctor directly. Please stay safe, okay?"

"Where else could I stay?"

Gwen grimaced at her mother's poor joke.

That night Lucy baked a rigatoni casserole. Claire felt disloyal admitting it, but without Gwen, the atmosphere was more relaxed. It didn't even bother her that Lucy drank glass after glass of wine. They acted like schoolgirls playing hooky.

"Did I tell you about this artist at the gallery? His name is Javier."

Claire was happy. On schedule, she drank an elixir before dinner. By eleven she broke out in a sweat, fearing indigestion. At midnight her head was hanging over the toilet. Lucy called the doctor on duty, then brought her a cup of Minna's tea.

"The pasta probably wasn't the best idea. Too spicy."

Claire nodded, hopeful that it could be something so simple.

"The doctor thinks maybe you're having hot flashes."

"Of course." The banality of the explanation made her angry. In her new dramatic circumstances, headache connoted brain tumor.

"Try to sleep," Lucy said. "Is it okay if I go into my old room to get some boxes from the closet? Her door is always closed."

"Don't touch anything. She bites Paz's head off when things are moved."

Lucy turned to go away. "I'm going to get a nightcap."

"Would you sit with me awhile?"

"Be right back." A few minutes later Lucy sat at the foot of the bed with a shot of tequila. "I never agreed with Gweny, by the way. I would be the same as you—stay where I drew strength and comfort. I'd do a lot of things before I'd agree to live under her roof."

"She doesn't like Minna."

Lucy sipped. "Sometimes people look a lot worse than they are. People do things to survive. Doesn't necessarily make them bad. Gweny doesn't accept weakness."

"How did I get such a brilliant daughter?"

"In the genes, I guess."

"She doesn't understand I'm trying to fix things."

But Lucy didn't hear her, lost in her own thoughts. "Gweny never got over being frightened that night. She told me they touched her hair. And she wanted to cut it off. Dad wouldn't let her. He said it would upset you too much. So she just held it all in. I told her you did the best you could for us."

"I wanted you to have a sense of belonging." Her parents had been permanent wanderers, making her feel an outsider. She wanted her children to feel the ranch in their blood, to have a bond so deep that it carried them through life and made them strong. "Was that so wrong?"

They sat in silence, the lamp casting a small circle of light around the bed, making the corners of the room dark, the night outside the open windows darker still.

"I saw him, you know." The words came out before Claire could consider the effect.

"Who?"

"Joshua."

Lucy nodded, her eyes getting larger, the pupils darkening. It crossed Claire's mind she might be taking drugs again. "Sometimes I think I've seen him. I imagine it was all a mix-up, and he's living in another state—like Utah—and has no idea how he got separated from us. Except he's always still the same age as when he left."

"Still a boy."

"Nothing extraordinary ever happened to our family except that. The one thing."

"I blame myself."

"We were just unlucky."

Claire had forgotten Lucy's request the next morning when she came into her room, insisting even in Claire's half-awake state that she had to come and look.

"It's okay . . ." Of course, Claire knew of the painted walls, knew of Saint Agatha, knew the effect of all this was like being transported to another world, but now a startling new density had taken place, a crowding of impressions that took one's breath away as if the room were alive, an organic thing, growing and developing with a logic known only to it.

The first thing to assault one on entering was a giant red heart painted against the turquoise wall. The red feral, punctured with black marks, making the whole room swim in front of Claire's eyes, but then she realized her mistake, shook herself alert to see—what she had mistaken for a long black bar was a sword plunged diagonally into the heart.

Although the effect should have been frightening, it didn't scare her. Instead Claire found something brave, fierce, even exhilarating, about it. Below the heart, in fine yellow lettering, was

the word EZILI. Below that were symbols, painted pots and cups, next to them a palm tree reaching to the ceiling, snakes winding up its trunk. On the yellow wall, writ large, were the words HE WILL COME.

"We're not in Kansas anymore," Lucy said. She walked around the room as if she were viewing an exhibition at a museum, stopping at the table in the corner. She motioned Claire over. At first glance it seemed a crowded jumble of junk. There were at least forty or fifty liquor bottles: Scotch, vodka, wine, beer, all sizes, some empty, some unopened.

"Maybe she's into recycling." Lucy giggled. The room had her jittery. "It's like a folk altar. I've seen altars like this in Santa Fe."

After looking more closely, they saw the arrangement was not random, was far from a cluttered jumble, was in fact laid out with great thought, and a kind of mad deliberation. At the center, among the bottles, was a crucifix, and behind it, taped to the wall, were dozens of religious postcards, some old and yellowed, some shiny new. On the table were a few burnt-out candles, and in the center of it all was the picture of Minna and Claire in Mexico, except the part with Minna had been torn off so that Claire sat grinning alone, her arm embracing empty space.

"That's mine!" Lucy said. An old doll's head was jammed atop one of the bottles; a corded, soft pouch was on top of another.

In a flat dish were the dregs of a noxious-looking liquid now dried brownish red, like the muddy bottom of a parched lake bed. On top of it lay a small clump of hair, more like the loose hairs pulled from a hairbrush than a clipping cut with scissors. Claire's.

A small pink book lay open at the side. Childish writing visible in purple ink. "My diary!" Lucy said. The date fifteen years before: *Josh is missing. Please bring him home. Josh is missing. Please bring him home. I promise not to lie anymore and to do my homework.* Over and over the same sentences for pages.

"I thought doing this as punishment would bring him back," Lucy said. "Why is she going through my stuff?"

Written on the wall behind the makeshift altar, because altar it was no matter how murky its intention, were the words OGOU BALANJO.

"She said she missed home," Claire said.

"She's not talking about Cambridge either."

Claire felt overwhelmed and ill, yet kept looking as if some key would explain it all.

Black figures were now on the yellow walls, one a man dressed in red, holding a long chain that ended around the neck of a smaller figure, walking away, head down. In his other hand, the man threatened with a long whip.

Claire stood, rapt, unable to fathom the message, and only wished she could have drunk in the whole impression alone, undisturbed. She felt protective, but of Lucy or of Minna she was not sure.

"This is seriously troubled," Lucy said at last. "Is this, technically, *voodoo*?"

It came to Claire like the welling up of an unsuspected, subterranean source—a ready ability for lies, deception. "Minna wants to be an artist. She's exploring the island's colonial past. Its history of slavery."

Lucy's experience in Santa Fe, working with artists, had habituated her to a certain driven, obsessive quality in the creative life. All manner of bad behavior, past and future, could thus be explained away. It made for such a comforting notion, Claire tried to believe it herself for a moment.

"How come she never mentioned it?" Lucy asked.

"She's afraid she's no good."

"It's powerful, isn't it? I could see this hanging in downtown lofts. Should I talk to the gallery owner?"

"Eventually. Right now, officially, we haven't seen it yet."

Lucy left the room, singing:

How do you do that voodoo
That you do so well

That morning, Claire's whole body ached, and when Lucy injected her she screamed, pain shooting all the way to the bone. She refused anything to eat and would only suck ice chips.

When a car rolled into the driveway, Lucy ran to the window. "It's Minna!"

Don's car in the driveway now a source of rescue. Minna had ensconced herself, made herself part of the family. Yet who was she? Minna stepped out, wearing a beautiful yellow silk dress, elegant and expensive, but the tightness of it undoing its intended effect. Her gold earrings and bracelets marked her as if with price tags—bought. Don walked in after her, carrying thick, glossy bags from designer boutiques. More clothes in service of creating what effect? What life was Minna preparing herself for? She seemed too far gone to return to the Spartan life of grad school.

When Minna saw Claire in the living room, she kicked off her high heels and hurried to the couch. "Oh, *che,* not so good? You're hot."

Claire shook her head, turned away, embarrassed at the fevered burn of tears.

"I'm glad Lucy called. I'll fix you right up."

"What's that on your finger?" Lucy said, grabbing Minna's hand and holding it high. "A diamond?"

"Don proposed." Minna laughed. "I said I'd take the ring and think about it."

Claire was startled that her earlier lie about a proposal had come true, as if she had conjured it. Minna changed back into her plain housedress, and the pain in Claire's chest lessened in the security of her being back. Barefoot, Minna walked into the kitchen to mix one of the herbal drinks. Alone with Claire, Don sat on the couch. "I want to apologize about Mexico. I just freaked out when you got sick."

"What are your intentions?"

"What?"

"Toward Minna?"

He shrugged. "I'm wild about her."

"But she isn't one of your Hollywood starlets. One of your waitresses. She's complicated."

"That's what I love—"

Claire held up my hand. "No one mentioned love. Complicated as in depressive. She's very high-strung. You and I have talked about the little discrepancies."

Don remained silent.

"I'm trying to look out for her interests since she has no family here."

Don shook his head. "This job will be over by the end of summer, right?"

"True."

A tendon in Don's jaw throbbed. Claire couldn't take her eyes off it, the gauge of his truthfulness.

He stood up. "The thing I always admired about you is that you minded your own business."

Had they become enemies so quickly, fighting over Minna? When Lucy came back into the room, he said a curt good-bye and backed his car out of the driveway in such a hurry he ran over a hedge of French lavender.

"You called her?" Claire asked Lucy.

"Yes, and good thing she did," Minna said, coming back from the kitchen. The elixir stank of rotting and was a thick, unappealing brown.

"I can't."

"You will." But Minna relented and poured sugar into it. "Where did Don go?"

"He'd had enough of our house of women, I guess. He gives his love." Claire thought she saw a shadow pass across Minna's eyes for a moment, but then it was gone. She couldn't possibly love someone like Don. Or was Claire hoping that? What kind of friend, mother, was she, not to look out for the girl's well-being? His ordinariness didn't fit Claire's romance-novel idea of her.

"Let's get you in a cool bath," Minna said.

Lucy helped Claire undress, seeing for the first time the scar across Claire's chest. Lucy grimaced. "Can I touch it? Does it hurt?"

Claire felt embarrassed, but Minna was blind to the amputation as if it were as commonplace as her own body and said, "Course you can. It doesn't bite."

Minna ran the bath, and they both helped Claire into the tub, full of greenish water on top of which floated large, crumpled green leaves, resembling a lily pond. Down at eye level, Claire saw that they were lettuce leaves.

"Takes the heat away," Minna explained.

"I feel like I'm in a salad."

"Which is better—butter or romaine?" Lucy joked.

Claire lay back, and the cool water did soothe her. Her insides felt settled for the first time since Minna had left, as if her very presence healed.

"Don't leave again," Claire said, then, sensing the desperation in her request, added, "Until I'm better."

"She needs you." Puzzlement was in Lucy's eyes. "She's never needed anyone before."

"How about a smoke? For the appetite?" Minna asked.

"How about just for fun?" Lucy said. She looked at Claire and clapped her hand over her mouth.

"It's fine this once. A little pot for medicinal purposes."

Minna went to her room, and Claire worried about their trespassing. Would she notice, and if she did, would there be tantrums? But she returned with no sign of having seen anything changed, a joint pinched between her elegant, long fingers. The two girls sat cross-legged on the floor on either side of the tub and passed the joint back and forth. Ashes floated on top of the water and stuck to the lettuce leaves, now giving the impression more of a rain-sodden, muddy pond. Claire wasn't above using her scar, her illness, to coerce Lucy into staying. In a way, wouldn't it be healthy to force an adult-size responsibility on her? Both of her girls seemed to have kept a certain childishness. Had she spoiled them, protected them too well? She felt remorse for her behavior with Don—had it really been interest for Minna's welfare, or had it been possessiveness?

Lucy whispered to Minna the new protocol after the emergency-room visits. Claire heard *white blood cells, impaired organ function, toxicity.* Instead, Claire would simply take the daily injections.

During this time, she would have to be kept isolated, with a minimum of people.

"I wish I could stay," Lucy said. "But Javier promised to take me to Tampa. We planned it forever."

"Who's Javier? Who goes to Tampa?" Claire asked.

Lucy looked hurt. "You never listen."

Minna smiled and took a puff of the joint.

"Of course I want you to go." The words did not sound convincing, even to Claire herself.

"I'll come back and visit."

"Tampa in the summer should be nice," Minna said, and started to giggle.

Lucy burst out in a laugh. "Okay, okay. It's a business trip, but you never know."

"Maybe you could come stay longer next time?"

"I promise," Lucy said.

Claire fantasized about cool, white foods—milk shakes and ice cream, creamy French Brie cheese with water crackers. "Can someone make me a grilled cheese?"

But neither girl heard her as they sat on the tile floor, leaning back against the wall.

"Donald seems taken with you," Lucy said.

"Oh, Don. That's nothing. I just magicked him."

"Why don't you teach me how to magic a man," Lucy said, laughing but serious. Claire understood with a pang that her baby girl was lonely.

"That's easy," Minna said. "Problem is, it doesn't get you what you want. In fact, it almost guarantees the opposite."

"I *want* lunch," Claire said, and both girls laughed.

"She hasn't kept anything down in two days," Lucy said. "And now she has the munchies."

"Let's go cook you something."

They sat in the kitchen watching Minna cook.

"I'm so hungry," Claire wailed. "Hurry."

Lucy reached up to the cabinet above the refrigerator and pulled down a chocolate bar. Claire had forgotten all about that hiding place when the kids were small. When Josh had discovered it, he used a chair to reach it, then stole the whole supply and ate it in the orchard so he wouldn't have to share with his sisters.

"I didn't know chocolate was still stashed up there. Please, my dear baby girl, bring that here."

Lucy packed to leave. She hugged them both good-bye. Minna had become indispensable, and not the paintings on the walls of her room, nor the nights spent out with Don, dissuaded them from the belief that they had come across someone true and genuine, to be treasured and held on to.

Claire didn't know what the words on Minna's walls meant, didn't understand if her relationship with Don was about love or money, didn't have a clear idea of her past, but Minna fed her, sometimes bite by bite, when needed. Although she did not love Claire, had not known her long enough except for a superficial affection, was not her daughter, Claire received more understanding at Minna's hands than she dared ask for from her own children, more kindness than she could ever have hoped for from a stranger, perhaps more than she deserved. If that disinterested tenderness was not some kind of love, she didn't know by what other name to call it.

Chapter 12

For Claire the time after the girls' second leaving held a kind of perfection. The awkwardness of new acquaintance past, Minna and she settled into a companionship that was in ways as satisfying as her early days on the farm. All the songs and poems of the world focus exclusively on carnal love, which in many ways is the frailest and most fickle of bonds. Maternal love, familial caring, friendship, are all less overwhelming to the senses, but capable of greater steadiness due to that reticence. But the two relationships had an obvious difference: Forster and she had created an ever-widening circle of people—family, friends, workers, children—while Minna's and her new world was ever contracting.

After a few weeks of cheerfulness, Minna promptly sank into one of her dark moods. If Claire had called them blue earlier, now they verged on soul-crushing, funereal black. More dissatisfied with things than ever before, she was lethargic to the point of immobility most of the day, but when Claire asked her what was wrong, she waved her off: "Some of us have to struggle in this life, *che*."

"Tell me what it is."

Minna scowled.

"If not me, can you talk with your family?" Claire prodded.

"The answers aren't comforting. They use money like bait, see, to get me to do what they want."

"And what is that?"

"They are disappointed that I didn't marry the man they had picked out. But he left me."

"I knew it." Claire slapped her hands together.

Minna looked at her oddly but did not elaborate. "You think I'm one of those characters in my great-*grand-maman*'s books. I'm disinherited. That's why I was working at the coffee shop when I met Lucy."

In this brooding mood that continued for days, Minna accused Paz of stealing one of her gold bracelets from her room. Things had been moved around and were out of place. "I warned her to stay out of my room," Minna said. Claire confessed that Lucy had gone into the room to retrieve her belongings. Perhaps she had moved things.

"Well, she didn't steal my bracelet, did she?"

"No."

Paz, confronted, broke down in tears.

"Tell her to empty her purse," Minna said, her order a tyrant's.

"Are you sure it's missing?"

"It's in her purse," Minna said.

Claire paused, at an impasse. She knew that if she stood up against Minna, a price would be paid in moodiness and bad temper. "No, I won't ask," Claire said. "I know it's not there. I trust her."

"She stole from me!"

Paz snatched the purse before Claire could stop her, dumped the contents on the kitchen table. Of course it was filled with only the most innocuous of things, no jewelry to be found.

Claire nodded. Paz quit anyway.

Claire begged her to reconsider, but she refused to listen, waving Claire's words away as she gathered her belongings. "I can't stand working here." As she walked out the door, she whispered, "Be careful. She is a *mujer malvada.*" Claire felt a sinking guilt but could think of nothing to remedy the situation. Soon Octavio, Forster, and Mrs. Girbaldi would hear of this, and then there would be an even bigger outcry.

Claire went to Octavio to explain, but he refused to discuss it. "I was not happy her working with Minna. It's time for the next generation to be off the ranch." He did not wait for a response.

After Paz was gone, Claire brooded in silence for a few days, angry, and complained about having to call around to find a new cleaning woman.

"Nonsense. We don't need someone getting you sick. I'll clean. I could use the extra cash."

"I don't think that's a good idea," Claire said, but it was too late. She knew that no matter whom she hired, Minna would be on the warpath with that woman.

Now Minna scrubbed toilets, mopped floors, talked to Claire less and less. Each time she passed her it was with a heavy sigh. When Mrs. Girbaldi came over with a home-baked pie, the two women sat in the living room while Minna vacuumed the room, pushing the hose under their feet, the sound making conversation impossible.

Mrs. Girbaldi watched and nodded to Claire. "Good job," she mouthed.

But Claire worried. Minna worked with a kind of fury that made Claire edgy. Minna knelt on all fours and rubbed lemon oil into the wood floor so hard the wood groaned under her pressure. When she finished, her hands were raw.

Late at night, Claire heard Minna on the phone, speaking in what she now recognized was French Creole. She never seemed in a better mood afterward. Neither of them mentioned these calls.

When Claire asked her to play cards, she frowned. "Are you going to pay me for my time?"

"I didn't hire you to clean. It makes me feel guilty. I don't even care how the house looks."

Those were the magic words, and the old Minna returned, walking with Claire in the orchards, lolling endless hours over coffee in the morning. The tension in the house was released as if a storm had blown over.

Minna didn't refuse the extra pay for the work that she now no longer performed, and Claire didn't want to upset the delicate peace by bringing up money. It was hard to explain even to herself how she came to accept the changes in their relationship. Perhaps it was just habit, the slow, creeping acceptance of the formerly intolerable. She was not an unintelligent woman, nor was she weak, but she supposed if she was honest, she would admit circumstances had revealed in her a hungering for transformation. Minna seemed integral to this.

For instance. A big surprise was the relief she found in no longer having to conform to outside expectations. Until then she had not realized how she'd made a prison of each moment of her day. Where had this compunction come from for sparkling countertops, scoured sinks, bleached sheets, socks and shirts folded neatly in their drawers? Whom was she out to please? Who was grading her? What an unexpected liberation to let dust accumulate, let the grass grow long and verdant, to allow birds to build nests in the eaves, to forget the grocery store and eat stew for three days in a row, or corn on the cob, or strawberries dirt-smudged from the fields. Minna's laxness revealed that it mattered to no one, and now least of all to Claire.

* * *

There had come a time, after the trip to Mexico with the girls, when Claire could no longer stand miming her way through the empty days. After Forster left, she sat in her bedroom, still in her nightgown at five in the afternoon, hair unbrushed, when Lucy, home from school, came into her room, sat on the bed, and held her hand.

"Mom," she said, "would it be okay if we just pretended we were happy?"

The shock of what she was doing to her girls called her to action. And that's what she did all those years—conformed to the world's expectations. Cleaned the house, ran the farm, took care of the girls, and smiled and pretended, pretended and smiled. Finally, pretenses were falling away.

Before she left, Gwen had stocked the freezer with meals she'd cooked, but over the next weeks, these ran out. For a while, Minna got motivated and cooked her own dishes: chicken and rice, plantains and beans. But these inspirations were erratic. Some days she would simply pick vegetables and fruit from the garden, and that would be what they ate. A few days they simply scooped avocado directly out of the shell, or smashed it on toast, drizzling it with lemon and salt. Ate oranges off the trees.

Minna no longer shut the windows or the doors, so it was as if they had no indoors, or rather that the rooms had become derelict and abandoned. A great interpenetration of the in with the out. Breezes fluttered papers on the couch, ruffled pages of an open book, ballooned the curtains. Sparrows tumbled through the windows and perched on the rafters, flying into furniture and walls until they found their escape. Feathers drifted onto the floor. Lizards sunned on the doorstop. It felt like living inside a ruin.

Yes, dirt collected on the tables, cobwebs in the doorways. A baby garden snake was found coiled in the bathroom. The floor was gritty, and the soles of Claire's feet turned brown after walking barefoot across the room, but she was happy as she had never been happy in her spotless house. Dishes crowded the sink and counter, mold bloomed in the shower, but a great peacefulness was in the hours. It was as if from sheer will they had somehow stopped the track of time. Literally, Minna had disengaged the grandfather clock, saying the counting of the hours depressed her.

One afternoon as they watched the news, street riots were shown in some small island country Claire didn't catch the name of. Minna watched, eyes widening till the whites showed, like the rolling eyes of a frightened horse. She got up unsteadily and turned the TV off. After that, they never watched television again, never listened to the radio. Claire got used to silence and for the first time in her life realized her own thoughts required a stillness she had never allowed.

Sometimes when they sat outside, they heard the workers' voices far away, but the noise was indistinct and melodious and of no consequence, like birdsong or the buzzing of bees at work. Only for a special treat would Minna put on a CD, and then listening to Mozart or to jazz or reggae took on a richness unimaginable. Was that what heaven would feel like if one believed in it?

As summer drew on, the house grew hot in the daytime, and they slept in later and later. Claire woke to the smell of earth from the fields, citrus baking in the scorching sun. When it was unbearable inside, Minna swam naked in the pool while Claire dangled her legs in the deep end.

One morning by the pool, she noticed that Minna was putting on weight when a noise startled her. The pool man stood there, unexpected, holding his net and scrubber, lewdly grinning. For a moment, Claire felt panicked, the shadow of a memory of male intrusion. She was unused to the eyes of strangers. The women both wrapped themselves in towels and hurried inside. Claire was surprised that Minna, despite her brazenness, hid in her room. After he left, Minna insisted on firing him.

"Who will clean it?" Claire asked, knowing already the deed was done.

"I will."

"But . . ."

"But what?"

And so with time, the pool, too, returned to its primordial nature, turned from blue to green. Leaves floated on its surface, and dirt collected on the bottom till it resembled a pond.

Claire added the pool man's wages onto Paz's wages onto her assistant's salary, with no protestations from Minna. None of this bothered her for the simple fact of Minna's increasing goodwill. She was simply buoyant, and her happiness transferred itself to Claire. They were like children going to camp during the summer, the ordinary, workaday world temporarily suspended except for the injections each morning that reminded Claire of her illness.

The heat grew so intense, they moved entirely outdoors, using the inside of the house only for storage. When the temperature passed one hundred, they lived on lawn chairs under the deep canopy of a large avocado tree next to the pool, mirroring Octavio's makeshift headquarters out in the orchard.

Minna went barefoot, wore cotton overalls cut off short on the thigh. Thin, white strips of cloth were threaded through her braided hair. Bare of makeup, shiny with sweat, she looked like a wholesome teenager. Despite the heat, Claire tried to keep covered. Minna looked at her perspiring face, then reached over and yanked off her baseball cap.

"Don't," Claire said.

"Enjoy the air."

After a minute, Claire had to admit it felt better, the air dry against her scalp. She tried to forget what she must look like. "I'm tired of being ugly and old."

"It feels the same when people stare at you because you're beautiful. Or because you're black. Staring is staring."

The next time Minna caught Claire despondent over her appearance in a mirror, she took all the mirrors down in the house and put posters in their place: the living room became Greece, and the den turned into Italy, and the dining room, which they never went into, languished as Finland. In the bathroom, Minna painted over the seventies-style mirrored walls with great swathes of blue-gray color so that one could only see one's ghostly shape moving as if through fog.

As the house fell into a swoon of neglect, Claire tried to take an interest in the farm, but it was no use. For years she had overseen and shared the decisions on the daily work with Octavio, but over the last months, as she spent less and less time out in the fields, everything ran just as smoothly as it had before. Trees were sprayed and pruned, the irrigation ran, the pickers came and went, all without her lifting a finger. Now when Claire forced herself, the long walks out in the field were difficult, and she arrived exhausted, unsteady, more nuisance than help.

She suspected that her previous efforts had been in vain, that Octavio had never needed her input, had consulted her as a courtesy. With Octavio's new coolness, Claire had to admit what she had never before considered. How could he not feel that three Mejia generations had worked their lives away on the ranch for nothing more than a decent living? Of course he wanted better for Paz. Forster's family had bought when buying was cheap, and that piece of paper allowed them the lion's share of the money, allowed them a home and belonging that was denied Octavio's family. In her new state, human arrangement and history seemed a strange and arbitrary thing. When did a person really own something?

One afternoon Minna and Claire were napping under the tree, lethargic from the heat. Claire dreamed of troubling things and woke to see Minna staring at the railing, specifically at two large fruit rats as large as house cats staring back. On the railing between them lay a half-eaten avocado. Both sides were quiet for so long that Claire began to think she was still dreaming, but when she moved her arm, the rats scurried away, the avocado falling onto the deck. Minna and she blinked at each other as if they had just woken from the same dream.

"Why are you so at ease with me? More than your daughters?"

"I can't tell them things, do you understand?"

"I do, *che*. You and I, we know pain."

"I want to protect them." Ever since the girls had left, Claire had been bursting with the desire to talk to Minna about her visitation. "I need to tell you something."

"Yes?" Her eyes were closed.

Claire pressed her hands together, plunged on. "While you were gone . . . the Fourth of July . . . one day in the kitchen . . . there was a flame."

"A flame?" Still Minna did not open her eyes, and her seeming disinterest egged Claire on.

"I saw him. My boy."

Now Minna opened her eyes, sat up with a big smile. "Good! Why didn't you tell me earlier? It's starting to work."

"What is?" Claire asked, confused by Minna's lack of surprise.

"Come."

She took Claire by the arm and led her through the broiling house, up the tinder-dry stairs, and into her bedroom. Each time she opened the door, Claire was again surprised by the changes.

Now the figures on the wall had multiplied again until they squeezed against each other, became as dense as a forest, so thick she could hardly tell the color of the wall for the profligacy of the creatures crowding it. The paint was so thick in places that the figures were beginning a life of three-dimensionality, beginning to lift themselves off the wall, like Michelangelo's prisoners freeing themselves out of stone. Minna directed Claire's attention to the middle of the room, to a large link chain, coated with a thick, gluey bright green paint, hanging from the ceiling and ending in a fabric-filled pail on the floor.

"This is the *poto mitan*. It attracts the *iwa,* the spirits, to come."

"You don't believe in this?"

Minna grinned. "Why not? No harm done, right?"

Claire turned and studied the figures on the wall. The silence stretched between them.

"Just fun and games, right?" Minna said. "Like a psychology course taught in pictures. No black magic or zombies."

They both laughed, thin, shallow, insincere sounds that bounced off the hot, dusty glass of the windows.

"You've never seen him before, your son, have you?"

"No. Never."

"It's not a bad thing. It's like a dream you make for something not finished in your real life. You finish it inside, in your heart."

Chapter 13

The intense heat continued, and that, coupled with the isolation of illness, made time become elastic. With it insufferable to be in the kitchen, much less cook over a hot stove, Minna and Claire ate bowls of cold cereal with milk, adding nuts and bananas and berries. When the milk ran out, they poured fresh orange juice over the cereal and finally succumbed to eating it dry right out of the box. When the cereal was gone, they finished the almonds, walnuts, and pecans out of the pantry by the handful, picked strawberries and blackberries from the garden, ate oranges, tomatoes, and avocados. Hungry, sometimes Claire ate fruit straight off the tree, not quite ripe, and suffered stomachaches. She pulled carrots out of the earth, held them under the hose, then ate them, warm and sweet. The absence of the debilitating effects of chemo resembled a return to health; hunger was a return of vitality. It allowed her to entertain the ironic hope that she would soon be strong enough to endure the poisoning again.

The girls called on schedule again. *Monday, Tuesday, Wednesday, Thursday. How're you? Fine. How're you? Great. Couldn't be better.*

Octavio was a shadowy presence, only intruding on them once a week when he would stop at the house, stand below the porch, and fill Claire in on the details of work. It was as if he wanted to emphasize that he understood that he, too, was only an employee, subject to termination at any time like his daughter. An aloofness had entered their relationship since Paz had left, but Claire planned to repair the damage later, as soon as she had energy enough.

When the time came to have her checkup with the doctor, Minna and she spent the morning showering and dressing in a combination of dread and excitement at returning to the world. Claire searched for her wig, but could not find it and had to resort to a scarf. Her hands shook with nerves, both from the upcoming verdict and at the jolt of unaccustomed activity.

"What's wrong here is that we need to get in the car to do anything. It would be better if we could walk to the grocery, to the laundry, the doctor," Minna said.

Claire shook her head. "No one walks in California."

"Well, they should." They giggled as if drunk.

"It makes people nervous to see pedestrians. It seems unreliable. They wonder what you've done wrong to not have a car."

They stopped at the IHOP and ordered two breakfasts each: one of eggs and bacon, the other of pancakes. Waiting for her food, Claire felt overwhelmed by the number of people around them, the noise. When someone sneezed a few tables down, she jumped. Had she become such a recluse? After their food deprivation, they now gorged until they could hardly move. But Claire only managed to eat half her portion before she was full to bursting. They sat back in their booth, giddy. Minna clowned, putting a smudge of whipped cream from a pancake on the end of her nose, while Claire laughed, holding her stomach in pain.

People in the surrounding booths turned and stared, but that only increased their hilarity, until Claire feared she would be sick from laughing so hard and long. Had she forgotten how to act in public? So-called polite society?

The waitress, a big, tired-looking Swede with graying blond hair, eyed Minna with distrust. Although Minna ordered for both of them, it was as if she were invisible. The waitress talked only to Claire, handed her the bill, returned the change to her, which she pointedly handed over to Minna. Unimpressed at the correction, the waitress turned her back on them. They revenged themselves with a nickel tip.

At the hospital, the doctor came in and sat studying Claire's charts, still holding a grudge over Mexico, refusing her any small talk since that disobedience. He stroked a thin goatee he was growing, reluctantly satisfied with Claire's white blood cell count but unhappy with the weight loss.

"Are you eating? Too nauseous?"

"Trying . . ." Claire said. Forgetting was more like it, she thought.

"After this much of a break, I don't see the efficacy in starting the chemo again. If you agree, we'll move straight to radiation. Provided you put on weight."

He could not see Claire was blooming from the inside, blooming and blooming, alive in a way she hadn't been in a long while. He could not see that she would no longer be defeated by anything as prosaic as cancer.

Bringing in the bags of groceries from the packed trunk of the car was like Christmas morning. Claire ate a few spoonfuls from the tubs of ice cream, a single butter cookie from each of the tins. Minna boiled a huge pot of spaghetti and meatballs; after three meals, the amount still in the pot was hardly dented. They did this with the knowledge that these were treasured feast days, following doctor's orders. Claire's appetite would wane as surely as the moon, a self-induced famine would inevitably follow because Minna would lose her will, forget, and let food run out again.

On a Wednesday, Claire picked up the phone to Gwen's call. When Claire told her that the chemotherapy was over, that now it was six weeks of radiation, Gwen started to cry.

"What's wrong?"

"Does this mean you're okay?"

"The worst is over." After Claire hung up, she stared at the phone. Minna walked by and asked what was wrong.

"I think Gwen loves me."

"What kind of daughter doesn't love her mother?"

In celebration of the end of chemo, Minna turned on the pool lights, which lit the now murky green into a romantic grotto. By candlelight, she brought out a tarnished silver ice bucket from the dining room—polishing silver another thing that had gone by the wayside. They popped open a bottle of French champagne Don had given Minna. Claire sipped one glass while Minna finished off the rest of the bottle. When the ice had melted, skeletons of insects floated to the top from the dusty bottom of the bucket.

"To Claire. The survivor."

"I feel more like the kid passed on to the next grade who didn't quite complete the work. But the chemo is over. Unless there is a recurrence."

"Don't say that word," Minna whispered. "Words have power."

"You're right. Survivor."

"A survivor is the most important thing to be. Nothing else matters."

Claire sipped her drink.

"The spirits are aligning."

They sat, the sky softening to a velvety blue. Clouds were coming in, the unheard-of promise of a summer shower. Birds roosted in the trees, feeling the change in the air in their bones, the promise of real moisture, unlike the irrigation. The pool was a mottled, embryonic soup, like the stirrings of a universe. Like housekeeping, cleaning the pool another useless worry to be let go. Claire decided she liked this more natural pond incarnation. Was that part of surviving, too, allowing things to morph into new uses?

"I think it needs fish," Minna said.

Claire shook her head. "They'd die in the chemicals."

"The chemicals are gone. Fish will eat the algae. Carp. Maybe koi. And goldfish. Except they get eaten by the bigger ones. A hard fish world."

"I want to give you something."

Minna grinned. "Aren't you the suitor."

Claire went into the house, which ticked in the cooling air like a car engine. When she turned on the light, a small lizard on the wall blinked. She dug in her closet and brought out a necklace Forster had given her years ago, a heavy gold filigree from Turkey, a place they had dreamed of going to but never did. The necklace consisted of semiprecious stones embedded in elaborate goldwork. It had always been too extravagant for her, and she thought Forster gave it to her in consolation.

"I can't take it," Minna said as Claire draped it over her collarbones, reaching behind her neck to fasten the clasp.

It glowed against Minna's skin as Claire imagined it would. Without thinking she pulled down the sides of Minna's T-shirt so that her shoulders were bared.

"You should never take that off. It was made for you."

"Wear only your necklace?" Minna laughed and pulled off her T-shirt. Underneath she wore her two-piece bathing suit. Only the necklace and covered breasts and the bulge of belly. She rose and unzipped her shorts. Although it was clear even in clothes how narrow-hipped Minna was, in her seminakedness she was surprisingly boyish, unsuited for maternity—straight torso, muscular thighs and buttocks, no rounded softness except for the stomach.

Minna jumped in the air and gave a yell, then danced around the pool, the glow of the pool burnishing her skin. Wind started to blow in the trees, and the moon was covered by swiftly moving clouds that bunched against each other. When she came closer, the candles caught the necklace, made it flash and spark as if on fire. Claire felt a great contentment seeing it on her, as if it had been returned to the person who could give it its due. How she would have liked to trade places and live her life in Minna's young body.

"Dance with me," Minna commanded, but Claire couldn't. Even though she took joy in the sight of Minna, her ease and lack of inhibition, it made Claire feel even more prudish, more nunnish. Minna's dance brought to the surface all Claire had never been, that was no longer possible. Had there ever been a time when she could have been more like Minna, less like herself? Why had she rushed into marriage, rushed into maternity, without any experience or thought to what she was losing thereby? She regretted nothing, except that making one choice canceled out the possibilities of so many others. As she continued to watch, there was the smallest opening in Minna's dance, like a dervish spinning for enlightenment, a pinhole through which Claire caught a glimpse of other possible lives than the one she had chosen.

After dancing a few minutes, Minna arched her body into a bow and dove into the pool, her dark form slicing the light open. Claire cringed, thinking of the necklace, but after Minna swam, she walked up the steps, glistening wet, and the necklace shone even more brightly. The things of this world were meant to be used, or they wasted. The necklace had always scared Claire—she would try it on, take it off, opting for something smaller, duller. Over the years, she had cleaned, preserved, and hidden it away in its velvet box. Wasted it. Minna was a perfect fit—the two matched in boldness.

"I'm so happy tonight," Minna said.

Claire realized that she was, too. So happiness could be like this, dependent on nothing.

"I don't want this to ever end. I never want to leave you."

Claire wanted to say, *Me, too,* but she didn't. "You're going to go find a man. If not Don, someone."

"I have Don. When I need him."

They laughed.

"This is as good as it can be," Minna said.

"Watching you reminds me of Antoinette swimming with Rochester."

"You and your books." Minna turned away, suddenly annoyed. "You ignore what's right in front of you."

Claire cursed herself for breaking the mood. They were silent, the harshness of Minna's words jarring both of them.

Minna stretched out on the concrete, water beading off her body. "There was a book," she said, her voice conciliatory, "that made an impression on me. Called *Temporary Shelter.*"

"What was it about?"

"Oh, I don't know. I never read it."

Now it was Claire's turn to be irritated. "Why not?"

"Because . . . the title told me everything I wanted to know. If I read it, and the author meant it to refer to the cost of cats in China, well, then the whole thing would be ruined, don't you see?"

"No, I don't see. That's absurd."

Minna lifted her eyebrows and sighed, summoning the infinite patience of talking to an especially dim-witted child. "What you want are the holes, the gaps, the blank spaces that your imagination can fill. There's nothing in life more deadly than finished."

"I can think of things."

Minna rolled onto her stomach, resting her head in her cupped palms. "What about men? I never hear about anyone. Was Forster the only love of your life?"

"That's all over for me."

"Why?"

Claire pointed to Minna's breasts. "I don't have those two lovelies."

"A woman is more than her boobs. There's what's between her legs, too." She reached her hand between her own legs and laughed.

Claire said nothing, the deep heat of a blush rising up her body.

"Would you like Don? I mean, he's a good lover. I could arrange it."

"Don't be absurd." Claire thought of Rochester, how he cast sidelong glances at Antoinette, how sometimes she seemed so alien. She did not like this side of Minna, this coarseness. Was she trying purposely to provoke? "Should I seduce him wig or sans wig?"

"I hate that mop." Minna wagged her behind back and forth, then carried the glasses inside as a few raindrops spat across the pool. "If you change your mind, he's yours."

"I don't understand you."

"Minna is Minna, that's all."

"I'm going to bed. I'm tired," Claire said. "If we're lucky it might rain."

August rain in California every bit as rare as the necklace around Minna's neck.

Dressed in her nightgown and in bed, Claire read. The sheets were crumb-filled and musty and hadn't been changed for a long time. Minna came in wearing jeans and a T-shirt. Her scalp was tan-colored and smooth, as if she had shaved her hair off, and Claire did a double take before Minna burst out laughing.

"I shaved the hair off," she said, pulling off the wig that was now a simple latex scalp.

"That was expensive!" But then Claire too, laughed. "Gwen will be furious."

"Don's picking me up."

"The bed needs changing," Claire said, grumpy, dreading the empty, creaking house overtaking her. She didn't want to have to go downstairs and languish in front of the TV to avoid the loneliness of early morning. "Have him sleep here."

"Here?"

"I don't want to be alone," Claire said, brusque, as if she were giving something away.

"Are you sure? I can send him home afterwards."

"No, I want you two here."

"Even though we are sinning?"

"I'm not that old-fashioned."

But Claire went to sleep right away, not wanting to be confronted with Don's presence after all. Despite what she said, a part of her wanted Minna's company to herself. Hours later she woke up to noises outside. Rain, a miracle in August. She went to the window to witness it and saw Minna and Don swimming in the murky pool. Quickly she took a step back.

They circled each other, tighter and tighter, and then Donald grabbed her, and she yelled, kicking at him as they struggled, then kissed. Claire stood in the lonely dark, unseen, and felt a molten thread. She had assumed desire was dead inside her. Was Minna testing? Taunting? She remembered those long-ago days when Forster's and her lovemaking had formed the center of their days and not just its afterthought, and later its memory.

She did not move away, but stood, riveted. Don carried Minna up the steps of the pool and laid her down on the lounge chair. He stood above her, gazing down, and Claire knew that loveliness that he looked upon. Even after all these months, Minna's beauty still had the power to shock. "Inside?" he asked. Minna shook her head. "Crazy girl," he said. Minna stayed absolutely still for the longest time so that Claire held her own breath, then Minna smiled and arched and spread her legs apart. Donald lay on top of her, unable to stand the separation any longer.

Claire's own legs turned liquid. A siren's call, the knowledge that she should move away quickly, but she didn't. What was wrong with her own sense of propriety that she stood there like a Peeping Tom? Minna pushed his face away from hers and looked up into the darkness of the window and then . . . smiled. Knowing and feeling Claire's watching. Yet another consummation between them.

Minna wrapped her legs around his hips, and Claire broke away, fled into the bathroom and barred a door no one would try to open. She sat on the cold, sobering tile with her back against the door. Of course, she could not stop seeing them, the image burned onto her retina. She turned on the shower, undressed, let the hot water pelt down on her. Tears mixed with water. The sight of them unspeakable and beyond lovely, a perverse, indecipherable gift.

Chapter 14

Minna, voicing alarm that Claire's weight loss might put the upcoming radiation treatments in jeopardy, went on a campaign to fatten her up. She cursed at her own prior laziness and went into a frenzied bout of cleaning and washing and cooking that lasted a week before sputtering out once again. During that period, she dressed up every day and drove to the grocery, coming back with improbably large bags of groceries for only two people. She cooked island dishes of spicy hot fish, basted pork chops, and baked a delicious dessert of layers of yellow cake, slathered with guava preserves, covered in a thick coating of whipped cream.

None of it gave Claire an appetite, but she couldn't disappoint her. That's what Minna counted on; each uptick on the scale was considered a personal victory. Her solicitude touched Claire, thinking no further to its root cause.

On one of those shopping days, Claire stood in the kitchen, making a stab at the piles of dirty dishes. The more Minna cooked, the more dishes stacked up, and with three or four meals a day being prepared, the place was in constant turmoil like a restaurant.

Claire scoured away at the copper handles of the sink, which had tarnished from neglect. When Octavio knocked at the back door, the disruption so startled Claire she dropped a plate against the dish rack.

Embarrassed, she straightened the scarf on her head. No mistaking the look of shock when he saw her up close. She wished there were a porch and screen in between them as at their weekly meeting, or that they were out in the orchards, with open spaces to distract them. Just moments before, she had felt stronger than she had in weeks, but still, health was a relative thing—compared to her former state, she probably appeared forlorn indeed. Her old robe hung on her like a tent; the skin at her temples was so thin and fragile that nets of blue veins were as visible as the lines on a map. Of course, there was the not-hair thing—not only missing from the scalp, but also not eyebrows, not eyelashes. A stripped and boiled look.

"Disculpe por molestarla—" he said.

"No, no. Come in. We haven't had a chance to visit."

"Esta ella aquí?"

"No." Claire knew that as observant as he was, he would have noticed the car was gone, had probably watched Minna drive away over half an hour before.

"There is something you must see. *Lo se estas enferma.*"

"Let me dress."

"Apurate, por favor. Before she returns."

Claire threw clothes on without thinking, dread in her heart, an echo of the first trouble, the one after which nothing was ever the same. After each large trauma, one was never as devastated, or as strong, again. Octavio, she feared, was determined to reveal something that there would be no recovering from.

She dressed and returned to the kitchen, steeled, ready to blame the messenger.

They talked of the recent rain as they headed, inevitably,

toward the portion of the farm that was unofficially off-limits. The explanation given to newcomers was not vetted by Claire; she didn't want to know how he chose to handle it. Sometimes she could tell the workers knew from their eyes, but now that pity could be for multiple causes. Many of the men came from rural areas of Mexico, religious and superstitious in equal parts. The death of a child was seen as a tragic omen. Octavio was too practical to make unnecessary difficulties for himself. Perhaps reticence was chosen as the most productive course.

As they continued walking, Claire noticed workers in ones and twos dropping the work they were at and mobbing behind them. Sweat began to form under her arms, at the back of her neck. Crowds now frightened her. By the time the asphalt road gave way to gravel, twenty or more workers were ganged behind them. At the last bend she saw the *vévé*, a symbolic drawing, on the ground, made from cornmeal that stood out yellow against the brown earth.

Since Paz's firing, Octavio had spoken carefully of Minna, but now he spewed a bitter list of grievances: "She treats the workers badly. Bossing, cursing, threatening to have them fired." Appalled at Minna's cruelty to Paz before she quit, her disregard for Octavio, her arrogance to those whose names she didn't bother to learn, still Claire had stood by and done nothing since her last chastisement to make sure the bad behavior ended. She turned a blind eye, and Octavio was no longer allowing that to continue. She felt both anger and gratefulness to him for forcing her to deal with that delinquency. Was it possible that Minna was really bad? Especially when she was capable of such tenderness to Claire?

She leaned on the further excuse that this was a cultural difference, that owning a plantation in the Caribbean implied very different things. Weren't there stories from the old days in California—ranchers who got it into their head they could play God? Who beat their workers? Took the laborers' daughters as

common-law wives? It was only a recent phenomenon that employees were prized and well treated. In a perverse light, couldn't the ranch be seen as a modern incarnation of a plantation? The Baumsarg farm had always had the reputation of paying high wages and treating people well. Claire had lectured Minna on this but suspected she only paid her lip service.

Now Claire stopped and stared down at the *vévé,* as intricate and temporary as a Tibetan sand painting that monks destroy at completion.

She recognized the figure's purpose from Minna's room—a drawing to call down the *iwa,* the spirits—but she dreaded to find out what more lay ahead.

"The men are not happy," Octavio said, but Claire no longer listened, driven by the sight in front of her.

The lemon tree had been transformed. The lower limbs sawed off, exposing the trunk, the cut spaces like wounds, the base saturated in red, yellow, and green. Figures were painted—a man with three horns coming out of his head, a mother clutching a child. Snakes and crosses. A rope hung from the fattest upper limb, and on it were strung empty liquor bottles. The rope and bottles couldn't be denied as resembling a noose, and the stubbed candles in the ground suggested miniature headstones. Nothing terribly upsetting after seeing Minna's room, yet here, in the open, the tableau had a menacing feel.

"The workers, they say this is *malo.* That she has cast *un espiritu maligno* on the ranch."

Claire laughed in his face, loud and scornful, so that the workers behind her were sure to hear. "I told Minna to do this. This is her artwork. An art installation. I can't help that some don't understand—"

"A few men have been in car crashes. Some of their wives have had miscarriages."

"Surely you're not going to blame those things on this?"

But Octavio would not back down. "She came and offered me money if I say nothing."

"Really?" Claire said, trying to hide surprise. "That's hard to understand because I already knew about it. Maybe she just wanted to surprise me when it was completed."

"She hit me when I refused to take her money." She saw his face turn a brick color, sweat beaded on his forehead.

"I think you misunderstood her."

"*A lo mejor,* maybe," Octavio said. "But some of the men see these things and think they make *maldición*. They don't want to work here any longer."

"Well. Well."

"Why do you let this happen?" he pressed. "This is something very dangerous here, *entiendes*?"

A car was speeding down the road; Claire had been straining to hear it all along. Absurdly, she wanted to bolt and run away. It came into view with Minna's tight face behind the windshield. She skidded to a stop in the gravel, jumped out of the car as if it were on fire.

"What are you doing out here?"

"I insisted Octavio give me the grand tour," she said, needing to lie to Minna more than to keep up pretenses in front of Octavio.

"Get in," Minna ordered.

"Why did you do this?" Claire said, not moving, and her tone, shrill and pleading and intimate at the same time, canceled the witness of the men around them.

A shadow passed the corner of her eye. Ready for the supernatural, Claire was surprised that it was simply a piece of rotten fruit that hit Minna in the neck. It burst wet against her skin, ran down her blue blouse; flecks of reddish gore even splattered as far as Claire's white T-shirt. A tomato.

"Who did that?" Minna yelled, but the crowd of men just stood, impassive and quiet as stones.

Claire turned to Octavio. "Help us."

As she spoke, a whole volley of oranges and dirt clods hit Minna in the back, on her arms, her legs. Hit Claire, as she tried to protect Minna with her own body. The words *bruja* and *puta,* and other words, until Claire's own curses joined the roar. Octavio yelled for the men to stop, then, when that proved ineffective, ran into the crowd and cuffed the nearest ones. Claire ran for safety, pushing Minna ahead of her, to the car.

By the time they reached the house, Claire was shaking.

"Why the tree? You know how I feel!"

"The spell needs to be in place."

"You tried to bribe Octavio."

"Never. He lies."

"You are crazy. You're making me crazy." The evidence of the tree had been a break in the trance—a moment when the frog realized it was boiling.

* * *

Claire sat in the chair on the front porch and waited, ready for more trouble. Another attack by men. Her mental state snapped so naturally right back to fifteen years before, it was as if the intervening years had never been. When Minna brought her a glass of water, she hissed at her, "Get in. What are you doing out here?" Turning Minna's words back on her. Minna's eyes filled with hurt, and Claire relented, all the while scanning the driveway.

"I should have told you," Minna said. "It's my fault."

"Of course not," Claire said, then wondered if it was. "What were you doing, anyway?"

"We have the spirits of the house on our side, now we must go after the spirits of the farm. You've heard of zombies? The spirit of a place can also be zombi; it needs to be courted with flowers, fruit, worship."

"It scared them."

"They're evil old goats. Ignorant."

"A misunderstanding. They are superstitious."

"There was a pregnant woman who worked on our coffee plantation. She went into labor in the fields and crawled into a curing shed for the beans, and then she goes ahead and dies in breech. So much blood . . . blood so that the floor stayed red no matter how many times we washed it. The shed was cursed. Workers refused to stay. My grandfather ordered that the green coffee beans inside be burnt along with the shed, and only that satisfied everyone. We lost money that year. He took it out of their wages the following season. See, he understood the old ways." Minna laughed.

"Why are you laughing?" Claire said, sickened.

"The air was scented with coffee for days and days. No one slept for a week. We inhaled caffeine with each breath."

"So I should burn down the tree? Or fire you? To pacify them?"

Minna turned her lip down, moody. "When I was a girl, our workers would get restless every year or so. Father said you could set the calendar by it. They would get lazy, threaten him with their demands. Then he watched a few days and picked out the one others listened to. He used a whip on him and made the rest watch. That broke their fever, and they would be peaceful and docile again for a whole year."

Claire couldn't bear to hear any more. "We don't do uncivilized things like that. Go inside now."

But Minna lingered at the porch railing, looking out at the fast-fading light. "Perhaps they will hurt me. Or you. Or worse."

"No one will hurt us. Octavio will get to the bottom of it."

"I'm scared," Minna said, but she did not look scared.

"Get inside." It was Claire who was now terrified.

"Octavio hates me after what happened with Paz. He says obscene things to me when you aren't around. You don't know him."

"Why didn't you tell me before?" Claire said, accusing.

"You wouldn't believe me."

"I'm tired. I don't know what to believe anymore."

"Men are men. It seemed harmless. Letting out his anger. I decided not to do anything to keep the peace."

"Really?" Claire said. "Is that the way it *really* happened, or are you maybe just exaggerating?"

"He told lies to the other men. To turn them against me. Against you. Lies about us."

"None of this is your fault?"

As they argued, Octavio's pickup pulled up to the house, and her answer was lost.

He stopped and peered out the windshield at the porch, took in the sight of Claire, distraught, in the rocking chair, and Minna balanced on the railing, one leg over the banister, a foot curled around the rung. He set his mouth, got out of the car, slamming the loose door, and took heavy, defeated steps toward them. Not until this last encounter had he understood that Claire, too, was afraid of this girl. But once again, he was helpless to intervene.

He glanced warily at Minna, and she smiled back at him as if to a lost friend.

Claire worried what Minna might do. "Get inside."

"But I should offer—"

"Get inside!"

Octavio nodded at her exit and sat down on the lowest step of the porch, facing toward the orchards. This was only a show of control on Claire's part. The girl would get what she wanted.

"Sit up here," Claire said, but he waved her off. She knew that moment that she had lost him.

"I do fine here."

"What happened out there?" she asked. Surprised when he shrugged and then chuckled.

"The men, one of them, Bernie, his car is stolen. Salvador, his wife run away. Easier to blame a tree for bad luck. They are just simple men from a country full of these superstitions."

"They attacked us."

"Her. You were in the way. They say she is from island where witches are. They say her black skin is *maleficio.* That she is a slave to the devil."

Claire could hardly sit, head and heart and stomach filled as if she would break apart. "That's disgusting."

"They are cruel, but that is their feeling."

"Are you leaving?"

When Claire first ran the place alone, Forster told her that the workers might not take orders from a woman. They would smile and joke but not obey. She had been proud of her bond with Octavio, thought it was beyond simple worker and boss. Over the years, they had formed, if not an equal at least a candid friendship. His attitude now made her feel betrayed.

"I don't care how they feel. They work for me. When they are on my property, I will not have any person attacked, do you understand?"

"*Entiendo,* but it makes no difference," he said, looking down at his thick hands, strong as small shovels. "Why didn't you stop her?" He pressed his palms together as if in supplication, certainly not to her, but to whatever power was making him sit there and suffer unjustly on those porch steps. Maybe this was the excuse he finally needed to return to Mexico?

"Why do they hate her so?"

"She cursed the ranch. They say she has dropped blood from between her legs onto the dirt."

"And what do you think?"

"I cannot stay. They no longer trust me. If I don't stand up for them, I lose their respect. Then I am useless to you."

Claire's head was spinning, changes occurring so drastically she couldn't imagine. Octavio predated Claire, Forster, all of them. "I want you to fire every man on the ranch. Because you've allowed this poison to fester, and all of them are contaminated. I can't trust them. Do you understand?"

"*Claro.*"

"Everyone will be paid a month's salary. Because it's unfair, the circumstances. I also want you gone."

He wiped his face and looked calmer now, relieved. There was no turning back for either of them.

As he got up to leave, Claire hesitated to reach out her hand. End their relationship by shaking hands, after all these years? Unthinkable to hug him. Minna would be watching from a window. Claire felt a galling spike of pride that Minna would see herself defended. Would Claire be the first person to offer her such unconditional loyalty?

"I will miss you, my friend."

He stood and remained silent for a moment, then walked to his truck. His heart was so full of things to say that of course he could say none of then. "*Ten cuidado,* be careful," he said, then jumped into the truck's cab and pulled away.

* * *

Claire moved as if underwater, grabbed a broom, and swiped at the wooden porch, stunned at the breaking of ties in a few minutes that had bound the farm together for decades. How quickly things could be destroyed. It all felt out of control. She had never intended to lose Octavio, and especially now when she could not afford to consider things outside and apart from her own body. His leaving felt like an amputation. Tears stung, but she had had no choice. The awful truth was she could less afford losing Minna. How treacherous one became in time of need.

The evening continued on its path, cruelly oblivious in its loveliness. Only Claire was estranged. The pepper trees on each side of the driveway bowed inward, the long trails of spiked leaves touching earth. Light daubed the mountaintops with pink, but she was in no mood to enjoy it. A heavy trail of orange and lemon mixed with the astringent of eucalyptus and the dull smell of dirt: the perfume of home. A squawking in the nearby grove revealed the wobbly, fluttering flight of a covey of wild parrots as they searched the unguarded fruit trees for their dinner. She loved this spot of earth more than anywhere else, yet for all her efforts she couldn't keep it still, unchanged, its inhabitants free of harm.

Minna came out of the house, meek, testing Claire's temper. She hummed a tune to herself and picked leaves off the wooden steps. "He's gone?"

"Satisfied?"

She walked over and knelt at Claire's feet, hugging her so tightly that the bones of her knees pressed against each other, causing pain. "No one ever loved me more than something else."

Claire's heart gave in just the slightest, although her words still came out harshly. "Because I fired a man unjustly?"

"You took my side. Like family. You didn't listen to his lies."

"I tried to take the right side. Which was yours?" Why did Claire persist now the act was done? A sinking feeling that could only be remorse. Lies all around her, and she had grabbed the most convenient one and called it truth. She kept seeing Octavio driving away, sure that could not be the just solution. "What'll I do now? We're going into high season with tons of work and no foreman."

"I'll fix it, my *doudou*."

"How? How could you possibly fix that? Like the pool? Like the house?"

"Trust me."

"Never mind, I'll call Forster." Claire stood up, eager to escape. She had coveted Minna's gratitude, but now that she had it, it made her uneasy. If Minna was the victim of lies, why was Claire the one to feel manipulated? Had she wronged a good man?

Minna sat, arms wrapped around her knees as if a chill were in the air instead of a heat wave. Claire waited, suspended, for the slightest signs of guilt, of acquiescence. Minna only drew her knees closer.

Chapter 15

A common misperception is that life on a farm is a lonely, isolated one, but rather it is to the contrary. In all the years Claire had lived there, she didn't ever remember longing for company but rather the opposite—dreaming of peace and privacy and a solitude that never came. Till now.

Usually upward of a dozen people were working in the fields and outbuildings at any time of day, with an endless stream of salesmen for irrigation equipment and soil amendment, and commercial buyers for the harvests. Farmers from the neighboring properties came over to borrow equipment or discuss a particular problem due to weather or blight. When they were still married, Forster had been involved in local politics, and neighbors often dropped by and stayed on for supper. Then the children invited friends, so that a gaggle of kids were always somewhere, up to some kind of mischief on the property.

With Octavio's defection and the workers' firing, Claire got to know the land in a new way, taking in its deep silences, its secret spaces. She learned the way light slanted throughout the day against the house, along the gravel drive, through the trees in the orchards. She had never before noticed how it hung in the branches at dusk, how it left pools of luminescence in the meadows. As well, she came to know the purpling shadows of night until they no longer had power to frighten her.

Minna disliked the constant strident voices of the television, so Claire agreed to unplug it. They carried it to the barn like a worn-out relic. Likewise, they disconnected the stereo and the radio, although Claire sometimes longed for music and regretted agreeing to that termination. The newspaper, too, was discontinued because most days it went unread, shunted away still in its plastic wrapper. The farm grew quieter and quieter, but, paradoxically, more alive.

Claire had called Forster to tell him about losing Octavio and the prospects for hiring a new foreman, and they got into a terrible shouting match.

"It's still my farm, too."

"You left it to me to run. I made a decision."

"Octavio was family."

"It was his decision." As she said it, she realized how much it had been a coerced one. "I'll start looking tomorrow."

"Who is going to supervise the workers?"

"I will." The omission that there was nobody left to supervise came easier than she would have thought.

But she found herself putting the burden of interviews off. When Forster wanted to come and check on things, she pleaded off for a week. Then another.

"Let me rest. I'm so tired from the treatments. Next week." That part wasn't a lie because the radiation drained her, and Minna had promised that she knew someone perfect for the job. This prospect was unlikely, but Claire agreed to wait.

Twice a week, she and Minna turned on the irrigation for a deep soaking. As long as the trees were fed, a few weeks of neglected chores did no harm.

Lucy called on Tuesday, promising to come stay with them, but one thing after another came up. She had returned from Tampa, lost her new job, broke up and reunited with Javier. Claire sat in the kitchen with Minna, talking on the phone. "You know I only have radiation left. Hurry home."

Minna hummed and chopped mint. Handed Claire the fourth elixir of the day.

"I worry about her," Claire said, after hanging up.

"Lucy? Lucy is the shining light. She glows."

"Think so?"

"If I ever saw someone destined for happiness, it's that girl."

"I hope so."

Gwen called on Wednesday. "Dad said you fired Octavio."

"It's a long story."

"How are you going to run the place?"

"I don't want to talk about it."

Lucy called on Thursday. "Don't you think it's time to get out from under this thing?"

"The cancer? Yes."

August had been the hottest month on record, and September burned with no letup, as if even the gentle shift of California seasons were broken. At first Claire turned on the air conditioner, but Minna quickly put an end to that, saying that the chemicals were harmful, the artificial chill unnatural. The temperature topped a hundred by noon, the scorching sun matching the scorching of the radiation machine against Claire's skin. She dreamed of ice and snow and the moon.

Each morning they drove to the clinic, and she put on their treacly pink cotton gown and sat with the metal beasts. A crescent moon was tattooed along the missing breast, and Claire sat in the machine's sights while a technician hid behind a concrete wall and pulled a trigger. Claire pictured a sun burning her from the inside out.

The skin of her chest grew into a tight, hard, red pustule. It ached, swollen. At home, Minna cut fingers off an aloe plant and dabbed the viscous fluid on with a cotton swab, the heat from her hand, her finger, too rough now. A tragedy to become too rarefied for human touch.

After the treatments, Claire came home late in the morning, exhausted, and lay in bed in her underwear, half her chest a red-hot, smoldering ember. She begged for the air conditioner. Minna plied her instead with glass after glass of iced tea or water, setting up three electric fans around the bed so that the pillowcase fluttered in Claire's face from the stiff breeze. Minna wiped her legs, arms, and stomach down with cold, wet washcloths. Fed her wedges of ice-cold watermelon and cantaloupe, then lay on the bed beside her. They gossiped over nothing because their only interaction with the outside world was at the hospital, which they pointedly wanted to forget.

Minna would begin, "See that hawk?"

"The one down by the corral?"

"He's returned."

"I wonder why he's down here this time of year."

"Visiting."

"A handsome one."

"Smart. Eyeing those rabbits heading to the garden to eat our lettuce."

"I hate to think . . ."

"He's gotta eat, too."

Sometimes Claire grew petulant. "I'm lonely. No one comes here anymore."

"People are overrated."

One afternoon Claire heard Minna speaking sharply on the phone, hanging up when she came by. "Who was that?"

"Wrong number."

Another time the phone rang while Minna was outside, and Claire picked it up. A man's singsong voice like cascading water asked for Maleva.

"Sorry, you have the wrong number."

He laughed. "You tell the girl her Jean-Alexi is calling her." The phone went dead.

Claire's heart beat faster. Here was a proof of her version of a handsome, moody island boy whom Minna had left behind. Or had she left him? When Claire later told her about the call, she jumped from the table and ran to her room, slamming the door.

Claire lost her appetite from the radiation, but it could also have been caused by the debilitating heat that kept them supine much of the day. Minna ate little more than she did, but as Claire lost weight, she gained it.

"What's wrong?" Claire asked at Minna's lackluster attempt to push the mop across the floor.

"Too much to do," she said, snapping the conversation abruptly off.

"No one's here to see the floors," Claire said, but in truth Minna already did little. The floors, and everything else, had remained untouched for a long while. The saving grace was the lack of witnesses to the disorder. They seemed to have discouraged visitors to the point that Claire had not talked with Mrs. Girbaldi since the girls left the last time. Once Claire thought she saw her friend's car in the driveway, but by the time she dressed and made her way downstairs, the car was gone.

"Who was that?" she asked.

"Someone lost."

"But it looked like Mrs. Girbaldi's car."

"I wouldn't know about that," Minna said.

That was another new theme of Minna's—disavowal of anything having to do with responsibility. The lack of dinner on the table, Octavio's quitting, the filthy kitchen, Claire's losing weight—Minna denied fault for any part of it. She acted the role of disinterested guest at a hotel going to ruin.

"The oranges need picking. We need a foreman," Claire said.

"I know that," Minna said.

"How long has it been?" Claire would spend a long, passive week somnolent, then wake up, driven and anxious by all she saw going wrong. The week deadline had passed into a month. Forster and she had shouting matches on the phone.

"Then do something about it!" Claire snapped.

* * *

Now she avoided Forster's calls because her guilt was overwhelming. Each day that passed made her feel a further constriction. The effects of the neglect were unavoidable: weeds crowding the driveway, dry cracks in the fields. Claire knew she would have to pull herself together. Yet how to explain that as soon as she relaxed her vigilance, she felt this deep pleasure in the moment, that as each former necessity was stripped away, it revealed itself to have been at some level less necessary than she had thought. As if weighted chains were being lifted off her. She knew she would have to return to the everyday, but for now she delayed.

"You're too sick to be worrying about such nonsense," Minna replied to her complaints.

"Forster offered to help."

"Why can't you wait till I'm ready?"

"The trees don't wait. Fruit doesn't wait."

"You want me to do *this,* you want me to do *that*. I'm only one person. Who's going to make your dinner?"

Finally Forster demanded they go out to lunch alone.

When Minna heard, she threatened to unplug the phone.

"What good would that do?" Claire asked. "He can drive over. He's insisting on a foreman. He's in the right, of course."

Minna pouted and claimed that what with the radiation appointments in the morning and all the work in the house, she hadn't had time to contact her cousin.

At noon, Forster's truck pulled off the road and started up the driveway. Claire rushed to find shoes, wanting to avoid his seeing the state of things, or, worse, meeting up with Minna.

They reached the porch steps at the same time.

"What the hell is this?" Forster said. She saw anger in him she didn't remember since long before. Claire had worried about his coming inside, seeing the chaos there, but now she looked with his eyes at the surrounding farm and saw the secret was out. She was astonished at the speed of the disrepair and disintegration.

Fruit lay rotting in the fields; the hot, melting sun tainted the air with a sweet, decaying smell. Weeds, dried to crackling, spread out between the trees, along the driveway, up through the bricks of the patio. On the porch, books and dishes wantonly covered the outdoor table, the swing, the chairs. Minna had left a blanket and book spread on the lawn weeks ago, and the regular waterings from the sprinklers had bloated the book into another kind of obscene, overripe fruit, past the point of reading. The blanket lay stiff and faded as a remnant on a battlefield.

Forster stalked the front of the house, his face broken into a sweat unrelated to the heat. His gaze searched in each direction as if he were expecting a gun to ring out, a ghost to appear. Claire wanted to laugh and shake him, wanted to say, *Don't you realize that everything bad has already happened?*

"Let's go," she said.

The cab of the truck was as chilled as the hospital, and Claire greedily aimed the vents at her face while Forster walked around and got in.

"What the hell is going on?"

"Wait till we get to the restaurant. I don't want to talk here."

"You're looking good," he said.

"I look like hell. Let's eat."

He chuckled. "Thank God you still sound like yourself." He drove east, away from town, to where it still felt like open, rural farmland. They passed the white clapboard church they were married in. Claire had not been this way in a long time and was surprised that the windows were boarded up, the parking lot chained closed, the church announcement board cracked and dirty. The letters, crooked and falling, only suggested an old and long-ago invitation:

We are people of God's extravagant welcome.

"What happened?" she asked.

Forster, lost in thought, looked over. "They sold the church. It's going to be demo-ed for a retirement community."

"How sad."

"That's the way things are going. Whether you hold on to that scrap of land or not."

"That scrap of land was our life."

They ended up in a chain restaurant in a strip mall. After iced teas were brought, Forster cut the small talk and got down to business, a trait that she used to find endearing and now found brutal.

"I don't know what's going on between you and that girl . . ."

"*That girl*'s name is Minna. What's going on is I'm trying to not die of cancer."

"I didn't mean that."

"Bad luck, having to replace Octavio. You of all people know how it is. No one is with you forever." She was determined to not let Forster see how guilty she felt.

"Running the place is a full-time job even when times are good."

"What do you expect?"

"The farm's legally still half mine. You're running it into the ground."

"Minna knows an expert foreman."

"What the hell would she know about running a farm? I'm concerned. More about you than the farm, but it's the same thing, isn't it?"

Claire picked at the club sandwich she'd ordered. No chance that she could eat it. She'd have survived for a week on that sandwich alone: one day eating the bread, the next the tomato, the turkey. Later on, if she needed, gnawing on the bacon. She had learned to deconstruct life to its basic components.

"Are you listening to me?"

"Yes." She had drifted, something she now was in the habit of doing.

"Do it, or it'll be done for you."

"Is that a threat?"

"If it was, I'd already have hired an attorney. Forced sale. You wouldn't have a chance in court. I'm trying to be gentle here."

For the first time, Claire got scared. They ate in silence.

"You have my word. A foreman by Friday. Come and see for yourself."

"What is it about this girl? Gwen and Lucy think you're infatuated."

"She makes me feel needed."

"Your daughters needed you, I needed you. We could have left. Started over."

"Do you think I would have chosen any of this? You called it running away at the time. And then you all ran."

"And you became the expert in *not* living. Turning the farm into a shrine."

They sat in silence.

"I'm not your concern anymore. You have a wife—not me—who you should be paying attention to. We've been playing this little game of ours too long."

"What game?"

"This unspoken thing. Like I'm your true love. Snap my fingers, and you'll come running."

Forster's face reddened, and Claire felt shame. She had grown ruthless these last few months. She ate a few more bites of sandwich, but then pushed the rest away. She continued on because it had to be done. It was her only way to ensure the farm stayed hers. "It's unfair to Katie. That she's some afterthought. Don't you owe her?"

Now it was Forster's turn to push his plate away. He folded up his arms. "Let's stick to business. Who's going to work the farm?"

"Do you really think I'd let this farm—the thing I have left—go to ruin? *My farm*. After the price I paid to keep it?"

Forster drank his coffee, not looking at her. She could tell by the set of his jaw that he would not forgive her saying those words aloud.

During their marriage, their only respite from the stress of the ranch would be to sneak off the farm to eat at the local diner, enjoying the novelty of air-conditioning, which Hanni didn't believe in because of the expense. They would hold hands across the table, unembarrassed, until their burgers arrived, and she'd eat his french fries, although she primly insisted on ordering cottage cheese instead. It was the loss of simple contact with him she grieved for most.

He gave her a hard stare. "It's dangerous when you love something too much."

This had been the rhythm of their fights—Claire's slow working up to the hurt that was preoccupying her, hurt niggling like a toothache, not allowing her to leave it alone, although it only caused them both more pain. Forster would endure the needling until it went on too long, then he would cut her with a sentence.

She finished the iced tea and signaled the waitress for the check. "I'll have a new foreman by the end of the week."

Driving back to the house, Forster let her off at the side of the road by the driveway entrance. "Can you make it from here? That's not my home anymore."

She got out of the car. "Hasn't been for a long time."

"Be in touch. I'll work with the new man. If you don't have someone by next week, I'll work the place myself." He drove off the moment she shut the door.

* * *

She walked down the long driveway through the crippling afternoon heat and smelled smoke from a distant fire in the hills. Fire was the thing ranchers feared the most, and yet a devastation just as thorough had occurred. The property appeared strange even to her eyes—derelict and abandoned. No people working the orchards, no cars parked by the barn, Octavio's lean-to dusty and blown over by the wind, as if something catastrophic had occurred to the place.

Closer to the house, Claire noticed with new eyes that the paint job had outlasted its prime—walls now faded and blistered—revealing the advanced age of the house. The annual repainting had been overdue since before Minna's arrival. Now windows were opaque, glazed with dust and cobwebs. Most were thrown wide open, as were the gaping doors. What she saw didn't look like home any longer, but it was like being a creature living deep in its shell—the inside known and secure, the only view possible outward. From inside, it appeared beautiful and right. How many times was one directly confronted with the surfaces of one's life, its appearance, only to find it strangely unrecognizable? One lived buried deep inside, cozy with one's illusions and justifications, one's fictions, and only when confronted by large events did one have to display oneself for the outside world's approbation. Was this where her new hunger for secrecy and privacy and concealment came from?

In the entry hallway, dizzy, Claire was confused at the sight of the pine cabinet. Didn't it belong in the bedroom? Why was she so confused? When had she moved it? Irresolute, nonetheless she laid her purse down on it, unsure of its physical reality, but the purse sat solidly atop it. No one must suspect these lapses. She had read in the brochures about "chemo brain," disorientation, short-term memory loss, and she was determined it would not happen to her. Walking through the emptiness of the living room, Claire felt herself falling deeper and deeper into a dreamland. The sad lunch and the promises to Forster receded like a foul tide.

Minna stood at the kitchen sink, not washing the crusted dishes that overran the counters, but peeling a peach.

Claire saw Minna, too, with new eyes. She had allowed her hair to frizz; it bunched out in an unruly dark halo circling her head, the ends orangey from sun. Claire's dark angel. She wore cutoff shorts that barely covered her bottom, and a short camisole, which left a gaping swath of newly protruding belly. This fact, like the others of the farm and the house, noted and acknowledged more from the inside than ever openly discussed. A fait accompli that new life was stirring on the farm. Claire's peculiar optimism in the face of so much dissolution had to be attributed to just that. Minna turned, her face brimming with joy.

"He's coming!" she said. "Soon."

In the orchard each year, some trees appeared to be dead, with bared branches, or branches filled with misshapen, curled leaves that bore no fruit. But they had learned to leave these trees for a season, and likely as not, the next year they would produce a luxuriant bloom. As if there were such a thing as a flora depression. Foliate trauma. Claire was not one for believing in miracles. The tree had not resurrected—rather, its life was simply hidden from the eye, beating deep in the soil, trembling within root hairs, in sap, wood, and bark.

When Minna declared he was coming, Claire had no doubt that *he* was her Josh at last returning. Her heart ballooned, swelled until she thought she would explode with unheard-of joy. She would gladly end in this delusion, but the next moment she realized her mistake. The idea of a foreman's coming relieved her out of all proportion to the fact because it made her feel her faith in Minna was justified.

This was what Forster, Mrs. Girbaldi, the girls, and everyone else on the outside failed to see. Failed because Claire, the lover of fictions and now concealment, had not allowed them to see. They only focused on the peeling house, the weedy driveway, all the things that could so easily be remedied.

Rejuvenation was taking place from the inside out. The seemingly dead trees were simply resting, as her own poor, suffering body was resting. The farm was perhaps temporarily fallow, but it was only in a shallow rest. It would be fruitful again. Claire refused to be a woman dying of cancer—she was a woman who had lulled cancer to sleep. Healthy new cells were forming, subdividing, growing on and on, creating new skin, new hair, new eyes, new heart. Could one's soul grow anew? Of course, Minna could not be left behind in all this—Minna the fecund, Minna the fertile, Minna the Caller of the Spirits.

Chapter 16

As they waited for the arrival of Minna's phantom foreman, the temperature continued to stubbornly climb each day as if the thermometer were broken, the mercury released from the ordinary laws of physics and burst from its glass prison. The Santa Anas blew fierce, scouring sandpaper winds that stripped everything before them. Leaves pulled from the trees in the orchard; what held on looked tattered and chewed. Blossoms and miniature green fruit fell off. The moisture in the air wicked away to nothing. Fires raged in the foothills, creating their own wind that spread more fire, more wind. Bullets of flame arced through the air. The sky boiled a yellow-brown inferno.

Their world fully contracted as Claire's radiation treatments ended, and there was no longer any reason to leave the house. The doctor had looked at the final blood work and declared her cancer-free. She would have to be monitored every three months for the first year, he lectured. He had shaved off his goatee as a failed experiment, and his manner was brisk. Clearly, she would not be his model patient.

Claire sat stunned that she had made it through.

"So it worked? I'm cured?"

"Cancer-free."

Claire put her arm around Minna. "She got me through this. The only way I could have made it."

"There's a chance, of course, that we already got it in the surgery. We never know."

"Then all of this would have been for nothing?"

"Unless we killed what was left behind. We work in probabilities, not certainties."

"Thank you," Claire said, and she took the doctor's hand and held it to her lips and kissed the back of it. "Thank you."

He pulled his hand away, embarrassed. On their way out, Claire averted her eyes to the chairs of sick people. As if they were on the island of the doomed, and she gratefully had temporary reprieve.

Claire called the girls, crying. "It's over." She insisted they get together, begging Lucy to come home. Things would be different, she promised. A new start.

Forster called every day about the new foreman, but he could not affect her elation. When she told him her news, he was quiet for a moment. "That's the best news I've ever heard."

The mood returning home from the doctor was strange—Claire supposed it was due to the fire and smoke, which had turned the sky yellow and bone-dry. Grit dirtied her skin after she walked outside.

The expected foreman had still not arrived.

"Are you sure . . . ?" Claire ventured.

"He is close."

Power lines had burned down so the electricity went out. Claire turned on a small gas generator, but they left the lights off through the house, only using what was absolutely essential. They sat on the lawn during those bright nights, under an orange, burning sky, and could hear the fire like an angry beast crunching brush in the hills.

They didn't bother to dress, wore odds and ends of clothes like rags. Minna let her hair go wild like a napped sculpture that caught bits of lint and leaf. Claire left her head bare with its new coat of peach fuzz. In a state of waiting, during the daytime they sat in the green gloom under the avocado tree. Minna stared up into the branches for hours, lost in thought.

"Do you know the name for these on my island? *Zaboka. Sa se youn pyebwa zaboka,*" she said, pointing at a clutch of avocados.

"*Zaboka,*" Claire repeated.

In absolute pleasure, Claire read and read, pure pleasure in escape, escape as in childhood, in early wife- and motherhood. Then she was drawn to tales of adventure, lost in Melville and Conrad, the open spaces of sea and exotic lands the only ones that echoed her own cavernous inside. Now she went with Antoinette to England, to the breaking of all illusions, dreaming of swans and snow. She felt an absolute freedom of self-consciousness between Minna and herself. They shared not their histories but their states: Minna, young and with child; Claire, ravaged but recovering.

"Tell me, Minna. Tell me what you want me to know."

They slept side by side on a mattress pulled outside, sheltered under the avocado tree. Their breaths intermingled. As much as it was possible for another person to share one's mortality, Minna had taken on hers. It had started with the disease and gone beyond that to new health. What kind of incalculable debt did Claire owe for that?

Alone now with Minna, not only did the preoccupation with cancer fall away, but so did the decades of her life. Claire felt they were contemporaries in a way she'd never felt with her daughters, who always made her feel older than her years. Each time she looked into Minna's unlined face, she felt it mirrored her own.

Through the world's reaction, one was informed of no longer being part of youth, part of what is vital, desirable. While young, it seemed a birthright, and those older had always been so (despite one's parents' faded pictures as evidence to the contrary). Passing into middle age was no different from being barred from one's beloved home. One's treasured children, now grown, banging a cruel drum in one's face. Shutting the gate and turning the lock. Not knowing to cherish youth until it was no longer. God's prank—to give the greatest gift at the age one can least understand it.

Why shouldn't one grow to love the time one is most accomplished, most experienced, most importantly *most* oneself? Why shouldn't there be an unseemliness to the twenties and thirties, the bareness of personality, raw, like uncooked meat, pure hormonal drives that canceled individual choice?

Claire was in her own fool's paradise with Minna, no mirrors to remember the lines on her face, no dissenting, disapproving outside. Minna telling her what she wanted to believe, filling her mind with fictions. She felt like a yogi deep in the forest, meditating on the heart of the universe, hidden and yet connected with everything.

Minna and Claire ate dinner on the living-room floor by kerosene lamp: cheese, crackers, and fruit. They ate like nomads, campers, travelers passing through a place they would not soon return to. Moths circled the room and singed their wings at the top of the lamp's glass chimney, leaving behind a smell like burnt hair. A large one hit the lamp and fell to the floor. He was furry brown, as big as a hummingbird. Minna picked him up in her hand and lofted him out the window. *The gay gentleman will be safe now.* Claire smiled, but then her amusement turned to confusion—had that happened before, or had it happened in the book? In the distance, they heard the wail of sirens.

"Tell me about Joshua." It had been so long—hours, days?—since they last spoke that Claire was startled as much by the sound of Minna's voice as the meaning of her words.

"I'd rather not—"

"I must know for the final ceremonies. That is the reason you are healed."

Earlier that evening, they had drawn the wooden gate across the driveway entrance in preparation for the possibility of fire reaching them, never even considering escape. They wanted to prevent invasion—even at the cost of their lives. Unspoken that they both felt in an enchanted place, untouchable. A stiff gust pressed against the walls, the windows, the doors.

"The smoke is heavier. It's getting closer," Claire said. "Are we safe?"

They went out on the lawn and saw that the night stars had disappeared in long, clotted valleys of smoke. Something hot landed on her arm, and she swatted it, thinking it was a mosquito. She lifted her hand to discover a piece of hot ash.

"The wind's coming our way."

Sirens circled closer, the wailing stoppering their ears. Through loudspeakers she heard garbled orders for an evacuation. The roof of the ranch house was thirty-year-old shingle, the sides wood, a tinderbox.

"What should we do?" Claire said.

Minna shrugged. "Go swimming, Agatha."

"Who do you mean?" From the novel, Claire understood enough that a renaming indicated a change of allegiances.

Minna went into the dining room and came out holding the two silver candelabra that Hanni had brought from Germany and had given to Claire on her wedding day. She dropped them in the deep end.

"What are you doing?" Claire asked, as Minna brought stacks of china and submerged them on the shallow steps. Soon, the two women were throwing in bundled sheets full of clothes. Claire took all her jewelry and dropped it in a pillowcase, tied it off, then plunged the whole thing under the diving board. Minna wrapped Raisi's samovar in blankets, taped it, and immersed it. They worked feverishly until all the valuables were underwater. Smoke lay heavy all around like fog.

Claire unzipped her shorts and stepped out of them. She waded into the shallow end, past the red, blue, and gold crystal wine goblets, wearing only T-shirt and baggy underwear. Minna came back out of the house wearing the necklace Claire had given her, shorts, and a cropped tank top that showed the hard roundness of her belly. Claire did not point out that if they were in need of rescue, or even if they perished in the fire, Minna would be better served covered to the eyes of the world.

They sat on the bottom steps in the shallow end, knee to knee, as if at a corner table at a restaurant, resting their chins on the surface of the water, alligator-style, enjoying a horizontal view of their fiery world. A curtain of orange flame appeared above the farthest treetops. A dread thrill that maybe the orchard would abandon Claire since she wouldn't abandon it. Her nose filled with the candied smell of burnt citrus. The last thing she saw was the glint of Minna's necklace under the water before she closed her eyes against the stinging air. The world shuddered a final contraction. Goldfish nibbled against her ankles as Minna hummed.

"He is coming," she said.

"Now?" Claire said, thinking of Minna's distended belly.

"Jean-Alexi. To run the farm."

Claire's mind itself caught flame, thinking of the phone calls and the man with the sliding voice like silver coins that she had talked to. The island boy of Minna's unrequited love. "If there's anything left," Claire said, trying not to show her excitement.

"Can I touch it?" She motioned toward Minna's stomach.

"Yes, Agatha."

"Why do you keep calling me that?"

"She is the saint that cured you. Jean-Alexi will take her dues."

Silence, and then Minna guided Claire's hand underwater. A shudder of electric happiness ran through Claire because new life was joy no matter its source. She put her other hand underneath Minna's belly, as if she were holding it aloft, as if she alone were cupping a world for safekeeping. Minna was right. No use planning. The future would find them.

The flames skipped over the ranch.

The wind changed direction, sparing most of the orchards. Famished, they got out of the pool, prune-fingered and stiff, and went into the kitchen to get something to eat. In the arctic light of the open freezer, they spooned mouthfuls of melting ice cream directly out of a gallon container into their mouths.

In the morning, Claire discovered a dozen blackened shingles on the roof, like rotted teeth on a Halloween pumpkin. An acre of citrus trees had turned to ash. Walking down the burnt rows, she found the coaled bodies of parrots.

Chapter 17

They had been alone together so long, had gone through illness and healing, Claire could no longer tell the difference between her white and Minna's black.

Chapter 18

Claire was Lazarus, come back to cranky life. Health had a slow gestation—she imagined a butterfly breaking wetly, clumsily, from her cocoon. The first glance of insect ugliness until the sails of wings unfurled, a veil of beauty hiding raw, violent birth. If illness was one kind of birth, returning health was another. Each a distinct new incarnation.

Her thoughts floated, both detailed and nonsensical as in a dream. The risk of normal thinking was as daunting as a sheer-faced summit, unapproachable. Concentrating on the mundane—grocery shopping, oil change for the car, fertilizing the orchard, the arrival of the new foreman, Jean-Alexi—beyond her. She dreamed of Raisi, relived her childhood apartment in the most minute detail—the carved armoire with the bear's mouth open where she used to hide grapes.

Where was that armoire? She would have given anything to look at it now. Why in the barn, why hidden? But then Claire lost herself again in contemplation of the clouds.

Had she pushed too many responsibilities onto Minna's shoulders, while allowing herself to revert to this childlike state? She felt as if she would split open at any moment and burst into flower. She had a mystical, almost supernatural feeling that something of immense importance was about to happen, either in her thoughts or outside in the physical world. Although the boundaries between the two were becoming less and less separate. Any manhandling on her part would interrupt what was preordained.

The doctor had explained this was chemo brain, this fog, the aftereffects of the drugs, and that she should not become paranoid. All enlightenments written off in one fell swoop as chemical imbalances. She scorned the doctor. Were his conclusions, his "probabilities," any less fantastic than Minna's magic figures and her elixirs?

Too, she began to suspect Forster's motives, his sudden insistence about running the farm. Probably his Katie had talked him into finally selling, and Claire was the last obstacle. She was beginning to see through Mrs. Girbaldi's perfidy. Hadn't she been one of the first to sell out? What could she possibly understand about being linked to the land? Neither Gwen nor Lucy would ever be persuaded of the ranch's value. No, the truth was that she was seeing more clearly than ever before.

Events were happening around her, unwinding like constellations, that she knew she would have to face. The screaming train of Minna's swelling belly, the likely paternity, was a fast-approaching future. Nothing like the approach of a child in one's life to mark time into neat, tidy increments of necessity. Which bedroom would be the baby's room? Birth a summons, not an invitation. Would that be a suitable excuse to delay selling the farm?

Another part of the constellation—Claire's emptying house, the implausibility of Minna's explanations. Why should her beloved things be packed away in the barn? Where, again, was the armoire? She daydreamed the grapes turned to raisins in the bear's mouth. Woke up in a panic. Why had the roses in the garden been torn out and green beans, tomatoes, ragged ears of corn, planted instead? Were they preparing for some sort of Armageddon? Why no electricity and only intermittent phone? Why had the farm become a place only fit for ghosts? Fruit hardening on the trees; juice distilled into sour syrup; earth turned graveyard. Claire took a pinch of dirt on her tongue but spat it out, the taste turned alkali.

At the time each change occurred, she accepted it, so that all became part of what already was and thus acceptable. The frog who overlooked her own boiling. Chemo fog. Minna so logical and persuasive that Claire accepted that she had been abandoned by everyone: Mrs. Girbaldi away on a cruise; Forster busy with a new business venture. The girls' calls always came when she was in the tub or taking a nap, which was most of the time. Tiredness such as she had never imagined, and she prayed it was a precursor to health. Minna warned that they would pressure Claire about selling the farm. Paranoia? The only way Claire could gauge how far things had gone off-balance was to imagine the circumstances through Gwen's eyes. Through her prim, judging eyes, none of this would do.

But all that was a diversion. Claire's real attention was focused inward, on her own resurrection, the swell of health tending her toward the mystical. Hadn't she been healed by magic, after all? She broke down in tears at the sight of returning golden, downy hairs on her forearms. The tissues in her mouth healed, and she could again chew. So unexpected, so delightful, the fading of the specter of death. As if it were a thing that could be overcome, denied, and forgotten for all time.

She looked with benevolence on the sun rising, the smell of sage scrub in the air, the shush of new leaves on the trees. Even Minna's strangeness, her lack of joy at the new life within her, could not blemish Claire's happiness. Her own pregnancies had been the most contented times of her life. Although she could not shake the light feeling inside her head—a constant vertigo that kept her from moving too quickly—she was able to sit for hours, caught in the sounds of birds, wind, caught in stillness. How to explain that each vestige stripped from her revealed itself to be less? As if she could finally take flight. She knew she would have to return to the mundane, but just not yet.

Minna broiled a large piece of steak in a roasting pan, and the smell of its cooking drove Claire into a frenzy, a sure sign she was getting better. She stood at the sink, turned on the KÄLTE faucet, drank deep gulps of the icy water, the only thing she could fill herself with freely. They sat at the bare kitchen table across from each other, the sole light from candles, the flames flattening with each breeze. Minna poured herself a large glass of red wine. Dark rings shadowed her eyes; she looked weary.

"Are you sure you should drink that?"

"Why not?" The flame's light contorted Minna's features, making her beautiful one moment, ugly to the point of fright the next.

"Your condition."

"I don't know what you're meaning." Minna plopped a large cup of the elixir in front of Claire so that it splashed on the wooden table.

"I'd like a little wine tonight."

"That's up to me."

"Please," Claire said, a stab of impatience. But she nodded, drinking the mixture down, already grown faint and tired from the coming effect of it. Hadn't Minna already led her so far, didn't it seem clear she knew better?

"What will you do, eventually? Go back to your family?"

"Don't know."

"Back to Berkeley?"

"Ready for me to clear out already? Want to wipe away all traces of me now?"

"No, no. I'd like you to stay here for a while. With the baby."

Minna rose and slammed the roasting pan down on the table. "Don't think that's likely. Gwen will throw us both out on our ears soon."

"The steak smells good," Claire said.

"Doesn't it?"

Minna speared the piece of meat, then attacked it with a hefty cutting knife, slicing a large piece and putting it on one plate, cutting a smaller piece and placing it on another. Claire knew better than to expect any vegetables on the side or salad or even bread. Again, a flash of impatience. She would broach the subject of taking over the cooking now that she was getting stronger. Maybe even insist on inviting over Mrs. Girbaldi for a meal when she returned from her cruise. But all in its time. When Minna was in a good mood. If it came to that, would Claire know how to deliver a baby?

"I'm so hungry," she said.

Minna set down the two plates on her side of the table and began to cut the meat, stuffing pieces in her mouth and chewing as she glared at Claire.

"I suppose you want some?"

Claire nodded, weak from the meat aroma and her hunger. So tired from the elixir it was an effort to keep her eyes open, keep her head from rolling on the table. "The carved armoire? The dining room table. Can we put them back in the house? I've changed my mind."

Minna cut more pieces, chewed them down and swallowed, following each with a gulp of wine. "You must've eaten like this all your life."

Claire's head, so unbearably heavy, rocked back against the wooden rung of the chair. "Forster used to make barbecue on Sundays. For a while the girls ate only vegetarian, then fish. . . ."

Minna let out a long, slow chuckle. "Quite a luxury—imagine choosing *not* to eat."

"You know how kids are . . ." Claire said, on the verge of tears. "About the armoire . . ."

Minna put her fork down and leaned close to her. The flame stretched her face into a long mask. "Do you know what real hunger is? I want you to feel it."

If only Claire could focus, she knew that Minna was revealing her own biography through the body.

"Oh, *che,* I'm afraid that medicine has gone to your head and made you sick. Best not eat just now. Vomit make me a lot of work."

Claire laid her head down on the table, willing herself back into the escape of sleep.

"I might just finish both pieces," Minna said. "Eating for two, after all."

Claire's impatience burst into flame, hunger making her reckless. "What do you mean? Two?"

Minna gave a broad smile, her mouth full of food. "Eating for you and me, *che,* what else?"

"There's someone else here. Why don't you speak it aloud?" Claire felt utterly helpless.

"You are just beginning to understand how it is," Minna whispered.

Claire staggered to her bed, which Minna had moved inside again. She now insisted they sleep separately. A nightmare woke Claire near dawn. She was being pursued, but her legs were so heavy she could not move. She banged on a door to be let in, but no one would answer. Then she was inside a house, struggling with a door to be let out. It was unclear whether she wanted in or out, but all the time the pursuer was catching up with her. She woke with a cry in her throat and lay on the bare mattress, wishing the nausea away, the stabbing of her stomach, the flutter and cramp of her intestines. Minna had urged her to wear a scarf, wrapped tight around the abdomen, so that she would not feel this pain she claimed was a spirit, but that Claire recognized was simply starvation.

Like a thief, she limped down the steps to the kitchen, opened the refrigerator, and pulled out a large round of cheese.

Sitting on the floor, paring knife in hand, she cut off hunks and shoved them into her mouth. But the cheese was too thick, too creamy. Starvation had dulled her taste buds. She gagged, then heard the soft pad of footsteps stopping behind her. It seemed Minna never slept anymore.

"What do we have here? A little mouse?"

Claire shrugged, past explanation. Guilty, dirty. As if she had let Minna down somehow.

Minna crouched down, stroked her cheek. "Is my *doudou* getting better?"

"I'm hungry."

"What about I make us some toast and eggs to go with that cheese? Would you like that?"

Claire nodded, ashamed, wondering if she had made the whole thing up, as Minna helped her up into a chair.

"The world is a hard place, my *doudou,* without mercy. But I will take care of you. I will be merciful."

The next day passed without incident, Minna feeding her so that she grew strong enough to walk around the house and then outside on the lawn and into the garden. She was ashamed of her doubts, her suspicions. With new energy, Claire took an interest in the orchard. What she saw hurt her—trees that had been nurtured for years now overgrown, the unpicked fruit going to ruin. She tried to see the farm in its new state as not necessarily a bad thing, but rather a regression to its former state of wildness.

"Somebody needs to work the orchard," Claire said.

"I told you. Jean-Alexi is here. He is studying the situation."

"Let me meet him."

"He's busy now."

Claire stopped and glared at her. "I don't believe anyone is here."

"You're going crazy."

"I need to call Forster. Why isn't the irrigation on? Why is everything dying? I told you to have the armoire put back in the house."

"You'll see," Minna said, walking away. "You be patient for once."

Again the elixir, and again she swooned into a deep, pleasurable torpor. Claire heard a man's voice when she woke from an afternoon nap. A man's voice like cascading water and then Minna's voice arguing. Claire stared at the stained mattress ticking, trying to gather enough energy to rise and go to her bedroom window. When she did, she could see nothing through the thick veil of overgrown trees. When had the coral tree got so large? So monstrous? Large enough to obstruct, large enough to crush the house? Was it a fairy tale? Paranoia? Then the voices stopped. Instead of going to investigate, and possibly angering Minna, Claire lay back down, promising herself she would get to the bottom of this. Soon she was back asleep, dreaming, and the waking time melded into the dreamtime so that she could not distinguish if the yelling had been real or not.

She found herself on the living-room couch—the last remaining piece of furniture in the room. Minna insisted Claire drink another large cup of the elixir.

"I don't want it."

"You must."

"It makes me sick."

"It's part of the cure."

"I'm healthy now."

"You are ungrateful." Without explanation, Minna carried in the small television from the barn, plugged it in, and left on soap operas to occupy her. The volume turned so high it gave Claire a headache.

Minna was in the laundry room when Claire poured the drink down the back of the sofa cushions and made her break for the front door. She wobbled on unsteady, rubbery legs but cleared the porch steps, shuffled down the road to the barn. As much as she knew anything in this life, she knew what she would find there. Which ended up being both true and not. When she flung the large slider door open, a black man spun around and shielded his eyes from the shock of sunlight, like a lizard startled from under a rock.

"What the fuck?"

"Who are you?" Claire said, her voice loud and false as if in a play. She felt as if she would fall over any moment.

She blinked hard at him, thinking he was some kind of phantom from her addled, fogged brain. But she could never have dreamed anyone quite like him—he was outside her imagining. One can only make up what one has some passing familiarity with, and he was as foreign to her world as the man on the moon. Bone thin and loosely jointed, he was like a raggedy-man doll strung together. His skin had a jaundiced, yellowish-brown hue. A network of tattoos spread across his chest and arms, partly covered by a T-shirt. Great, dusty coils of hair sprang along his head, gathered and partly tucked inside a large knitted tam. What she saw in his eyes terrified her. Eyes like shattered glass. Crazy eyes. His look answered all the questions she'd been avoiding.

"You *fou,* woman?" he yelled.

"Who are you? You are trespassing." Of course, she *was* crazy. But she was returning. She had simply been gone, lost somewhere in her coiled mind, the labyrinth of illness. She backed away.

"It's cool, lady. You talk to Maleva, and she introduce us proper like."

"Maleva." Claire nodded, backed away, stumbled, then ran. He did not follow, but stood in the gaping passageway, his jaw working up and down like a puppet's.

Part Three

Chapter 1

Maman, she tell her daughter the story of the olden days when the sun was like a sweet orange in the sky. All the days back then were buttery, she sang, the rivers ran like honey, and the people were as often happy as not. *Maman,* she tell that when the Troubles came, even God in his house could not help them, and he squeezed down on that orange sun, but the juice that should have been sweet, when it met this world, it turned to salt, it filled the oceans, it came out of the people's eyes. *Maman* say, "Marie, all your life you must look for the sweet, it is there for the finding."

Marie's *maman,* Leta, was always singing, a throb of sadness in her voice that felt like softest suede brushing against bare skin. She sang because she did not wish to remember how her life had changed.

Ersulie nain nain oh! Ersulie nain nain oh!
Ersulie ya gaga gaaza, La roseé fait bro-
dè tou temps soleil par lévé La ro seé fait bro-
dè tou temps soleil par lévé Ersulie nain nain oh!

Leta's fondest wish as a girl was to become a teacher at the convent—a place of peace and order. Her life till then was a small circle made up of her family's house and her friends' houses; the girls were chaperoned on special trips to the beach or the mountains. She was raised a stranger to her own country. She studied hard and the Sisters praised her for her studiousness, in time allowing her to teach a class. The first colored teacher, necessary now that the danger in the country scared foreign missionaries away.

Each day Leta rose in the darkness to ready herself, preparing meticulous lesson plans and memorizing each student's name on the first day. Leta always wore a crisp white blouse and a pressed, dark blue skirt because she felt so privileged to teach, wanting to prove herself worthy. Each day she picked her way through the dirty streets to the school, avoiding the piles of trash, avoiding the stray animals and the straying eyes of men, avoiding the open sewers by walking on the rickety boards fording them, trying also to avoid the sun darkening her creamy skin. An implied lesson that lightness was closer to God.

Her family's house was not large but not small either, not in a rich neighborhood but not in a poor one. A house perfect for as much happiness as living in the capital would allow. One day, walking home, a car sped by and spattered mud over her skirt and shoes. Near tears, Leta stopped and looked down as a young man jumped out of the back to apologize. A famous politician who was running for election sat in the back and tapped impatiently on the window.

"We are sorry," the young man said, although the driver in front and the politician in the back did not seem the least bit sorry. "What can I do? Can I pay you?"

"To wash the mud away?" Leta said, and looked up, laughing.

If her mother had had the ability of foresight, to look at her life as Marie was able to later, backward and forward, she would have known to turn and run, that mud was the smallest price by far she could pay out of this meeting, but of course she knew no such thing. Instead, she looked up into the handsome young man's eyes as the car spun its wheels and took off, the politician tired of waiting on his love-struck assistant. Mud now spattered the young man's pants, too. What she noticed was the way his suit fit him. Noticed also that rare thing—he treated her like a gentleman.

"Looks like we are in the same boat," he said, looking into Leta's moss-green eyes brimming with tears, then at the flashing white teeth of her laugh. How to explain that he fell in love with how easily her emotions transformed one to another. A useful gift in a troubled country.

Marcel had just been made judge when they married; they had had their first baby, a girl named Marie, when the next elections again tore the country apart. The politician whom he had supported lost, this time narrowly, and beat a fast exile to Miami. The military scoured the streets each night, disposing of his supporters to avoid a coup. They had a name for this from when Duvalier left, *dechoukaj*, uprooting, like what the peasants did when they pulled the manioc roots from their fields, except it was never clear who needed to be uprooted, or rather, it depended on who momentarily held power.

First Marcel was fired from the position he had been promoted to, Court of Appeals. A week later arrested at his house during dinner. The Tonton Macoutes waited patiently while he pushed his chair back and laid down his napkin, kissing his young wife on the forehead before he left. One of the Tontons grabbed a chicken leg on his way out. They would not let Marcel go to the bedroom to kiss his baby girl good-bye.

Alone, having nothing else to do (electricity out as usual at night, phones not working), Leta cleared the dishes. In her vanished Marcel's place, she found a puddle of urine soaking the chair cushion and the floor beneath.

The next day, the mother superior called Leta in. Mother had a big, round Irish face and innocent blue eyes that refused to acknowledge the horrors in front of them. An accommodationist's salvation. *Dechoukaj.*

"You must fire me," Leta said.

"Otherwise they said they would take the girls. They will burn down the church."

"I'll be gone in five minutes." Leta went for a last time into the empty classroom and cried the way it is only possible when you are sure what you have lost is gone forever. She stole a blackboard eraser and put it into her purse. She did not care if mother superior forgave her.

That night her husband's family home was burned to the ground. Marcel's body was found macheted and set on fire on the Grande Rue.

Leta borrowed money from her parents and boarded a *tap tap* with little Marie bundled in her arms. She headed north since that was the direction of the first available bus. She was going to the *pevi andeyò,* the outside country, an exile into a country she did not know. Wherever she ended up, it could never again be in the capital.

Marie grew up in a small, rickety house by the sea, with a corrugated-tin roof. She was not saddened by the way *Maman* now was because she didn't remember her any other way. What she was told when she was older was that upon coming to the poor village of her great-*grand-maman,* Leta handed over the baby and refused to care for her again. What had brought her such joy before now only reminded her of *no longer,* as in she was *no longer* a schoolteacher, *no longer* a wife. Her bright future gone, never to reappear. But *Grand-Maman* would not give up. She forced Leta to attend the ceremonies, and for the first time in her young life Leta experienced what her parents had tried so hard to keep from her—the wild, irrational strength in powerlessness.

Leta saw women who begged or worked all day long in rags come to the ceremonies in the middle of the night freshly bathed, dressed in immaculate white. They beat their drums, they sang, they danced, with a freedom and dignity she had not imagined for them. The first time a goat was sacrificed, the blood drained into a bucket, she was horrified, but then she remembered the horrors she had fled, and she understood that this was nothing worse than the truth that had been kept from her before.

Now she wore the loose dresses of the peasant women, kerchiefs over her head. No one would ever guess what Leta had been before, and that was as she wanted it, because as the saying went, *revenge has long arms,* and a widow was considered vengeful. After a year of dancing and spirits and magic powders, Leta came one day to *Grand-Maman*'s house and took back her baby girl. Then she began instruction in the old ways.

During the years of the drought, food was scarce, and *Maman* would boil up yam, next day boil the peelings from the yam, then, if they still didn't get lucky, sugarcane, or bitter plantain. She convinced Marie the jellied, sweetened water was the most wonderful food in the world, manna from the gods, and she was the luckiest of girls to have it. Marie was ashamed to admit her stomach still stabbed with hunger because that would be a breach of faith to *Maman*. Instead she wrapped the hunger belt tighter around her waist. On the darkest days *Maman* would bake dirt cookies, mixing a pat of butter and bit of sugar with clay that tasted like the ghost of food. Only a cook as good as *Maman* could make starvation taste good.

* * *

Their luck seemed to change when the *blans* in the pink house were looking for a new cook. They despaired of hiring another French, one who wouldn't endure being out in the hinterlands. A friend of *Maman*'s knew her skill and suggested her. After that, at least there was no more hunger. Growing up, Marie always saw *Maman* working, either cooking at the pink house or healing as *medsen fey*, leaf doctor. After *Grand-Maman* passed five years later, *maman* also served as a priestess. She had become another kind of teacher, knew all the people of the village, and helped them through her new abilities. Understood it was always the choice of the gods, the *béké,* if a ceremony worked or not.

Marie's happiest memories as a young girl were watching her mother painting sacred figures on walls, doors, or *drapos,* flags. Often the two of them went off for the day into what remained of the ancient forests to search for the ingredients in her *remèd,* her powders and elixirs. They would walk single file, hiking the steep trails for hours, stopping only for a simple meal of fruit and bread. At those times, resting under a tree and holding Marie in her arms, Leta could recall what happiness felt like.

"The trees are sacred," she said.

On Marie's eighth birthday, *Maman* took her to a sacred *mapou* tree. "This is the forgetting tree," she said. "Like the ones in Africa but different. When anything bad happens, I want you to come here. The tree is where you leave the bad memory behind so that it doesn't poison your life."

Marie fidgeted, wanting to go home, but Leta shook her.

"Listen to my words. My words are all you will have someday."

Marie was forbidden to go to the ceremonies deep in the forest. She lay nights in her bed, falling asleep to the soft drumbeats, which comforted like a mother's heartbeat. In the daytime, no one acknowledged the ceremonies happened because the military had banned them, and this was how the young Marie discovered what a secret, hidden, or even double life meant. Finally one night, Marie, unable to resist any longer, snuck out of bed and followed the sounds past the sacred *mapou* tree, past the trails that she knew so well from their gathering trips, deeper into the forest than she had ever before been.

The drums grew so close she felt their vibration in her body. She hid behind a bush and watched her *maman* in the middle of a crowd of people. In white, she was dancing provocatively back and forth around a large fire, flames nightmarish in the fierce heat, encouraging the drummers to beat even more wildly. Her face, strange and distorted, was unfamiliar: lips pulled back, eyes rolled up into her head, whites visible, head canted as if listening to words instructing her from the open night sky. Marie broke out into a sweat, her eight-year-old's heart beating madly like a small animal's. She was about to run into the crowd to rescue *Maman* when a man joined the dancing. Back and forth they moved, snaking their bodies around each other, and Marie had the frightening thought that this stranger might be her father, that maybe it was he she was being kept away from. Again, she rose from her place of hiding, ready to run to her now reunited parents, when *Maman* ripped off her shirt.

Marie had seen her mother's body many times before. *Maman* had always told her to be proud of herself, her natural beauty, proud enough to keep it covered from others' eyes. To see her mother's nakedness in front of such a large group shook the girl. Having this man who might or might not be her father dancing closer and closer to *Maman* unnerved Marie, and she closed her eyes, paralyzed about what to do.

When she opened her eyes again, *Maman*'s shirt was back on as she gracefully dipped her bare arm into the fire, kept it there until Marie could clearly see the wrist gripped in flame, until she had to turn her eyes away. Now a large knife appeared in the man's hand, and a scrawny, trussed chicken was brought from the crowd. As the head was cut off, Marie vomited into the bushes, then turned and ran home.

The next morning, *Maman* cut mango and laid out French bread for breakfast, mild as could be. Marie looked hard at the purple of the skin around her bandaged wrist.

"It's nothing, *doudou*. A burn from the stove."

"You're lying."

Maman's face sharpened. "Watch yourself!"

"I saw you. You said that such was devil. To stay away."

"You know that *Grand-Maman* taught me the old ways."

"But—"

"We abandoned the old ways. I didn't know better. The vodou healed me. It is about my relationship to god, to the villagers, to you, to nature. Remember our days under the trees? What did I tell you?"

"They are sacred."

"They will save you when nothing else will."

Marie lowered her voice although they were alone in the one-room house. "Was that Papa?"

"Where?"

"Dancing."

"That was just a man. Vodou brings your father close to me. He is watching over us. Remember that."

The first time Marie saw Jean-Alexi, she was a girl of ten. The village was celebrating, a wedding or a new car; any excuse was welcome. She was playing with the other children on the beach, and some boys stole the coins *Maman* gave her to go buy *fresco*, ices with her friends. As she cried, Jean-Alexi, teenaged with lean muscle, walked along smoking a joint, and looking at the pretty *tifis,* making loud noises to his gang. He swaggered, his pants riding provocatively low. His hair was done in dreads, which one hardly ever saw in the village. He was tall and thin, loose-jointed, so that he was all arms and legs and head coming toward you, like a fighting rooster. His skin was light almond yellow, his face small-featured, with a pointy chin that bobbed as he chewed—gum, tobacco? When he came by them, he saw her tears and bent down. "*Ou byen?* You okay? What make this little face go down, *mwen petit fi?*"

"They took my coins."

In short order, the boys had their arms pinned back painfully, one of them had his finger broken, the coins urgently handed over to Jean-Alexi. "Okay, little Erzulie, what you want happen to *des* boys?"

"Kill them," Marie screamed. She recognized the name Erzulie—the vodou goddess of love, always beautiful—from her *maman*, and his calling her that made her feel for the first time grown up.

He chuckled. "Oh, my Erzulie, she has a hot blood, *moun*."

The boys cried like babies.

"Okay, tell you what. You crawl to her, and you kiss her feet, and maybe we let you live."

"Non!" Marie screamed, jumping up and down on the sand, drunk on the new idea that she could inflict pain on those who hurt her. "That's not what I said. *Touye* them, kill them."

"Enouf this. You one spoiled girl child." Marie pushed her chest out and tied her shirt up under her ribs. *"Ou,* titty too *jenn,* too baby. Maybe in couple years." Jean-Alexi winked and threw her a piece of candy as he took off after an older girl who wagged her hips at him. The boys scattered free. Only later did Marie figure out that Jean-Alexi did not give back her coins.

Chapter 2

The pink house was built forty years ago for an English bride whose curls by then had turned white. *Maman* had been cooking in the pink house for five years when the old, white-curled lady, a schoolteacher way back, said to her, "Bring me someone ignorant to teach the Queen's English to, someone to convert into God's lamb," and so *Maman* brought her own Marie each day. *The rain in Spain stays mainly in the plain.* Marie was taught that everything in England was heaven, and they on the island could not be helped for their ugliness, their sin that showed skin-deep.

The old lady told the young girl this even though she had lived on the island all forty years of her married life, lived there so long England was as much a fantasy as heaven, all her relatives long buried, she herself long forgotten, and the girl believed her. Marie was so good at English, she read out loud the silly Brontë and Austen stories (full of young women holding hankies and waiting to marry rich) the old woman loved so much that she lay back in her bed with a smile, as if she were already dead and in heaven.

* * *

Maman was such a fine chef because she knew the best dishes used both the sweet and the salt since that was the way of life. She told Marie of the time when she was a young girl, and the light in the deepest forest was gold, burning like a necklace around a rich woman's neck, and the country was full of hope, but how after, it turned the dark of iron. In *Maman*'s mind, the country's happiness and her own were the same, and the Troubles that came destroyed both. Some think bad luck comes like lightning, once in a lifetime, but *Maman* knew it was more like a rock slide, one thing setting off another until the end of one's days, and so it was for them.

One of the village women grew jealous of *Maman*, her schooled ways and her healing, how she kept back from the rest as if she were slightly better, how even though she hid her pretty shape under sackcloth, it was still visible. That woman did some talking back in the capital and informed the Macoutes that Marcel's widow was agitating in the countryside.

Ten years after she had come there, the men, on the way to somewhere else, decided to stop in the little village and settle old scores. They followed *Maman* into the forest, and as she gathered healing leaves, they gathered her. Because they were simple, brutal men, and she was defiant and unafraid, they killed her quickly, afraid of the rumors that she had magical powers.

That was how the men caught her in that black-bitter iron forest, the despair-filled dark jungle. After, just in case she might recognize them in the afterlife, they carved away her face. Marie thought maybe that was better—God had mercy and did not make her look back at the despair of her life.

When *Maman* died, sans face, everyone was too afraid to mourn for her in public. Whoever picked up her body, that one would be killed. Whoever buried her, also. Whoever mourned, too. Like the long line of begats in the Bible. Marie sat alone under the *mapou* tree in the rain and watched the road away from town, watched the dirt turn to liquid mud, and wondered if that was the road

Maman had meant, the long road to Guinée. If she walked it, could she join her? How would *Maman* make her way, blinded, faceless, on such a road?

After Marie's *maman* was gone, the girl became a *restavek,* forced to live in her aunt's house. On the island, family was a rubber-band kind of thing. Since Marie's great-*grand-maman* was gone, a cousin called aunt was perfectly acceptable. When Marie tried to run away, hiding under the sacred tree, each time they found her and dragged her back, beating her. "*Timoun se ti bet,* kids are animals," Tante Josie said. Uncle Thibant was the opposite of *Tante* in every way—slight where she was wide, quiet where she bellowed. He was whip smart, too, and understood how it was to have life go against you. He winked at Marie and passed her a coin or two for candy, but he would not lift a finger against his wife.

Tante Josie took over cooking the meals in the pink house on the hill. She did not want to lose the good wages, but *Tante* was not a chef like *Maman,* she used too much salt, every dish came out bitter, and she knew her days were numbered, so she looked around and bartered the sweet, not her own dear daughters, *non,* but Marie, now fourteen, up to the house. No more time for English classes or reading either, but the white-curled lady never raised a question, turned her cataract-clouded eyes to the wall, because nothing could be truly spoiled if it wasn't English first.

Tante had her mop the floors, rub lemon oil deep down into the grain of the wood, but mostly she left her in the greenhouse on long afternoons, alone in a babyish, white crocheted dress and frilly pink panties, alone with the old lady's son, a man with his own hair gone salt and pepper already, because the sweet of their same family blood didn't matter to *Tante.*

* * *

Another village by another name, where *Maman* had taken her for *fresco,* ices, but now where the man-on-the-hill took her when he wanted more privacy than the greenhouse allowed. First, he sat in the bar and had a beer, talked with the men while she sat outside on a chair or crate or, if there was no room, on the curb where her legs would get dusty. Sometimes he sent a Pepsi out. Then he rented a room in the town's only hotel, but this was no news since he had rented rooms there many such times, so the only gossip was adding Marie's name to the long list of ruined. She felt light-headed with dread. A small room, bare, except for a wobbly table by the window, one chair, which he sat on to untie his shoes, and a bed barely wide enough to hold one weary body.

The man-on-the-hill was kinder when he was away from his large pink house and his fancy people. He showed a definite tenderness toward those he would use. His face was soft and pink like the belly of a pig. Marie looked down at his bare feet, the toenails thick and yellowed. He pinched her earlobe between his thumb and forefinger as he ruined her the first time, so that she wouldn't feel the true pain. "Marie, Marie, Marie," he whispered in her ear till she grew to hate the sound of her own name. He made her whisper back his name and the English words his mother had so carefully taught her. "Edward, Edward, Edward." *The rain in Spain stays mainly in the plain.* Afterward, he pulled out a small pair of gold-plated scissors and cut out a section of the stained sheet, which he neatly folded and put away in his jacket pocket. Marie pictured a wooden box filled with the scraps of other girls. While he smoked, he ordered her to strip the rest of the bed and bundle it for laundry, treating her as maid, as if the act were simply another service provided by the hotel.

When Marie started throwing up in the mornings, *Tante* took her down to the curing shed where the coffee beans dried. She worked a metal wire between her legs and that was the end of that. So much blood, maybe this would be her end . . . the floor stayed red no matter how many times she made Marie wash it afterward. Tante Josie stood by and smoked down her cigar. "Shame on you," she said. "You *bouzin*. At least there won't be babies." That was the first time Marie felt herself grow strong by hate. *Tante* let Marie stay home that afternoon, resting on the porch, while she brought her cup after cup of coffee to fortify her blood. By now, Marie knew better than to mistake this for kindness; *Tante* was protecting her investment.

After a time, maybe two years, the man-on-the-hill was done. The white-curled lady lay dead in the weed-covered foreigners' graveyard. She would never make it back to her England or know the wickedness the island had allowed to fester in her son. Now he only wanted fresh goods, *Tante*, with her pebble eyes, said to Marie. Josie was a regular businesswoman bartering with Marie's body. Next she offered the girl to man-on-the-hill's son, a pimply boy scared of his own shadow. Then after, to his friends, until after a time it didn't matter to Marie anymore—what was Marie was gone like a kite after the string snapped.

As Marie was handed down, there was less and less kindness, as if the thing that had been done to her were simply a fact of nature or self-inflicted character. As if she had been born ruined and was maturing into it. Soon not even shabby rooms were rented, but dark alcoves, hallways, stinking alleyways. Taken for granted that she was what they saw before them, had always been that, and nothing else. Treat someone as if they're worthless, soon they believe it. By the time Marie got to the woman in Port-au-Prince, even Tante Josie pretended away her part and blamed the girl for her state.

* * *

After the men in the village were through, *Tante* cut a bargain with the woman who ran girls to Port-au-Prince. A regular establishment of whoring. Marie packed a kerchief and boarded a *tap tap* for the capital, a reverse of her *maman*'s escape. When Tante Josie and her daughters waved good-bye, Marie turned her back.

Although Marie had not seen Jean-Alexi again after the beach encounter, she had heard talk of him through the village gossip. From small-time criminal and drug dealer in the village, he had been recruited by the local Macoutes to turn his attention from cruelty to things to cruelty toward men. He "disappeared" some of the men who were making trouble for local politicians collecting taxes. For his appetite for ruthlessness, he was rewarded with a Jeep, an Uzi, and a few acres of land. These he quickly converted to cash to buy drugs, doubling his wealth. At about the time *Maman* was murdered, Jean-Alexi was on his way to the capital to continue seeking his dark fortune. Unlike Marie a few years later, he did not go empty-handed or without connections.

Madame Zo, Madame Bones, the woman *Tante* sold her to, was impatient as she met the *tap tap*. "You are late, stupid girl." It was dark already, the noise and crowds of Port-au-Prince overwhelming to a girl from the country. But Marie remembered the happy stories *Maman* had told her of her younger days there—could life get any worse than it had been in the countryside?

Madame Zo walked her to the edge of the park, what she later learned was the Champs de Mars. "Get in a few customers before we go home." Marie was dirty, hungry, and tired. The walkways around the grass and trees were crowded by the dark shapes of other girls, and each time a man passed by, voices moaned and pleaded. Marie hung back against a building, her sack of belongings clutched over her chest, till Madame Zo found her. "Nothing? Too much to hope for."

She held on to Marie's hand and marched her through the nightmare of La Saline. Marie had never imagined such a way of living because, although they had been poor, there had always been space; here there was none. They wound their way through a maze of narrow, dirty passageways, a chaos of noises and smells, and all she could think was how she would escape. Sanity would be when she was back in open spaces, back under her sacred trees. They came to a rusted-iron, padlocked gate. The house was built of plyboard, supported by leaning on its neighbors; the roof was corrugated iron that in the rain dripped puddles of orange rust. In the alleyway, a dozen girls lounged on low plastic stools in various states of undress. A few listened to calypso on the radio, a few played dominoes. None of them bothered to look up at Marie's arrival.

"You don't work here—you do your business in the park. This is home," Madame Zo said.

Some of the girls snickered. Home was the size of a large closet, and thirty to forty girls were to call it their place of living. No matter where Marie rested, she pressed against other bodies. At night they slept *dòmi kampe,* what they called stand-up sleep. The first girl in rested against the wall, padding her cheek with an arm or a piece of clothing. The next girl came and rested against her, so on and so on, until the last packed herself against the opposite wall, sometimes seven or eight bodies thick. When they were in tight enough, one could relax, held up by others, and not fall down. At first the contact repulsed Marie, used to the luxury of space in the village, but after a while her insides grew so lonely, the contact comforted. It didn't much matter which girls she leaned against, they were all sisters in misfortune.

One day that was especially fine—the sun hot but the trade winds carrying off the humidity, Marie walked to the public fountain to wash her dress while she wore the other one she owned. A customer from the night before had given her a generous tip, and she treated herself to *fritay,* fried pork in dough. Out of the corner of her eye, she saw a swaggering, loose-jointed walk and dreads that could belong only to one man. "Jean-Alexi?"

The young man turned and studied her with a smile, trying to place her. *"Bonjou."*

"Don't you know me? From the village?"

He shrugged, lifted thin, muscled shoulders. *"Koumon ou rele?* What's your name?"

"Marie. From the village." Their brief meeting had been years ago; they had never exchanged names. News of Jean-Alexi had created a relationship in her mind. "You protected my money from some boys on the beach."

"Good for me, *nuh*? I'm late now." He didn't remember her, but as he turned away, she became desperate to hold on to someone from the old days.

"I'm Leta's girl."

His face broke open in recognition. "Why didn't you say? Say hello now to *Maman.*"

"They killed her."

He nodded as if this were part of the everyday, no *who?* or *why?* needed. *"Mwen regret sa.* I'm sorry."

"I have no one to tell," she said.

"Grown up as pretty as your *maman.*" He looked at her closely, then looked away as her tears began to fall. Only in front of someone who understood did she feel free to cry. "Let's go."

They walked out of La Saline and through downtown, grabbing rides from trucks and cars whose drivers beeped in recognition of Jean-Alexi. Inside the vehicles, the men sat in front and discussed business, ignoring Marie in the back, which was just fine with her. This was her first chance to see the city as a whole, and as their journey slowly led them up the hill, the details that were so hard to bear up close grew smaller and smaller. From a distance, the brightly painted shantytowns almost looked tolerable next to the rolling blue of the ocean.

Halfway up the hill, Jean-Alexi jumped out of the pickup they were riding. Marie had not imagined an area as nice as the one they now found themselves in. Palm trees swayed overhead, bougainvillea and hibiscus formed crowded hedges at street level. Although the houses were run-down, many abandoned, there was a sense of ease that didn't exist down below. Jean-Alexi led her inside the crumbling walls of a compound.

"These were your people. Look how we sliding back in one generation—you turned *bouzin*."

The main house had been condemned—a fire and then a few years later an earthquake made it unsound—but on the grounds, families had set up shacks, squatters' residency.

"I like it here," Marie said.

"You should. This is your papa's house. Or was, long ago."

"Did you know him?"

"I was just a kid. But he was a great man. Gave people hope."

They walked through the empty rooms, looted of everything of conceivable value. In the kitchen, the stove gone and a pile of coals on the floor. In the bedroom, an old stained mattress. Marie liked it that way—the place hollowed out of meaning. Too painful to consider what could have been her life.

"I come here sometime to be alone. Now you should come. This is all that's left you. Your *maman* was a good woman. Like *tante* to me."

Marie stood at the open window, stripped long ago of shutters, glass, and screens. The only thing that couldn't be stolen was the view of the glittering ocean far below.

"Is this rich neighborhood?"

"Ah, *non*. You go on up to Pétionville for that. You headin' up in the world, you go there and then next stop Miami."

"Miami." The name rolled in her mouth like something sweet and undreamed of.

"Hurry goin', girl. This La Saline life goin' eat you up fast."

He rummaged in a corner and came back with a bottle of *tafia,* homemade rum. As the sun sank into the ocean, they sat side by side on the mattress and passed the bottle.

"How about I stay here with you?" Marie said. "Not go back to La Saline. Nothing for me back there."

"*Mwen* leaving tomorrow, next day. Big time waitin' for me in Miami."

Marie nodded at the fact that Jean-Alexi would always be just ahead, out of her grasp.

"You ever hear 'bout the *chimère* in Cité Soleil?"

Marie shook her head.

"Don't want to. Just means I have a mark 'bove my head same as your papa and *maman*. Time to be moving on."

"I get so scared," she whispered.

He nodded. "When I used to get scared, I killed it right away. Kill it, that's all I can tell."

Halfway through the bottle, she realized she was drunk for the first time in her life, and the worry that was a constant in the pit of her stomach was gone, or at least unfelt.

"You can kiss me," she said.

He shook his head. "You like *mwen sè,* sister."

Jean-Alexi rolled over and fell asleep. She had wanted his kiss. The chance to feel desire herself was new, instead of serving as the object of it for others. Love, too, as impossible and out of reach as a big house on a hill.

Loud chirping woke them the next morning. They searched the empty room until Jean-Alexi found a cricket high up in the rafters. Carefully he cupped it in his palms, carried it over to the window, and opened his hands. It just sat there, big and brown, warming in the sunbeam it found itself in. It started to rub its wings and sing

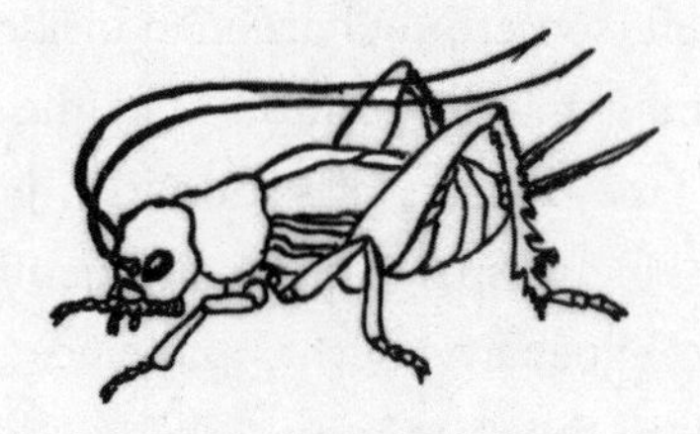

again. "Get goin'. Don't know a good thing when it happens." He blew on it and the insect flew straight up and out into the sky.

Jean-Alexi didn't leave but neither did he touch her. She wanted to be touched by someone she chose. Nothing more than that. Too much. Instead they lived chastely side by side in the abandoned house for a couple of days. It was the happiest time of Marie's life. One night after he took her out for a big dinner at a friend's restaurant, they lay in bed and held hands.

"That day on the beach I told you about?" she said.

"Listening."

"You were so beautiful that day. I wanted you for *mwen* boyfriend, but you don't even look."

Jean-Alexi smiled and closed his eyes. "You were just a girl-child, I think."

He leaned over to kiss her, then kissed her more. "I'm leaving here," he said.

"It's okay," she said, and covered his mouth with hers. She made love to a man of her choosing. This is it, she thought, this is what it should be. The other times were such a sad fake. Women did it to eat, but why did the men buy? Compared to the real, it was worse than nothing.

After a time, the moon drifted up, and she was so peaceful in the quiet room, she fell asleep. In the morning, she woke up, and Jean-Alexi was gone.

* * *

After Jean-Alexi left, something hardened inside Marie. She went to a higher-class madam who paid off Madame Zo, and soon she was walking the fancy streets of Pétionville. Jean-Alexi's prophecy haunted her—she wasn't going to let the life eat her up. She saved to buy one expensive outfit, and once well-dressed, she worked her way into the restaurants. She would sit alone and order dinner and hardly ever was she alone by the time she finished, check taken care of.

A French aid worker took a fancy to her after several times together and made a deal to have her to himself when he was in town. He was an older, important man in local politics; she heard him give interviews on the radio, speaking of aid and saving the Haitian people. Although he did not care enough to keep Marie his when he was gone, he insisted on owning her body when he was there.

He would arrive and open his rented apartment that remained empty and locked against her while he was gone. Each day when he left, he turned the key from the outside, imprisoning her no matter how she argued that she would like to take a walk or visit with a friend. When he returned, he filled a washbasin with warm, soap-filled water and motioned Marie over. He bathed her as gently as a mother: her feet, her elbows, behind the ears, although she had already made herself clean for him. Then he would have her spread her legs apart, and he would rub only there, and at that moment he changed into lover. He brought her food, delicious food, and took pleasure in watching her eat, sometimes feeding her himself, but each day he brought less, so that finally Marie was starving even as she ate.

She could have tried to jump out the window, but she would only have succeeded in breaking her neck. And what was she escaping to? She could have pounded and yelled at the door, but the crafty landlady was against her. People's hearts tend to understand the side with money, the side that pays the bills. What is another young, ruined girl, after all?

* * *

Often the Frenchman drank in the small room, and the alcohol would make him homesick for Cannes, for his wife and two boys.

"Why don't you stay home then?" Marie pouted.

He narrowed his eyes at her, as if considering the implications of the question. "Because I never love them as much as when I am here."

"*Tanpi*, too bad," she said, smirking, and then he would hit her. It always ended like this, and so after a while she found herself hurrying to this point to get it over.

Afterward, he would be filled with remorse and passion. His eyes would tear, and he would give her extra gourdes to buy herself something nice. "You don't understand, *ma petite nègresse*. I've never loved anyone like I love you."

Marie wondered at the horror of this being true.

One time only the Frenchman took her on a trip out of the capital. They traveled to the coast, to a resort on the beach where one of his UN buddies was giving a party. Marie was excited because this appeared a step in making their relationship public and permanent. He parked the car in a gravel lot with a long dirt track to the beach, fenced jungle on either side so the locals were kept out.

As they walked, small girls appeared from behind the trees and pressed against the fence, holding bunches of bananas. When the Frenchman came close, they began their chants: "Baa-naaan-nan. Baaa-nan-naan." Up and down the road they sang like birds, small girls who reminded Marie of herself at seven or eight years old. Would they, too, eventually become the girls moaning and pleading in the dark along the Champs de Mars?

The Frenchman laughed and pointed, thinking their hawking charming, but Marie shook with fury. She hissed at them, "*Pe la!* Shut it!" But of course the girls saw her nice dress, her well-fed stomach, and wanted that for themselves, ignoring her.

Finally the Frenchman chose an especially scrawny girl who looked half-starved and bought the largest bunch she had. When they arrived at the resort, a crowd was out on the terrace dancing. Most of the men were European; all the women were black.

"I've brought the banana girl," the Frenchman announced as Marie carried the bunch in behind him.

She burned with humiliation, but she could do nothing. All eyes were on her, expectant, so she lifted the bananas on top of her head and danced slowly around the floor, pulling off and handing a banana to each man and woman she passed. The Frenchman clapped, delighted, but Marie understood she was nothing more than those girls standing in the dirt.

When the Frenchman wasn't around, she often went to her father's abandoned house. In its cloistered emptiness, she tried to see a future that wasn't the obvious one she was headed toward. She tried to recall the days spent there with Jean-Alexi, the only bit of happiness she could summon. When the Frenchman returned to the island the next time, she wore her best dress, and as soon as he had a few drinks, she broached her plan.

"I'd like to go to France."

"Yes?"

"Could you help me? I want maybe to be a teacher, like my *maman*."

"A teacher doesn't have a *pute* for a daughter."

She wanted to slap him across the face, but she knew it would cost more than the momentary satisfaction was worth. "That's the problem with you people. You believe history only moves in one direction. Sometimes it slides backwards, sometimes it just gets mashed up."

"I like you right here. Waiting for me."

* * *

Next, Marie turned to her only other hope, Uncle Thibant. Since he couldn't read, she hired a messenger to tell him her request—pay for her boat passage to Miami or she would come to the village and tell everyone what Tante Josie had done to her. Not only that, Marie would be sure to get her fired from the pink house. "No matter what it takes, I will ruin *Tante,* tell him that. But tell him I love him."

When Uncle Thibant showed up in the capital, he looked older and more frightened than she remembered. It was his first time in Port-au-Prince. She took him out for dinner, and he fidgeted, not eating a bite. "I never knew what she done to you."

"You knew, or you didn't want to know. But I never blamed you, Thibant. I figure you and me are just the weak in the world."

"I find a boat through *zanmi* Jean-Alexi. So they don't steal from you, he pay at other end."

Her heart was pounding so hard at the reality of leaving, she hardly heard him, didn't care for the details. A good omen—Jean-Alexi would be on the other side for her.

They hugged to say good-bye. Thibant such a country peasant he insisted on sleeping at the side of the road all night to make sure he caught the first *tap tap* out of the capital in the morning.

"You tell *Tante* this is the money she owes me. This makes us square, okay?"

Uncle Thibant moved off quickly, and Marie realized with a sting it was to get away from her. No matter that she had been the one wronged. Especially in the country, people tended to condemn a person for her misfortune; it was easier that way. Thibant didn't want proof of who *Tante* was. Easier to pretend when Marie was out of sight and gone.

Victim turns into monster, and they don't want themselves to blame for it, *wi*?

Chapter 3

The horror of the boat trip was forgotten because Marie thought at last her life would change. "Change, life, change," she chanted under her breath, to the rhythm of the waves, until the other girls thought she was singing, and they hummed along searching for the melody.

The slosh and thump of water against the boat's hull, the constant fear of the mosquito whine of a Coast Guard boat coming to turn them back, or the equal fear that the smugglers running the boat would take advantage of the women, all vanished at the first sight of land. From far off the orange halo over the cities of South Florida looked like giant bonfires lit to signal them in. Magic names—Miami, Key West, Delray, Boca Raton—like incantations. No one waited for them, or wanted them. They stole in like thieves. But Uncle Thibant promised Jean-Alexi would be there to pick Marie up.

Grateful to have someone to take her away from the beach and the danger of police, she didn't notice until later that he was also chatting up the other women in the group—the thin, young ones—who crowded into the back of the waiting van with her.

Behind the tatty front seats, the van was pure island, stripped out with nothing more than a filthy metal floor to sit on. At first, the most fussy of the group, those who had saved clean clothes to be worn after the landing, if there was a landing, tried to squat and preserve the impression they had struggled so hard to make—white blouses and dark, printed cotton skirts—of well-behaved convent girls. But the quick driving, the hard turns, knocked them over and into each other. Marie had to brace her legs against the side of the van to avoid landing on top of, or underneath, other bodies. They were like chickens thrown carelessly in a box on the way to the butcher.

The two men who crowded together on the passenger seat did not introduce themselves, did not follow polite island custom. They sat, squat and muscled, with blue-black skin, and hungry rat eyes. Marie knew such men from Port-au-Prince. They sat and drank till they were filled with lust, then they picked luxuriously, like choosing cuts of meat, and went up the stairs, and the girls didn't talk for a long time afterward.

Jean-Alexi didn't seem to recognize her. Or if he did, he wasn't letting on. Not that she'd expected a honeymoon meeting. He'd lost weight and put on years—he looked old and tired for twenty-four. His eyes were scattered and hyped. The old cockiness gone.

The main thing she noticed was the increase of his dreadlocks—now enormous and dusty-cocoa colored, billowing up large like an engorged cockscomb, bundled in half with a tie like a huge crest. His hair frightened and fascinated her. A shantytown rooster. As she reached to touch one braid, unable to guess if it felt stiff and hard as rope or soft as fur, he grabbed her wrist hard.

"Now, little Erzulie, what kind of trouble you looking for from your Jean-Alexi? *Nuh,* girl?"

Marie tried to pull her hand back, but he held the wrist fast as with a band of steel, a deceiving strength from such a banty man, strength hid like a strand of spiderweb.

He looked back at her, foot tapping, other hand thumping the wheel, his eyes a cracked gold that didn't seem right. Then he pulled her hand to his lips, stuck out his tongue, and ran it along the inside of her wrist.

"Hmmm, homegrown sugar, that's what I miss the most of the island."

At this possibility, the other two men looked at her for the first time, appraising.

"Too bad you're Thibant's folk," Jean-Alexi said, and dropped her hand roughly.

"Not mine," one of them said.

Jean-Alexi looked at him hard. "Way too precious for you, brother."

Marie was confused at this behavior after the way he had been before and wondered at the change. Was this fierce new look and behavior some kind of act in front of the others?

The past gave her a flicker of courage. "We're hungry," she said.

"Well, let's feed you," he said. "Don't you know? Now you're in the land of plenty?"

His crazy eyes studied her, but she convinced herself he meant no harm. No love, either. She remembered the candy he gave her that day on the beach—a dried-out, pink piece of taffy too stale to eat.

There was whispered discussion up front while in the back the girls and Marie exchanged wondering looks. A few minutes later, they pulled up to a brightly lit building with glowing neon. Jean-Alexi rolled down his window and talked at length into a speaker box that crackled back answers to his words.

When he drove around the building, a girl was sitting in the window. Marie guessed the same one he'd been talking to through the box. Her skin was pale and blotchy, her eyes a drained blue, her whole appearance suggesting something uncooked. Greasy, long hair, the color of brass, was held up out of her eyes with black bobby pins. But Jean-Alexi spoke to her as if she were the most enchanting princess, and Marie felt a stab of something—embarrassment for him? Jealousy? Here he was, courting the lowliest of white women.

"How you doing this night, beautiful lady?"

"That'll be fifty-two fifty, please," she said, expressionless.

Marie liked that she wasn't buying his stupid flatteries.

He handed the window girl a crisp one-hundred-dollar bill with a flourish. "How about I take you out after work sometime, pretty lady? Take you for some real food?"

Marie thought that maybe the girl only heard words through the earphones, that in person, communication was only one way, outward.

The girl blinked at the bill and hesitated, then took out a fat highlighter pen and ran a yellow line over it, then held it against the fluorescent light. She signaled back to her manager, who was busy shoveling fries into small paper pockets. He shrugged.

"I'll have to get change."

Marie looked into the main building where the tables stood under the scrubbing light that killed any shadow. Each detail—a crack in a plastic seat, a man's stubbled chin—showed in stark relief, like looking at grains of sand under the clear ocean back home. The people at the tables seemed to be moving in slow motion as if they, too, were underwater. Eyes half-closed, they ate their food out of paper and avoided looking at each other's face. The night was hot yet they were bundled up in long sleeves and jeans and jackets. They did not seem to know the temperature outside, to know where they were. Marie could tell them—she who still had the smell of sour bilgewater on her feet, who'd risked everything to arrive at this very spot. *You are in the land of dreams come true.* What would they make of her sacrifice? The thought came up inside her, unwanted: What if this place cost more than it gave, what if it was really no better than what had been sacrificed for it?

The brass-haired girl came back and gingerly counted out the green bills into Jean-Alexi's outstretched hand, avoiding touching his long, curled fingers. One of the men in the passenger seat turned on the radio, and reggae blasted out. Maybe to convince her that it was like a regular tropical vacation in the van?

Large, white paper bags were handed from the manager to the girl to Jean-Alexi, who turned and gave them to Marie to pass out.

"You want extra ketchup with those?" the girl said. Already she belonged to someone else, her brow furrowed as she listened to a new order through her earphones and punched it in on her plastic board.

"You lose a big, fat chance at happiness, girl," Jean-Alexi said, when the last tray of drinks crossed over.

"Would you mind moving your car ahead, sir? So the next customer can pull up?"

The van stood idling, Jean-Alexi tapping his fingers along the steering wheel as if he were sending out a message in code.

The girl cupped her hand over the mike and leaned over the counter, her head partway out the window. "I don't do black fellows, hon."

Jean-Alexi stepped down hard on the accelerator, jumping over the corner of the curb, and shouted, *"Bouzin sal!* Dirty bitch!" out the window. The bounce of the van tilted the big, papery cup of soda, which spilled down Marie's shirt, but already she was smart enough to say nothing.

They parked in a deserted corner of a lot, and the men got out to relieve themselves against a dumpster. They smoked while the girls huddled in the back and ate their fill of hamburgers and fries. The girls trembled and asked Marie if they would be safe, and she assured them yes, even though she had no idea. They threw the paper remains out the window and curled against each other like stray puppies and fell into a desperate sleep.

* * *

They, twelve girls old and new, shared a single bedroom in a cinder-block apartment building. One had to step carefully because someone was always either lying asleep or sick. The girls marked their floor space by spreading out sleeping bags, or towels, blankets, pillows. But for all their efforts, the places they fought for still ended up being only the size of a coffin. There was hell to pay, and fists, if anyone touched another's belongings. The net effect of their jealousy was that the room never got cleaned, the floor on which they slept turned grimy with grit and dust, dead insects and loose hair.

They were so possessive because they had nothing else, and this was no *fanmi,* family. Girls disappeared with alarming frequency, to be replaced by others, and so they became aloof and protective and tried not to get too close.

Maman's girl, Marie felt too far from God in that filth, and she spent the first week negotiating the permission of each girl to mop her section of the floor on condition that each possession be guarded and then returned to its rightful place. Jean-Alexi, impressed by her leadership abilities, gave her special jobs.

Amélie, a girl already there when their group arrived, had a single possession that made her the envy of all—a pair of red, patent-leather high heels. She and Marie became friends because they discovered they had each lost their *maman* within a few months of each other, suffering much after that, until finally ending up in the cinder building. Amélie was light skinned, with soft eyes like a deer, and a straight, thin nose. Men stopped in the street and stared at the way she rolled her hips as she walked by. She talked all the time of becoming a model, but first she needed to save money to have her teeth fixed.

The first afternoon that they found themselves alone in the apartment, Amélie allowed Marie to try on her shoes.

"How you know Jean-Alexi so good?" Amélie asked.

"From home. We shared time together."

"You sweet on him?"

Marie ignored the question by looking at the shoes. She had never before worn such things—thin, shiny straps that cut across the toe, a strap that choked the ankle, and a four-inch heel as thin and sharp as a dagger. She walked around the living room feeling like a giant, tripping forward as if she were on stilts.

The front door rattled, and Jean-Alexi walked in, followed by the two from the van, Zac and Lolo, carrying pizza boxes. When Jean-Alexi saw Marie, his eyebrows shot up.

"What you think, brothers? She take to them shoes like fish to water."

Quickly, Marie sat to take them off, but he stopped her. "Keep walking. Get a hang of those things."

Amélie made a face and went to the bedroom, slamming the door.

Jean-Alexi moved around the room on his toes, like a dancer, giving her advice on how to swing out her legs from the hip so that her stride would be like that of Amélie, who moved smooth as a cat. Starved, Marie basked in his attention.

"Tomorrow I take you shopping for some of your own girl stuff."

"I don't have money."

"Don't you worry. Jean-Alexi will take care."

The next afternoon, he came back from his business appointments early and took her downtown, buying her lunch at a Jamaican restaurant in an alley. She ate jerked pork and dirty rice and drank cold beer, and she thought that her American life had finally started.

"Why don't we eat at Haitian restaurant?" she asked.

"They all in bad neighborhoods. Too, the owner here owes me monies."

He watched her lips as she wiped them with a napkin, then leaned in quick and gave her a kiss. He tasted of cigarettes, but she didn't care because it was a kiss she wanted, not one she was paid for.

"So you remember our time together?" she asked.

"I know I had a sweet night with you."

"But you don't remember me on the beach. I was a little thing, and you said I was too young and small."

He leaned over and squeezed her breast as if it were a peach. "You *tête* just right for me now."

Marie swallowed her disappointment.

Jean-Alexi shook his leg as if it were on fire. "That years ago now. I'm a whole other person now."

She cleared her throat for the speech she had been practicing: *Maman*'s dream for her to work someplace quiet, someplace filled with books. She had decided on a library, although she wasn't sure what one did there. *Maman*'s idea of success was doing something that didn't give you calluses on your hands. "I need to find a job. I want to go to school."

"All in good times. You don't need that now. Soon I going to have good businesses. You work in family place."

"I'm not family."

Now he slung his arm across her shoulders as they walked and nibbled on her ear. "Might be, *nuh*? You liked being with me, didn't you?"

Jean-Alexi took her to a clothing store that played loud music, the fast, thumping kind foreigners danced to in nightclubs in

Pétionville, and a girl with a round mahogany face framed by long platinum hair came up to Jean-Alexi and gave him a wet kiss on the mouth. She kept her wolf eyes on him, and Marie guessed they'd been lovers, but now he was all business and told her to find Marie something real pretty.

"One of your new girls?" the women asked.

"I'm his girlfriend," Marie said, and they both laughed at her.

When they got back home, Lolo and Zac were eating ribs out of an aluminum tray and watching basketball on the TV in the living room.

"What should we call her?" Jean-Alexi asked.

"Why call me anything but my name?"

The Two Fools, which name Amélie and Marie used behind their backs, were stoned. They threw their dirty dishes in the sink for the girls to clean as if they were slaves. Now the fools giggled and smirked while Jean-Alexi framed Marie between his fingers as if he were going to star her in a picture.

"You rename something to give it power," he said, but Marie knew from her *Maman* one renamed to take power. "You are my lead lady. How about Maleva?" he said, plucking a rib from the tray.

"I don't want my name changed," she said, but he didn't bother to hear. When she reached for a rib, he slapped her hand away.

"Got to watch that figure, girl."

The fools laughed and stamped their feet. "*Wi, wi*. Yes, yes."

Marie took her shopping bags and went into the bedroom, intending to lie down for a nap and wait for Amélie to come home for dinner. She worried about this given name, worried Jean-Alexi might try *obeah,* try to take her soul away. When he came in and insisted she dress in the new clothes and they go out, she told him she was tired.

His face grew mean with displeasure. "How you going to get a job and go to school when you're so lazy? How are you going to be my lady?"

So she put on the white halter dress and the shoes as tipsy high as Amélie's. Jean-Alexi looked at her critically and made her put on more mascara and lipstick, then handed her some silver hoop earrings that belonged to another girl.

"That's not mine."

"None of this belongs to any of you *tifi,* get it? Jean-Alexi's property."

Marie did not ask him questions because she didn't want someone who held her future to think that she didn't trust him. Gossip among the girls was Jean-Alexi wanted her to be his partner. When young ones were brought in, he took Marie to the kitchen and showed her how to grind up little white pills and mix them in juice to calm the girls down. Best way to ease them into the business with the least fuss. Too, she felt sorry for these girls, not introduced to the life before like she was. She cooked up big pots of spaghetti, trays of chicken and rice, the way *Maman* had taught her, so that they might feel some comfort.

Surely he didn't see her like the other girls. They had a bond from the island. Maybe he was only an island cousin, which meant nothing more than someone you knew from the island, but he knew she was Leta's child. Maybe he was wanting to settle down with just one, and she could be that for him. He told her over and over she was his *bijou,* treasure.

He said he wanted to celebrate, and they pulled into a hotel parking lot by the airport. Marie did not take the bait of asking, celebrate what? Getting out, she felt the hot wash of a plane's wind as it passed low overhead to land. The bar was dark after coming in from the blinding afternoon sun. The blue lights overhead made soothing pools along the tables. Maybe this was not such a bad place after all. But the air had a sour, refrigerated smell—she shivered in the thin, new dress. Would it be so bad to be the girl behind the counter, all cool and dressed pretty, serving rainbow-colored drinks to people?

Jean-Alexi broke into a large smile—a perfect row of white, snapping teeth—and put his hand on the small of Marie's back as he steered her through empty tables toward one occupied by a middle-aged man. Under his breath, Jean-Alexi said this man was going to help him get a liquor license. The man seemed squeezed into the suit he wore, rolls of fat overflowing the collar of his shirt. His baldness and full cheeks gave him the look of a baby, but when he looked up at her, there was no smile, no kindness. The shadows around his eyes were cruel, and Marie stepped back as if he'd growled.

"Don't be afraid of César." Jean-Alexi laughed. He jived and bobbed back and forth, and she saw that he was deferential and weak in front of this man. The transformation of Jean-Alexi from a minor prince of the slums to this depressed her.

Perhaps César was the owner of the hotel, or the manager of the bar. Maybe Jean-Alexi would get her work as a maid, a waitress, a bartender? But the table in front of César was empty except for a glass that held a thumb's worth of amber liquid. No, probably she was César's business that day.

"This is fresh Maleva that I promised you," Jean-Alexi said, bending to give him a handshake and private words.

Marie turned and ran. She heard a name called out, but kept running, only later recognizing it was her newly christened one. A name she would not be using. She stood by the van until her breath came steady again, her heartbeat slowed. Goose bumps gave way to sweat in the heat. No one chased after her. After a while her feet hurt from standing in the heels, and she pulled off her shoes and stood barefoot on the hot asphalt.

After half an hour, Jean-Alexi, all bull confidence, strolled out as if he had enjoyed the visit with his friend as intended. He smiled at her and waved at the passenger door.

"Get in, get in."

Watching the cars flying by on the interstate, the lights from the city beyond, the glowing windows of the hotel above, Marie understood she did not know another human being there besides him. She had no choice but to climb inside.

"You're not *fou*, mad, at me?" she asked.

"Surprise, surprise. He liked that little act. Makes it more believable that you're some virgin off the island. He say rest up a few days, and he'll pay double."

"You do this to me!" she screamed. "*Yon fanmi!* Leta's girl."

"Enouf."

"I'll tell Uncle Thibant what you do."

"From what I hear, this is better than spreading your legs in chicken coops the way you did back home. Thibant sent you over on credit. You work off that boat ride, roof, and eats on your back."

"Non!"

"Listen to me, we're all 'cousins' over here. Just 'cause you and me bed don't mean nothing if you can't earn food in your mouth."

They drove in silence.

Gentle Thibant cheated her after all. Sent her to a different corner of hell, collect. Marie looked out the window at the miles of city that she didn't know. "I thought you liked me."

He said nothing.

"I can clean for you."

"Don't need no maid."

"I take care of the girls, dope them up for you. They trust me. I run drugs—no one expect a pretty little thing like me, right? Work off the debt slow."

"Don't need mules," he said.

"I want to work in library."

Jean-Alexi reached his arm so that Marie thought he was going to hit her, but he grabbed behind at a scrap of newspaper. "Read this," he said, a dare, jabbing his finger on the print. When she began to read aloud, he slapped it out of her hand. "Reading a dime a dozen here."

Marie dragged up the stairs behind him, went alone to the bathroom. She took off the dress and shoes, careful because they were not hers, and sat on the edge of the bathtub in her underwear.

The tub and the sink were ringed in filth. Trash overflowed with women's personal. *Maman* had taught her cleanliness and modesty. Even in the worst times, she always turned away to dress, even if a man had ripped the clothes off so that the buttons scattered across the floor like teeth. She stared at the makeup piled on the shelves, the lotions and curlers and other fake the girls used to be beautiful. This was the life offered to her, the same life she'd tried to escape. Look at what Jean-Alexi had become. If she took it, how long before a better one offered itself? When would what she did finally become who she was?

She walked out of the bathroom wearing the clothes she had arrived in. She handed Jean-Alexi the dress and shoes. "I'm going."

His chin went up and down rapidly, biting down on something nasty. He nodded. "Then."

She took her bag of possessions to the front door, but now he shot up and followed her.

"I didn't even fuck you to get *mwen lajan*, my money, back. Just suck me off then. At least there's no chance of a idiot coming out nine months from now."

"Non."

"Don't want to hurt you." He banged his fist on the wall behind her head.

She looked at him then, but no longer saw him. "You'll have to kill me first."

He howled but let her walk away, down the stairs. They both knew that she had reached the point where she had nothing left to lose, and he had no chance bargaining that.

"You think you're something special, but you'll find out. It's bad out there, *fi*. You'll come back soon, unless you *mouri*," he yelled out the window.

"Coming back won't happen."

"I be here when you're begging. Price go way up then," he screamed down the block at her retreating back. Did he sense he might be losing someone true? *Non*.

When she could no longer hear his shouts, she sat on the ground and shook, as if she had just scraped by with her life. She wasn't brave enough for her own actions.

After a time, Marie heard footsteps. If it had been Jean-Alexi, she might have gone back, but it was Amélie with another girl.

"Jean-Alexi kick you out?"

She nodded. The whole story in her eyes.

"I work at this place before here." Amélie scratched around in her purse, then grabbed a piece of newspaper off the ground. "It's bad, but they don't ask questions. My sister, Coca, worked there. I don't know anymore. Go early. Early bird gets the poison. You have someplace to sleep?"

Marie shook her head.

"Be careful. Careful out here. Not like back home." Amélie took her aside. "If you see Coca, tell her I work as a model in a department store downtown, okay? This is just temporary, don't want them to worry." She emptied a few crumpled bills from her wallet into Marie's hand. "What do you have?" Amélie barked at the other girl, who made a face, but added a few more. "It's all I can." With that, they walked away.

Marie found the building when the sky was still dark. Many hours from Jean-Alexi's apartment, and she had spent the whole night in slow movement toward it, like a ship tacking in the ocean, asking for directions that were more often than not wrong. Nobody in this city of foreigners seemed to know where they were. That night they were all lost. Under the sickly orange glow of streetlights, the concrete building appeared squat and defeated and did not seem promising of any kind of future.

She sat against the chain-link fence, her bag in her lap, and fell asleep. She woke to a gentle kick on her thigh and looked up into the not-unkind face of a young Hispanic man. Marie showed him the address and said, "Amélie," but when she got no look of recognition, she said, "Coca," and he nodded.

Inside was a jail, small cages packed tight with dogs. The dogs barked and howled, their noises echoing and amplified against the concrete floor and walls until she felt a humming inside her head as if it would split open. The overwhelming smell of urine and *kaka* gagged her.

The man, Jorge, handed her earplugs and a stained plastic apron. The job was to shovel out the cages, then hose down the floor and the dogs. Afterward, she filled the metal bowls with dry food. The dogs cowered in their cages, the muscles in their hind legs twitching with fear, but when she unlocked the doors, they bared their teeth and growled.

By noon Marie finished and was handed a twenty-dollar bill and a stale sandwich. As she stood eating in the shade of a coral tree because it reminded her of home, a pretty girl walked in. She hung on the arm of a short white man with tattoos down both arms. His teeth, brown and crooked, were ringed in gold. Marie saw the girl's resemblance to Amélie, except this girl did not have the fine bones and clear skin of her sister.

"Coca?"

Her eyes narrowed, and Marie saw the polite island ways were not followed here.

"I am *zanmi* of Amélie."

Now she smiled. It was only this place that made her wary. "How is Amie?"

"She told me to come here."

Her boyfriend ignored them. He picked his teeth, then swatted Coca on the behind. "Come on. You have a paycheck to earn."

When he had gone inside, Coca bent her head to Marie. "You in trouble?"

"What is this place?"

Coca lit a cigarette, and Marie admired her red-painted nails. "They steal dogs, pick them off the street. Even pretend to adopt them, but the shelters are starting to catch on. They sell them to the clinics. Cram lipstick in their eyes." She laughed.

Marie looked back into the cages.

"It's *travay,* work." Coca shrugged.

"You find me somewhere to sleep?"

"Our family is close by. Go introduce yourself to Papa. Use Amélie's bed."

For the next two weeks, Marie worked the morning shift from five till noon. Coca worked in the front office, but Marie was buried in the back. After a while, she got to know the dogs individually: this one would calm down once she entered his cage and another could be coaxed with a bit of food. She took out her earplugs now because she recognized the different barks, they were distinct voices, and she knew their cause and no longer found the noise frightening.

A reddish-gold pit bull mix wagged her tail each time Marie

came into her cage, and she stole an extra half cup of food for the dog every morning so that her ribs wouldn't poke out so sharply against her skin. After the first week, the dog let Marie rub her ears, one ear shorter and frayed, probably from a dogfight. Under her breath she took to calling her Rolex, the most precious thing she could think of in this new country.

The workers were forbidden to interact with the dogs and were supposed to treat them as things. Jorge said they were no different from cattle in the stockyards, but Marie did not see the point of it. It seemed to her that especially the condemned were entitled to any little kindness so maybe their last memory of this earth and their jailers was not so damning. Why else did the executioner allow a last meal, or a cigarette? The man in the pink house, if he had stayed kind and loyal, he could have used Marie for life; she didn't know better. Sweet with salt; the smallest bit of love with hate. That's the way one made a true slave.

Marie tried to ignore how Jorge and the other men roughhandled the animals, holding the leashes tight till they were swinging by the neck, bodies dangling like the stripped bodies of pigs or cows from butcher's hooks in La Saline. If the dogs were mean, the men kicked them with their heavy boots, and sometimes they kicked them even when they were not mean; it did not much matter to the men either way.

She rooted for the mean dogs. She wished them luck in their bites because either way they were doomed, and after a time she thought they, the humans working, were equally doomed, and the dawning knowledge that life could be as hard and ugly in America as it had been back home packed her chest so tight she could not breathe.

At the end of each week a van would pull up to the back of the building, and the dogs who had been there longest were pushed into the back in plastic crates and driven away, never to return. Then the process of refilling the cages would begin again. Marie was given overtime to stay and clean up after the dogs were hauled away. If *Maman* had been there, no doubt she would have felt the spirits, despair so painful Marie had to hit herself in the leg or arm so that she could bear it.

While she waited for her paycheck, she talked to Coca in the office, glancing at the lists, and saw it was Rolex's turn to go the next week.

Marie slept in Amélie's fragrant bed—a bed carved by Amie's father from a special wood only from the islands—its narrow hold like a boat transporting her back. She was in *Maman*'s kitchen, watching her make one of her special dishes, chicken with rice. They were hungry, so looking forward to eating, but no matter what spices *Maman* used, the dish grew saltier and saltier until it was finally inedible. *Maman* tasted it, tried to give Marie a spoonful, but it was impossible. Tears were in *Maman*'s eyes as she watched their bodies grow thinner by the minute, and she begged her daughter to fix it. Marie woke at dawn, exhausted.

At work, they led Rolex to the shower room to clean the dirt off her; Marie heard snarling and the men's threats. She walked in and spoke for the first time in two weeks. "Let me wash this one."

"So the Dog Girl talks."

The men were glad to take a break. Rolex, backed in the corner, crouched, teeth bared, eyes hating, and at first didn't recognize her. Jorge threw Marie the dog's chain in a challenge and went off to smoke a cigarette. "Don't get your hand chewed off."

She squatted down. "*Doudou*," she whispered. "It's okay now. I take care of you now." She picked up the chain and led Rolex under the showerhead and shampooed the filth off her. No one could have guessed the luster of her clean coat. The men stood around watching, thoughtful and sullen as they smoked their cigarettes.

"I'm going to take her on a walk to dry off," she said.

One of the new boys said it wasn't allowed, but no one else seemed to care.

"Give it a break," Marie said, scornful, because any show of softness would end them. She walked out of the shower with dripping Rolex, collected her purse while Coca watched under thick eyelashes. She walked down the street alone. After a few blocks she turned and saw no one behind her.

They ran.

She ran faster than she thought she was able, buildings and cars melting past. The faster she ran, the more Rolex stretched out, took longer strides, as if the new space allowed the dog to grow, heading straight ahead as if she knew this was her fate all along and had simply been waiting for Marie in her slow human way to figure it out. Marie ran faster, air a hot piston through her lungs, her bag banging hard against her side. They came to a park, and she veered off into the grass, the softness relieving the terrible pounding in her feet. She slowed, and Rolex slowed, as if they were a single body. They trotted, a slow jog, then walked, blowing out breaths like professional runners, shaking out legs, and when they came to a fountain, she let the dog drink deeply from the water.

They spent the whole day in the park, resting under a tree with large, spreading branches. The neighborhood they had invaded had bungalow houses set back on grassy lawns, palm trees that made pools of thick shade. Marie watched blond, blue-eyed mothers wheeling their babies through the park. Some of the babies were being pushed by dark women, some from Mexico or Central America, others from the islands. The sight of these women calmed her and made her feel safe. She was sick of the world of men. She fell asleep under the tree, holding Rolex's leash, dreaming she was back home.

When she woke, the dog was sitting, watching a young black woman pushing a pram with a yellow-haired baby. Marie called out, "What time is it, sister?" and the woman answered, "Five in the afternoon. Time to quit loafing."

Marie laughed at the tease, and the woman laughed back. She had skinny, bowed legs, with a big space between her front teeth. She struck a match against the pavement and lit a cigarette. "They don't let me smoke in the house. Is he friendly?" she said, pointing at Rolex.

"She needs to be, doesn't she?" Marie said.

"Be careful. The police don't like our faces around here unless we working."

"I hear you. Any chance your people would want this dog?"

The woman looked at Rolex as she shook her head. "No chance. The woman don't like any dirt in her house."

"That's too bad."

"It is."

"You get good job here?"

The woman nodded. "Many Haitians *nan Florid*. But we're all still dreaming of the promised land, *nuh*? Got to get going."

She walked on. Marie took out her lunch, ate half and fed the rest to Rolex. The dog gulped without chewing, looking for more. No more here, Marie thought. It was too sad to want to give more than you had. Sitting under that tree, she was as happy as she'd been since leaving home, but she knew that she would have to move on again. If the island was about standing still, America was about moving, even if you were past dead tired.

She walked through the park to the edge of a long street of houses that looked like mansions to her, like the palaces of kings in the Bible. Grander than the pink house on the hill even. Marie could tie Rolex to a streetlamp, but she worried that this would make the dog helpless, and perhaps only the police would rescue her, take her back to the shelter from where she started.

No, Marie thought as she untied her, Rolex is wise enough to recognize kindness when she runs across it. Marie had not seen much of it herself since she'd come here, the only god she saw worshipped so far was money, but this freedom was the only gift she could afford to give.

Sometimes it felt as if they were both dumb animals, lost and alone in the world. She felt the flame of good in the world was riding lower; lately she felt it guttering, about to blow out.

Maybe Rolex would walk up to that big white house with burning lights in the window, and she'd curl up on the porch by the door, and the pretty yellow-haired family that lived in it would come home and find her curled asleep, and they would see that she was precious, and they would take pity, which was the most that anyone could hope for.

Maybe after weeks and months of comfort, Rolex would be restored to herself, to the way she was before Marie ever saw her. She will only remember her shower, Marie's hands rubbing shampoo into her fur, only remember their run, the sharp, clean air as they fled. She will recall as her true beginning the day in the park, their nap as her resurrection, and Marie her weak angel, who brought her to the life that was surely waiting for her, the life that should be promised to all.

Marie took off the ribbon that held her hair and wrapped it around Rolex's neck and tied a bow so that anyone looking could see that she had been loved.

Rolex strained ahead, sniffing the night air as Marie unclipped the chain from her collar, and then she was gone.

Chapter 4

The less you have, the more the pain in losing what remains.

Marie stood alone in the park for an hour, hoping Rolex would return and hoping she would not. At last Marie started walking, one foot in front of the other, and found herself at Coca's house. When Coca saw her—a ghost at the door—she dropped the plate she was drying, confirming that Marie's hold on this life was weak.

"*Kisa ki rive ou?* What happened to you? Why did you come here?"

"Where else?"

"You took the dog. They'll make trouble now."

"It doesn't matter."

"If they see you here, I'll be fired."

Marie gathered her few shirts, a toothbrush.

Coca watched, biting her lip. "*Ou byen?* You okay?"

"No loss. I couldn't work there another day."

"Wait." Coca walked into the next room. Marie heard her on the phone, wondered briefly if she was turning her in, betrayal now a commonplace, but then Coca came back with a big smile on her face. "There's this lady I worked for. She called, asking if

I wanted to come back. Problem is that you have to live there, and I have family, my boyfriend, to look after. It's far on the other side of town. But for you . . ."

"Can't be far enough now."

"Just cleaning her house. She lives alone so there's not much mess, only dust. But don't do anything crazy, like with the dog, *oke*?"

Marie was shaking now, relief unlocking her bones. Already sure that she'd run out of last chances. "I can clean."

"Course you can," Coca said.

"*Mesi,* thank you. You save my life."

Marie started to cry, but Coca brushed her away. "One does what one can. Look, I tell the lady you're my cousin from Trinidad."

"I'm Haitian. She'll never believe me."

Coca looked at her, eyes disbelieving. "Don't you know, girl, we're all the same to them?"

Marie borrowed money from Coca for the bus and walked to the station. It didn't matter if she waited hours or days because this was the only slip of life she had left to try. She spent her last dollars on a sandwich and a Coke and even bought a candy bar in a spike of reckless hope.

Two hours later the bus dropped her off in a fancy suburb outside Miami. A warm night, the terminal was open to the air, brick and lacquered-wood benches scattered under a roof of grapevines. Marie slumped down on a bench and slept until the janitor poked her awake at dawn and told her to leave. That was what she was learning of this new country—no matter how lovely the place, one could never stay long, but had to keep moving.

She clutched the piece of paper with the address as if it were a lottery ticket. She wandered the streets reading the signs. Finally a garbage truck stopped to load cans, and the men were from Cité Soleil. They smiled, and they greeted her like long-lost kin—*Bonjou! Komon ou ye? N'ap boule!*—the taste of familiar words in her mouth gave her strength. They read the address and pointed the way, offering a ride, but *Maman*'s girl couldn't arrive for her new life with the garbage, so regretfully said no. Other than the trash truck, nothing moved in the silent, empty streets. The houses were set behind high walls, barricaded behind prickling, thorny hedges of bougainvillea.

At seven in the morning, Marie was staring at a white building that looked as if it were a set of child's blocks stacked one against another, filled with silvered glass on all sides. She checked over and over to make sure this unlikely place was the address on the paper. Unsure, she walked up the bleached-rock driveway that shushed under her feet like a rocky beach and dropped the fish-shaped knocker against a copper door, heard it echo through a large, empty space.

No one answered. She stopped and studied the street, then turned back again to the knocker, which she lifted and let fall, and heard a gunlike bang ricochet on the other side. The door gave way under her knuckles, and she dipped forward as a thin, tall woman wearing a white robe squinted down. Her face was tanned and sculpted, the skin shiny tight over the bones. When she smiled, it was quick and painful, her eyes remaining fixed and cold.

"You're Coca's cousin?"

"Yes, ma'am."

"Come in. Get out of the street, for Christ's sake." She waved with a skeletal, clawish hand. Her nails were short and lacquered a dark gray. A band of diamonds glittered on her finger like a tiny collar. Marie walked into a room unlike any she had ever dreamed of before. The walls, couches, table, carpets—everything white. The ceiling was of glass, and the walls, too, everything leached of color and substance. Sunlight blazed all around them as if they were trapped together inside a bottle. It was the most terrifying and peaceful room Marie could ever have imagined.

"Let's do introductions later. I'm going back to bed."

"Yes, ma'am."

"Enough *ma'am*. You make me feel like someone's grandmother. *Me llamo* Linda."

Marie nodded.

The woman did not ask her name, only looked at her face briefly and looked away. Her eyes were such a light blue they seemed to have no color at all, like the room itself, and like the sun they were hard to look into for long. Her hair was the palest blond, also drained of color, and it swept along her chin like a delicate cloth.

"I'll show you your room so you can get settled. Since you'll be living here, I require you to take at least one shower each day and wear a uniform. Nothing silly—just a polo shirt and white jeans, white sneakers or loafers. Give me your sizes, and I'll take care of it. Is that okay?"

"I always wear others' clothes. Don't know my own size."

"More information than I really wanted." Linda sighed. "I'll guess. You're about the same as the last girl."

"Yes, ma'am."

The woman frowned. "Maybe we both need sleep."

The maid's room was not like the other parts of the house—the ceiling was low, the beams exposed, the walls painted a gloomy mustard yellow with figures and words scrawled across them that told Marie that the girl who had drawn them (she did not think it was Coca) had been from the islands also. She pried the window open, struggling with the warped wooden frame. The only sounds outside were of a lawn mower and the ocean in the distance. She sat and let the silence wash over her. The window looked out at a thick, coarse lawn, the blades so fat and sharp they looked as if they would hurt bare feet, and at a corner of the swimming pool, blue like a chip of island sky. Marie lay back on her single bed, the mattress covered by a balding chenille blanket. A closet, a scarred desk, a sagging chair, nothing else in the room. The most beautiful place she had ever been.

She fell asleep and did not wake until she heard an impatient rapping on the door.

It flung open before she could get up, and the woman stood in a white pantsuit, her only bit of color a pink scarf trailing down her neck. Now her eyes were rimmed in kohl, her lips a silvery pink, and Marie thought her perfect like the pictures in magazines. The woman was like her house—untouched, with no sign of time passing and leaving its imprint. "Do you normally sleep all day?" she said, lips in a frown while she raked through her small purse.

"I'm sorry. . . ."

"I hate people apologizing. Just don't do it, okay? Let's move to the living room, please."

Marie jumped up and tried to smooth her clothes as best she could, jogging in her hurry to follow the woman's long strides.

"Cleaning supplies are in the pantry off the kitchen. I'm sure you'll figure things out for yourself. Coca said you have experience, right?"

"I know cleaning."

"The number one thing to remember is that I prefer not to be bothered with details, okay? Unless it's absolutely essential. Is that clear?"

"Yes, Mrs. Linda."

"This isn't a Southern plantation. Linda."

"Linda."

The woman pulled out a dark pair of sunglasses from her purse and put them on. The room was so bright Marie wished for her own pair.

"I'm late for lunch so we'll continue with this later."

"Yes."

The woman opened the front door, then turned back. "My God, I forgot to ask—what's your name?"

Marie hesitated, her mind empty of possibilities. "Maleva?"

"What a pretty name. A pretty girl. You'll do just fine. I'll be back at five."

Coca was right—the woman did not leave behind much dirt. Marie's biggest job was to go over her own cleaning of the week before, vacuuming and dusting, replacing wilted flowers in vases that were never looked at, plumping pillows on the sofas that were never sat on for guests who never came.

Linda was gone most of each day, and at night she sometimes brought her boyfriend home. They went into the kitchen that Marie had cleaned after it had not been cooked in that day, and they stood and drank water out of bottles before they went into Linda's bedroom and closed the door behind. When she came home alone, Marie would often hear her crying, and sometimes she watched her outside in the hot tub, drinking from a bottle of wine.

"Are you okay, Linda?" Marie would ask.

"Just need to take my happy pills. Men get mad over nothing."

"This is true."

One night Marie snuck into the kitchen in the dark to take a cold apple from the crisper. By the weak light of the open refrigerator, she stood deciding if she should have a piece of chocolate cake also. She could still not get used to how, as much as she ate, there was always more, and she was growing plump. Already the loose clothes Linda bought were getting filled in. Suddenly the overhead light came on, blinding her, and there stood the boyfriend in his underwear. He was slim and olive-skinned, with curly brown hair. He was as young and carefree as Linda was not.

"Hello?"

"Sorry, sir," Marie said, dropping her eyes and backing out the door.

"Don't leave. Get what you came for." He smiled. "You're the new one."

Marie nodded, ashamed of her old cotton nightgown.

"Stats?"

She looked up, confused by the question.

"Name?" he said.

"Oh. Maleva."

He grinned. "Bad girl. You must be. I was shocked to find food in Linda's house."

They both laughed. It was true, until Marie's coming the cupboards and refrigerator were empty.

"She gets mad when I cook anything here. Cooking smells bother her. It reminds her of people actually living in a house. I'm James, by the way."

"Maleva," she said again.

He nodded. "Since you're living here, watch out for Linda's drinking, okay? She takes antidepressants, and she's been known to take too many."

Marie looked at him, blank.

"The last girl had to call an ambulance."

He tapped his hand on the phone. "You know 911, yes?"

"Okay."

"Good girl. Eat away." James took a bottle of water and turned away. "Don't worry—I won't rat on you. We both need the job, right?"

In Linda's bedroom was a table piled high with books, and some days she stayed at home and sat over these books, reading and writing.

"You like to read?" Marie said, bringing folded laundry through the bedroom to the closet. She always warned Linda of her presence with a few words because the habit of aloneness caused Linda to startle and get angry as if Marie were an intruder.

"Oh. My dissertation. For my doctorate. In case James doesn't offer a ring."

Marie shook her head, not understanding.

"Matrimonio, entiendes?" Linda said, tapping her ring finger. "I'm writing a biography about an author. Then I graduate."

Marie continued to the closet.

Linda yawned. "Actually, you might find it interesting—the author Jean Rhys. Pretty obscure. I needed something off the beaten path to get my topic approved. She's from Dominica, your part of the world." Linda looked down at the paragraph she was marking with her finger.

"Yes, I would like to read sometime," Marie said.

"Hmmm." Linda had already forgotten her.

Marie was sure Linda would not remember because she never remembered their talks, repeating instructions to her over and over, although Marie always pretended to hear them as if for the first time, never telling her that French, not Spanish, was spoken on her island, but the next day Marie found a book on her bed, *Wide Sargasso Sea.*

Once she opened the book, she was home. She knew Antoinette's mother-loss, but also knew the peace of her childhood in abandoned Coulibri, the joy of nature, living under trees, how it made the hatred not sting so much. She understood how the convent felt like a refuge, *a place of sunshine and of death,* because Linda's house felt the same way to Marie. She never wanted to leave. Would her fate in Florida turn out better than Antoinette's in Rochester's bitter England? She would make something of herself, she hoped, she prayed.

She did not remember her work that day, much less to eat. For the first time, she had the experience that another human being had felt much the same as she did, that her life was not so unique. Never again would she have to feel so alone. This was the release of art, what *Maman* must have felt while she painted vodou figures. Loneliness had stuck in her bones since *Maman* died, and this was the first time the pressure released just the smallest bit. Parts of the novel made her cry, and when she bent her head down close to the pages, she imagined the tears on the paper smelled of the island's flowers. Was it a lingering trace of Linda's perfume or her own longing for home?

When Linda had left that morning, Marie had stayed in her room and did not clean a single thing, and when Linda came home that night, she absentmindedly praised Marie's work, saying the place looked perfect. She was right because it was unchanging, never anything less than perfect. But reading that book, Marie was more exhausted than if she had cleaned without stopping all day.

The day before Christmas, Linda packed for a trip with James. "Tomorrow clean out my closet thoroughly so it'll be straightened when I get home."

"Tomorrow is Christmas," Marie said.

"Oh, I forgot." Linda went into her bedroom and came out with a hundred-dollar bill. "Here you go. I always have some stashed for a rainy day. Polish my shoes, too."

Marie learned to adjust to silence and quiet. The only people she saw each week were the people who serviced the house—postman, gardener, pool man. They waved at Marie through the windows, and she waved back. Once a month, she called Coca, who invited her to family dinners, but the trip back and forth was too long for Linda not to complain of the inconvenience of not having her. Marie went twice: for Christmas Day and again in the spring for a funeral.

But Coca and Marie did not really know each other. When Marie was lonely, she called Jean-Alexi. Sometimes just to hear his voice, then she'd hang up. Sometimes she'd cry on the phone. He would not comfort her, but he would not hang up either. When he was in a good mood, which was less and less frequently, she got him to talk about the island, the village, and Port-au-Prince. Their days in her father's abandoned house grew into a missed opportunity, something she knew was false from reality, but they both allowed this. The story of the lone cricket turned into a whole orchestra of crickets that serenaded their lovemaking. Eventually Jean-Alexi would ask her where she was or suggest they meet, and then she would quickly hang up. She knew her loneliness and homesickness were misleading her. But he was the only link to who she was.

Linda finished the long paper on Jean Rhys, and James threw a party at a restaurant because she did not want the house dirtied. Although it was at a Caribbean restaurant, with food and music of the area, they had not thought to invite Marie. Afterward, Linda put a signed, first-edition copy of *Wide Sargasso Sea* in a glassed shelf of her bookcase—a present from James. When she left for work, Marie took the book out and stared at the signature, thrilled at this proof that the actual person who had expressed her deepest thoughts had held those pages. She imagined the yellowed paper smelled of spices.

What confused her was that she could not complain about her living conditions or the ease of the work—she had never dreamed such luxury possible—but the lack of human company made her feel as if she had already left the earth and existed in some kind of limbo. Wrong to say she wasn't grateful to leave the filth and poverty, but she had also left the company of other human beings. One morning as Linda rushed out, Marie could not contain herself.

"What do you believe in?"

Linda stopped in her tracks—exasperated, irritated. "What do you mean?"

Marie regretted the question. "What makes you happy?"

"James. My house. All kinds of things. I don't think it's an appropriate topic."

Linda never asked a single question about Marie's life and clearly did not want to know. Marie might spend the rest of her life in that house, and she would die unknown, a stranger.

As soon as Linda left each morning, Marie turned on the televisions that were in every room, each tuned to a different station, so that as she moved through the house working, it was as if she were moving through a crowded village. She would stop and catch up with the goings-on in each room. Talk back to the screens. A soap opera on one; a game show on another; the news; a movie; a talk show. Her speech improved rapidly, moving from the stilted Queen's English to American casual.

When her work was over for the day, she usually found herself lingering in Linda's closet, looking at the clothes. Knowing that Linda would be away the whole day, at first she would try on a coat, a dress. Eventually, she grew braver, putting on whole outfits with shoes and makeup and jewelry. The girl that appeared in the mirror was unimaginable to her. This time she christened herself: Minna.

She did not intend it to happen, but the outside world began to fade, and the imaginary one created in the mirror became the only one that satisfied. Her dreams were the dreams of the girl in the mirror, not the real one dressed up in someone else's life.

One day she opened the small drawer in Linda's nightstand and found a gun. Heart pounding, she picked it up, surprised at its cold heaviness and how soothing it felt in the hand. She carried it carefully, marveling at its weight and how invincible it made her feel. It almost made her want an invader to break into the house so that she could prove her bravery. Each time she came upon a mirrored image of herself, she took aim, pretending she was one of the pretty actresses on television who aimed guns and were never hurt. What, she wondered, could frighten Linda so much, living in this perfect world that Marie found as safe, if dead, as heaven?

Although she knew her time here could not last forever, she hoped it would be long enough to plan what to do next. Almost two years had passed when Linda called her into the kitchen one night after she came home, and Marie saw something unfamiliar in Linda's eyes: happiness.

"James and I are getting married!"

"That's so good." Marie felt honored that Linda was announcing it to her, as if they were family. She assumed her life would not change, except she would be cleaning after two people now. She liked James because he talked to her as if she were more than the girl who cleaned Linda's house, as if she were a person with her own desires, as if they were in the same boat somehow, and once in a while he would slip her a couple twenty-dollar bills and say, "Go have a little fun."

"We're moving to Sarasota. A broker is listing the house."

"What is Sarasota?"

"Where I'm moving, silly. I'll give you two weeks, and then the movers are coming."

Marie reached out and, much against Linda's will, hugged her. Marie hid her face. When Linda felt her shaking, she patted her back.

"You sweet, sweet thing," Linda said, then walked out of the room.

Later Marie wondered if she could have asked Linda to take her with them. But she always was too busy, too distracted, to listen. Always looking past Marie to more important things. But Linda was Marie's whole life. Or rather, her house was. For a few days, Marie went through her usual routine in a trance, frightened. The threat of the outside world was too real, and she had grown cautious. She could not imagine going back to Coca or the dogs or Jean-Alexi. Her best hope was when she cornered James in the hallway one morning.

"Would you ask her to take me?"

He smiled and looked at her polo shirt. "Oh, sweet Maleva," he said, and raised his hand to touch her breast through the fabric.

She let it stay there. After all, she knew the ways of the world. She even moved her hand toward his pants because this was how she knew to survive. A caught breath made her look up just in time to catch a glimpse of Linda's face in the crack of an open door. They both heard the click of Linda's bedroom door shutting.

"But I don't need this kind of temptation in my house," James said, pulling away.

Marie planned the time carefully—one of the days Linda would not be home till late evening.

She woke that morning, heart empty but light. Dusted the dustless house, then she clicked off the television in each room, one at a time, as if bidding adieu to acquaintances. She shut off the omnipresent air conditioner that tightened her shoulders and made her skin pock into goose bumps, made her nose run. That made living inside the box-house like living on the scentless, atmosphere-free moon and made the outside, with its bugs and smells and humidity, unreal and finally intolerable. She cranked open the windows; the rusted metal struts stuck, then screamed from long disuse as she forced them open; the panes of glass angled out like stiff, broad sails in the wind, letting loose a small universe of cobwebs never before visible.

She unbolted the shiny, brass latches on the French doors and spread them wide in a gesture of welcome, but of course no one was there, just the blast and tumble of hot, boiling air pushing its way in. The smell of wet grass and flowers, hot-baked, like perfume, calmed her. More faintly, the bite of salt, the flat sea smell of rocks and kelp, all of this shoving itself where before it had been denied—inside the sepulchral white box.

Marie prepared herself breakfast. First, four pieces of toast, greasy with butter, and on each piece she swirled a different jam: strawberry, blueberry, apricot, and plum. She drank from a carton of orange juice, ate a bowl of cereal, with blueberries and bananas. She made strong coffee, then poured cream into the entire pot, took that and a mug out on the patio. Sitting on a chair under an umbrella, she drank cup after cup until the pot was empty, savoring that morning more intensely than she had any other day in her life.

When she was ready, she made her way into Linda's bedroom.

She took off all her clothes at the foot of Linda's bed, then, on a whim, crawled onto the mattress, sprawled out in a big *X* with her head nested on the down pillows as she looked out the French doors to the pool beyond. She wondered what it must be like to have another life, Linda's life, to marry James and live happily. But it was useless. Salvation, even salvation so close that one can see, hear, touch, and eat it, but that's not one's own, was maddening. Salvation just out of reach undoubtedly one of the first causes of cruelty in the world.

How to explain that this new life was harder than the one Marie left? Because here there was plenty—denied. Nothing here for her, simply a caretaker of other people's things. Nothing that didn't come with a price tag that would destroy the little that was left of value inside her.

She rolled over and picked up the phone, called Jean-Alexi's number. More and more lately, he had been strange and jacked up on the phone, barely hearing what she said. Coca said that he was more involved with selling drugs, taking them, too. His liquor license fell through. He was losing himself. No one answered.

She rose and moved into Linda's bathroom, turned on the lights, and saw her blackness reflected many times over in the mirrors. Those feet, those legs, hips, breasts, that throat, that kinked hair, none of it worthy of belonging in that bathroom? Wouldn't James gladly exchange Marie for Linda in his arms? Wouldn't he rather fuck her? Marie, who had never had sex with a man she loved, except maybe one, and even him she was not sure of. Love a luxury not allowed the desperate. Who had now been celibate for over two years. Why was she undeserving of love? She took a long bath, scented her skin with the expensive oils from Linda's cabinet, then dried herself on the plush towels that she washed and stacked, but was not allowed to use. She walked into the closet, turned on the light, inhaled the scent of the lavender sachets that she herself had put in those drawers and shelves so that Linda didn't have to smell her own odor.

She pulled out shoes and put on one pair after another. She chose a pair of strappy, gold sandals with a tall heel that made her legs look a mile long, the calf muscles bunched. Her stride was long and graceful thanks to Jean-Alexi, and she walked back and forth in front of the mirrors, mesmerized by her own feet. Those feet belonged in that room. How was it that the smallest of changes could transform how one felt about one's place in the world?

She searched for the dress she loved more than any other—a long, dark dress that had large flowers in red and gold twisting around the body. She felt at home in that dress, having worn it countless other times for games of make-believe, pulling it over her head, letting the silky fabric slide over her skin. The straps, thin and dark, were invisible on her shoulders. Almost as if the dress were painted on her. She searched through the drawers and put on black lace panties, a lacy black bra. She sprayed herself heavily with Linda's most expensive French perfume. At that late date, she was not too modest to say that she had never looked finer. The woman in the mirror belonged in that house.

She swept the bottles of pills in the medicine chest into a towel and took them with her to the living room. She stopped in the kitchen and took the smallest, sharpest paring knife—the one capable of cutting an apple peel as thin as a strand of hair. In the bar, she opened the best bottle of French red wine, poured a glass until it was filled to the brim, and took a deep drink to fortify herself.

She swallowed down two bottles of pills with the wine, then rose to refill her glass. In the sudden calmness, she was sure it was enough pills, but needed more wine to celebrate. The blade ran smoothly across her skin, so that she had to hold her wrist close to her blurred eyes to see the delicate thread of blood swell.

She sat in Linda's long, black dress. Black dress on black body on white couch in white room. A black speck in a white universe. Carefully she held the glass of red wine because if it spilled, it would be the same color as her blood. Red on red on black on white. That simple. A tragedy of color.

Time passed through her mind like a needle pulling thick thread so that it seemed either a blink of an eye or an eternity. She thought of pouring the wine on the carpet, a *vévé* to bring Papa Legba to open his gates for her. The sun was higher, beating overhead, unbearably hot. The room humid as a greenhouse. All she could feel was a sensation of floating, as if she were one of those colored balloons that skinned its way across the ceiling when let loose. She longed to burst, to be released.

She thought of home, *lòt bò dlo,* going to the other side of the water, for the first time in a long while. She could bear the current pain because she knew she was about to return to the small house by the ocean where she was raised, loved in *Maman*'s arms. The sun made the tin roof a burning semaphore at noon. As unlike the room she breathed in that moment as two rooms could be. Burning and hot and blinding. Her *maman*—had she ever been so young? Prettier even than the Minna in the mirror. She felt a stab of happiness that had not been hers since early childhood.

Maman used to say when someone died that they were returning by the slow road *lan Guinée,* to Guinea. She told of her grandparents in Africa having been made to circle the forgetting trees so that they wouldn't pine away to go home. That's what the slaves said, and what was Marie if not a slave in every sense that counted?

A dream of her own death released Marie. Finally she would meet *Maman*'s younger, inviolate self on that road, and they would move on to a freedom never granted in this life.

In the dream, Josie and Thibant, and even Jean-Alexi, appeared, and Marie forgave them all because they had the excuse of poverty.

Empty stomach trumped all.

No one would mourn Marie, either. Just as it had been for *Maman*. Linda would call one of the services that drove white trucks to the house and carted away all that was broken, offensive, unsightly.

Those things disappeared from the neighborhood as if they never existed, to keep the illusion of perfection: a mildewed carpet disappeared this way; a drunken, violent husband carted off; a baby alligator coiled under a hibiscus bush disposed of in a metal box. It would be as if Marie had never lived in that house, her presence scrubbed away as diligently by the next girl as she had scrubbed away the dirt left by the unknown one before her, the one who had saved Linda's life from overdose. A long succession of disposable beings. Perhaps Linda would tell James that Marie was troubled (although he understood Marie was only hungry). Perhaps Linda would hear things from Coca, or she might mix up Marie's story with the pasts of her other cleaning girls, or more likely, she would simply forget, uninterested. The memory of Marie landing neatly in the detritus of Linda's past.

None of this bothered Marie; it was just a story that happened to someone else. She had sunk easily into the sea of black faces in Florida, all of them uprooted, blowing like weeds, some coming to rest in cracks where they grabbed hold—grabbed hold for life but never wanted, easily pulled loose again. Or rather wanted only to clean houses but not sit across the table to break bread. To nurse but not be cared for. To fuck but never, never, be loved.

She felt a violent downward twisting of the earth. Her stomach turned on itself, devouring. All the contents of the morning—breakfast, pills—came up and created a purplish death-stain on the rug. Her thoughts pumped as slowly as her blood, and there was another deep drag in her intestines. She cursed herself that she worried about the stain on the carpet. Clear that this would take too long. The end. She grew ravenous for it.

The gun, cold and heavy as a stone, welcoming, hidden away in the drawer by Linda's bed. Before, she had not considered anything so big and violent, but now she was eager to leave this agony. As long as she didn't disfigure her face. A bullet to the heart would be fine. Her legs were rubber as she staggered back to the bedroom, the floor like a moving ship, and she pulled hard on the drawer so that it flew off its tracks, contents sprawled across the floor. She shoved papers aside, impatient, but the gun was gone. She broke into tears as a manila envelope taped to the underside of the drawer swam into her view. Angry, she ripped it off, tearing the envelope, thoughts pumping slowly, her head packed in cotton. Green bills fluttered down into her lap. Hundred-dollar bills. Many, many hundred-dollar bills.

She crawled to the other side of the bed and pulled out those drawers, found another envelope, more fistfuls of money. Now she staggered to the toilet and gagged herself to vomit the rest of the contents in her stomach. In the kitchen, she drank glass after glass of water. Could luck in one's life appear in such sordid ways? Salvation by such dark means? She kicked off the high heels, hiked up the long dress, and moved like a madwoman, yanking drawers out, sending the insides flying—pajamas, panties, bras, socks, shirts, scarves. No other envelopes to be found, but the two were enough.

She took an empty purse from Linda's shelves and stuffed the money inside. She took nothing else than the dress and the gold sandals, strapping them back on and wobbling through the living room. On a whim, she grabbed the signed book out of its glassed prison. The book was hers, belonged to her through shared pain, and no one like Linda deserved to own it. Some things belong to one because life had earned it off one in blood and sweat. Marie made her way out the front door, careful to lock it behind her. She walked outside—a black woman in an evening dress in broad daylight. If a policeman stopped her, she would have confessed and turned herself in. She had nothing left to fight with. She would have accepted being sent back home or to prison. She would have let them kill her as they had *Maman*. Perhaps their line was simply not made up of survivors.

Not a single person spoke to her. As usual. She walked on as if invisible, for over an hour, till she reached the bus station. Her feet ached. She asked for a ticket and pulled out a crisp hundred-dollar bill. The woman behind the glass was overweight, with damp skin and glasses that kept sliding down her face. Marie guessed from her eyes that she also went home to an empty room. The woman nodded as if she were about to fall asleep.

"Can't break a hundred, unless your fare is close to that amount."

"Where will this much money take me?"

The woman blinked behind thick lenses that magnified her drooping eyes as she studied the timetables. In that affluent area, the people who went out by bus always had unhappy reasons for escape. "Where you headed? North? Not much South left from here. Key West. Not much East either, matter of fact." She said this in a jokey way that Marie could tell had been repeated thousands of times before so that it had lost its meaning.

No other explanation for the woman's lack of surprise except that each day she was confronted with people who had no requirement to be in any one place—no pull of family or job or particular inclination—but instead chose place as a substitute for freedom, for meaning, for love.

"Someplace warm," Marie said. "Like this but as far away from here as possible."

The woman sighed, considering the proposition. "Two of those bills will get you to California, how about that?"

Chapter 5

Minna didn't believe in the past, it was just a story that happened to someone else, to a girl named Marie, whose mother lost her face in the iron forest, but when she first saw Claire's farm, she thought it was the most beautiful place in this world. She did not want to take off her sunglasses because tears of homecoming were in her eyes. Far as the eye could see there were oranges and more oranges, and she remembered *Maman*'s prophecy now come true—they would be returned to the time of sweetness.

She was the Antoinette of the novel; the book, too, become prophecy. Antoinette goes to the convent. *My refuge, a place of sunshine and of death* . . . Marie had traveled to a foreign land only to be returned to the original Garden, her own place of sunshine and of death. Only words stood between her and the coming sweetness. Words that she had learned to use like a knife.

Claire's eyes matched the pale of the foreign sky. Although she was sick, her daughters only thought of going away, tending their own wounds and interests. To them, too, the sweet of their own blood didn't matter. Marie would be the one to stay. She would be the devoted daughter that she could not be to her own *maman*. They thought she was one of them because she talked like a little Englishwoman, like the queen herself. *The rain in Spain stays mainly in the plain*. She talked as if gold coins were dropping out of her mouth.

After everyone had left the farm, Marie could finally feel peace. She heard the breathing of the trees in the morning and felt the slow, dry bake of the earth in the afternoon. The sun was again like a sweet orange in the sky, and the moon hung high like a crisp sheet. All the days were buttery. She had not known such happiness since she was a girl in her *maman*'s arms. She assumed Claire's silence about her past, about the small mistakes in her story, was a form of acceptance, and Marie's care was a form of love.

She mopped the floors and washed the dishes and went to the store where she could buy as much food as would fit in the kitchen. No one cared, no one watched over her. A crime, but there were no punishments, not even a harsh word. She wiped the windows and made the beds and picked up each book on the shelves to read just one page. If she lived to one hundred, she would not have time to read all the books in that house. This was eternity, but she had not died yet or become angel.

Claire and she lived together, and she was content. It was as if two people shared the same life. Inside this life, it was impossible to believe the hate of the world outside. That must be what it meant to be protected. When Claire grew sick, Marie hurt because Claire was like her own *maman*. It pained her that Claire couldn't enjoy all the riches in her life. But Marie reminded herself Claire would get better. And once she did, there would be no more need for Marie.

In America she would never get over how many things each person had. The same dress served a woman at home to marry, christen her children, and then be buried in. Here one person owned more plates and cups, more knives, forks, and spoons, more dresses and oranges and books, more shoes, than the person would ever know, or miss. Cleaning, wiping, worrying over Claire's things, made her dizzy—so Marie took them. Claire would never know or care.

Those months of living on the ranch were the happiest in Minna's life. They lived surrounded by trees, and she felt *Maman*'s spirit. She gorged each day on sweet kindness, and the salt slowly leached out of her. Claire cared so little about Marie's blackness that for the first time she knew what it must be to be white. To not have to think of skin color at all. Marie forced herself to look in the mirror each day and remind herself she was still poor, she was still black.

In the months of living with Claire, Marie grew a relationship, even a kinship, with the objects under her charge. Touching each thing, she felt richer. She thought of cleaning as a meditation each day: she mopped floors and vacuumed Persian carpets; feather-dusted the piano, shuddering the black and white keys; ran a rag over mica lamps and Chinese vases; plumped pillows on the sofa into inviting shapes. She pretended she was a novitiate, and these were her tools toward salvation, but with time this feeling began to grow smaller, meaner. With time, she was no longer in awe of these objects and grew tired of them, in the way one gets with things of too little value compared to what one thinks one deserves.

Marie cleaned less and less, and finally skipped the dining room altogether, with its large crack down the center leaf of the oak table, the showiness of the bright colors in the Chinese vase that she learned from the antiques dealer showed it was a cheap reproduction. The china cabinet with its stacks of eggshell-thin plates. Wasn't whoever bought these things trying to put on airs? No one had eaten in the room since she had lived here. She left the mica lamps unplugged because they were so poorly wired they were fire hazards; she decided they should drink out of jelly jars because the English Staffordshire coffee cups had handles so brittle they snapped off under the least pressure like bird wings.

The sagging sofas in the living room, the tarnished brass coatrack in the hall, the dusty rows of crystal in the bar, turned out to be lies because Claire never used them. Barren things whose only human contact was Marie in cleaning them, and then cleaning them once more.

When the crew Forster hired came to clear out the charred trees, Marie paid them extra to move the dining-room table and chairs, the china cabinet, the sofas, and the piano into the barn.

Claire was weak as a small bird after the radiation, and they spent the hot days after the fires outside under the *zabokas,* marooned on lounge chairs in the hot shadows. Don came and sat on the porch looking hangdog. *Tante* had been wrong about her making babies. Marie knew this thing tugging inside her was because of him, and he would start feeling he owned it and her. If she knew one thing in this world, it was that she would never be owned again. She told Claire to make him go away, that she couldn't stand looking at him anymore.

"But what about our weekend in Santa Barbara? I don't understand," he said.

"What about it?"

He looked at her belly and said he wanted to marry her. That would go away if he knew the truth of what she had been. All these spoiled people in love with their lies. Or maybe he was the rescuing type, but she had no interest in being rescued. He turned angry and said he couldn't live without her anymore, as if she were his bad drug or something. *Menti,* liar! Marie laughed and laughed in his face, never hearing anything so ridiculous.

Claire backed away from life as she always did when it wasn't to her liking. She read that novel over and over with a dreamy look on her face, as if it were going to reveal some truth she wouldn't get at by just looking around her. She would understand me, Marie thought, if I were a character in a book.

Marie wanted to shake her by the shoulders until all the illusions came rattling out. Instead she peeled an orange, feeding Claire a section at a time, the sight of the juice on her fingers making her nauseated.

"I can't eat any more," Claire said, and rolled away.

"You must." But Marie gave up, threw the rest of the fruit under a bush.

"I don't understand these women Rhys writes about. They're so destructive. Why don't they just ask for help?"

"Life's a lot harder than books."

"You're not listening to me."

"No, I'm not." Marie closed her eyes.

"I understand about hiding things. People can be cruel."

That opened Marie's eyes. "What would you know about that, silly Claire?"

"She writes about the colonials on the island."

Marie shrugged. "I didn't know those people so well. Those were the old-timers. Tucked away in their pink houses. Reading Austen and Brontë. They didn't mix."

"Your pink house?"

Marie forgot her lie about the pink house being hers. "We were isolated."

"You never talk of home—it's like you've forgotten it."

"I'm not a forgetting person."

⋆ ⋆ ⋆

Forster kept calling, kept circling. No one cared until someone else did. Marie told Claire to go have lunch and get him away. She used the time alone to call the antiques dealer in the paper, who came with a checkbook and took away the French bombé chest in the entry hall with its paw feet and gilded corners. The man had roving eyes, and he lit on the dark armoire in the living room. Marie hated it because it was so tall and hard to clean. The carved animals on it gave her the frights, especially the bears with gaping mouths. The dust always pooled in the bottom of their maws. The man nodded, and she said why not. A fat check for five thousand dollars deposited in her checking account that afternoon. Later she found out the haul was worth more like twenty thousand.

Nothing to put in the armoire's place, but she replaced the bombé chest with a frail pine cabinet from a bedroom. She put back the picture frames and lamp in the exact same positions they stood on the chest, but it was a poor replication. The albums and tablecloths from the drawers she crammed on the single exposed shelf. When the cabinet could not hold another thing, she put the rest in paper bags.

Most were things Claire couldn't miss: faded ribbons that had never been used to decorate birthday presents; a shot glass with the name of a town in Mexico and an agave plant painted on its side; a salt-and-pepper set embossed with a bronc-riding cowboy on each egg-shaped cylinder; pads and pads of paper with the names of real estate companies printed along the top. Why keep a calendar a decade old with pictures of kittens and beaches and a California poppy unfurled, its petals like the skirts of a dancer? Claire hoarded for a time of need that never came.

Marie thumbed the albums that contained everything expected with the raising of two daughters. She felt a stab inside her, wishing that she had been that family. How was it that an accident of birth caused happiness, or its opposite? Why shouldn't it be her and her *maman* in those pictures? No possibility that Claire would be found a victim in the iron forest, or that Gwen and Lucy would ever have been *restavek*. Even the loss of the boy would have had to be shrugged off to survive back home. Injustice an everyday happening. Marie closed her eyes and swallowed the bitter that would otherwise overwhelm her.

She laughed at the jauntiness of a young Claire, chin jutted out at the world. She did have *spunks* then. A Claire long gone before Marie arrived. Was it the losing of her boy that changed her? In a wooden box like a treasure chest was a handful of old photos. A scrappy boy stood perched in the dark sunlight of each picture, white-blond hair and tanned face, the matching mischief of his young mother's eyes, the same jut chin. In Marie's favorite, he wrapped a wiry arm around Claire's neck as if consoling her for soon leaving. Joshua. Marie looked closer, but there was no sign he knew his fate.

At the bottom of the chest was a manila envelope softened by age, full of folds, with a singe name, Hanni. Inside were pamphlets to such places as Spain, Bora-Bora, Thailand, and Paris. Some of them dog-eared from having been looked at many times, but none were written on. Most of them new as if they had been buried before they were ever considered. She found a picture of white people in Martinique drinking cocktails from glasses bristling with umbrellas. The women had hairdos from the fifties, and big, rounding skirts, and pump shoes shaped like boats. She read the prices and realized it was a trip no longer possible to take because now it was more a journey in time than place.

When Claire came home from her lunch with Forster, she paused where the bombé chest used to stand. A thrill of scare went through Marie at the prospect of being caught at last, but then Claire, deep in thought—resigned?—laid down her purse on the pine cabinet and moved on to the living room.

* * *

Claire always wanted Marie to talk, but she wanted to hear what she already imagined. Marie was supposed to speak in postcard descriptions: fiery sunsets, silky white beaches, smiling black faces. Already Claire's mind was filled up and rejected what wasn't already there. Something in Marie wanted to break that, push out the ugly, bloody, squalling truth. Wanted to talk about the heat and the flies, the violence, the shit and the dirt. The stuff they didn't tell on pretty travel brochures of spiky cocktail glasses and women in boat-shaped shoes. How hard the earth floor was, how loud the shanties were with hunger, how heavy a grown man laid on a young girl's bones. Favorite food? Any, when the norm was starvation. Marie wanted to lay the mewling thing, truth, at Claire's feet.

Instead: "The flowers are big, big as your outspread hand."

"Oh," Claire said, pleased.

Marie hated her those moments, felt cold inside, like seducing a man one didn't love. "Oh, Agatha, you're just wanting to be charmed, aren't you?"

"'Agatha'? Why are you calling me that?"

Marie frowned, not about to tell her that renaming took away one's soul. "Don't you remember, *doudou*? The patron saint of breasts? I'm giving you her powers."

"I don't like it."

"They only mention Rhys's marriages in the biographies. They don't tell how she abandoned her children. No one wants to hear the less than pretty details. What if my great-grandmother lost her husband when she was still a young wife? Very hush-hush. And she goes to hide on the other side of the island? What if she is killed? The baby left alone to be raised by distant family. Doesn't make a very good story, does it?"

"No." Claire seemed disappointed. The bitter of the world too much for her.

"The biographies don't tell that she was a selfish woman, that she never looked back, never thought of her baby girl again. That she wasn't mother material. They want to make her all romantic-seeming. Poor, dreaming Agatha. In love with a ghost."

"Stop calling me that!"

"What if my grandmother married a black man, and my father married a black woman. Only a small bit of Rhys blood left. But in your eyes, I'm all her."

Marie could tell Claire didn't like these answers. And just like that, the truth urge went stillborn. Marie would not disappoint again. The habit of story was stronger in her. She was used to begging for her supper this way.

"But you have your great-grandmother's eyes. And the same set of the mouth," Claire said. Stubborn, like a child. "I looked at her pictures."

"I wish I had her money, too."

Claire laughed, both of them relieved.

They were sweeping up the ash from the fires off the back patio when a fireman in yellow gear walked around the side of the house, startling them. He looked like the man on the moon, squeaking rubber with each step, arms angled forty-five degrees out from the bulky trunk of body. For a moment, all three froze at the unexpected sight of each other.

"Excuse me," he said finally. "We're checking fire hazard at all the area homes."

Marie wore a crocheted tank top, bare underneath. His eyes hovered at her bulging middle, not daring to look up, not trying to look away.

"We weren't hoping for visitors," she said.

"The place looks boarded up from the road," he said. "Abandoned."

Claire coughed, and he slowly moved his glance from Marie's stomach to Claire's face.

"We were worried about looters," she said. "We belong here."

"Incendiary. You have a lot of burned trees that need to be removed."

"That's true."

He kept staring at Claire as if *she* might be in need of rescue. She did look pale and sweat-soaked in the harsh light. "Excuse me, ma'am, but are you okay?"

"I have cancer." Claire was thinking that was now a lie; the cancer now an excuse. She was cured.

"Oh, I'm sorry—" His reddish skin turned a dark brick shade.

"That was a good one," Marie said. "Real smooth."

"It's my job," he mumbled.

"Agatha and I are just fine," Marie said, watching Claire flinch just the smallest bit, as if she had been pinched in secret. "Snug as bugs in a rug."

"No offense taken, Officer," Claire said. "My name is—"

"Baumsarg it says here. Agatha?"

"No!"

"Can we offer you a glass of water," Marie interrupted as she pulled a T-shirt over her head.

"No, thank you," he answered. "I won't take up any more of your time."

"A crew will clear the trees next week," Claire said.

He nodded and pulled out a notebook. "I'll mark that down so no one bothers you again. Lots of fire danger this year. Can't be too careful."

"The smoke was bothering me. Me and my baby." Marie stroked the small bulge of belly. She gave that up to keep Claire quiet.

"A baby? You're pregnant?" Claire said.

He scratched away on his notepad, retreating even further

into his officialdom. "Well, I've marked you down. Good luck to you both. Stay safe."

After he was gone, Claire sat on the diving board, giggling. "He thinks we are in need of rescue."

"It's hot."

"A baby! So many plans to make."

Marie sat on the diving board and took Claire's hand in her own, pecked the bony back of it with a kiss. "I don't like them snooping."

"My secretive Minna. I need my drink. Now we need to bring all the old baby stuff from the attic—cribs, bassinets."

Marie obliged and went into the kitchen, making up the tonic that Claire was now convinced brought her health. In truth, it was no more than the spice shelf at the local supermarket—ginger, cilantro, basil, mint—steeped like tea. Then Marie added cinnamon and star anise and ground-up aspirin. Claire drank it down as if it were elixir, hungrily and with such ardor that Marie herself almost believed there might be something healing in it. The mind is an ever-hoping thing, leaning toward faith like a plant toward the sun.

"Tell me more about your family."

Marie sighed and for a reluctant moment she considered it. "My mother used to take me to town, to Ravine Froide, every Saturday, for coconut ice."

"I don't know that name."

"Sometimes we went to Massacre."

Claire's face lit up. "I know it! Massacre. That's where Rochester and Antoinette stopped on their way to the honeymoon house."

Marie shrugged. Claire spoke about imagined events taking

place over a hundred years ago, things that took place only in an author's head. A made-up love and a made-up madness. Marie could not understand Claire's childlike preoccupation with make-believe. On the island, it was different—dread reality outstripped any kind of fantasy. One couldn't afford to dream of anything except escape.

"I don't remember that part of the book," Marie said. "It must have been only a small part."

"I pictured it so clearly." Claire jumped up with more energy than she'd shown in weeks and rifled through the living room till she found her book, sway-backed on the chair. "Here it is." She frowned, squinting. "Get my glasses."

Since the chemo, she had become more forgetful and impatient when she misplaced things, so Marie solved the problem by buying multiple pairs of reading glasses at the drugstore. They were scattered all around the house, tending to migrate into a pile on Claire's bedroom nightstand, from where Marie then redistributed them. Marie hesitated when she found a pair placed on the pine cabinet in the entry hall. Was it a sly signal from Claire? But, no, she was oblivious, and when she had the glasses on her nose, her face relaxed, and her voice grew strong and confident as she read the words: " 'I looked at the sad leaning coconut palms, the fishing boats drawn up on the shingly beach, the uneven row of white washed huts, and asked the name of the village.' "

Claire frowned and flipped the page. "Here's more: 'The rain fell more heavily, huge drops sounded like hail on the leaves of the tree, and the sea crept stealthily forwards and backwards.' "

She kept flipping pages.

"That's not much," Marie said. "Could be describing anywhere."

"Here: 'Everything is too much, I felt as I rode wearily after her. Too much blue, too much purple, too much green. The flowers too red, the mountains too high, the hills too near.' "

Claire slapped the book shut, satisfied. "I know that place better than places I've actually been."

"Yeah?"

"Like the facts you've told me about yourself. They don't explain the Minna I see in front of me."

"Those last words were Rochester's. He hated it there. She didn't feel that way about her island. But to her—no matter how ugly, how haunted, it is home. We find something to love in it because it is what we have. She saw kind faces—Caro's, for instance, in the village—where he saw only ignorance and sin."

"I thought you forgot that part?"

"You never forget. That book is in me. It's just buried."

Claire nodded, somber. "Don loves you."

Marie shook her head. "He has no idea who I am. You only love what you understand."

"Then explain yourself to us."

"You. I know your pain. Not just the boy, or the girls, or Forster, but your own failure." Marie, now gentle, caressed Claire's head, put her lips against Claire's ear. "That day I touched the tree, it told me. We understand each other, don't we, Agatha?"

The time of the fires marked the end of the radiation treatments. Claire more exhausted now than ever before, eyes like a bed of ashes. Marie had counted on the time of the treatments to be enough, that she would be bored like a stray dog, ready for the adventure of the road again. But as the time came and went, she had grown soft, used to the deep sofas and china cups, beds with sheets the dull white of bleached bone. She resented that she would soon be expected to move on.

She felt a deep feeling for Claire, but did not recognize it was love. Comfortable, she knew she didn't want to go back into the

Uncertainty, could not imagine going back to the Troubles. She started to think she was whom she pretended to be. That was why she kept calling Jean-Alexi—to be reminded she was nothing.

While Claire slept, she called him to come. Although she knew what he was, she missed him. Couldn't he change again? Change back into the boy in her father's abandoned house, the one who serenaded her with crickets? They were the same, after all.

A month after the radiation, waiting for Jean-Alexi to show up any day, Claire began to have enough energy to run the farm again. Marie had to hurry and dull it. She built Claire up to drinking two "elixirs" a day. It would not do to have Claire full strength when he finally arrived. Back in Florida, Marie had discovered the uses of Valium. Claire floated through her days, lost in her own dreamworld.

"Where's the dining-room table?" she asked, her eyes faraway.

"Remember, we discussed the rooms were too crowded?"

"Oh, yes," Claire said, trying not to appear forgetful or suspicious.

The next day while she lay in a drugged sleep, the same people who bought the bombé chest and armoire came out with a truck and wrote Marie out a bigger check for the antique farmhouse table in the kitchen, a set of cherrywood rocking chairs, plus the big silver samovar that always needed polishing. Even while they were driving away, Marie stood in the driveway thinking there was again as much to take out of that stuffed house: barrister bookcases, sleigh beds, mahogany library tables.

With the house emptier, Marie was tempted to take up cleaning again because at last she could see what was left. Like her childhood home it was bare, but as *Maman* said, as clean as God's own house.

With money sitting in a safe-deposit box, Marie felt safe for the first time since she had left the island, but how to make that last? Claire, when not asleep, stared into space and asked her relentless questions, and Marie spun out fairy tales in answer. When the girls called, Marie held up the receiver to Claire's ear, but she lost attention quickly, and Marie made excuses, making a note to herself to lower the dosing. Claire agreed that the house felt roomier with the furniture "stored." Time growing shorter, Marie grew more bold, went into Claire's closet, tried on her clothes, but Claire was not like Linda in Florida; she had always been a woman without vanities, and there was nothing to Marie's taste.

She sat on Claire's bed and watched her sleep. She was the first person Marie had loved since her mother. She would be sad when this time was over. Tears formed in her eyes.

Claire was lethargic, her breaths sweeping shallow like a bird's, and she whimpered in fear that the cancer had come back. Why else feel so strange?

But Marie could only dose Claire's mind; her body fought on with a vegetable vigor. She did not recognize these were the growing pains of health. But Marie saw the change. Undeniable as the turning of the winter solstice—even one day later, the darkness was less, and beyond the physical darkness, one felt in one's bones that light was gaining in the world, conquering. Looking at Claire, one clearly saw that her life was returning—her color was pink instead of sheet white, her gauntness caused by hunger, not lurking death. Her skin had a fuzz of peach, the chick fluff on her scalp enough to make them both laugh. Marie had nursed her baby back to life, and she was proud as a mother and terrified as a mother—a matter of time before she was no longer needed. What came after? Why didn't she deserve a home?

Claire got too weak, hardly wanting to leave her bed to relieve herself, and they were scheduled to visit the doctor in a few days, so Marie lessened the dose in the elixirs, and Claire walked around the house like a plucked bird, humming. Marie felt drunk with power like a tiny god. This smallest reprieve, and she had never seen Claire so happy. Joy is a thing that can be delivered in small slivers.

"Having the house empty helps me think," Claire said. "Maybe I should redecorate. Start all over. Or travel? Maybe go see Lucy in Santa Fe? What do you think?"

"You should rest," Marie said.

"How about some of your chicken and rice. I could eat a horse. I could eat a whale." She giggled at her health, unsure if what she felt inside was real.

The night Jean-Alexi arrived, Marie put triple the dose in Claire's elixir. She vomited, and her blood pressure dropped extremely low. Marie had to measure it twice to make sure she'd read it right. She was scared, frightened she had gone too far.

Claire cried Marie's name in the night, and she went to her.

"Climb in bed and keep me warm." Tears ran down her face, but they were healthy, glistening tears.

"Here I am, *doudou*."

"I dreamed I was dying."

"We're all going to die someday, *che*."

"You know what I mean," Claire said, her eyes accusing, and Marie thought her secret was found out.

"Recurrence," Claire hissed, accusing, as if the word held all the pain of the world inside it.

"Don't talk like that." Marie wiped Claire's tears with her fingertip, put it inside her mouth. "It's just a bad dream. Let me tell you what I see. I see you healthy in the future."

"I get so scared." Claire whimpering like a child, and Marie could not help the revulsion that lay sour in her throat. She lifted Claire off her arm and chest, and when she grabbed at Marie's shirt, she thumped her cheek with her middle finger, a hard pluck off the thumb that shocked Claire into silence.

"That's enough. I need to sleep, too."

"Please," Claire moaned. "Don't leave."

"Selfish, selfish, Agatha. Only thinking about yourself while the world is burning."

Marie walked to the door, looked back at the dumb pleading of Claire's face, like an animal kicked for no reason. Almost enough to turn around and give in and coddle her, because Marie did love her. But this was the way of the world; Claire better learn it. It sickened Marie to see such innocence in such old eyes. Why should Marie take pity when no pity had been taken on her?

She slapped off the light and shut the door. As she went downstairs to warm herself a cup of milk with rum, she heard the muffled sounds of Claire's sobs. Later, Marie went back to her room. Claire was deep in sleep, her forehead furrowed and sweaty as an infant's. Marie slid into the bed, and Claire rolled against her and sighed.

Marie poured cornmeal on the living-room floor to form the *vévé* for Papa Legba, opening communication with the spirit world. Was the vodou real? Yes and no. Marie knew as little about it as the man in the moon, only what she had stolen from spying on *Maman*, yet it had become more real to her than time spent in church. Why? Claire and she pretended for each other that it was real, that both felt its power, and that made it so. Wasn't that what was meant by faith?

It is complicated to be a survivor. Sometimes you have to pretend in magic. You have to find a way to bury the dead.

Maybe the vodou had worked on her as well. After Jean-Alexi came, she realized too late she had changed.

Part Four

Chapter 1

Minna came to Claire's room, folding away fresh laundry in drawers for the first time in months. "You met Jean-Alexi, *nuh*?"

"You decided to do laundry?" Claire nodded. "He's the father?"

Minna looked down at the bulge of her stomach as if in surprise. "Oh, no. No."

"Why is he here then?"

"Our new foreman. He was a very good farmer before on Dominica. He won't cheat us. He can be trusted."

Claire thought about this changeable thing, trust. How she had squandered it so freely on a stranger who was more a figment of her imagination than a real self. But as she looked into Minna's face, she knew that the woundedness was real; Claire simply did not know the source or the outcome of the hurt she was hiding. This girl was made up of motivations Claire had no way of guessing. Paranoia? All she could feel was a longing to go back to the way they had been before the man's arrival because she sensed he would change everything.

She did not mention that the barn, supposedly packed full with the furniture from the house, including Raisi's armoire, had been half-empty.

That night Minna set the table for three. But only the two women sat down in the usual candlelit semidarkness. After waiting for a long time, Minna, skittish, finally gave the signal that they could eat. She had been waiting for an appearance by the man that did not materialize. Clearly she wasn't in charge. Dinner was the usual hodgepodge of food—smoked sausage and the wheel of cheese, refried beans and rice, oranges.

"You must have spilled some of your drink. There was a stain on the back of the couch."

"I don't know," Claire said, digging into the bowl of beans. She, too, had learned the art of not answering.

"Jean-Alexi doesn't scare you," Minna said, a statement rather than question.

"Should he?"

"He needed a job. A place. Only for a little while. I needed to repay him a debt."

Claire stared at her plate. "But you're supposed to be looking out for me, too. Are you?"

"His wife and daughter are gone away. Macheted by bandits. Their faces taken off."

"Oh." This explanation stripped off her anger. Claire wondered if this explained the wildness she saw in his eyes.

"He is a lost man."

When Jean-Alexi finally appeared from the barn, he and Minna exchanged angry words rapid-fire in a patois French Claire couldn't understand, but she smiled up into his face, ignoring his dirty hands as he touched the food, the reek of his unwashed body. Away from him, Minna paradoxically appeared timid, subservient; in front of him, she became defiant, combative.

The women made small talk while Jean-Alexi wolfed down his food, ignoring them.

"Enough woman talk." He shoved his chair back with such

force it banged against the wall behind him. The room shrank as he rose to his full height. He seemed like a caged animal indoors, not-of-his-place. "Go make us coffee."

"I think later—"

"Go!" he yelled, and Minna flinched as if he had hit her, bowed her head, and left them alone. Paralyzed, Claire felt her heart press against her lungs, her breath come in shallow spurts.

"I told Maleva here, it be a good thing if you sign over the farm to her. To make the working of it go fine."

"Why do you call her that name? That's not her name."

"She take good care of you, *non*? Better than that worthless family of yours."

Claire processed that her family had been discussed between them, judgment passed. Something terrible was dawning on her, a pressure behind her eyes that made the objects in front of her swim—Jean-Alexi's face distorted into a fun-house mask. "It's not my farm to give."

"There's ways, lady. Anyway, Maleva alone in the world like you."

Finally something from him she could grab on to, control the direction of the conversation. "Tell me. She won't."

But he shook his head, determined on his own narrative. "The ways I see it, lost got to help the lost in this world."

"Yes." She couldn't help but agree with him. His power both attracted and terrified her. How could an innocent girl such as Minna hold out against the likes of a Jean-Alexi? "Is that what you two are doing? Helping each other?"

"You got it wrong, lady," he said, coming up close. "*I* am not lost. *I* am one of the conquerors of this world. Don't forget it."

"You won't let me forget it, will you?"

"There's work to be done."

"The farm belongs to my husband's family. I'm calling him to come meet you."

"No need. I just passing through. Don't want any trouble for Maleva, do you?"

"What do you mean?" she asked, but he smiled, picked his teeth, and walked off. A terrible, strutting little rooster.

Minna came out, watched him walk away, shaking her head. *"The devil must have his little day . . ."*

The next days passed in a game of cat and mouse, Jean-Alexi conducting business out in the barn on his cell phone, coming into the empty house only for meals. During those meals, he always waited till Minna was out of the room, then broached again the subject of signing over the ranch. It did not seem possible that Minna was unaware of these efforts, and Claire put it to delicacy on her part to refuse to acknowledge them.

When she was alone with Minna, she pleaded that he be sent away.

"Got to be careful what genie you let out of the bottle," Minna said. "Jean-Alexi goes the opposite way he's told."

"He's asking me to sign the farm over to you."

Minna bit her lip. "That's his making. I was foolish calling him. He's too lazy to work the farm. He'll be moving on."

"But why did you call him?"

"Why? Why?" Minna mocked her. "He's home. He's familiar. No matter how bad, he knows me. You can't escape your history."

Now it became clear to Claire that the elixirs were doing the opposite of what they once had, now the cause of her tiredness, but she did not exactly blame Minna for this, figuring instead that in her zeal for Claire's health, she was unaware of the side effects and maybe even desiring them. Perhaps Claire *was* safer asleep, out of the range of Jean-Alexi and his obsessions. Nonetheless she went on a campaign to dump the drinks when the two were out of sight. Her strength built, and one morning, feeling the strongest yet, she dressed before Minna came into the bedroom.

"I'm going to visit Mrs. Girbaldi." It came as a shock how long it had been since she had talked to her old friend, or Forster for that matter.

Minna quickly shut the bedroom door. "Not a good idea."

"I'm tired of being shut up in here."

"Don't make him angry. For me." Genuine fear was in her eyes.

Claire was so pleased that Minna was finally talking truthfully to her, acknowledging the reality of their situation, that she hardly comprehended the admission of the danger they were in. "Tell me, what's going on?"

"I made a mistake, calling him. He wants more than he's owed. That's where my money went."

So that was the explanation of the mystery. "You only assumed he'd help. All alone in this country," Claire said, already on her way to making excuses for her. "You forgot not all people are like you."

"Once he realizes there's nothing more to get, he'll leave."

"We must get rid of him," Claire whispered. "Police?"

The awful panic in Minna's eyes was something Claire had never before witnessed. "Please, for me, no. They will take me to prison, too. Or send me back. Give me time. If you care anything."

"So it was all a lie? Jean Rhys, Cambridge?"

"Would you have allowed me in any other way?"

"That's not true."

Of course she was right. The beautiful false life had sanctified the skin color. As if poverty and misfortune were contagious. Claire thought of fate—the one that killed Josh and brought her cancer, but also the one that insured each of her children would not be born in want. Minna more beautiful and shining than most babies, but of course that didn't count. The world shunned those born in misfortune. The unfairness of it shamed Claire even now as she suspected she might be made victim of the victim.

Claire sat on the porch. Minna was in the kitchen, satisfied she had won Claire's obedience. Still Claire wanted to test the boundaries of the situation. She refused to feel fear, and in fact Forster or the police were only a phone call away. Unattended, she started to walk down the driveway. Quickly, Jean-Alexi was at her side. Confirmed, the realization that it had come to a kind of velveted house arrest.

"Where we going, lady of the house?"

"To visit a friend."

"That's fine. But don't you be complaining." He touched her elbow.

"Don't ever touch me!" She looked down and saw his dusty, cracked bare feet. Calloused feet unused to shoes, used to hardship, backbreaking labor. Feet that told of chasms of life experience between them.

"Or I call the police and tell them about our little Marie. She ever tell you about the Florida woman? Stealing from her?"

"I thought you cared about Minna."

He laughed in her face. "Only a rich person can afford to think like that."

That night, Minna and Claire sat alone in the empty living room, candles throwing monstrous, grasping shadows across the ceiling from the winds. "Tell me about this woman in Florida," Claire started, interrupted by a banging on the door. They looked at each other in confusion and dread, neither of them daring to move.

"Mom! Mom, you there? Anyone home?" Lucy's voice.

Both women scrambled to their feet; Minna raced to the door and threw it open.

"Surprise!" Lucy said, her arms full of flowers and presents. She looked more gaunt than before. Dark circles under her eyes and unwashed hair screamed relapse.

Claire's heart buckled at the sight of her. "Why are you here?"

"I promised I'd come, didn't I?" Lucy walked in and looked around. "Remodeling?"

"Things are complicated right now."

Lucy put her hand on Minna's stomach. "Oh my God, I had no idea! You both are just glowing. Mom, you look so much better."

"Oh, baby." Claire hugged her, then hugged her tighter. In some strange corner of her mind, the situation had remained an experiment until now. Lucy changed the rules.

Steps behind them, and Jean-Alexi was sprawled across the doorway, arms folded over his chest, head wagging. *"Kisa ou ap fe isit?* What do we have here?"

Lucy and Claire broke apart in their embrace. Instinctively Claire stepped in front, partially shielding Lucy from his sight.

The answer out of her mouth sticky, reluctant. "My daughter."

"What a beauty," he said.

"This is my cousin," Minna said.

Lucy blushed and ducked under her mother's arm, walking over to him. "So nice to meet you. We love Minna."

"Oh, come closer," he said, and swallowed her in a big, long-armed embrace that almost took her off her feet. "It's all family here, love."

★ ★ ★

Despite Claire's misgivings, the next few days went by in an almost celebratory atmosphere. Now Jean-Alexi abandoned the barn and his cell phone and spent time in the house. They ate meals together, island music playing, and he flirted shamelessly with Lucy. Claire saw another side of him, the raconteur, spinning one charming story of their life in the islands after another. Was it possible that she had overreacted? That the solitude and her sickness and the drugs had deluded her mind? Or was he cunning enough to insure his safety by attaching himself to what she loved most in the world?

"So were you at Cambridge also?" Lucy asked.

Jean-Alexi closed his eyes to slits, staring into the candlelight, chewing thoughtfully. "No. My part of the family wasn't the fancy one."

"What is the name of your village again?" Lucy asked.

"Jérémie," Jean-Alexi said.

"Isn't that in Haiti? Not Dominica," Claire said.

Minna said nothing, simply got up and cleared the table. The reproach clear. What was Claire trying to prove? If she caught him out lying, would she throw Minna into the street? Would she call the police? What, exactly, did Claire want? Did she want to be begged? Did she want to be the all-merciful Claire? Did she want to be the savior, to be responsible for another human being's fate besides her own? Or was it simply hurt pride that Minna did not believe in her enough to tell her the truth?

"What you got to understand is that we've got family scattered all along the islands."

"Tell me about you two as children," Lucy demanded.

"All the women were in love with Jean-Alexi," Minna said. "That time on the beach . . . ?"

Jean-Alexi threw his head back in a howling laugh. "This is a story you must hear. This is my little Maleva."

As they both took turns telling the story of the coins and the boys and Minna's death order, they all laughed. Claire watched, mesmerized, as yet another Minna emerged than the ones she thought she knew or had imagined.

"The taffy," Minna said, chuckling, dabbing tears from laughing so hard. "Remember that dried bit of taffy you gave me? I didn't realize you had stolen my coins."

"Those were your dues for protection, little sister."

Claire was lulled against her doubt of the nature of the relationship between the two. Still, at other moments, she had an urge to pick up the phone and call the police. For what? He was a powder keg that might go off at any minute. She wanted him gone, but she was afraid for Minna's sake. Now Lucy was involved. How to warn her away without frightening her and stirring Jean-Alexi's wrath?

At night, Lucy slept with Claire in her room. They gossiped together like girlfriends, as they had so many years before.

"Why did you come?" Claire asked.

"I wanted to see you. And the gallery closed. Javier and I broke up."

"It's good you came home."

"I don't understand what's going on here," Lucy said.

Claire didn't answer.

"Kind of a commune feel. That's cool with me, but you don't want Gwen to see this."

"He'll be leaving soon."

During her days there, Lucy's assuming normalcy affected the others to pretend the same. She plugged in the phones and called Gwen, told her about the charming Jean-Alexi, spent hours with him getting the irrigation lines back in working order. She convinced him to move the remaining furniture back in the house, assuming Claire had sold the rest, and Claire did not contradict her. She screwed in lightbulbs, found a used piano in the want ads to replace the one that was sold, according to Claire because it no longer held a tune.

Forster came over, and although he was unhappy about the state of things, Lucy and Claire's acceptance made him hold his objections. Privately he told Claire he was starting the search for a foreman. In a few weeks if things didn't improve, he would have the man replaced.

Once Claire caught Jean-Alexi and Lucy smoking a joint on the porch and giggling, stopping when she approached. Another time, she saw Jean-Alexi cup his hand over Lucy's elbow as he talked to her. Was this another subtle threat? Seducing the daughter?

Another Jean-Alexi would approach Claire when she was alone. He came into her room, unbidden, late in the mornings and stood over her, businesslike and menacing.

"Time for you to sign, and I get leaving."

"We don't seem to be communicating. Ask Forster to give you his ranch."

His face grew pained and tight. "I got things to do, people to see. Can't spend much more time here."

"That's too bad. I'll hate to see you go."

"You have money in your bank account. Jewelry. How about a loan?"

"Can't."

He sighed, stretched, swayed his hips. "That's one juicy daughter you have."

Claire said nothing.

"Thinks I'm quite the man. I'm this close," he said, pinching his thumb and index finger closed. "Told her I'm goin' to perform a vodou ceremony. That got her hot and excited."

* * *

Alone in bed, Claire stroked Lucy's hair. "I don't want you spending time alone with Jean-Alexi."

"Oh, Mom."

"I'm serious."

"He's fascinating."

"He might be . . . he *is* dangerous." Lucy's face immediately dropped, and Claire recognized that long-ago look of fear in her eyes. Whatever Claire did, she needed to keep this from her, otherwise her distrust would give them away. "I just mean Minna tells me he's a real ladies' man. I don't want you hurt."

The furrow between Lucy's eyes relaxed. She dropped her head back on the pillow. "Oh, Mom, I'm a big girl now."

But the isolation of the house was getting to Lucy. "How about we go out for dinner?" she suggested.

"I miss Minna's cooking," Jean-Alexi protested.

"I'm sure she would like a break, too."

"I'm fine," Minna mumbled.

"You cook," he said.

"Let's all just go to a movie or for drinks."

"You and me go. Minna and *Maman* want to stay home and take it easy."

Lucy hesitated. "That would hurt their feelings."

The next afternoon, arguing could be heard from in the barn. Minna came in with a swollen eye, holding her stomach.

"What happened?"

She looked around the room, disoriented. "I tripped and hit the corner of a table."

Neither Claire nor Lucy said a word, but Claire squeezed her daughter's hand.

"Jean-Alexi has decided it is time for the ceremony."

"Ceremony?"

Minna handed them a crudely lettered piece of cardboard.

YOUR INVITED TO A HEALING
FOR ERZULIE, SAMEDI, AGATHA,
N BRIGETTE POST YA TIME SOON

"All the spirits need to be thanked."

"No, I don't want to do that," Claire said.

Lucy clapped her hands, relief on her face. "Oh, how fun. Can I help?"

Surprisingly many mirrors accumulate throughout a house over the years—in bedrooms, closets, and even in dark hallways to give the illusion of openness and size, to give onlookers time to organize the face they show to the world. Minna had returned the collection that had formerly been banished in the barn, and it felt like coming full circle, from being denied to being forcibly shown. The mirrors were spaced out along empty floors, substitutes for bodies of water, which attracted and reflected the spirit world. In addition to that, Minna said they were lucky to have the pool, especially in its new brown-green opacity, which reflected one's face back as detailed as any mirror.

As Claire passed between the mirrors, she caught glimpses of her underneath self—rosy chin, delicate, short, curling hair. If one didn't look too closely, she resembled the young girl she was when she first moved into the house, returning health giving her a false youth. When she crossed Minna alone, she hissed, "I know he hit you. It's not just you alone now. Let me call the police. Or at least Forster."

"No, please wait. If you care for me," Minna begged.

"I won't let Lucy be hurt." Claire bided her time.

As it grew dark, they were summoned by Minna, dressed all in white, a priestess, the house lit by hundreds of tea candles on the floor, multiplied in the mirrors' reflections into thousands. Jean-Alexi came in dressed in his usual rags, but he had added a straw hat and a pair of sunglasses. One lens in, one out, so he could see in both worlds at once. He held out his hand to Minna. *"Ma femme, Maman Brigette."*

Solemnly he led them single file up the stairs and into Minna's room.

It was a mystery that now the room was empty it still felt so dense, so teeming. Candles everywhere giving movement to the figures on the wall as if they pulsed and writhed in their own anticipation. In the middle of the floor, a brazier dragged in from outside on which wood was burning. Smells of cinnamon and nutmeg, grass and flowers, the unmistakably oceany tang of salt. In a bowl on a small table lay the gold necklace Claire had given Minna.

"Come here, Agatha," Jean-Alexi said, and Claire started at the name but went to him and allowed him to drape her in her old yellow bathrobe. On his breath, she smelled alcohol. So clear to her that this was a bit of fakery, a B-movie set piece. Minna set a jug of the elixir between them and poured out cups for each. Lucy hesitated and Jean-Alexi reached over and tipped the bottom so that she had to gulp it and still it dribbled down her chin. Claire's heart was beating so hard she thought it would explode in her chest, as if one could overdose on fullness.

Jean-Alexi turned the transistor radio on and flipped channels till he stopped at some techno-disco stuff. Lucy giggled, and the two did some bump-and-grind dance while Minna poured another round of the elixir. Now she made a paste of nutmeg and lime juice and came to Claire, taking off her robe, but when she tugged at her shirt, Claire resisted.

"I've had enough of this."

"It's part of the rite," Minna said.

"Not in front of him."

"He's a priest—"

"*Non,* it's okay. I step out for smoke." He got up and held his hand out to Lucy. She rose on her feet unsteadily, and he put his long, bony arm around her waist for support.

"I need you here," Claire said, and Lucy looked disappointed but stayed. She swirled the contents of her glass and drank to the bottom.

Minna took off Claire's shirt and bra, then began to apply the paste while mumbling words. "Just go along. Pretend." Staring at the closet door, Minna spoke under her breath. "It is complicated to be a survivor. Sometimes you have to pretend in magic. You have to find a way to bury the dead. Jean-Alexi should have remained buried in my life."

Claire nodded but didn't understand, except that the danger had engulfed them—already Jean-Alexi was back in the room, distracting. She was unembarrassed now, did not turn away her brown-smeared chest, as if her disfigurement were a layer of protection. Let him look. She had never felt less naked. Minna lightly placed the robe back over her. "You must look within. Inside. You must take action. You must use the cleansing fire of the sword, sword of fire, do you understand?"

Another round of elixir. The percussion of the awful music timed perfectly with the throbbing in her temples. Claire could no longer sit upright but lay prostrate on the bare floor. Her body tingled, her mind spun and cawed to visions, but her stomach cramped, grew unbearable. In the corner, Lucy retched and ran out of the room. Minna handed Jean-Alexi a large glass in which she poured straight rum.

Minna put down a small, framed picture of Joshua, the one from Claire's bedroom, next to her. Up close: the brown eyes, sly grin, half-moon scar, crooked teeth. Next Minna put down a huge bowl of misshapen lemons that could have come from no other tree. Minna stirred the logs and a flurry of sparks went out. The air turned stifling, smoky. Lucky if they didn't asphyxiate. Lucky if the house didn't burn down, Claire thought lazily.

Lucy returned as Minna talked.

"Agatha, he visited me."

Claire looked at her, accusing. "What are you saying?"

"In the kitchen last night after you went to bed. He had the darkest brown eyes, and a half-moon scar along his cheek. He held a dead parrot in his hand. He wanted me to give him a chocolate bar from the cabinet above the refrigerator. How could I know this? It was him." She put the lemons on the fire, and their acrid, sour smell nauseated Claire.

It was so ridiculously made up. Claire saw clearly how false this was, trumped-up, compared to what had gone on before, between her and Minna alone. This was a big fake, and Claire was letting Minna know she knew the difference. But she heard helpless sobs from Lucy.

"Why would he visit *you*?" Lucy said. "I've missed him so long."

"She's lying, Lucy. Can't you see that?" Claire said.

"*Maman* taught me to believe that death is only change. That the departed still bear weight on the living. He showed himself to me because I was open and your mother is resisting."

"Did he say anything?" Claire asked, against her will. She knew she was on the long, treacherous slope of gullibility but could not help herself.

"It's not like that. More a feeling. Possession. Of paying reparations. For being healed. For being allowed at last to rest with the dead."

Time passed. Lucy was asleep when Jean-Alexi stood next to Claire and lifted his boot to set it down on her skull. "Give her all the money, all the jewelry, or the spirits will take their revenge."

"I'll get the money from the bank tomorrow."

"Or else." Satisfied, Jean-Alexi left the room with the gold necklace in his pocket. Minna went on her knees, lifted Claire's head, and wiped off her sweat. "I never meant to let him hurt you or Lucy!" She put a pinch of salt on her tongue. "The bitter to set things right again," she said, and followed him out the door.

Black stars swirled around Claire. She closed her eyes and saw the purpling orchards, felt the cool, gritty dirt under her back. Heard the labored breaths from a drugged Lucy asleep beside her. Thought of Minna's unborn child swimming in its cocoon of sea. The child was hope, to be protected at all costs.

Claire lay dreaming of herself in a long, white nightgown of bast material that made the body inside it, poor battered body, both solid and ghostly, both of this world and beyond it.

What the cancer taught her was the need for destruction before healing, the need to burn away every bit of the disease to prevent recurrence. She knew every ash that fell on the ground would enrich the soil, that with time it would become sweet and fertile beyond all imagining.

With only the guttering light from the logs and the candles for illumination, Minna shook her awake. Terrified, Minna led her out in the hallway where Jean-Alexi lay, face twisted in a grimace. Claire looked at her for confirmation.

"Il est mort," Minna whispered, as if the devil were lying there.

She was trembling, shuddering. A low moan came from deep inside her. Claire had never seen such fear and despair in a person.

"How?" Claire asked.

"Dead."

"Are you sure?"

Minna closed her eyes in a swoon. "Valium in the rum. Rifle butt to the head."

The monstrousness of what had occurred. "Don't lie to me, Minna!"

"Him or us. I didn't realize he was no choice. He only understood violence, pain. He would never have left without punishment. . . . I owed you that much . . . to not bring harm."

"Is that the truth?"

"He was all I had in the world."

How did one ever come to the final truth? There was none. One flew blind, never having all the information. "You will be safe." Even in Claire's previous suffering, she had remained privileged from the greater world's tragedy, but what she had learned in this last stripping away was that, unlike her, Minna had been doomed from the beginning, and for her there would be no justice in the world other than Claire.

The closet door appeared to be glowing, and she knew before opening it what she would find there. Ten large containers of paint thinner, an amount in excess of anything that would gainfully have been needed, an amount that was a clear summons.

Chapter 2

Especially in California, one was reminded of the fragility of one's tenure on the land. One felt the rattle and rock of the earth's crust, saw hairline fractures appear like visions in concrete driveways, plaster pools, rock walls. One made a pact with the devil to stay on borrowed time, while the honeycombed cliffs crumbled into the ocean, while giant, unseen excavations hollowed out sinkholes that suddenly devoured a car. Foolish to pin all one's love on an orchard or a house.

Claire walked straight to the lemon tree, its branches covering the silvered moon shadow of her. She touched the black, scorched part that she'd managed to burn so many years before. It had never healed, simply became part of the new growth. This time she would be successful. The magic had returned as if Minna stood there beside her, but she would not allow company. Hungry, dried, famished leaves gobbled the fire. Her neglect forming kindling.

The golden light warmed her although she was already warm, hot, was burning. The silver moon shadow reappeared as she walked away, back to the house, black-smudged fingerprints on white nightgown.

Returning to the house, her body was fatigued by even this exertion, but there was still so much to be done and so little time left. As she mounted the porch steps, she looked over to the east where, a mile away, the lemon tree now glowed a sunny halo in the blue-black night sky. She tried to think of the steps required of her and knew that sleep was still a far-off reward.

In Minna's room, Claire avoided the shrouded figure in the middle of the floor by the brazier. She laced the floorboards with the noxious liquid, splashed the walls, regretting that the artwork was a necessary sacrifice. She doused the contents of her own room, bloating the mattress, creaking the floorboards. Fumes stung her eyes, burned her hands, wet her nightgown to an opaque where liquid had spattered. She fought with the swollen window and banged it open, as a noxious cloud of chemical swept stinging her eyes, burning her nostrils.

She ran through the hallway, wetted the Persian hall runners, lacquered a carved-oak finial at the head of the stairs. There was music in her head, she was humming Minna's song, one she did not even realize she had learned, a rhythm from far away, and she danced the liquid in time to it. In the living room, she sat on the returned yellow sofa, all thick, down pillows and heavy damask cloth, and looked at the golden, floor-length silk curtains that framed the windows, the golden velvet piano scarf draped over the used stand-up Lucy had found. History turning and replaying itself over and over, and she, Claire, determined to take it off the spindle once and for all. No place for her in such a room—it was cold and beautiful and empty as a hotel. Upstairs slept the guests, some temporarily, some permanently, and she was the arthritic porter, there long past her useful tenure.

She sat in her white nightgown on the yellow couch in the golden room and had never been so sure what needed to be done.

A madness masquerading as sanity, or sanity as madness. A rescue fifteen years delayed. That moment it felt as if Minna were inside her, as close as the air in her lungs, the blood in her veins, the thoughts in her brain, so unlike how alone she had felt long ago. Minna who was already in the throes of escape.

It took minutes that seemed to stretch into hours to empty the last of the cans, and she chided Minna in her excess zeal. Where at first she had been careful and miserly, now she grew sloppy and profligate in the abundance. The kitchen towels drooped soggy. What temperature would it take to melt the copper sink, the ceramic faucets with their antiquated lettering of HEIβE and KÄLTE? The daybed in the den reeked like a swamp; the coats in the hall closet dripped like laundry on the line; still there was splashing in the can. The wood floors grew dark and oiled, the grain magnified and lustrous; the doors, wet, groaned heavily on their frames. Claire had never loved the house so much. It was not so much a destruction, but a leave-taking, like sending off grown children, like burying one's parents; an accomplishment necessary in its time, though painful. Its dignified accomplishment a thing greatly to be desired.

The air in the house had become so acrid, so fume-laced, that if she had lit a match, her lungs would have ballooned into flame. She could have blown them all into a high-treeing cloud that would be seen through the whole length of the valley. She stated the obvious to herself so that it would be clear what she did *not* do. Did *not* blow Lucy or Minna or even herself up. Later, there would inevitably be the character assassinations, the *I always figured* and *She seemed funny* and the rest. But what she was determined to do at that moment was to save what had value, in the only way she thought how. What she did do, in sound mind and body, was scream to Lucy to quickly leave the house.

Lucy stumbled out in shorts and a T-shirt, hair rumpled. "What happened?"

"A leak—gas. Get out now!"

Bewildered, Lucy had the milky breath of childhood as Claire led her down the stairs and outside.

Minna was nowhere to be found.

Claire struck the match in Minna's room first, to pay homage. Overturned the brazier onto the shroud. Out of the most unlikely hands sometimes salvation could be delivered. A gold blaze licked across the floor, stopped and puddled in dense places, burst into blue, then gold again, and moved on. The beautiful figures on the wall began to erase themselves. The single-breasted warrior curled and went black. Claire had to fight a terrible urge to stay inside the room. She closed the door, too enamored of it to witness its passing.

Glancing out the window, she saw Lucy at the end of the driveway on her cell phone. Time was running out. Soon the sirens would begin. Soon the fire engines and the police cars and the great suck of public attention would come to rest on the ranch once more. Claire dumped the entire box of matches on the sofa. The whole went up in a great swell of flame like sunburst. Past due to leave, she couldn't tear herself from the surreal beauty of the room—walls warmed by flame, curtains blazing, the soft sofa in the center now a burning coal. The down feathers swirled like black snow in the wind created by fire. A strange, alternate universe. A piece landed on her arm, crystalline like a black, skeletal snowflake. How had these objects, this building, acquired such a hold on her?

Clearer in its destruction that all that she had held on to so tightly had been mere illusion. Did one fight for a sofa, or a house? Even the land was strangely indifferent. Later they would accuse her of being crazy, the madwoman in the orchard, but she would have been crazy only if she had forgotten the people. If they had ever accused her, she would immediately have pleaded guilty, for so many past things it didn't matter what she was charged with in the present. But that never came. The story of the new foreman, Jean-Alexi, drunk, setting the house on fire in anger, then asphyxiating from carbon monoxide fumes from the brazier, came so easily to one as adept at untruths as Claire had become, was readily accepted by those shocked at her previous poor choices. One only had to look as far as the state of the farm to know she was unhinged. Lucy unknowingly corroborating the untruth by saying she heard Minna and him fighting.

The piano screamed and groaned, chords possessed as if played by a madman—the room had an eerie feeling of life. The floorboards upstairs thrummed like the bleachers at a racetrack when the horses went thundering by, struts popping after the unbearable climaxing pressure. With a gentle sigh, they sagged through, an avalanche of fire and board, the convention of division, of upstairs and downstairs, rendered false. It was now inside versus outside, heat and light and creative destruction against the cold, indifferent blackness of the world.

She stayed as long as she could. As if the heat and flame, by eating up the house, were releasing its secrets. And she still thirsted to learn more. She didn't feel the loss of one thing, simply the gain of knowledge pouring into her. A rocking chair became a fiery throne, the spokes glowing hot orange before the whole crumbled to ash. "So that's the way it is," she said, feeling that she knew the essence of the chair at last before it disappeared.

She heard the sluggish wail of sirens in the distance. For a long time, the farm had become a nuisance, an eyesore, to the planned communities around it. The Baumsarg ranch was living out of its time, an anachronism, and as with all things not of their time, there would be a sigh of relief at its passing. The world broke what it could not change. But for a beautiful moment, she had returned the place to its sacrosanct emptiness.

Behind her there was the tinkling of glass as each upstairs window burst out. She stood on the edge of the orchard, holding her arms around trembling Lucy (saved!), and beheld their former home, now lit up like some macabre jack-o'-lantern, the windows and doors like swelling eyes and mouth, the fiery shingle roof like a shock of electric hair.

As the fire trucks pulled up the driveway, Claire saw in the beam of their headlights a figure running away through the trees. In the false dawn of the fire, the dark figure seemed to hesitate, wave an arm, to look backward in adieu. The figure grew smaller and smaller, a dark heart beating in the darker night. Then Claire lost her.

Chapter 3

The day had been long, first Paz's chaotic church wedding, with so many people that the overflow ended up standing outside on the sidewalk and into the street, then the even bigger celebration at Claire's house. All of Octavio's married sons with their families, all of Sofia's extended family; Gwen and her family; Lucy reunited with Javier; Forster and Katie; Mrs. Girbaldi; practically the rest of the county. The rooms hardly allowed movement, and people took their plates of food out onto the cooler veranda, the pool area, across the lawn, and some sat under the shade of the lemon trees.

Octavio motioned Claire with his head, and they both carried their champagne glasses to his pickup and jumped in.

They stopped at the end of a neighborhood cul-de-sac, and Octavio came around and opened the door for Claire as she struggled in the new long dress she had bought for the wedding. The first dress in years. They walked through the late-afternoon light to the fringe of the remaining orchard that had been left for decoration around the outer edge of the new development: Baumsarg Estates. After the fire, the ranch, minus a ten-acre set-aside, had been sold.

They walked down the rows, Claire trying not to look through at the lines of houses. The trees were left unpruned for privacy; the oranges went unpicked. The fruit was small and yellowish. Neither of them could bear to taste one.

Claire had gone away after the sale, when they wrapped the ranch in chain-link fence and then withheld water till the trees slowly died of dehydration. Claire had seen such things in the past—long rows of trees petrified to kindling. Only Octavio understood the physical pain of witnessing this as she did. Each tree was an individual, with a personality, and this treatment seemed a desecration of nature. When the trees were dead, dried out, bulldozers came and tore their roots from the earth, piling them into a big heap, from where they were trucked away to be shredded for compost.

The family's legacy now shrunk to a remaining ten acres devoted to organic lemons, with a small, Spanish-style house built in the middle for Claire. On her veranda, she could look out in each direction and not see the houses that crowded all around her. With the money from the sale, she had given a generous retirement to Octavio, although at that point they had not spoken in a year. To her surprise, he had asked if he could work the ten acres. The pace would be leisurely; much of each day spent on the veranda, discussing crop yields, exotic graftings, dishonest packers, and selling direct. This work gave them a deeper pleasure than anything else.

Old friends again, they talked freely of everything except Minna. She remained inexplicable and Claire's alone.

Claire returned to see the land, denuded of orchards, being recontoured, lines of small plastic flags to denote streets that had not yet been named. The original rootstock tree, the Agua Tibia, cut down, the root ground out of the earth. Each time Claire walked by, she could swear the air was still fragrant where it had stood.

Octavio and Claire sat on a bench in the shade to rest.

"It was a beautiful ceremony. Paz looked like an angel."

Octavio grunted, pleased. "Can you believe that's my baby? Where did the time go?"

"My friend, you're asking the wrong person."

Hours had turned to days turned to months. Each moment, Claire had prepared for Minna to burst through her door, regal as a queen in diamonds and satin, while a man in sunglasses waited for her in a sleek, foreign car. Her arms would be spread wide in riches. *Where have you been?* Minna would cry, as if they were the ones who had not been there all along, waiting. She flattered them that they had more in their lives than her. Or else she would show up straggly haired, with dark circles under her eyes, shoulders bent, the marks of a hard world on her. Her hand holding the tiny hand of a shy, sniffling toddler. It would make no difference to Claire.

A year after her new house was built, Claire picked up the telephone to crackling reception, accepting a collect call. She could not understand the language other than a few French words sprinkled here and there, but she thought the voice was very like Minna's.

"Is it you? Is it you?" she yelled, but the voice went on, unintelligible, crying, then abusive. Claire stood and listened till her ear grew numb from pressing the receiver so hard, but finally she replaced the receiver in its cradle, gently, knowing how it would pain the hurting soul on the other end. Although she had no regrets over what had happened, still she wanted Minna to come and prove to her that she had done the right thing. Claire could not say with certainty that she ever knew the real Minna, though even if Claire had been made aware of each and every fact of her life since birth, it would not change the essential mystery of her. Claire would be loyal to that mystery to the end of her days, because it was identical to the mystery of life, which one loved without ever fully comprehending it.

Although there was beauty in rootedness, Minna had taught Claire that another kind of beauty lay in being free.

As the sun began to set, Octavio drove Claire back to the wedding party. The serious drinking and dancing had started. Tired, Claire in a lawn chair, relaxing, when she saw her. Minna walked up the driveway slowly, her smile so big and calm it was as if she knew every detail of the farm and the family during her absence, predestined, and she only remained out of sight long enough for its fruition.

She wore the black dress with the gold and bloodred flowers that made her look so regal. On her feet were the golden, high-heeled sandals with her toes hanging slightly over, and around her neck was the necklace Claire had given her. Since years had passed, Claire was surprised by the lack of change in her, but then she reasoned Minna wore those clothes specifically for old times' sake, for memory, for her.

Her face took Claire aback: a face not only unchanged during this absent time, not only the same, but younger, more vibrant, more the ideal Minna who had already passed by the time they met. No getting around that they were both already damaged by the time their lives intersected. Instead of asking Minna any of the more pressing questions, Claire wanted to ask about that—*what fountain of youth did you find, and was it worth it, and are you happy?* Minna's happiness haunted her. But the questions, of course, died on her lips. She could do nothing but go on staring; how her eyes hungered for that face. There were things she wanted to whisper—*you are among the loved, you are remembered, in my heart you cannot perish.* But the look of tenderness on Minna's face as she looked at Claire did not fool her. She was not there.

* * *

Claire had never before allowed herself the possibility that Minna was no longer of the world. That Minna was one of the lost, and her attempt at rescue had failed.

Claire needed to believe that out there somewhere, the enigma of Minna remained and kept being added to, so constant and palpable was her presence in Claire's blood, behind her eyes, in her breath. Surely this vision was not a leave-taking, a sign that she had passed over. Surely it was a product of Claire's overheated day, too much champagne and wedding cake. Without country, without kinship, without name, how could Minna survive? Claire was brokenhearted as she at last closed her eyes in good-bye, certain Minna would be vanished when she reopened them.

Claire felt her leaving then, a cold breeze, and the lonely, motherless pull of Minna wanting her to come with her in exile that fiery night. Adieu. But Claire was already home. Home made out of the walls of connection, not boards or plaster, or even rows of orange trees. A home now stronger because it was built on forgiveness, with the full knowledge that it hung over an abyss that could reopen any day. Wherever Minna was in the world, Claire would remain at that exact spot on the earth, her land, diminished but real, a lighthouse to signal her in. Claire burned a candle in the window, Raisi's flame, reignited to light the way for yet another daughter finding her way. Minna only had to see it and be returned. Come. This is the only place. The beginning and the end. Home.

Acknowledgments

I am indebted to many excellent books in my research. One of the seminal books that made me want to become a writer and provided the inspiration for this book was *Wide Sargasso Sea* by Jean Rhys. For the biographical facts of her life, I referred to *Jean Rhys* by Helen Carr and *Jean Rhys: Life and Work* by Carole Angier. For my understanding of citrus farming: *A Citrus Legacy* by John H. Hall; *Oranges* by John McPhee; *Pay Dirt* by J. I. Rodale; and *Orange Empire* by Douglas Cazaux Sackman. Books that were important in my understanding of Haiti: both the fiction and nonfiction of Edwidge Danticat, most especially *Create Dangerously, The Butterfly's Way, Krik? Krak!, The Dew Breaker*, and *The Farming of Bones*; Bob Shacochis's *Swimming in the Volcano* and *The Immaculate Invasion*; Amy Wilentz's *The Rainy Season;* and *Tell My Horse* by Zora Neale Hurston, especially for the lyrics to "Maitresse Ersulie." Also instrumental to my understanding of Haiti were the documentaries *Aristide and the Endless Revolution* by Nicolas Rossier; *The Agronomist* by Jonathan Demme; and *Ghosts of Cité Soleil* by Asger Leth. The excerpt from "I Love You Truly" was written by Carrie Jabobs Bond. I would like to thank Katie Shull, John Northrop, and Gina Vela for answering endless questions. I would also like to give a special thanks to Rabih Nassif for his patient listening through numerous drafts. Sandrine Belanger for being my North Star. For the artwork, I'm indebted to my husband, Gaylord Soli. I would like to thank Hilary Rubin Teeman and Dori Weintraub for making me feel well cared for. Lastly, thanks to Nat Sobel for being in my corner.

THE FORGETTING TREE

by Tatjana Soli

About the Author

- A Conversation with Tatjana Soli

Behind the Scenes

- "The Second First Novel"
An Original Essay by the Author

Keep on Reading

- Reading Recommendations
- Reading Group Questions

For more reading group suggestions,
visit www.readinggroupgold.com.

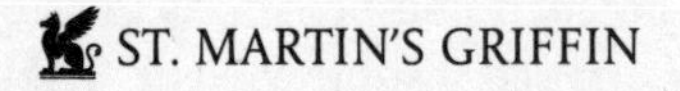

A Conversation with Tatjana Soli

***The Forgetting Tree* is your second novel. Was it easier or harder to write than the first?**

I joke that it is my second first novel (as you'll see in the "Behind the Scenes" section of this Gold guide). I had written drafts of it before my first novel was accepted for publication. So, at the time, I felt free to do something that interested me, without really thinking about audience. I had just completed my MFA, and I wanted a different challenge than my first book. Writers I admire such as Jennifer Egan and David Mitchell reinvent themselves with each book, and temperamentally that appeals to me. I was interested in combining realism with mystery and fantasy elements. This is an area that Southern writers freely write in, but I was also thinking of the fantasy or poetic realism in books that I love, such as *Wide Sargasso Sea*, *Jane Eyre*, *Wuthering Heights*, even *The English Patient* and *Housekeeping*.

"Writers are foremost entertainers."

What pleased me was that my editor immediately said she recognized many of the same preoccupations and themes as my first book, yet the books are entirely different in subject and tone. In terms of being easier, no it wasn't easier at all. If it was, I'd be worried that I wasn't taking enough risks.

You mentioned the combination of realism with mystery. Would you talk about that?

I do think *The Forgetting Tree* is a mystery, both on the level of plot and character. There's a line in the book: "Exotic is on the inside." In my first book, *The Lotus Eaters*, the exotic was on the outside, and in this one the setting is very domestic. Yet, as the story progresses, it becomes strange, exotic, violent. I joke and call it California Gothic.

Where do you get your ideas?

It's always different. With this book, I really wanted to explore the clash of cultures. People with wildly different life experiences and behaviors living side by side. The relationship of the powerful and powerless. The temptation of victim to become oppressor. So the relationship between Claire and Minna is almost an allegory. For Claire, from a middle-class American background, there is this myopia toward the larger world.

In your last book, you gave balanced points of view between Americans and Vietnamese. In your latest, you give us both an American point of view and a Haitian point of view. Is it difficult to write across cultures?

I find it very hard and potentially scary. Yet it is the story that fascinates me as a writer. So I drive myself, and everyone around me, crazy with research to try to get it right. As essential as it is, it is not a documentary; the factual is only the foundation on which to build the fiction. The particularity of characters is also a saving grace. Claire certainly does not represent every middle-aged, white woman in southern California; by the same token, Minna is not a representative of every Haitian woman.

How do you see the writer's role today?

I always surprise my students when I say writers are foremost entertainers. I mean simply that we are competing against so many other things for attention that we must give the reader an experience he can get nowhere else. My new favorite quote is from an article by Askold Melnyczuk: "However he identifies himself, every good novelist is at heart an anarchist."

You wrote that your favorite new question at readings is "What's next?" So?

When I get asked that question, it reminds me that writing is a continual process. I'm much happier and saner when I've got my head working on the next project. I've had the idea of expanding a long short story into a novel for years. Slowly I've been researching and jotting notes, and finally it's obsessing me so much now I can't bear to put it off any longer. That's my mental home for the next few years. I'm too superstitious to say more than that.

Photo © Marion Ettlinger

An Original Essay by the Author

"The Second First Novel"

Readers can be forgiven for believing that books are published easily, that authors take a grand view of the world around them, choose a subject—*mix and bake*—and two years later a beautiful new book appears. The reality, like life, is always much messier and more complicated.

I'd devoted a good six years off-and-on to writing my first novel, *The Lotus Eaters*, about a photojournalist in Vietnam. The book had been roundly rejected, and my agent told me none too gently (he's of the tough-love school) that I needed to move on and write something new. I was in mourning. The first lines in *The Forgetting Tree* are Octavio's, but to a much lesser extent my own feelings of loss at the time were mirrored in his.

But he also was in mourning for the missing boy.
Did they not see?

What I did during this difficult period in my life is the same thing I do almost every day when home—take long walks in the regional park where I live. When I first moved to this area in Southern California, one could walk through orange, avocado, and eucalyptus groves and rarely run into another person. It was incredibly beautiful and peaceful except that over the years it began to change. A eucalyptus grove on top of a hill where we used to picnic is now a gated, luxury development where we can no longer walk. The flat, sandy bed where my puppy loved to run is now paved road. One of the most painful sights that I can remember was driving past bulldozers tearing out orange trees. This scene found its way into the book:

Each tree was an individual, with a personality, and this treatment seemed a desecration of nature. When the trees were dead... bulldozers came and tore their roots from the earth, piling them into big heap from where they were trucked away to be shredded for compost.

One of my favorite writers, J. M. Coetzee, writes, "To imagine the unimaginable" is the writer's duty. Novels grow from complex root systems. I don't know what the turning point was, but during those walks in the groves the story of the Baumsarg ranch, and the struggle of its owner, Claire, against the dark forces that confronted her began to form in my mind. Hers was a family torn apart by tragedy and time. The crown jewel, though, was Minna, who appeared to me like the Indian god Shiva, both creator and destroyer, concealer and revealer, ultimately unknowable. At this stage these were all simply pieces that would take months to put together into a story, but they captured my imagination.

"The story burned inside me...."

The tree had not resurrected—rather, its life was simply hidden to the eye, beating deep in the soil, trembling within the roots hairs, in sap, wood, and bark.

So I wrote my "second" first novel not with the idea of an audience, or the idea of it being published, but because the story burned inside me, and the writing of it was the thing that fulfilled me as a writer. As I finished a first draft of this book about Claire and her search for redemption, I got the surprise call of my life that my first novel had sold. Was I ecstatic? Of course. But I had already proved to myself that even during the most fallow times, story could appear mysteriously. What made one a writer ultimately was the daily laying of those words on the page.

Illustration by Gaylord Soli

Recommended Reading

Jane Eyre **by Charlotte Brontë**

Yes, it's a classic, but it's so much fun to reread. It was considered ahead of its time in its exploration of a strong female character's feelings, a proto-feminist text. Plus, you need it fresh in your mind as you learn about the madwoman in the attic, Bertha Antoinetta Mason, for the next book.

Wide Sargasso Sea **by Jean Rhys**

My college professor said reading this book will change you, and I agree. The imagery and prose are stunning in their own right, but it is in the telling of an alternate history of the above that the novel really gains its power. Our assumptions and prejudices of the infamous madwoman are turned on their head. It is considered a post-colonial novel in that it tells the story of those whose voice is usually silenced. It deals with racial inequality and displacement. The relationship between the two texts inspired much of the structure of my book.

Housekeeping **by Marilynne Robinson**

This is one of my favorite novels of all time. I'll admit that I took a long time coming to it; the plot description of two young girls growing up in a small town in northern Idaho doesn't begin to hint at how beautiful and profound the writing is. Hiding in the trappings of a domestic novel is a deeply subversive story about the freedoms to be found in nature and in throwing out society's expectations. Ruth and Sylvie will haunt you long after the book is closed.

***The Dew Breaker* by Edwidge Danticat**

Danticat is an exquisite writer. The book is a series of linked short stories. The title comes from the Creole nickname for torturer, in this case referring to the Tonton Macoutes of the Duvalier regimes. Danticat was born in Haiti, and although she has lived in America most of her life, she writes about Haiti's history with beauty and thoughtfulness.

***The Rainy Season* by Amy Wilentz**

This is my only nonfiction book on the list, but it is a fascinating look at Haiti after the "Baby Doc" Duvalier regime and the rise of Aristide. The added bonus (especially for readers of my last book, *The Lotus Eaters*) is that Wilentz is a female journalist navigating a dangerous and tumultuous country, and her vivid writing brings the experience alive for us.

Reading Group Questions

1. Why do you think Soli named her novel *The Forgetting Tree*? How does the meaning of the title relate to the characters in the book?

2. How does the Baumsarg citrus farm shape the characters in the novel?

3. How does the loss of Josh Baumsarg affect the family? Forster and Claire react differently. How do you feel about the way they chose to live their lives afterwards?

4. Describe Minna. What is it about her that makes such an impression on Claire and her daughters?

5. How does Claire view herself as a mother? Did this perception change after losing Josh? As her daughters have grown into adults? In what ways did Claire's relationships with Gwen and Lucy evolve throughout the novel? What particular dynamics between parents and their adult children does Soli seem interested in exploring?

6. Describe Claire's relationship with her mother, Raisi, and her mother-in-law, Hanni. What life lessons does she learn from them? How does she pass these on to her own children? To Minna?

7. The novel is structured in four parts. Why do you think Soli chose this way to tell it? What do you think of this technique? Does it change the way you experience the story?

8. In Chapter 17, Claire "could no longer tell the difference between her white and Minna's black." What does she mean by this, and how does this suggest a theme of the novel?

9. Does knowing Minna's past absolve her from responsibility to Claire? Do you think she overcomes these motivations by the end of the novel?

10. Jean-Alexi states that the "lost got to help the lost in this world." In what ways are Claire and Minna lost? In what ways do they help each other out of this state? In what ways do they fail?

11. Why does Claire eventually let the farm go? Do you think this is a good or bad thing?